Stealing Fae Hearts and Secrets

FAE THIEVES AND CROWNS
BOOK TWO

JOANNA REEDER

REED IT & WEEP

Also by Joanna Reeder

IN THE RAVEN COURT:

FAE THIEVES AND CROWNS

Courting Fae Thieves and Crowns

Stealing Fae Hearts and Secrets

RAVEN COURT

Exiling a Fae Queen

Imitating a Fae Queen

Hiding a Fae Queen

Evading a Fae Queen

Becoming a Fae Queen

LEARN ABOUT JOANNA'S OTHER BOOKS AT:

joannareeder.com

Reed it and Weep

Stealing Fae Hearts and Secrets
Copyright © 2023 Joanna Reeder
joannareeder.com

Cover Art by Angel Leya
angeleya.com

Map by Hanna Sandvig
hannasandvig.com

Edited by Kristen J. Dawson and Madeline Mortensen

Kickstarter Edition

2024

To everyone who backed this project, breathing it to life... thank you.
    —Joanna

To Gladys
#teamwings

THE REALM OF FAERIE
Summer Court
SIGMUS RIVER
INFERNUS FOREST
AURA POND
ISI AURA
Spring Court
SIGMIS LAKE
CLIO
HERDAN
OHM MOUNTAINS
EMERALD RUN
ORIS LAKE
ERATO
The Sea of Neptulus
VERDANTHEARTH
CALLIOPE
ROSEWIND
CARBONNE CHANNEL
EUTERPE
MOIRA RIVER
MELPOMENE
TERPSICHORE
THALIA
Winter Court
Underwater Court
THE GRAY VAULT
FROZE MOUNTAINS
THE HARSH LAND
NEPTULUS
LUMINARIA
ADIUM LAKE
CERAUNA LAKE
Autumn Court
CAVALA
AUTUMN WOODLAND
GRAYCREST
TUMAL DESERT
FORESTS OF NIGHT
ATMOS MOUNTAINS
SANDTIDE
N
W
S
E

One

I'm the first to walk away from the prince. I should stay on the beach a little longer and eavesdrop on conversations between the remaining Consort Tourney contestants. But my insides squirm with lies and secrets threatening at the back of my throat.

After tonight's invitational, ten are left—including myself. Three from both the Summer and Winter Courts, two from Autumn, one from Spring, and one from the Underwater Court. I should continue spying and learning, but I must get away.

The gems on my violet skirts jangle together as I walk through the corridors of the Isi Aura palace. After the loud crashing waves at the shore, the cacophony of the clanking beads pushes back the bitter silence.

There's no reason for me to say goodbye to the four who are leaving—I don't need to see Raine's tantrum, nor do I dare risk a repeat of the labyrinth with Clove. I barely know Aqualis or Lily, and they'll want to return to the water realm as soon as possible, anyway.

My thoughts and my heart drift back to the impressive creature—my cabyll ushtey—that Prince Rion gave me tonight. I can hardly believe the formidable water horse is *mine*. She might be the most wonderful gift I've ever received. Of course, the prince had to give me something since the king's secretary, Gnacia—the fawn who is the mediator between the king and me—likely told him I must stay tonight. Even so, Rion remembered my love of these dangerous creatures. Now something inside me has shifted. Softened? No, *that,* I cannot afford.

Nor can I dwell on it.

Amberle, focus.

If I'm to free my father, I must assess the contestants. I identified a threat, but my warnings were dismissed. So, I must find Gnacia. *Now.*

Frost Niege cannot stay. She's a potential danger to the other contestants and the royals. I'd reported her, but they allowed Rion to keep her. Why?

What is the point of bringing me on if my reports fall on deaf ears? Why bring me here at all? I can't demand answers from the king, but Gnacia is not my sovereign and I demand to be heard.

But I'm making it easy to avoid me with my thundering, jewel-clanking dress announcing my presence across this entire wing. I turn on my heel and head to my rooms to change out of this noisy gown.

As I whip around a corner, a firm hand grasps my wrist. The motion pivots my direction, sending me flying toward a tall flower arrangement. An arm stops me short, just before I career into the vase.

"Why are you in such a hurry?" Wyn asks but doesn't release his hold. "What's wrong?"

Recognizing my friend, and not the mysterious murderer, my momentary panic turns to fury. "Trying to make me smash another priceless treasure of the crown? Clumsy as always, Wyn?"

"The vase is fine," he says, lifting a shoulder and releasing his grip. "There's something I wanted to speak to you about."

"Not now. I need to—" I briefly close my eyes and shake my head. "Never mind." I turn to go.

"You need to... what?" he asks, stepping in front of me to block my path.

"I just..." I grit my teeth and resist the urge to lash at him for holding me up. "I just need to speak with someone."

Wyn hooks an eyebrow, then folds his arms and grins. "You need to speak with... Gnacia?"

I can't stop the panic that crawls up my throat, but I can control the steadiness of my gaze and the coolness of my smile. "King Estelar's assistant?" I hate that my voice comes out too high pitched. "Why would I need to speak with her?"

"Because the winter fae, Frost, wasn't eliminated."

"None of the winter fae were." I move around him to continue down the hall.

"Amberle, stop." He lets out a frustrated sigh. "Amberle, *I know*." He leans heavily on the word. "You don't have to deceive me or skirt the question."

I bite the inside of my cheek, fighting the terror licking at my heart. He *knows?* How much does he know? Slowly, I turn back toward him.

Wyn casts a glance around—as if to ensure we aren't being overheard—then steps forward and mutters, "I know why you're here. In the Tourney. The king told me why he ordered you to come."

I press my lips together when he steps back to read my expression. I don't assume he knows *anything*, but my stomach clenches; my childhood friend can destroy me with a few wrong words. I frantically feel for winter magic—the projection magic watching every moment of the competition—but between my flustered thoughts and trying to keep my face neutral, I can barely sense my toes, let alone magic.

When I don't answer, he rolls his eyes and leans forward, cupping my ear with his hand. "He's asked you to be his little spy."

I yank Wyn's arm, surprising him and throwing him off balance as I drag him down the hallway.

He laughs nervously, but doesn't resist. "I thought we agreed that you'd *control your passions* around me, Amberle. This feels scandalous."

"Oh stop, Wyn."

"Stop what? I'm well aware of my rugged handsomeness."

I twist to glare at him. "Don't flatter yourself."

He snorts. "Where are we going?"

We're going somewhere we can talk without being watched, I want to add, but I keep my jaw clamped. I scan for winter magic, but don't feel it. But would I, with my temper flared?

Wyn plants his full weight abruptly, so I'm forced to stop when he does. He throws a look over his shoulder, then pulls me through an open arched doorway to a small balcony that overlooks the distant lavender fields.

"What—"

All joking gone, he lifts a finger to silence me, then pulls a small piece of flint from his pocket. He steps to the wall and strikes the rock against the stone. The spark that's thrown doesn't surprise me, but I'm stunned by the brilliant blue color and the way it inexplicably expands into a fireball as he cups it in his hand.

My wings twitch, and I step back as it grows with some sort of summer magic. I might be part summer fae, but fire still burns.

"It won't hurt us," he assures me as it engulfs his fingers that hold the flint and keeps growing up over his arm.

I step closer, watching as it expands. It dims and becomes more and more translucent the larger it becomes.

It has almost completely engulfed Wyn when the edge of it reaches me. I suck in a breath as the fire heats the air, and when it brushes over my face, it tingles, but doesn't scorch.

I exhale.

Within moments, the strange fire bubble encases us both.

"The winter magic can't see or hear us while we are within this barrier," Wyn explains. "We are essentially invisible to it. We're invisible to all fae, in fact."

How can I get one for myself? I wonder, but refrain from asking. For now.

"What if it saw us before you created the barrier?" Though I hadn't sensed the winter magic, I'm not an expert at recognizing it.

"That could be problematic, but the winter magic is likely focused on our prince and the fae who are leaving tonight," he assures me. "This magic won't last long, but we are safe for now."

"I hope you're right," I say. "Spill, Wyn. What do you know? I thought it was the prince who sent for you. How do you know…" I point to myself but can't seem to say it out loud, even after Wyn revealed he knows I'm a spy.

"Yes, Orion sent for me, but when King Estelar learned I was in Isi Aura, he summoned me." His eyes drop to the ground. "I told him why the prince asked me to come."

I step closer, as if someone might still overhear us. "Rion doesn't know why I'm really here."

His green eyes lift back to mine, and he frowns briefly. "I'm aware."

"So, what happened? The king just decided to tell you why I'm a part of the Tourney?" I throw my hands in the air.

Wyn squares his shoulders. "Like you, it seems I'm now here on official—but secret—business for the king."

My arms drop. "What business?"

Wyn lifts a dark eyebrow. I don't think he'll tell me. He'll play it off like some sort of game.

"The crown has tasked me to help the prince find an appropriate match," he says, surprising me by being direct, then pauses, gauging my reaction. "While throwing suspicion off those who have the same task. It seems that one of you is having trouble." Instead of a teasing expression coupled with that remark, he looks unsettled.

The realization slaps me; Wyn is talking about me.

The king doesn't trust me to do my job. I turn away with heated embarrassment and bite down on the corner of my lip. *And why should he? After I threw myself at Rion in the garden? After the mistakes I've made? After the way we danced at the revel—*

What does this mean? If King Estelar is recruiting others like Wyn, will he no longer need me?

And if so, what does that mean for my father?

A cold pit forms in my gut. I twist my center at the discomfort, but it's difficult to breathe. I stumble from the protective bubble and lean against the balcony. Steadying myself against the railing, I attempt to stretch the stiffness out of my wings, but the movement doesn't help. I doubt the king has told my old friend the full terms of my deal, and I don't dare ruin my slim chance of success by crying on his shoulder about my father.

Wyn joins me, putting the fire orb around me again. He rests his forearms on the rail so we're near shoulder-to-shoulder. "Since we're both working for the kings now, we're in this together. Let's just get out of it alive."

Together. Yes. I could use an ally. Someone I trust.

"How many spies are there?" I ask, keeping my voice even. "Who else are you watching?"

"There's just one other…"

Just one. That's encouraging.

"But the king didn't reveal who they are."

"I thought you said you're here to throw off suspicion!" I shout, but then catch myself. Wyn said the winter magic couldn't penetrate the fire bubble, but he said nothing about it blocking the sound from any nearby fae. "How can you do that if you don't know who the other spy is?" I hiss.

Wyn's face is taut with anger, his eyes filled with fury. "Because the other spy isn't fumbling every step along the way!" His nostrils flare. "You are the *wrong* fae for the job, Amberle. You shouldn't be here."

I lift one eyebrow and hitch a hand on my hip. "I thought it didn't surprise you that I'm here."

"You shouldn't be here in *this capacity*, Amberle." He pauses, then drops his chin and his tone when he asks, "Why are you doing this? Why would you do this to—" He stops himself, then amends his words. "What does the king have on you?"

"What does he have on *you*?" I throw back at him. I'm too heated to trust the curse won't activate again and force me to blurt out the truth.

"Nothing but his orders and my wish to keep my king happy," Wyn says to the summer night air. "That, and the prince is my friend and I want to help him." He looks back to me. "But *you* disappeared nearly a century ago without a trace. If you wanted to keep in the king's good graces, you would have come back a long time ago. So why now? Why are you here *now*?"

I need to calm down, so I turn toward the lavender fields and watch as the deep violet ripples with the wind like waves of the sea. The breeze wafts the calming scent toward us, and I close my eyes, breathing it in deeply as I scramble for a response.

"I thought, perhaps…" Wyn says, but doesn't finish. When I glance at him again, he turns away and scrubs his hand over his face.

Hopefully that means he's decided not to pressure my answer.

I take advantage of the pause to turn the subject back on him. "Does Rion know the king asked you to help him pick a mate?"

"As far as Orion knows, I'm here at his request, doing him a favor to find out who killed the Faeven girl. He won't be suspicious if I offer my opinions about his contestants, too."

I stare at my hands, gripping the rail. "And what are your opinions so far?"

He shifts to face me, resting against the rail on one elbow. "I don't want to talk about that now. Let's focus on the Faeven girl first."

I study his face. My first instinct is that he's hiding something, but he basically said he doesn't trust me. Why would he share information with me if he didn't trust me? He's here to watch me.

But I want justice for Juniper. "Fine. Do you have any leads?"

Wyn frowns. "Not yet. Will you show me where you found her body?"

"I can. Do you think the prince is still distracting the winter magic with his goodbyes?" Speaking with Gnacia will have to happen later.

"The king wouldn't want this investigation broadcasted," Wyn assures me. "At least not until we have some answers. We won't be watched while you show me. He's the one who gave this to me." He lifts the flint, then covers it with one hand, extinguishing the fire bubble.

I push down the bitter anger that threatens to engulf me. Why didn't the king give *me* a magical piece of flint? Why is Wyn so special?

But I know the answer. The king doesn't trust me.

No one trusts me.

I must change that. I must prove myself.

Shoving my pride aside, I steel myself and lead Wyn back inside. Helping Wyn find Juniper's killer is a start. I have information that might help.

Perhaps if I prove myself in this, I can regain the king's trust.

Three

The corridors are quiet as I lead Wyn through the palace. I'm still practicing at feeling for the winter magic, but I feel none of its buzzing energy. No cold spells. Just a warm and comforting summer night in Isi Aura.

I wonder if any of the eliminated contestants are pleading their case, trying to convince the prince to let them stay a little longer, while I'm skulking through the castle. Part of me is sad I'm missing the drama.

"Juniper was the first to go on a date with the prince," I whisper as we walk.

"That alone could give someone cause to attack her," Wyn says. "Was there anyone who was particularly jealous of her?"

I think back on that morning after Juniper's date when all fifteen of us were crammed around a small table, everyone hanging onto her words with raptured attention as she related the details of her time with the prince. Juniper was enamored. And she was convinced the prince was in love with her, too.

But none of the fae seemed spiteful or angry.

"Not that I noticed. I think most were just envious that she earned time with him." I hate that I can't give him more.

As we draw closer to the corridor where the autumn fae reside

—the corridor that conceals a hidden passageway where I found Juniper—my hands begin to shake. I realize I have not been here since that day, and it pricks at my memory.

"I overheard a conversation between Tierney and Cerule before I stumbled upon Juniper," I say, distracting myself from my churning emotions. "Tierney complained, calling the prince shallow and admitted she was unimpressed with him." I remember that part of it, but there was something else I must have buried deep in my mind.

They said Juniper knew a secret. A secret she revealed to them.

The king deserves to know…, one had said. *Someone should tell him…*

What thing should the king know?

Juniper said if you look hard enough… if you look past the glamour, you can see it.

See what? Was it this *secret* that got Juniper killed?

"Amberle?" Wyn shakes me from my thoughts, and I realize I've slowed to a stop. I snap my attention to him. "Was there something more?"

"Secrets."

He steps toward me. "Secrets? What do you mean by secrets?"

"That morning…" I start, but don't dare say more, and hold the air in my lungs.

Wyn looks up and down the hallway, then re-ignites the protection fire bubble around us.

I exhale.

"Go on," he prods.

"That morning when Juniper told us about her date, she told us that she and the prince were interrupted by someone." I lift my eyes to his. "She said they talked about a *secret* and that Faerie should know about it."

"What was the secret?"

I lower my eyes. "She never said."

"Well, that's something. Perhaps if we find out what the secret is, we can figure out who killed her." He lifts a finger to his lips, gesturing that I say no more, then he extinguishes the fire bubble and points at the wall. "Where did you find her?"

"Just up here," I say, walking swiftly again and pointing at the hidden door I slipped behind that day.

I move to push the door open, but Wyn stops me, holding up a hand and gestures that we both step back. He stares at the concealed entrance with his arms folded and his brows furrowed. Almost like he can't see it.

I look at the concealed doorway, then back at Wyn. Then back at the wall.

He steps forward and fumbles to open the door, but he's way off. I join him and assist, but avert my eyes when it swings inward. Surely, they removed Juniper's body, yet fear grips me.

Wyn steps back, looking into the narrow darkness while clutching his chin.

"What is it?" I ask. "Do you see something?" I force myself to look but see only an empty passageway. It's exactly as I expected it to look that day I slipped inside to hide from the autumn fae.

He shakes his head, then walks inside, beckoning with one finger for me to follow.

I take a deep breath and pull my wings tightly at my sides so they don't brush against the cold stone as I cross the threshold and plunge myself into the dim, musky space.

"Who do you think knows about this specific passageway?" he asks quietly.

"What do you mean?" I match his volume.

"You knew about it. You knew it was here."

"Well, yes, I grew up here—"

"I spent a lot of time here as a youngling too and I didn't know about this one."

I look at him. *Is he accusing me?*

"I knew about many of the other secret doors and passageways around the palace," he continues. "But not this one."

"Wyn..." I speak slowly. "I didn't kill Juniper."

"Oh, no! I didn't presume you did, Amberle." His face

scrunches, looking incredulous before his attention returns to the space. He runs his hand along one wall as he thinks aloud. "It's just curi— Wait. What's this?" He bends down and examines something tucked between two cracks in the stone.

"Amberle!" Gnacia's voice right behind me causes my heart to nearly leap from my chest. "Here you are! I wanted to speak with you."

I press a hand against my now racing heart and twist myself to face her. Why didn't I hear her coming? The faun is not known for her stealth. I realize too late that the acoustics don't carry the sounds of the corridor into this space.

I wonder if it's reversely true. If the sounds within the secret passageway are silent to anyone in the hall.

Gnacia's hoof clacks against the stone as she leans to pry past me, her attention cutting to Wyn.

"I see that you've shown Wyn Firetail where you found that poor fae's body," she says with fake grief. She doesn't seem to notice that Wyn has shifted his body to keep one hand hidden behind him. He's hiding something. *He's found something.*

Funny how I was desperate to talk to the king's assistant before running into Wyn and now I can't wait to get rid of her. What is Wyn holding? And why doesn't he show his find to the king's trusted servant?

I need just a moment. "Yes, Wyn asked for my help—"

"And now we can leave him to his task," she says with clipped and impatient words, then gestures with her hand. "Come. We have things to discuss."

"I—"

Gnacia's eyes narrow. "Need I remind you—"

"I'm coming."

She owns me.

Reluctantly, I step back into the corridor, but glance behind me once more in time to watch Wyn tuck a bit of parchment into the sleeve of his shirt.

Four

I don't have time to wonder about the piece of parchment Wyn found because we don't go far. I expected Gnacia to wind through the palace to her office, but we stop abruptly a short distance down the autumn fae hallway. She lets me into a room that looks similar to mine, but larger. And colder. Instead of blue, the furnishings are covered in various shades of orange and yellow.

"Whose room is this?" I ask when she shuts the door. "Won't they be back soon?" I left the Invitational ages ago, and it must be wrapping up by now. I can imagine Cerule's sylph flying ahead of her and slipping under the crack in the door, discovering me. Even worse, Tierney might send her squirrel to scratch at my face. I shudder, knowing what pleasure Tierney would take in plotting her revenge.

"We won't be interrupted." She waves a dismissive hand. "I've brought you here for a report."

My gut twists. "What do you mean? *Why* won't we be interrupted?"

Gnacia's eyes narrow.

"This is Juniper's room, isn't it?" I wrap my arms around

myself against a sudden chill and look around as if her ghost might appear.

Gnacia sighs. "This was the closest place we could go to where the winter magic is blocked. Would you rather trek across the palace to my office? Or take the stairs to your room?"

"Actually—"

"Countless fae could stop us," she interrupts, lifting a hand and blowing out an exasperated breath. "There will be questions about why I'm escorting you through hallways. And we might have to deal with your servants if we go to your room. But in here..." She lifts a hand, gesturing at the forever vacant quarters of Juniper Faeven.

"No one will interrupt because Juniper doesn't require servants anymore," I say.

"Exactly."

I saunter toward the sitting area near the window. The area is spacious—Juniper could entertain half a dozen fae with ease— and the massive window overlooks the sparkling sea.

This is what the room of an actual potential mate of the prince looks like.

A gold-colored cushion lines the sill of the window where Juniper can sit and marvel at the Summer Court foliage outside.

Or rather, she *could*. Before she was killed.

"I need a report," Gnacia says. "Any information about anyone who cannot make a good match for Prince Orion."

"What about the information I learned about Frost?" My volume rises and my wings flutter, pain pinching in my back. "I *told* you Frost was a threat. I *told* you she is not here for the right reasons, and she cannot be trusted. And yet... Prince Orion gifted her a *cu sith*."

The fawn steps forward with a finger aimed at me. "You are here to do a job, Amberle Kindra. And your job is not to question Prince Orion, or myself—which implies you question the king."

"Fine." I close my eyes briefly. "But I need a clearer objective. I agreed to spy and gather information to ensure the prince ends up with the female King Estelar approves of. But..." I suck in a breath. "I need an *end date.*"

Gnacia raises an eyebrow and walks toward me. Her hooves clomp loudly against the floor. "What you need is a reminder of your place here. You do not make demands of me or the king. If you want your father released, you will leave when your task is complete. You will stay until the king says you can leave."

What happened to *you're only guaranteed to last one invitational?* Now I must stay until the king says I can leave? What changed? To keep my temper and my frustration under control, I clench my hands into fists at my sides.

"How long?" I ask. I'm not sure how much more of this I can take. "How many contestants must be eliminated before I can go? Give me a number."

"If the king says you must stay until the final three, you will stay until the final three."

Three? Wyn's words echo in my head. Gnacia, or rather the king, imagines me inept. This is proof of it.

"Surely you don't want me included in the interviews the final five must undergo?"

The faun smiles. The edges of her mouth parallel to the tips of her horns. "I trust you can manage a simple interview."

I step toward her and spread my wings, even though it makes my injured one ache. I stare unblinkingly at her, hoping my intensity masks my fear. "But if it is revealed what profession I'm in, it could create a problem."

For me and anyone I'm tied to, I don't add. My mind flashes to anyone I've worked with in the past seven decades. To the many clients I've stolen for. To my half-dozen temporary partners like Ralvano.

To Clay.

What will happen to my freckle-faced friend if I'm revealed as a thief? And now a spy?

Gnacia directs a gaze at me with the same potency. Her lips

twist into a cruel, threatening half-smile. "Then keep your profession a secret."

"That will raise questions about why I'm here!" I shout. "We both know the king doesn't wish for that. He'll have my head!"

"All the more reason to mind your words." She lifts her hands and purses her lips. She's pleased with herself.

It makes my blood boil. It's unacceptable and I won't take it.

I step toward her again and stretch my wings further. "If I'm still here as one of the final five and I am forced to reveal secrets I don't want known... I will take you down with me."

"You would threaten me?" Gnacia presses a hand against her breast and steps forward. "Do you understand who I am?" One of her eyebrows twitches despite her flippant laugh. Is it a sign that she's afraid?

I lean into it. "Yes, an autumn fae who clawed her way to the top. Everyone knows the higher the climb, the farther the fall."

"You will give the king a full report of the final five contestants before the interviews," Gnacia says, shaking her shoulders, straightening her spine, and lifting her chin. "You will leave when six remain."

"And what if Rion won't send me home at six?" My heart jolts. That's dangerously close to the final five who will be subjected to the interviews. "Certainly, I can learn more information even before the next invitational." I ignore the part of me that resists the idea of leaving so soon.

Any trace of possible fear vanishes from the faun's face and is replaced with determination set between her eyebrows. She won't be cowed. She's a biloko disguised with her seemingly harmless bell, ready to convince me to offer a slice of my flesh for her evening meal. "Fine. You will stay until seven contestants remain."

"Seven isn't much of a—"

"But the compromise will cost you," she snaps. "If you are to leave when there are only seven, we need more information."

I cross my arms, indignation flaring.

"In two days, you will have a full report on everyone remaining."

"Two days?" I struggle to appear calm as I grapple with the implication of her words. "You can't possibly think—"

"I don't need to remind you that you are not the only one hunting for information."

Right. Wyn and the secret spy.

"If I feel like this is something you cannot do, it won't hurt much to send you away now."

"What? You just said I must stay until seven remain and now..." I pause, watching her as a horrible realization creeps into my gut. "If you send me home now, what happens to my father?"

Gnacia lifts one brow. "He will remain where he is if you don't hold up your end of the bargain."

I keep my chin held high, but the weight of her words presses against my chest like a boulder, threatening to crush my ribs.

"Now. If you have nothing else of importance to tell me, I suggest you get some rest because tomorrow the prince is taking you on a special outing." She pauses. "Faerie has been waiting to watch the two of you reminisce about your past. So you will give them what they want, while showing them you and the prince will *not* make an agreeable match."

"Tomorrow? But you just told me I only have two days—"

"That's enough talk for tonight." She claps her hands and walks toward the door, then opens it without interlude. "Now, run along."

Five

A buzzing energy startles me awake seconds before my curtains are unceremoniously jerked open and the morning sunlight streams in and bathes the room in an infuriatingly joyfulness. The feeling is only accentuated by the shuffling of maids who flit around my quarters, filling the bathtub, readying fragrant perfumes, and carry in armfuls of dresses that they hang carefully in the wardrobe.

It's maddening.

My head pounds from all the stresses of last night. Frost is still in the Tourney, Wyn's presence might make my position moot, and Gnacia—and the king—suddenly shifted what they want of me, and expect me to do the impossible while putting on a performance in front of all of Faerie.

Two days. Gnacia has given me two days to find out more information about the fae, but she really means one day because half my time will be wasted during my date with Rion. How am I supposed to spy when I'm separated from those I'm spying on?

We'll be alone. The prince and I. Just him and me.

That's why I took a risk last night after Gnacia dismissed me. After ensuring Princess Shay had retired, I snuck into the room on the upper floor of the library with her secret magic disc. I camped out, hoping to learn something, *anything*, about the remaining fae. But every single fae had retired to their rooms; apparently, I was the only one breaking the unsaid curfew. I spent hours watching the different court hallways until my head hit the table. Finally, I dragged myself back to my rooms.

I lost sleep for nothing. I learned nothing. I might fall asleep on my date today for nothing.

And now I'll only have one day to learn enough to free my father.

I sit in front of the vanity while Kenna brushes through my long, still-damp tresses as she shares kitchen gossip with the spring maid, Posey. With what energy I can muster together, I focus on figuring out how to end my date quickly. I might have the remainder of the day and evening to eavesdrop on the others if I'm successful.

Yes. Make the date short. Some quick jaunts down memory lane, easy, friendly smiles that broadcast to Faerie that we can be nothing more than just friends—while making sure Rion doesn't send me home immediately. Simple.

A groan escapes my lips.

Kenna frowns, and I quickly flash a smile. "I'm just... ready for breakfast."

"Aren't you always?" Kenna jests before continuing her chatter with Posey. For a human, she's certainly grown comfortable here. She acts just like any fae servant. "I heard Ava talking in the hallway with Brecken after Didi Beechriver's date."

The mention of my friend's name captures my attention.

"Wait." Posey says. "Ava and Brecken aren't the Beechriver's maids."

"Right. They oversaw Clove Farabella. But the spring contestants' attendants are all thick as thieves. Anyway, they said Didi might be the prince's favorite if not for—"

"Kenna," Posey interrupts and, in the reflection, she nods in my direction. They know I'm listening.

"If not for… what?" I ask, turning my head to look at them both, pulling my hair from Kenna's grasp.

They stare at me with open mouths.

Because she's a star fae? I dread hearing the words, but I must know the truth of the rumors. Can Didi not win the favor of the prince and the crown because she is a star fae? Does that fact deem her not good enough?

"It's no secret that you're the favorite," Posey says nonchalantly.

I suck in a breath, a mixture of feelings screaming for my attention.

Posey continues, "Everyone looks forward to watching the two of you together today."

Kenna nods, grinning widely. "It's so romantic," she says, then sighs as I turn back to the mirror. "Childhood sweethearts-turned lovers."

"W-wait. We're not—"

"Hush," Posey snaps, but her smile fills her entire face. "We all see it. You may not be lovers *yet*, but you can't deny that it's coming."

"Yes. You will be queen someday," Kenna says wistfully.

My cheeks heat and remain inflamed while Kenna twists my hair in a loose, but elegant arrangement, and continues to simmer while Posey helps me into the pale pink dress. Compared to many of the ornate gowns brought today, my maids select a relatively simple dress with a narrow waist. It covers part of my shoulders and flows down into a court neckline. Although tight around the bodice, it offers a modest décolletage in the front with a larger one in back—for my wings. The sleeves are loose from top to bottom and the skirts widen below my waist and reach to just below my knees while slightly longer in the back. When my face eventually cools, I'm nearly ready, but a light knock on the door sends my heart hammering and a flush rushing right back through my veins.

Kenna covers a nervous giggle, while Posey straightens *her* skirts as if she is the one who needs to impress the prince. My spring fae maid moves to open the door.

Rion is dressed casually in soft leather black trousers. His thin mint green shirt hangs slightly open at his throat and its sleeves billow around his forearms and biceps.

My simple dress was the right choice for the day.

When my eyes catch on his tousled walnut-colored hair and his golden eyes that shine in the morning light, my breath hitches.

Give Faerie what they want. Give them a story, a history while convincing them we cannot make an agreeable match, I remind myself. *But not so much that Rion wishes to send me home today.*

Easily done, right?

I take a deep breath.

"Amberle," he says brightly. "You look lovely." He dips his head.

"Shall we?" I ask, standing quickly and tipping over a crystal perfume bottle on the vanity.

Rion smiles.

"Where are we going?" I ask, covering up my clumsy faux pas.

"Calliope Island," The prince grins, showing his pearly-white teeth.

Calliope? I can forget about spying today. I'll be lucky if we're back with enough time for me to learn anything tomorrow.

For the love of Vejo, Gnacia. She had to know the prince's plans. So why is she so hell-bent on watching me fail?

Six

The prince offers me his elbow and a radiant smile, causing a warm feeling to churn in my belly. I slip my arm through his and look away from his golden eyes, unable to meet his fervent gaze. The staggering feeling of warmth is twisted by the crackling iciness of the winter magic surrounding us the instant we step from my chambers and into the hallway.

Whoever is controlling the magic has made it even more suffocating today. It's clear that Faerie doesn't want to miss a single moment of this date. Going from the *Silver Shadow*, who was never seen by anyone, *ever,* to a 'contestant' in the Consort Tourney and being watched by every fae is dizzying.

"Any chance we're riding cabyll ushteys to Calliope Island?" I ask, attempting to distract myself from being overwhelmed by all of it. At least the magic can't follow us on the water, though I imagine it will be patiently waiting when we arrive at the island. Also, I've been dying to see the water horse Rion gifted me last night.

"Not today." He nudges me, probably seeing the pout I didn't mean to display. "But soon," he whispers low. "You haven't named her yet."

A thrill runs down my neck, but I'm sure it has more to do

with my excitement over my yet-to-be-named water horse and not the closeness of the prince.

Soon we're on the deck of one of the royal schooners headed toward the summer islands that span the gap to the other tip of the Summer Court. It's surreal to be on board when I've only ever viewed the massive ships from afar.

Leaning with my hand firmly clasping the rail, I close my eyes as a salty breeze picks up, lifting tendrils of hair away from my face. Rion is next to me, but his presence isn't distracting or unwelcome.

"What is in your thoughts, Amberle?"

I look at him and see a smirk playing on his lips. His tone is more flirtatious than teasing.

"I'm just enjoying myself."

His mouth twitches and he twists to face me full on, leaning on one elbow. "Oh?" He tries and fails to hide an amused smile and I sense playacting as if we're being watched. "Would you care to elaborate on how *enjoyable* this date is so far?"

A brownie with butter yellow hair tied up in a neat bun, approaches us with two glasses of sparkling wine. I wait until the brownie is back below deck before continuing.

Lifting my shoulders, I turn to mirror his stance. "I always thought being on a ship, trapped at sea, would be my worst nightmare. But it has surprised me. It's freeing. After living in the shadows and always planning an escape route in any situation—"

"*Gah!*" A wave rocks the ship, and the prince spills his drink all over his shirt.

I lift one eyebrow at him and sniff my drink, but don't smell the thing that inebriates the fae. Then I laugh. "Did they add cream to the wine?"

He eyes me and accuses the sea. "I didn't expect that enormous wave!"

"I think you're just clumsy."

Rion lifts his shoulders as if confirming my words as truth.

"Do you want to call for someone?" I ask. "Change your clothes?"

"No." He shakes his shirt to fling some of the liquid, then dismisses it and turns to lean both elbows on the rail, looking at the horizon.

I stand next to him and notice his hands have a subtle tremor.

When he glances at me briefly, I catch the split-second warning in the wider-than-usual slits in his eyes.

Are we being watched? Was his flirting for more than the brownie who brought our drinks? Did he interrupt my words because I was about to reveal my secret identity?

A shudder runs through me, but I suppress it, then rub my chin against my shoulder, covertly looking behind me. But I see no fae eavesdropping. It can't be the winter magic; we're too far away from the shore. But the mere thought heightens my senses, and I feel it behind me on the deck of the ship. Safe from the water. My wings twitch, and the injured one smarts a bit. It's nothing compared to my spike of unease.

I'm a fool to think Rion and I might have had this time on the ship in privacy. And now I understand why we couldn't ride water horses to the island. It's obvious. Traveling by ship meant the magic could travel safely with us.

And Prince Rion just saved me from telling all of Faerie that I'm the Silver Shadow.

My feeling of freedom is snuffed. But I shove my disappointment from my mind because this is the job. I shouldn't have allowed myself to hope for a break from prying. There's no room for error or complacency.

"To answer your questions, I've never actually been on a ship," I say. "I'm just enjoying the moment."

"You've never been on a ship?" Rion's eyes widen, then his eyebrows pinch and his mouth twists. The disbelief in his tone is potent.

I shrug. "I never had a reason to travel on one."

He studies me as if sensing some deception or untruth, but he'll find none.

"I am not the crown prince of Faerie, *Prince Orion*." I remind him with a tilt of my head.

Rion frowns.

"It was never my duty to travel with my father to other courts." I wave a hand toward the waves without taking my eyes off him. "Or a leisure opportunity to take a holiday to Terpsichore."

"You cannot help but remind me of the gap in our stations." He shifts forward and leans against the rail on his forearms. His head slightly lowered.

"I only tell the truth," I say softly. Now's not the time to upset him. "*You're* the one who brought it up. I simply made a statement. I wasn't lamenting that I had never been on a ship—"

The soft pressure of a warm hand resting on mine stops my words. "Let's start again," he says, his tone apologetic. "Even though we lived under the same roof for so long, it is only recently that I have learned your upbringing and mine were worlds apart."

My words come out airy when I agree. "They were."

His fingers slide across mine, then hook underneath, grasping my hand. I can't help the flutter of my wings, so I quickly wrap my fingers around his to cover my slip of emotion.

"I want to know more of it, Amberle," he says, then lowers his head toward me and his tone is barely above a whisper when he says, "Was it so bad living in Isi Aura? Did you really hate it so much?"

I lift my face to his, but my breath catches when I see the crease between his eyebrows and the vulnerable pleading in his eyes. Matching his volume, I say, "I never hated living in the palace, Rion. It was my home."

I wonder if he heard my slip, saying his nickname, instead of his proper one. The thought flees when his eyes flit down to my lips, accelerating my pulse. I jerk my hand away and my head toward the sea, my eyes focusing on the horizon. But immediately regret the action and briefly close my eyes.

Why am I pulling away? My instincts are warring, and I'm failing.

"Then it's just me you hate."

His words are so quiet, I know the winter magic can't hear them. I'm not sure even I heard it. But I snap my eyes back to his and immediately grip both sides of his face before I realize what I'm doing. Heat rushes through my core and up my neck into my cheeks. My mouth goes dry.

I hear the king's and Gnacia's voices shouting in my head in unison with my own thoughts. *What are you doing?*

But I ignore all of it. "I don't hate you."

I'm almost shocked at my own words. I *don't* hate him.

Rion's smile is small. Quiet. He blinks and puts one hand over mine. But his expression softens, and I think he sees my panic. We're close, and I only seem to show bursts of affection. But instead of teasing, he removes my hands from his face, but keeps one hand cupped.

"Come," he says, threading my arm through his. We stroll on the deck in silence for several long moments, the crackling winter magic keeping pace as I scramble to come up with something, *anything,* to talk about for the fae to hear. But my mind is still a muddled mess.

I might not hate Rion, but the lingering hurt is real. He never understood the power dynamic between our families and he *definitely* doesn't know now. Even if he's realizing my childhood wasn't as privileged, he doesn't know his father is holding the keys that's keeping my father locked up. Even so, if the complications of our families were stripped away, would I want to be Rion's friend?

Nieven Morphyra pops into view from the lower deck and claps his hands once. His sunshine-yellow smile is wide as ever.

I give Rion's arm a quick squeeze before relaxing my arm in a distant, respectable manner.

"Just the two fae I was looking for!" Nieven calls.

I look at Rion, but all I get is a tight smile. He's nervous. I thought the announcer was coming for something on the island, but he's dressed as if he's on stage with a glistening blue jacket that complements his skin tone and his midnight black hair styled into sharp spikes.

"Shall we get started?" Nieven asks.

"What does he mean?" I ask the prince.

"Well, there are certain things Faerie wished to know about our shared past, so Nieven here is ensuring that we answer those questions."

"We're being interviewed?" I stiffen. We're not naturally talking about our past; being prompted to answer some questions could be problematic.

"I'd like to call it guiding the conversation," Nieven says, flashing a smile at the winter magic, then at us. "Shall we begin?"

With little choice, I smile and play along.

The announcer turns back toward the winter magic and lifts both hands. "If you're just tuning in now, I'm with Prince Orion and one of our lovely contestants, Amberle Kindra. The two of them are traveling across the Sea of Neptulus for an exclusive, one-on-one outing to see if they might make an agreeable match and whether Amberle could become Prince Orion's chosen bride."

Well, I won't actually be the one chosen, echoes in my thoughts, but a stabbing sensation slides between my ribs at the mention, anyway.

"But for those of you *underjordiske's* who have been stuck in your mounds while the Tourney has played out, you should know that Amberle was not a stranger to the prince when her name was called at The Choosing." He pauses as if waiting for audible gasps from an invisible crowd. But only the cry of sea birds and a distant siren song can be heard. "That's right. Amberle Kindra grew up in the palace as a youngling with her family and was an occasional playmate to our crown prince."

Fear ices through my veins at the mention of my family, but I'm able to keep my wings still and my expression neutral, so when Nieven turns toward us I manage a nod while Rion bows his head and smiles.

"Tell us, what was your friendship like as younglings?"

I keep quiet, letting the prince lead the storytelling. It might not be the smartest strategy, but I don't know which things would be worse to reveal about my past.

"Well... Amberle is quite the prankster."

I snap my head to him, intending to protest, but the glint in his eyes cools my ire. "Yes, well, you're no human saint, either."

Rion laughs.

"Now we're intrigued," Nieven says, glancing at the winter magic, then back at us. "Did Amberle ever prank you, Your Highness?"

"More times than I can count, Nieven." The buoyancy in the prince is exhilarating and contagious.

"Ooh, do tell. Give us a story."

But whatever lightness Rion brings is layered with my anxiety about what he intends to share.

"Amberle liked to steal away to the lavender fields," Rion says.

"The fields where the labyrinth task took place?"

"The very one! Whenever I wasn't busy with my princely duties, I would follow her to the fields." I feel the prince turn toward me. Knowing I'm being watched, I meet his gaze. "I think it irritated her," he says, lifting both eyebrows in one quick motion matched with a half-smile. More flirting.

Without thinking, I flash a twisted smile. I hadn't realized he saw right through me back then.

"What made you think it irritated her?"

Rion holds my gaze for a long moment—causing pixies to swarm in my stomach—then turns back to Nieven and the watching magic. "Because she trapped me in a faerie ring once. I was stuck for a full day and half a night."

"That's a dangerous trick for a commoner to pull on a royal," Nieven says.

"No! It was endearing," Rion says quickly. "And we were just younglings. But I think it was payback for the trick I pulled on her with a biloko bell."

A pit weighs heavy in my gut. *No. Not this story.*

The prince leans close and whispers to me, "I still don't understand why you've never forgiven me for that one."

"No secrets! I think Faerie deserves to hear all of it!" Nieven protests.

"Do you want to tell the story, Amberle? Or should I?"

Seven

I finally trust my wings enough to catch me if I fall, so I perch on a once-precarious top branch of a tree in the center of the Infernus Forest. A flock of harpies cry and bicker in the distance.

Father is busy with the king for the rest of the day, and since both Wyn and Arielle are away with *their* fathers, my favorite play-mates are gone.

The princeling is free. He called out to me when I entered the forest, but I pretended I didn't hear his calls. He's too fond of his pranks lately and I need a respite from him.

Stretching my wings and my arms, I rise to standing and walk —one foot in front of the other—to the end of the branch. My weight makes the branch bow very low and my feet slip, so I flutter my wings just enough to hold the bulk of my weight and allow the branch to straighten again.

My insides swell with pride knowing I'm on my way to mastering balance and flight.

"Gorwin said there's a *biloko* in this forest."

I grind my teeth and groan hearing the prince's voice. He's found me. "Go away, Rion."

"Gorwin said we shouldn't be out here alone."

"Then obey your father's assistant and go away! How did you even come into the forest? Where are your servants? Where's your tutor?" My good mood is plummeting like a stone tossed into the Sigmus River.

"I told them I needed to look for you."

"And they let you?"

"I sent them on an errand and told them I'd find you myself."

"You're going to get me in trouble."

"You might already be in trouble, *Amberle*! What about the *biloko?*" He whisper-shouts the last part, then glances over his shoulder with dramatics.

"A biloko can't get me up here!"

"They ring their bells. They make you want to follow them with their hypnosis—which will be harder for you to resist since you're half-human."

"I'll be fine." I prick at the insult. "I'll immediately fly away if I hear any bells." I don't even try to hide my annoyance and close my eyes as if the action will miraculously cause him to disappear. Too bad I don't have *that* kind of magic.

"You won't be able to fly away! It'll lure you down. It'll make you follow it to its den and convince you to butcher pieces of yourself for its dinner."

I shut my eyes tighter.

"Come to the river with me," he whines. "I've got a new pirate ship and a royal schooner. I want to try them out, but Wyn and Arielle are gone, so I can't ask them."

I'm glad he thinks of me as his third choice. "You mean your little toy boats?"

He nods, flashing his teeth with his enthusiastic, yet feverish, grin.

"I think I'll stay here."

"I could order you to play with me," he warns. His smile has vanished.

My fear spikes briefly, but dissolves just as quickly. "You can't order me to be your friend, princeling. Only your father can, and we both know you don't want that."

He quiets, allowing a bit of guilt to snake inside me. *No! He doesn't get to order me around! I'll play with him later.*

"Fine. Stay up there!" Rion shouts. "Just don't blame me if you lose a piece of your arm or leg because you were too stubborn to get out in time."

He stomps through the underbrush, and I grin. I've won! Perhaps I do have magic to make him disappear. Relief floods me —I'm free of him.

Thank *Vejo* Prince Rion wasn't born with wings. Now that mine have finally developed enough strength to hold my weight, perhaps I can escape him whenever I want!

My spirits leap triumphantly.

Rion wasn't so bad before, when the four of us played, but now that he's learning his place in the court and the realm, he's become insufferable. He's become spoiled and entitled and feels as if all of Faerie revolves around *him* and *his pleasure.*

"Yes, Prince *Orion,*" I mock, singing to the trees. "Whatever you say, Prince *Orion.*"

Perhaps Faerie does revolve around him, but I won't submit to it.

Father said to be kind to all creatures. That I should be kind to the prince, especially because I don't know what he suffers. He also reminded me that Rion might someday be king, and that I should remain in his good graces.

But maybe I don't want to be in his good graces!

Father also told me to be kind to the pestering pixie who taunted me in my bedroom three weeks in a row. Eventually, she chopped off a chunk of my hair in my sleep, then bit me when I offered her a pastry from the kitchens. That's where kindness got me. Sometimes it's better to watch my back.

I continue practicing my balancing with the aid of my wings. Walking as light as a will-o'-the-wisp on branches as thin as my thumb, then jumping from tree to tree. It's getting easier with each leap and I'm able to fly over increasingly larger gaps.

"Amberleeeeeee!"

My heart jolts. It's Rion again. But he sounds panicked. Terrified.

"Amberle, heeeeelp!"

His voice isn't coming from the direction of the palace, it's coming from deeper in the forest. Between his cries, I finally hear it. The faint ringing of a bell.

My heart pounds against my ribcage. *Oh no.*

I leap to the ground, rattling my knees and slamming my feet hard into the forest floor. My soles sting with the impact. My wings are getting stronger, but my feet are still far more reliable and faster.

"Prince Rion! I'm coming!" I bolt through the trees.

Weaving through the foliage, my face and arms are lashed with branches and thorns. My wings might help with speed in a barren field, but they'd only slow me down in here and would risk looking like my face and arms, so I keep them tucked tightly behind me to block the assaults.

I hear the bell again but ignore its ring to risk falling into its hypnotic trap too.

I hope I'm not too late. The prince might be a pestering, tricksy phouka, but I don't wish him harm. It's probably the human part of me. Or maybe my father's influence.

"Here! Amberle!" He's on my left.

I pivot, rushing in his direction and promptly clasp my hands tight against my ears to prevent myself from also being pulled in the biloko's spell. Terror shoots through me. What if he's fallen into the very trap he feared? I can't even think of what he might look like, what he might be *doing* when I find him.

But when I finally catch up to the prince, I'm confused.

Rion sits at the edge of a large boulder covered in moss, swinging his dangling legs back and forth with both hands braced behind him. He's at leisure. He doesn't *look* like he's in peril.

My steps slow and I search the forest for the small creature with hair and a long beard the texture of grass. There isn't one, but there *is* a shiny brass bell with a wooden handle next him on the boulder. Finally, I drop my trembling hands.

It wasn't the biloko they warned us about. The prince rang the bell. He was never in any danger!

Rion clutches his middle and bursts into laughter, pointing with one hand. "You should have seen the expression on your face!"

My still racing heart pumps fire through my face and limbs. "Why would you do that? I-I thought you were really in trouble!"

But he only laughs harder for several moments before calming himself. The prince then grips the bell and hops to the ground. "Now that you're done playing in trees, care to join me at the river? I have two boats. You can play with one."

I grit my teeth, but keep my lips closed. My fists are clenched so tightly, my fingernails dig into my palms. Was he using my humanity to manipulate me? *How could he?*

Turning on my heel, I stalk away. He keeps up, tripping over branches and attempting to get me to stop, but I flutter over a small ravine to get away from him. Without wings, he'll have to go around. I've effectively lost him.

I storm through the forest, my blood boiling. Other emotions creep in and tears threaten as I emerge from the forest.

Captain Shinyfleck stops me at the gate with a stern tone. "I thought His Highness was with you?"

I scowl, using my anger to mask other emotions I can't risk unpacking right now. I hook a thumb over my shoulder. "He's behind me."

Captain Shinyfleck grips my shoulder when I try to pass him. "Not so fast. You left him *alone* in the Infernus Forest?"

"He followed me, I—"

"Elm!" the captain snaps at another guard, springing all of them to sprint toward the forest while he keeps a firm grip on me.

"He's fine, really. The prince isn't in danger," I say. *Other than being clobbered by me for what he just pulled.*

"You'd better pray to *Vejo* that he is."

"What? It was his servants who let—"

"His servants said you lured him. That you tricked him into playing one of your games!"

"I—"

"Enough!"

I fold my arms and blow out a breath. Obviously, his servants threw me into the dragon's mouth to save their own hides.

Several minutes later, Rion strolls between the two guards who ran after him. They're overreacting. But my heart still races with the possibility of being punished for *his* foolishness.

The prince is frowning, and darts his gaze around as if he's nervous, but when he spots me, has the *gall* to smile widely and then *wink!* If punching the smirk off his face wasn't a capital crime, I'd pull away from Captain Shinyfleck's grip and do it this instant.

"What's all the fuss?" the prince asks. "Did she tell you what happened? It was just a prank." He lifts the bell and rings it again. "This is an ordinary bell. A human relic. There's nothing magical about it, let alone biloko hypnosis."

He doesn't wait for a response and pushes past me a little too hard.

I shake my shoulders, waiting for the captain to release his grip so I can run off—or fly off—and find somewhere to scream, but his fingers only dig harder.

"You don't think I'm letting you go after that, do you?"

I gesture toward the irritating, retreating figure of the spoiled, cruel prince. "You heard him! He just pretended a biloko wanted to make a meal out of him to get back at me for refusing to play with his stupid boats!" *Okay, maybe I shouldn't have added that.* "He was never in danger."

"But there *is* a biloko in the Infernus Forest and you've just put the crown prince in danger by luring him out there."

"I didn't—"
"Silence! This cannot go unpunished."

Eight

RION

The color in Amberle's face has drained. I thought this would be an innocent story to tell Faerie, but Amberle has lost her spark. Could she be feeling ill? Although star fae can succumb to sickness—mostly human diseases—it is rare.

"I'm not proud of what I did, but at the moment, it seemed like a good idea," I say, reaching over to take Amberle's hand. I hope the gesture is reassuring. At least that's what I tell myself. Really, I just want to touch her.

Her fingers tense and I fear she wishes to pull away, but she relents and allows me to cup her hand. The near-rejection smarts, but I focus on the way she gripped my face before Nieven popped up on deck a few moments ago to tell me she _doesn't_ hate me.

Vejo, I wanted to kiss her right then. I want to kiss her now. But I won't risk it until I'm certain she wants it too.

My chest tightens as a shard seems to twist in my gut.

"We were younglings, and I had this idea that everyone wanted to be my playmate because I'm the crown prince," I say.

"That is a fair assumption," Nieven says, grinning, then turning to address the audience. "Tell me I'm wrong, but I think most fae would _kill_ to be close to the prince."

Amberle shifts beside me, so I pull her hand slightly and squeeze her fingers, prompting her to look at me. When her bluebell-colored eyes—that are more sapphire today—lock with mine, I feel a jolt, but manage a friendly smile. "Not everyone."

"So, what was it, Amberle?" the announcer asks. "What did you dislike about the prince?"

"I uh... I mean, I didn't—"

"There's no need to be coy," Nieven assures her. "Prince Orion already told us he thought your pranks were endearing."

The announcer eyes me, but I already feel the heat scorching through the veins in my neck. I duck my head in a failed attempt to hide it. *Am I so transparent?* Can Nieven, and all of Faerie, already see that I'm already a pathetic fool for this girl?

"I think it's safe to say that you, *Amberle Kindra,* are one of His Highness's favorites," Nieven continues. It's a gross understatement, but I don't correct him. "Tell us about the biloko bell." Fortunately, Nieven is addressing Amberle because I'm still composing myself.

She begins by explaining she was just learning to use her wings. Unfortunately, she's animated, and she pulls her hand away to gesture. When she flutters her wings, it's slight, but I notice her wince at the motion. She's still injured. Anger floods my body, radiating from my core. It's unacceptable. She should be healed by now. I must speak with—

"...The prince found me practicing in the Infernus Forest." Her words interrupt my thoughts, and she pulls my gaze. Her eyes quickly search mine, her pupils constricted. I think she's trying to communicate something, but I can't read her. "He wanted me to go with him to play with his new toy boats."

I was so proud of those ships. They were a gift from the king of the Underwater Court as a tribute to accepting me as the crown prince—as the next high king. I didn't realize the magnitude of that gesture until later. The Underwater Court is excellent at uncovering secrets.

"His other companions were away that day, so I was the only

one he could ask." She shrugs, her hands up, slightly more exaggerated than her usual self. A performance. I hate that I can't talk to her privately.

"That's right. Although Princess Arielle and Wyn Firetail were your playmates too," I say, reminding her that we are all friends. "They were both away from Isi Aura."

Her hands fold in her lap. "Yes, so he had no one else to seek out."

"Amberle," I say, leaning closer to her, my heart suddenly pulsing against my ribcage as I lay my hand atop hers again. Her fingers twitch and she turns to me. I lower my eyes. I shouldn't admit this, but I want to. "I was grateful for the excuse."

"The excuse for what?" Amberle frowns, creating a slight crease between her eyebrows. I itch to reach up and smooth it with my thumb, but resist.

"The excuse that I could ask you first." My voice is low. Vulnerable. I move my hand around hers, taking her fingers and interlacing them between mine.

I don't expound, but Amberle must know what I'm implying. I wanted to ask *her,* not the princess whom everyone *expected* me to spend time with. Nor Wyn, who was the easy ask, without expectations or risks.

I look at Nieven, needing to look away from *her* because it's too much. His jaw is slack, and he's blinking rapidly. But I can't allow myself to react, other than plastering on a smile. I'm not saying what he or anyone else expected. I try not to think about my father's reaction to this moment. Even if Faerie doesn't understand my insinuation, my father will. He'll be furious.

When I turn back to Amberle, the frown and the crease are wiped away, but what remains is neutral. It's maddening.

"It sounds like you had a special kinship. Dare I wonder if this fae had a piece of your heart even when you were a youngling?" Nieven leans close, his previous jovial attitude returned.

"She did." I straighten.

Amberle stiffens, jabbing another painful pierce through my chest. *She doesn't feel the same.*

"But the other fae in the Tourney are intriguing and beautiful in their own unique ways," I admit. *For someone else.*

I hope no one catches my careful use of words. The others have their virtues. But they're not Amberle. They're not enough. Not to me.

"Yes, of course," the announcer agrees. "And perhaps you've had special moments or will have impactful experiences with the others that could become more than an infatuation from when you were young."

He makes it sound so trite, so much *less* than it is, but I cannot agree. I force a smile. I attempt to say *perhaps,* but the word won't lift from my tongue.

"Now, I thought this story was about a biloko bell," Nieven says, eyeing me and Amberle. "All you've told us so far is about Amberle's fledgling wings and Prince Orion's new boats." He turns to the winter magic. "I think we need to hear more of this story, don't we?" He asks the audience, lifting his hands as if waiting for invisible cheers.

"Well, I might have been scheming in my attempts to get Amberle down from the trees." I look at Amberle. I don't let the lack of emotion on Amberle's face stop the laugh that escapes. "I told her she shouldn't be in the forest because a biloko had been spotted recently."

"By the tone of your voice, I'm assuming it didn't work," Nieven says, matching my amusement.

"It didn't."

"I was stubborn," Amberle says, crinkling her eyes. She's finally participating. "So the prince tricked me by ringing a bell and making me think he was being eaten by the biloko." She's smiling, but something is *off* about her voice.

"You weren't too thrilled when you discovered I'd tricked you," I add, goading her. I want her to say what's on her mind.

"Who would be?" she snaps, pulling her hand away again. But

then she softens and turns to the announcer and the winter magic. "I was a youngling." Amberle shrugs and plays it off with a now-forced smile. "Naïve to the joke. I truly feared the prince was in danger."

"It shows your loyalty." Nieven sobers. "A proper response for the future heir. But perhaps that you cared for the prince too?"

Amberle nods but twists her mouth. I catch the glisten in her eyes before she stands abruptly and says, "Excuse me."

"She was not keen about that prank, Your Highness," Nieven says as we both watch her rush to the far starboard side of the ship, ducking under the foresail boom. "No one can be surprised that she secretly loved you, even then."

Was that why she couldn't forgive me? Has she cared about me all this time with the same depth I've felt for her? Could she not forgive me for making her think I might be hurt?

"If I could, Nieven, I'd like to go after her."

The announcer gives a knowing smile and lifts one hand toward the winged fae who holds my heart so tightly. "By all means, my Prince."

Nine

RION

I only catch part of what Nieven says as I trip away toward Amberle, but I swear the announcer tells the winter magic that he doubts any other contestants even have a chance.

He's not wrong.

Amberle can't go far, so I catch up to her, gripping the rail as she works her way to the stern, rounding barrels of oranges and lemons destined for the star islands. My pulse quickens and a churning feeling settles in my gut as I draw nearer to her. A jasmine-like fragrance wafts from the tendrils of her silver hair that lift in the sea breeze and mix with the citrus of the fruit. It's intoxicating. As is the idea that she might have cared for me all this time.

"Amberle. About that day—"

She whips to face me with glistening eyes right as the winter magic catches up to watch.

I offer both hands palm up. "If I had known—"

"But you don't know!" she snaps. But when she looks behind me, she straightens and sniffs a few times as she blinks rapidly to rid the brimming tears. Then, folding her arms, she lifts the edges of her mouth, but nothing else. It's not a genuine smile.

"I don't know what?" I ask, moving a half-step toward her.

Her head lowers to the side with eyes closed as if she's bracing for a beating. It's only for a tiny moment and she quickly rights herself, replacing the careful mask.

My gut wrenches, but I step closer, taking her hand and whispering so only she can hear, "You don't think I would hurt you? Do you?"

Amberle's wings flutter. "Not you, no."

Not you? What does she mean? "Then someone else? Do you think someone else will hurt you?"

"Rio—*Prince* Orion, your actions that day..." She pulls her hand away as she trails off. Keeping the rest of the words to herself.

"They hurt you. *I* hurt you."

She looks at the winter magic again. It clearly bothers her. She doesn't enjoy being watched.

"Don't worry about that," I say, waving a hand to block it and stare intently at her. "It's just you and me here. You can say what you need to say. Whatever it is."

"Yes, I was concerned for your safety," she says, wringing her hands. "And I was angry at you for pretending to be in danger..."

I attempt to fill in the blanks. "But there was more than that?"

She glances between the magic and me again. Warring with herself.

Without thinking, I grip the side of her waist, then pull her toward me. "Tell me. Whatever it is," I breathe into her ear. Then I whisper, "I'll protect you."

Amberle looks up at me. My breath catches. *Dear Vejo, she's breathtaking.* It's all I can do to stop myself from pulling her closer and kissing her. Right now. But I know she's doesn't want it—yet—and now is not the right time. Her eyes flit back and forth between mine, but by the tight line of her mouth, I finally realize I've misread something.

"Like you protected me *then*?" Her quiet words prick with painful truth.

I release her as if I've been stung, then swallow over the hard lump. "What happened to you... then?"

She folds her arms, putting a barrier between us and steps back, bumping into the rail. I step back to give her space.

"There are consequences for putting the crown prince in danger, of course," she says. "As there should be."

"What do you mean—"

The cold look in her eyes stops me.

"But you didn't put me in danger—"

"Forget it." She waves a hand, as if brushing off my questions. "It was a long time ago."

What feels like a mass of stinging eels swirls in the pit of my stomach. It's like the feeling I get when I've had too many pastries, and my gut wants to purge them. "W-what..." I reach for her hand. My instinct to touch her is too strong, but I pull away. *Now is not the time.* "What was your consequence?"

Bile rises at the thought of Amberle being punished for *my* games.

She hesitates, but in one quick motion, she bridges the gap between us and moves her face toward mine. A shiver runs up my neck as she passes my nose and I wait for her lips to brush against my cheek or my jaw in a kiss, but her breath and her words tickle my ear when she whispers, "I cannot tell you while they watch."

I pull back so I can see her eyes again. Our noses nearly touch and her mouth parts slightly when my gaze briefly flickers down to it. Clenching my teeth, I force myself to look up again. "I'll. Protect. You."

Her entire posture falls. She feigns a grin, but it doesn't light her eyes.

"Remember the time when we slid your toy soldiers down the banister and knocked down a mirror?"

She has forced a change of subject. I step back, releasing her as quickly as I gripped her. I look away, up over her shoulder at the blue-green waves of the sea as the magic crackles behind me.

The magic mocks me. There's no escaping it.

I turn back to Amberle and her smile cracks, likely because I'm not playing along. I hate seeing her under duress, so I won't press her. Not here.

"We kept that mischief a secret for decades." I chuckle and I hope it doesn't sound as fake to Faerie as it does in my ears. "I guess there's no time like the present to tattle on ourselves. But I can't imagine my tutor punishing me at this point."

This is our time to be alone! This is our time to be away from the other contestants! When I am not required to divide my time and when I have no other responsibilities other than to reminisce about mine and Amberle's shared past. When I only need to entertain Faerie with our stories. But I cannot get past this heavy thing that obstructs us.

"Ah, yes," Amberle continues, her smile strained. "Growing up in the castle had its perks. Even if the consequences for each of us were never quite equal."

Nieven pipes up from behind me, "Well, of course, a full fae prince has loftier standards and expectations from the king."

Amberle lowers her gaze, as if agreeing with Nieven, but her posture is stiff.

Is it this *punishment*, whatever it is she endured after my little prank with the biloko bell, that has kept her at arm's length all this time? Has she held this resentment toward me ever since that day? Is that why she said we were never friends? Because I hurt her without knowing it?

I can't help but think about *what might have been* if it had never happened. If I had never played the trick on her. Would she have stayed? Would she have come back?

Would she love me now?

The imagination is worse than reality and I cannot continue with this day until I know what Amberle's punishment was. I may not earn forgiveness quickly, but I can make reparations now if I know the truth.

I look back at her. Her eyes have fallen to the deck of the ship, her hands fisted. There's an invisible weight that pushes her shoulders and her wings down and I just want to take it away—whatever it is.

It's painful to watch and I can't help but tear my gaze away, back at the waves. Back at the water. At the blue green—

The water.

I grab Amberle by the waist with both hands and lift her up and over the rail. She's surprised, but her wings catch her fall, and she hovers. Thinking quickly, I hoist the nearest barrel, tumbling it over the side, then leap from the deck.

Whoosh! The water rushes into my ears and cuts off my senses. The world goes dark. My body is instantly alert in the chilly water as I spiral downward.

When I've stopped falling, I propel myself to the surface, waving my arms with clumsy flapping and kicking my legs wildly. But my head only barely breaks the surface when my inexperience pulls me back down again in a pathetic flail.

What was I thinking?

I can't swim.

Ten

Every curse word I can think of runs through my head as I stop hovering and dive down to save the foolish prince–effectively saturating my wings. Pulling him to the surface, I sputter and cough up salt water. Bright yellow balls float all around me, and I realize I'm surrounded by lemons. My wings, heavy and useless, now drag me down, so I do the best I can with my arms and legs to help me tread water. But I won't last long.

"What the hell, Rion!" My voice is raspy. I scold the prince, but he's slipped back underwater, beneath the lemons, so I wait. *Lemons?*

His face pushes through the surface, scattering a half dozen fruit in all directions.

"Rion! What were you—"

But his head is immersed *again*. When he bobs back up, he gurgles something muffled I can't understand.

The foolish prince is *drowning*.

I yank him up by the back of his shirt, pulling his head to the surface, but keeping us both above water is arduous.

"Amberle, the lemons," Rion says, between violent, quick breaths. "They float."

"That's great for them, but I don't think they can help us, Your Highness." I lose my grip on his shirt, and he slips under again. Frantically, I dig under his arm to get a better hold but push myself underwater in the process. I struggle back up and take a big gulping breath, just in case I go under again. Then, flexing my wings behind me, I flutter them slightly to aid in treading. It smarts with the movement, but *not dying* and *not letting the prince die* is more important than further injury to my wing.

"The barrel," Rion gasps.

"Help!" I shout to the ship, ignoring him. Surely someone saw us. All of Faerie watched. Everyone knows we've fallen overboard. "Someone heeeeellp!"

"Amberle! Get the barrel."

Rion is twisting his body, making it difficult for me to keep his head above water, so I turn and see a mostly empty barrel floating close to us.

A half dozen lemons still float inside it.

I curse under my breath as I pull the barrel closer to the floundering prince. *Leave it to Rion to get himself killed!* Of course, I'll be held responsible and find myself in a prison cell next to my father if he drowns.

"Grab it!" I say.

Rion slaps the barrel with his hand, spinning it and pushing it further away while going under again. The trajectory of the spin toward him doesn't push it too far, so I'm able to stop it and hold it steady.

Finally, in one flash movement with his other arm—that clearly takes all his strength—Rion grips the open end of the barrel tightly and pulls his head and his body back up.

I swim to the other side and pull myself up to drape over the center of the barrel. I lift my other hand so I'm laying partly sprawled over it. Rion adjusts, so he is lying over it too and our left ears are close to each other. With our weight hanging on opposite sides, the barrel won't spin out from under us.

Without warning, the prince bursts into laughter even though his breaths are still short and violent.

I stare at him. "What's so funny?"

He doesn't answer, but looks at the barrel and all around us, continuing to laugh.

It's contagious, so I can't help but crack a smile.

"That was so foolish!"

"Forgive me, but I'm afraid I have to agree with you. Why did you jump off the ship? Now is not the best time for a swim."

"That's not why..." he trails off and stares down into the water.

"Then what—"

"Tell me now," he interrupts, his expression serious again when his head snaps back up to look at me. "What was your punishment? The magic can't hear us in the water."

We're in a life and death situation and he still won't drop this?

"Is *that* why you pushed me in?" I shout, spitting water in his face. "Is it why you jumped in? Is it really *that* important to you?"

"Yes. Amberle, I *must* know."

It's hard to focus on the emotion in his voice over my irritation, but it's also hard to forget the things he said only moments ago on the deck of the ship. *Before* he nearly killed us.

I glance at the schooner and see frantic scrambling on the deck as the ship nears us, but the entire thing feels ridiculous. Foolish.

"Amberle," Rion prods. "We have little time, and I doubt we'll have this opportunity again." He gestures at the scrambling crew who are lowering a small rowboat onto the water. "They're bound to be furious—"

"That's just it! You don't think about the consequences!" I interrupt but, in my anger, I jostle the barrel and nearly tip myself off.

Rion's hand jerks out to grasp my arm, pressing it firmly against the wood. "You're right, I didn't think this through—"

I pull my face closer to his until his slit pupils dilate and I can see the different shades of gold in his irises. "They're going to blame me!"

"They won't, I—"

"It doesn't matter! They won't listen!"

His amusement falls.

"You don't understand, Rion." I turn away and my volume drops. "This is what happens. You do something like this, you jump into the sea and nearly drown, but *you* won't face the consequences."

His eyes bore into mine as he holds my gaze.

Then, in a voice I can barely hear, he asks, "What was your punishment?" Pause. "*Back then?*"

I stare right back. Daring him to look away when I respond, "An oubliette."

The waves become turbulent, and the barrel rises and falls out of our control.

"How long?" His eyes darken and his voice breaks.

A sharp breeze whips my hair across my cheek, and rivulets of water cut lines down my face.

"Five weeks."

I spent five long weeks in that dank, dark, and oppressive oubliette for *him*. Later, I learned they sent away every servant involved in disgrace. Servants whispered that even the captain had received an invisible, yet painful punishment.

My father tried to plea to the guards to reduce my sentence, that I was young, and it wasn't entirely my fault. But my father's pleas fell on deaf ears. *It's hardly a sentence at all,* they said, and *she won't be in there forever.*

Five weeks is nothing, they said. But to a youngling, it might as well have been five decades.

The prince jerks like he's about to fall in, but I flip my hand and grip the sleeve of his shirt to keep him on the barrel. He wanted to know and went to ridiculous lengths to find out. He's not escaping so easily.

"But it was worse for some of the servants who were disgraced and dismissed after their time in the dungeon," I add, with venom.

The rowboat is in the water with two fae frantically rowing in our direction.

Our time is up.

"And now I'll surely be punished for this." I release my grip on his shirt and drop back into the water.

Eleven

My once-carefully arranged hair is a sopping mess around my face, and the fabric of the soft pink dress clings to my skin. But I'm more worried about what comes next than the state of my appearance.

The prince holds my hand as we're taken back to the schooner. He offers a reassuring squeeze, prompting me to turn to him, but I only manage a slight smile. My heart pounds against my ribcage even though we're now safe from imminent death.

I don't know what awaits me when we're back on the ship— or back at the palace. The oubliette so long ago might have felt like a luxurious getaway compared to the punishment I'm handed this time.

There's no question that I'm out of the competition, but if the king makes me disappear, who will even notice?

The prince is ushered onto the deck by frantic guards, and then servants swarm him with blankets. I watch from below, taking deep breaths and scrambling for the right words to get out of this alive. I stand and square my shoulders, then move toward the rope ladder. My wings are a useless mess of soggy, wrinkly gossamer. Otherwise, I'd fly to the deck—or fly away. They weigh me down even more now that we're out of the water, tugging at the muscles on my back and making the effort even more grueling, but I put one hand and one foot in front of the other and make my way up the ladder.

But a hand with long, thin fingers is suddenly in front of my face, palm-up, offering assistance.

I glance up and nearly fall backward when I see the way the prince is looking at me with his walnut hair plastered to his forehead, streaming water that runs down the sides of his face. I avert my eyes, but get caught on the way his drenched shirt clings to his chest and force myself to look at his face again. He watches me as if I am the only fae in the entire world, in any realm, and he would be lost and cease to exist if I did not take his hand now.

He pulls me to the deck, then lifts a gray wool blanket over my shoulders and an arm around my waist, drawing me close. Even wet, his body is warm pressed against mine.

"I won't let them blame you for my actions," he whispers, his breath like a warm summer breeze against my cheek. His face stays at my ear a half's breath longer than his words linger before he faces forward.

The announcer approaches us.

Nieven claps his hands together in front of him—his smile more serious than it was during the interview—and I feel the buzzing magic keep step with him and turn to us. I attempt to lift my shoulders again but can't help that I probably looked like a drowned gryla standing next to the crown prince who nearly lost his life.

"Your Highness—"

"Before you say a word, Nieven," Rion says, tightening his grip on my waist and lifting his free hand as he speaks. "I want you and everyone watching to know that the little dip in the sea was entirely my fault. *Mea culpa*. It was foolish and dangerous, and I could have killed myself and Amberle both. But I take responsibility."

I can't help but stare at the prince. By announcing this in front of everyone, being broadcast to all of Faerie, there can be no dispute. If the prince had merely waited and told the truth in private later, the king and Gnacia still could have gotten rid of me, citing this incident as an excuse.

"I... I'm developing strong feelings for Amberle," he continues, and I bite down hard on the inside of my cheek to keep myself from showing any emotion. "She will not be eliminated for what happened today."

A maelstrom of warmth and bubbling churn at my core. If his request is taken seriously, I'm likely safe from being sent home in two days as a failure. I still have a chance to save my father. *Mission accomplished.* But by the prince voicing his feelings for me so publicly in a forum that is being watched by *everyone*, including the other contestants, life in the Tourney will become complicated—and likely uncomfortable—for me very soon.

"The king has requested that we turn back to Isi Aura at once, Prince Orion," Nieven says.

Rion must notice that I inadvertently suck in a breath because he holds me tighter. "Nor will she be punished."

"I'm sure you can discuss all of this once we've returned." Nieven waves a gracious hand and bows slightly,

The prince dismisses the announcer, and we stand shoulder to shoulder at the stern, looking at the wake of the boat behind us. I'm pleased that I can sense the winter magic at our backs, that perhaps I can sense when it's around and take advantage of situations when it's not, but it makes me feel vulnerable. Trapped. Living in shadows for so long, the light is painfully bright.

But I fear it's the least of my troubles to come.

"It shames me that my actions have caused you so much pain," Rion says to the sea.

I turn toward him, but he keeps his gaze locked on the white-capped waves that fan out behind the ship, so I turn away again. A mer with a turquoise-blue fin leaps from the water and arches over the waves before disappearing back into the depths.

"Actions always have consequences, but they can be different depending on your station."

"Thank you for helping me see that."

I feel his eyes on me, but that's not why my head snaps to him. "Rio—*Prince* Orion, you just—"

"*Thanked* you, I know." He smiles and turns his entire body toward me. "I *want* to be indebted to you, Amberle. I *want* you to have power over me until you think of a way for me to fulfill my oath, my *thanks* to you."

My insides do a little flip in my chest. He *thanked* me. The fae do not use those words unless they wish to be indebted to the fae they thank. And it usually ends badly. Kings have handed over crowns for those words. Wars have been lost. Kingdoms have been destroyed.

"But Prince—"

"When we are alone, I prefer you call me *Rion.*"

Rion might have hurt me in unforgivable ways in the past, but I see he has changed. And not because he just put himself in my debt. I've tried to ignore evidence of Rion's growth, but he *has grown*. He was changed before I met him in Rosewind, but I've seen the increase little by little as I've snuck my way back into his life.

"Rion, you didn't have to—"

"I know." His golden eyes burn. "Amberle, I..."

Panic spikes inside me. No, no, no. Rion can't confess any more *feelings*. His father would surely make me disappear. Tonight. Forever.

Rion licks his bottom lip before continuing, "There's no one I'd rather—"

Pushing up on my toes, I quickly press my lips against his cheek, near his jaw, in a quick, forceful kiss. It does what I intended. It stops his words and shuts down anymore.

But I realize my mistake too late.

I've just kissed the prince. What have I done?

/ welve

The prince's entire body is rigid. Stiff. Statue-like. I can't look him in the eye when I slowly step backward, but he captures my hand in his. Keeping me close.

I kissed him! Sure, it was on the cheek, but I *kissed* the prince!

My soaked wings hang heavy behind me. I should look for a patch of sun on the boat deck to dry them out, but I can't seem to pull myself away from him.

When his eyes lower to mine, urging me to look at them, I'm trapped in a golden brilliance with a hint of pleading that shreds my heart. A fluttering of dragonflies settles in my belly with a warmth I force myself to ignore because he *can't kiss me here.* Not now. Not like *that.* Not with all of Faerie watching.

Maybe not ever.

No, Rion, the words catch on my throat, unwilling or unable to escape.

The corners of his lips lift. Is he encouraged?

Please don't.

I fear I'll have to claim his vow to me now and cash in the thanks he offered only moments ago. I shake my head slightly as I pray to *Vejo* he'll read my expression correctly. His eyes darken and his face moves closer to mine.

No. Rion, you can't. Things will be so much worse if the prince kisses me and not only for me and my place in the competition. My father might be punished for *my* actions.

I touch the swirly inked promise mark near my eye.

Pressing my lips tightly together as if hiding them can stop him, I balk at the stark contrast of this moment against the one in the garden all those nights ago when I threw myself at the prince, terrified of being thrown from the competition. I *wanted* him to kiss me that night. *Desperately.* I would have done anything to convince Rion to keep me in the Tourney and I was prepared to defend my actions to Gnacia, and even to the king, with that argument.

"Kisses can be lies," he had said.

The memory makes my head fuzzy because something changed that night. I felt something.

Then lie to me.

Remembering that change isn't helping my current situation.

My soaked wings twitch and with my free hand, I clutch the crystalized sunbeam—that he gave me—below my throat as I panic and scramble for a reason to stop his kiss.

"It's a miracle I didn't lose this in the water," I say, fumbling with it.

Rion lifts my unoccupied hand, bringing it to his lips without breaking eye contact, and presses them against my knuckles.

I slowly and covertly let out the breath I held captive. I don't want the prince—or Faerie—to see my relief, but I can't bring myself to be entirely happy about a chaste kiss either.

"My actions were foolish. Reckless," he says, then, "It's a miracle I didn't lose you." His muttering is so quiet, I'm not sure I heard him right.

Then, with the moment over, we stand at the rail, shoulder to shoulder, watching the water behind us in silence all the way back to Isi Aura.

When we dock, hordes of waiting guards meet us. And also, a handful of Tourney contestants. I'm glad to see Didi, who bounces on her feet, clutching her cait sith in her arms. She might be happy to see me *and* the prince back on dry land, but I know by the way Princess Mora's raven *kraa's* and the stiff stance of the two autumn fae, Tierney and Cerule, that the three of them wish I'd drowned.

Wyn is also at the dock. He looks relieved to see us both. Seeing him reminds me of the slip of parchment he found in the secret passageway. I instantly itch to escape everyone and find out if it's important. I'm jealous that Wyn already knows if it has a clue to the mystery of Juniper's death.

A raven—Stjarna, the prince's raven—glides from his high perch on the mast of another docked ship to Rion's shoulder as we walk down the gangway. Mora's bird *kraas* sharply again.

"Our pets are already in love, Prince Orion!" Mora sings, then rushes forward and pulls on the prince's arm, looping hers with his and their backs toward me as if I'm not even here.

My chest tightens.

Stjarna adjusts his position on the prince's shoulder to turn and stare at me with one black, glistening eye. Up close, I recognize the bird. I blink, surprised, but there's no mistaking this creature. He's the same raven who was outside my window early in the competition. I cock my head, wondering why he had visited me. Stjarna was not yet the prince's pet when I lived at the palace, so he could not have recognized me. We'd never met. Perhaps it was a mere coincidence? Perhaps the ledge of my window looked the most appealing that night? Or perhaps I'm reading too much into it.

I brush it off as unimportant to my task, nothing more.

"Your Highness," Wyn approaches the prince and I'm not sure if I imagine Rion's relief at having his conversation with Mora interrupted, but the uncertainty gnaws at me. "The king wishes to speak with you immediately."

"Of course," Rion says, reading his friend's gravity. He lifts a hand, which forces Mora to release his arm, and turns back toward me. "But first, I want one more word with Amberle."

A guard steps forward. "Prince Orion—"

"You will grant me this!" His tone is firm and his expression is stern. King Estelar's orders always trump the prince's, so I expect them to ignore his wishes, but no one objects, and Wyn and the guards closest to us step back.

Even Mora occupies herself by talking quietly to her raven, but her bird takes off after Stjarna when he *kraas* and flies away.

Rion turns to me with lifted eyebrows and gently takes my hand and pulls me close, leaning down as he speaks. "I'm sure to get an earful from my father," he says, his eyes flitting back and forth between mine. "But I'm glad you told me—" He halts his words and glances up. We're surely being watched by winter magic now. "I'm glad we talked," he amends. "I'm glad you're here. That you're back and that—"

He's interrupted by one guard clearing his throat. The prince turns to snap at the guard, but I pull his hand.

"We'll talk later," I say, trying to sound demure and submissive, exactly the type of attitude that should be least likely to anger the king. "The king is waiting for you."

The smile he parts me with is physically painful and I'm forced to clutch a fisted hand to my chest when he walks away with Wyn to quelch the ache. The scowls shot at me from Tierney, and even Cerule doesn't help, but they both turn on their heels in a huff and walk away.

A guard approaches me. He's a trouping fae who barely reaches my elbows, but he's not without presence and looks up at me through thick, dark eyebrows. "Don't think you've gotten away with this, Amberle Kindra. The king is displeased with you." My pulse quickens and my palms clam up. Fortunately, I cannot feel the buzzing energy of the winter magic. "Putting the prince in danger cannot go without consequences."

"I understand." I take a deep breath. "What consequences will I face?"

"That is yet to be determined."

I nod.

Then he leans closer to whisper, "And Gnacia Evernet hopes you remember your instructions and your deadline?"

Gnacia is sending messages through another fae? Even though Wyn was just here and could have done it for her? It worries me, but now I know the reason for the absence of watching magic. The king doesn't want this conversation broadcast.

"I remember."

The guard grunts, then stalks away with his arms swinging and his nose in the air.

Didi skips toward me, juggling her feline familiar to one hand, to wrap the other arm around me and pull me close. "What was that about?"

I bite the inside of my cheek and force a smile.

"Wait." She looks around us as if feeling for the winter magic. "Are they blaming you for what happened? We all saw it! The prince threw you off the ship, then jumped in himself!"

I shrug as my senses pick up the faint crackling of returning winter magic. Wyn has also broken away from the prince and appears to be waiting for me to catch up, which will save me from needing to track him down.

"Well, it doesn't matter. What happened on that ship..." Didi whistles low. "There aren't words."

"I agree, and yet, I was there," I say, glancing up at Wyn who isn't within hearing range yet, then force out a little laugh. I struggle to keep my attention on Didi's words. I'm eager to speak with him. "My wings still haven't dried."

"I am not talking about your little dip in the water. I'm talking about how obviously the prince is in love with you!"

That brings my focus snapping back to her. "Didi, I—"

"You cannot deny it. Yes, you were there, but you weren't watching like the rest of us. Seeing you and him... well, it's undeniable that you are the prince's favorite."

I press my lips together, waffling between a strange, warm

elation blossoming at my core mixed with unbridled terror. Also, I'm not so certain Wyn didn't hear her.

Rion cannot love me. I cannot win. That was not the plan. That is not the job.

"The king might insist that he continue on with the Tourney as planned, but I think he'd pick you now if he could end it."

"Amberle," Wyn interrupts and the two of us look at him. "Can I steal you away for a moment?"

Didi's clear eyes appeal to me. *Do you want to be stolen away?* She seems to ask.

"Wyn Firetail and I are old friends," I assure her, grateful for the interruption. For more than one reason.

Thirteen

My back muscles ache with the heavy, still-drenched weight of my wings as I walk beside Wyn toward the palace.

"How was your date with the prince?" Wyn asks. His eyes are on Didi, who is retreating, but still within earshot. I itch to ask him about the slip of paper he found in the hidden corridor, but we cannot discuss that when we could be overheard.

"You should really start watching the Tourney, Wyn." I tease. "The king did order all of Faerie—"

"Oh, I saw everything that happened on that ship, Amberle Kindra," he interrupts, wagging his eyebrows. "What I mean was, how was your time in the water? You *know*, the part the winter magic *couldn't* hear?" He leans closer to me and adds, "And the lemons?"

"In Prince Orion's defense, he thought the buoyant lemons would help us float." I hope he doesn't see the way my cheeks burn, even though I'm not sure why I'm blushing.

Didi is long gone, but the energy of the winter magic is strong. We're being watched.

I don't know why anyone wishes to overhear mine and Wyn Firetail's conversation—the magic usually follows the prince wherever he goes. But... perhaps the king doesn't want his tête-à-tête with the prince broadcast, leaving the contestants—myself included—as the entertainment.

The magic can be in more than one place, of course, but I'm also "special" at the moment because I had the most recent one-on-one time with the prince. I hate feeling so exposed and wish I could crawl back to my shadows, but I can use this to my advantage; I'll give Faerie what they want while doing some damage control with the crown.

"So, what did the two of you discuss while you were in the water?" Wyn asks.

"Survival," I quip. "I also might have scolded him for tossing me overboard." I duck my head briefly, considering my next words. I must paint Rion in a positive light while edging myself away as his *potential mate.* "You know what it's like being friends with the prince. When he has his mind set on something..."

"He can be stubborn," Wyn finishes.

"Yes, but that attribute is also favorable in a good ruler," I point out.

"Of course."

"I imagine Faerie would love to know what it was like being friends with the prince as a youngling," I say, waving a hand at the watching magic. "Why don't you relate a story to them?"

"I'm sure Faerie would love to hear more about *your* feelings toward the prince after your time with him, Amberle."

"But Wyn—"

"I'm sure Faerie would also much rather hear stories about Prince Orion as a youngling from you, not me." Wyn always knew how to ruin my games and plans. And now isn't any different.

But I'm distracted when Wyn veers in a direction I don't expect. "Where are we going?"

"A healer."

He points at my injured wing that flutters at the attention. The action aches and I can't help the "*Ow!*" that escapes.

"We aren't finished talking about you and the prince, but

Prince Orion insisted that I take you directly to the infirmary," he says. "How did you injure it?"

"It's an old injury," I say, flicking my wings again to downplay the severity and expel some of the water, but I bite down hard on the inside of my cheek to prevent myself from crying out.

Wyn tilts his head expectantly.

"I-It happened when I found Juniper—" I can't finish the sentence.

His hand drops to my arm and tugs me forward.

"Wyn, it's fine. Really, with more sunlight and—"

He whips on me again. "Under different circumstances, I might agree with you, but Amberle, a fae *died*. A contestant in the Consort Tourney *you* are a part of." He ushers me through the corridors, silent and refusing to be stopped by anyone. I don't realize he's taking me to the royal healers, the ones reserved for the *royal* family, until we're marching through the infirmary doors.

"You should have taken me to Kali Islandwort," I mutter under my breath, feeling the flushing of my cheeks in full force.

"Appearances," he says, just as quietly. Then, he speaks up when he says, "As a potential *royal*, you should become accustomed to being attended to by the *royal* healers."

"He's right." A summer elf greets us. "And you should have come to us *much* sooner."

I'm too stunned by their statements to argue, especially as the elf has such thinly veiled distaste in her eyes. Her long, stick-straight, dark navy hair swishes past, undulating back and forth a bit like a snake as she walks around me.

"Had Prince Orion not been summoned by the king," she says cooly, "I'm sure he would have brought you to me himself."

She flashes what might've passed as a smile at Wyn, except it's a sneer-with-teeth. I could've sworn thorns literally extended from her arms before retracting.

I know her act is all for the magic and favor of the prince. That if we weren't being watched, this healer would have sent me away immediately, and Wyn wouldn't be holding back his barbs for this elf who clearly despises us both.

She escorts me to a bed near a tall window, then orders me to sit. "I must gather some supplies," she says, "but this won't take long."

I obey and lower myself onto the bed as she walks away. The sunlight streaming in from the window hits my wings. The warmth and healing power always feels rejuvenating, so I adjust until both wings are directly in its path and close my eyes. The winter magic is still strong, so I can't ask about the parchment yet. Or ask Wyn what he knows.

But I can do one thing: damage control. Perhaps I can talk my way out of a punishment for what happened today.

"It was my fault," I say, praying Wyn takes the bait.

He does. "What was?"

"The reason the prince and I ended up in the water," I say, opening my eyes. "If I'd just told him what he wanted to know, it never would have happened."

I hope they heard my admission of flimsy guilt with mercy and not further fire to get rid of me. It'd be easier if I could just lie.

"What did he want to know? What your punishment was... back then?" Wyn's expression darkens, and he blows out a breath. He knew about the oubliette. "When I heard they—"

Don't. I shoot him a stern look and shake my head slightly. *Please, don't say it.* I'm trying to extinguish the fire, not fuel it.

Wyn moves to sit next to me, jostling the bed with his weight. "Prince Orion might be my friend, but when I heard what happened, I wanted to wrap my hands around his little—"

I grip his wrist with my nails. He grimaces, but I only dig harder. We need to have a private chat soon. Wyn shouldn't be talking negatively about Rion. Not with so many listening. I hope he gets my meaning.

"So he never found out?" Wyn's voice has dropped.

"Not until today." I shake my head, then look down and release my grip, noticing the bracelet of red crescents I left behind;

they might've saved him from his own dungeon. Getting back to my task, I feign that I'm as ridiculously forlorn as I dare.

"I should have told him so he didn't... so I didn't... " I pretend to search for words. "It was my fault. I just hope my punishment doesn't pull me from the Tourney." Breathing out a sigh, I hope it's enough to appease the king to keep me around. My job isn't done. I look up at Wyn and suddenly hope they *are* watching. "Because I'm not ready to go yet."

His eyes narrow.

"As the prince's old *friend,* there are things I need to do before..." I let viewers imagine what I'm thinking. I hope I've hit the right notes so that the king won't hate me, and when my father and I return to society, we won't be shunned.

Wyn frowns, then stands and walks to the other side of the room as the elf with a navy waterfall of hair returns. The healer's assistant trails behind her, carrying an armful of linen. They're clearly identical twins.

"We will dry your wings first," the healer says as she and her sister approach them.

I lean forward with my eyes closed tight and brace myself with both hands clutched around the edge of the bed as the elves make quick work. Using the linen, they pat-dry my wings, and by the warmth I note they're using summer magic too.

Then, one stretches out my wing. Pain radiates like a thunderbolt. I cry out, my back arching.

The bed jostles and someone has taken my hand. Wyn.

"It'll be over in just a moment," the healer says.

Then the burning starts.

Unlike when Kali uses her healing magic, *this* searing magic is agonizing and fills my entire body with molten, fiery pain.

Squeezing my eyes shut again, I scream. Whatever part of me insists on bravery—it's gone. All I know is boiling, vomit-inducing torture that blots out all other senses and threatens to swallow me whole.

But then it's over. The pain has completely vanished. All of it.

I take a tremulous breath and open my eyes slowly. I blink several times before Wyn comes into focus. He's wincing, his face red, and lets go of my hand. He shakes it out and I wonder if he regrets letting me cut off the blood flow to his fingers. Then I realize there's something he left behind; the rough feel of the paper he slipped into my hand pushes out all other thoughts.

Has he just passed me the paper he found in the corridor? My heart skips a beat, but I can't let my face show anything to give it away. Everyone expects me to test my wings, so I use it as a distraction from my churning thoughts. Looking over my shoulder, I stretch them both to their full span. There is no lingering ache, no smarting sensation, no pain.

I've spent most of this Tourney with an injured wing. But not anymore.

The twin healers give me tight smiles when I stand and nod at them, then they gather the linens and shuffle away.

Wyn and I walk out of the Infirmary with the winter magic dutifully following alongside us. The paper he passed to me is pressed against my wrist as I hold it concealed at my side. How can I talk to him with the magic watching? How can I read what's on the paper? I understand Rion's reckless actions of throwing me overboard so much more, but we're not on a ship right now and if we walk to the shore with the intention of speaking privately, suspicions will rise.

"I think it would be wise for you to retire to your rooms for some rest," Wyn says. He glances down at my hand that holds the note.

"You were always such a good friend to be concerned for me," I say, grateful for the easy excuse. "I think I will rest awhile."

It's all I can do not to sprint to my quarters, but soon I'm in the safety—*and privacy*—of my rooms. I feel for the winter magic and only sense its absence before I fumble, unfolding Wyn's note and feel two pieces of paper. The top one is short. It's from Wyn and merely says,

The gardens at dusk. Southern wall. - W

The second one is in a scribbled, hurried hand.

I fear the secret I've uncovered is dangerous. It's clear the reason for the Consort Tourney is more than it seems. It's a distraction from a truth the fae deserve to know.
Send help or advisement.
Juniper

Fourteen

Wyn didn't explicitly state that I should get to the gardens without the magic following, but it's implied. We can't speak freely until we know we're not being overheard.

So, with freshly healed wings, I opt for the window.

There's no way to open it, but that's never stopped me before. Shattering it would be quickest and easiest, but it'd draw guards and the winter magic running. Cutting the glass is my best option.

It just takes something sharp and hot.

A poker from a fire and some cold water can do the trick in a pinch, but there isn't a fireplace in my rooms. A full-blooded summer fae could easily use their magic—which sends my thoughts fluttering back to Rion. It's only a half-formed whisper of an idea that I would never truly consider, but part of me wants to ask for the prince's help.

I have neither a poker, adequate summer magic, nor Rion to lend me his, but I have the next best thing. Crystalized sunbeams are made with powerful summer magic and contain a flicker of the heat of the sun. Although rare, I have one looped around my neck.

In a way, the prince *is* helping me.

I toss a pitcher of water on the window to wet the surface. Then, lifting the gifted necklace over my head, I use the edge of the sunbeam to score a small hole just large enough to fit a finger through. Which is what I do next, hooking my left index finger on the outside to grip the glass. Then, with my right hand clutching the sunbeam, I score a large square that starts and ends at the windowsill so I'll have a perch to fly from and eventually land when I return. It would be better to remove the entire glass, but it's too large for me to handle safely.

I make a mental note to ask Gnacia to replace the glass and perhaps install it with the ability to open and shut.

Once the glass is cut, I gently pull it toward me, hearing a satisfying *shloop* as it separates.

Carefully, I place the pane on the floor against the wall. I have ample time before any servant will return to prep me for dinner. I hop up onto the opening and brace my hands against the sides. A strong breeze cuts across the face of the palace, whipping silver strands horizontally across my face.

Leaning forward in a crouch, I curl my toes along the edge of the windowsill, watching until a distant guard, the size of a wisp's trail below, disappears around a corner, then I leap.

There's a brief pause, a moment of silence, a space between time when my feet leave Faerie and before the air captures my wings. It's peaceful and serene and nothing else matters. There are no clients, there are no jobs, there is nothing to be stolen, not even a breath. Nothing exists in that moment except for me... and a single heartbeat. It's been so long since I've lived in that space between time. My throat tightens, and my eyes burn.

When the moment ends and my wings grab the wind that *whooshes* past my ears, my pulse suddenly races because this time, the moment was different. Something else shivered within my elation and echoed within the depths of my bliss. A word or a name spoken with the rhythm of the single beat of my heart.

No. It was nothing. Just my imagination because he came to mind a moment ago.

I stretch my wings out. After trying—and sometimes failing—to keep them still for so long, they feel good and *whole.*

The gardens aren't far, so my flight doesn't last long. It's disappointing, but it won't be the only time I fly tonight. I lower onto a cobblestone path, knees bent, and feet disturbing a small puff of fine dust that lifts briefly from the ground.

When I straighten, I pause and feel for the winter magic. It's still absent. *Good.* It might not be aware that I've left the palace, but I move through the gardens silently as I make my way to the southern wall.

My limbs and head buzz with the aftereffects of my first flight in ages, and I can't help the giddy smile that spreads across my face.

Wyn isn't immediately at the wall when I arrive, but a dark form lands on the ground in front of me when I near it—he jumped the wall. After a brief glance at me, a spark ignites against the stone and fire spreads outward. I recognize it immediately as Wyn's fire privacy magic.

"You shouldn't talk like that," I say when we're engulfed in the fire. Safe from listening ears and observing eyes. "It doesn't matter who you are or how close you are to Rion, if they hear you speak ill of him even about something in the past—"

"You're right, but now I can speak freely. And about something in the present. The prince is being a *fool,* Amberle," Wyn quips. "What was he thinking pushing you off a ship, then jumping in after you? Especially when you have an injury?"

"He wasn't thinking," I admit with my own bubbling frustration and remembering all the moments Prince Rion came to my rooms when he wanted a private word. I much prefer that over half-drowning in the waves of the sea. My chest tightens and I realize just how much I miss those unexpected visits.

"This is a precarious and delicate job, Amberle. No matter

how many times Orion promises to protect you, he does not know the extent of the danger you're in." Wyn lifts an eyebrow.

"I know."

"*You* don't understand the extent of the danger you're in either." He watches me, frowning. "What are you thinking, sneaking around looking for the murderer of a Tourney contestant—when you're supposed to be undercover as a *Tourney contestant*? It's very, *very* foolish."

I cross my arms and clench my jaw. He didn't know Juniper. He didn't find her body. Wyn doesn't understand why I need to find her killer.

"And with an injured wing, no less," he adds.

"It was healing," I argue.

"Then why did Rion task me with taking you to the royal healers? Why did he insist they attend to you immediately?" One eyebrow arches in my direction.

I shrug.

"Prince Orion didn't realize the extent of your injury until you were back on the ship, Amberle. The moment you disembarked; he ordered me to take you." His voice has softened, but he huffs out an exasperated breath, then shakes his head and smiles.

"What?"

Wyn pushes away from the wall and unfolds his arms, donning a smirk. "First, admit that you were acting foolish by not getting it healed sooner. You should know better! The palace, the Consort Tourney, and your job in it isn't a youngling's game."

"I know."

"Admit it."

"Fine." I lift both hands. "I was a fool. You're right. Now what was that look for?"

Satisfied, Wyn leans his shoulder on the wall again and hitches one foot flat against it. "Orion wanted to take you. He was *desperate* to go with you, but he was also panicked that the king might send you home. He needed to obey the summon of his father if he has any chance of keeping you here."

A jolt of fear rushes through me. I run a hand over my forehead, brushing loose strands of hair away. I suspected my position in the Tourney might be in peril after Rion's stunt, but to hear the prince is also worried spikes my anxiety. *Can he save me? Or are my moments numbered?*

"You don't see it, do you?" Wyn tears me from my musing.

"See what?"

"That Orion was *desperate.* To go with you. To save you."

I shake my head. "So?"

"So... Prince Orion is clearly in love with you."

"But he can't..." I say as pixies jostle around my belly and my mouth fills with spiderwebs. Didi said something similar, but she's wrong. They're both wrong. "No. He's not—"

"It's not really something you can argue, Amberle. And it's not why I asked you here, but it's a problem that needs to be dealt with. Later. You may not have come for Orion, but he doesn't know that, and the king has clearly paid little attention to his son."

The king couldn't have known what would happen at the Tourney—seeing into the future is only possible for select underwater fae—but it doesn't matter. Rion isn't in love with me. They're misreading the situation. The prince and I are friends and have a fondness for each other, but it isn't...

I take a deep breath to clear my head.

He might have forced it out of me, but Wyn is right. I should have pushed to heal my wing quicker because I have a dangerous job to do in a situation that already cost one fae her life.

"You're right," I repeat. "I should have more information now, but I've been using my injury as an excuse..." To play along with the Tourney instead, but I won't admit that to Wyn.

But I'm not a contestant in the Tourney. Not really. I must get back on task.

Wyn sobers and takes a few steps toward me. "It's not an excuse. It's a reason. A good one, but you must spy for the king. Whatever comes, you must give detailed reports on all the contestants." He pauses. "I've seen what happens to those who fail King Estelar. You cannot fail him. I'll help you if I can, but you must do better."

I can't admit that Rion is affecting my decisions more than I'd ever intended. And I don't dare to bring up my father and how his fate is intertwined with my success. So, I nod and change the subject.

"We should discuss the note." Juniper's broken body flashes across my mind.

Wyn sighs. "I wanted you to know of its contents because I knew you'd pester me until I showed you, but you aren't acting on anything we learn from it. Do you understand?"

"Wyn, I think Juniper knew she was in danger—or that she was dying—and shoved the message into that crack in the wall before she could get it to whomever she intended it for."

"I deduced the same, but Amberle—"

"Which also means whoever she intended it for never got the message."

"Yes, but—"

"What do you think the secret is? Shouldn't we be finding that out?"

"*We* aren't doing anything. Do you understand? Whoever killed Juniper doesn't want the secret revealed," Wyn warns.

"But it gives validity that there is a secret. The Tourney is a distraction for something else. Something bigger," I say. "If we find the killer, we could learn—"

"Did you not hear what I said? *We* aren't doing anything!" Wyn steps closer but doesn't decrease his volume. "The king asked me to help Orion with the Tourney and choosing the right mate and he also asked that I keep *you* in line, but Prince Orion asked *me* to investigate Juniper's death. He didn't ask you. *You* will stay out of it."

"But, I could help."

"You could also be killed for snooping around where you shouldn't." He reaches for my shoulders and squeezes them. I fold my arms in defense. "Amberle, you are being watched closely. Likely closer than most." Wyn drops his tone. "You must focus on *your job*, which entails the Tourney contestants, and which is qualified for the prince. I will handle investigating Juniper's murder. Alone."

He's right.

I hate that he's right.

I turn to leave.

"Where are you going?"

I look over my shoulder, a half step away from the fire barrier. "To do my *job*."

To his credit, Wyn keeps a smug expression from appearing, but I don't miss the way his forehead smooths in relief. "Good."

He might have won, but he's not shutting me out. I turn, squaring my shoulders as I face him. "But you will keep me apprised."

"If I don't think it's something—"

"Wyn. Whatever you learn might help me understand the contestants. You *will* tell me what you learn."

"Of course, I will, Amberle."

Satisfied, I turn on my heel and push through the protection fire. Taking a few moments to feel for the winter magic, I only feel its absence. So I crouch down before pushing myself back into the air, stretching my wings to lift away from the ground.

I have some spying to do before Gnacia's deadline.

Fifteen

RION

I *will not be intimidated by him.* I steel myself as I march to the king's private office. I wish I could tend to Amberle and bath the sea water from me first, but I'm ordered to go now. My father promised that it's my decision who I choose as a mate and future queen, but I don't want to tempt him to meddle unnecessarily by disobeying him.

When I enter, I immediately spot my father's corn-yellow hair as he stands at the entrance of the massive balcony that overlooks the sea. Other courts protect their royals deep within their citadels, but the summer king must always have easy access to the sun. With his back to me, his hands are clasped behind him in one of his favorite regal stances. In his confidence and arrogance, he doesn't even glance to ensure I'm not an enemy come to assassinate him and steal his throne.

"Leave us," he commands the guards without turning. "This is a private conversation between me and the prince."

I walk toward my father and hear the doors shut quietly behind me. When I was a youngling, I used to stand next to him, mimicking his stance. I'd visualize what things might be like if something ever happened to my father, making me king. I envisioned how I would rule the realm—just like my father—

and the outlandish demands and flippant changes I would enact.

Fruit-filled pastries for every meal, long epic voyages to far-off places, or a week-long annual trickster festival with the sole purpose of every fae pulling pranks.

But as I grew and learned some painful truths, that vision shifted. I still wish to rule someday, however I now desire to make weighty changes. But with his immortality, the throne might never be mine.

I glance at the column to the right, the place where I usually lean against with arms crossed while my father berates me for some misstep of my duties or stumbles in appearances. I've made it a regular occurrence over the past several decades, but it's difficult to care about duties and responsibility when I don't foresee my father dying and passing the mantle to me.

Today, I stand beside him. Hoping the reminder of who I was as a youngling—a loyal, dutiful son—will aid me back into his good graces.

"Orion, tell me how you perceive the success of the Consort Tourney." The king doesn't move; he speaks to the breeze.

I fear Amberle's presence at the palace depends on this conversation and my thoughts immediately go to her as I rub my hand over my opposite forearm, feeling the stickiness of the lingering salt water. By some undeserved luck, we were put in a position where a union between us is not only possible but might be accepted. But I know my father well, and I know when his words are two-edged. I clear my throat. "The success?"

He glances at me briefly, then back at the view. "Leaping from ships is foolish, Orion. Especially for the crown prince."

While I know this is the reason he summoned me, it feels like the silent calm before the raging blaze. A respite before the king's wrath.

"Because we could have drowned?"

"Unlikely."

"So, it was because of the Underwater Court?" I ask, tilting my head. "Because they could have taken advantage of the situation and dragged me to be held hostage or executed?"

"Now why would the Underwater Court risk kidnapping the crown prince when one of their own has a chance of being next to him on the throne someday?" He finally turns to me with a slight smile. "I remember you gifting River Lyn a harbor seal."

He's right, but River hasn't even crossed my thoughts since that moment. No one has except...

My thoughts flit back to Amberle. To her guarded expression and the genuine smile set free once or twice over the course of these weeks together. To the intensity of her blue eyes when I'm lucky enough to capture them for more than a moment. To her wings—I bite the inside of my cheek as a wave of remorse fills me and I pray Wyn obeyed my request.

"Let us start again." Father steps toward me with frustration lining edges of his mouth. "Tell me, Orion, what is the *purpose* of this Consort Tourney?"

I scold myself for becoming distracted, but refuse to be cowed by his condescension. "I'm not a youngling. I don't need to be reminded of its *purpose* and I am doing everything expected of me."

"What is expected of you is not to be running around with that halfling and jumping from ships with her." The king's smile has vanished.

"I had to get away from the magic. Just for a moment."

He turns back toward the sea. He pauses and my shoulders tighten, waiting.

"She told you about her time in the oubliette?"

"You knew." It isn't an accusation, just a statement of fact. He's the king, of course he knew. "Why? She was a youngling."

"She put the prince in danger. She was lucky you weren't killed that day." His voice is irritatingly calm.

"There was no biloko that day!" I shout. "I was *never* in danger!"

Father turns and rushes at me until his face is inches from

mine with summer fire in his eyes. "And she would have faced worse if you had been!" The anger emanating off him catches me off guard. Deep down, my instincts scream a warning. I've rarely witnessed this side of him, and the burning hatred under the surface feels like I'm skating on ice. Thin ice with a monstrous div laying in wait, smelling blood. "She's a *commoner.* You are the *prince!*"

"*Mea culpa,*" I say evenly without stepping back. *I will not be intimidated by him.* "It was my fault, then. It was my fault today. Amberle should not be punished for my actions."

Something that looks a lot like respect flashes in my father's eyes before he smiles again and steps back. "Fine. She will not be punished."

I take the win and dare press further. Something about Amberle has him rattled and I am willing to risk his wrath to find out why. "And about the *halfling* you say I've been running around with? In case you've forgotten, that *halfling* is a contestant of the Consort Tourney."

"Orion." Father warns. His voice is smoother, his fury boiling just under the surface. I dread that his outburst is truly related to Amberle, not a shallow projection redirected from some other annoyance.

"We invited all the contestants based on different merits," I reason. "Amberle might be the one—"

"Orion, you will be silent!"

My mouth clamps shut. I realize with a growing horror that the king might not actually approve of every contestant.

"You are not an idiot, son. You know the reason I summoned you."

"I'm not so sure I am," I say, keeping my voice steady. "I thought I was summoned because of my actions on the ship."

"It is because of your actions... with *her.*"

"What actions?" Nausea threatens. I bend my knees, but not enough that the king will notice. "With all due respect, Father, Amberle is a Tourney Contestant. If the purpose of the Consort

Tourney is for me to connect with the fae I intend to spend the rest of my centuries with..." *The remainder of my existence...* "Then my actions with her... are acceptable."

The king pinches his nose, taking a heavy sigh. Then he turns and rests heavy hands on my shoulders. "Spend more time with the other contestants," he says. Something under his calm tone sets me on edge. "You don't know everything about your former playmate-turned-*Tourney Contestant*." I don't imagine the half-sneer that emerges. "Explore your other options. Trust me. I only want what's best for you and the kingdom."

"What do you mean?" I ask as my father drops his hands and turns away. "What don't I know about her?"

"Have you spent time with the winter princess? Shay Malov? A union between the summer and winter fae could prove to be a powerful combination, both politically and for the sake of the bloodline." When he looks back at me, a different, easy smile greets me.

"Father, what don't I know about Amberle?"

"Well, for one, she did not enter the Consort Tourney because she wished to be with you."

A sharp, javelin-like prick pierces my chest. "Yes, I'm aware. She told me she originally came because of her father."

Though she's since professed that she is here for me.

Father tilts his head. He's mocking me with his faux pity, taunting me. "Are you certain that's all?"

"I mean, we've had our differences." I choose my words carefully. "I'm learning that her upbringing in the palace was worlds different from mine. Because, as you said, she's a commoner and I'm the prince."

He studies me for several moments, then nods. Satisfied. "She hasn't told you. Good."

My heart plummets. Is Amberle keeping something from me? Or is this a deception, a trick from my father to dissuade me from choosing her? I can't help but ask, "She hasn't told me what?"

"Tell me, Orion, how you perceive the success of the Consort Tourney?"

I hide my fisted hands behind my back along with my frustration—the king has simply referred to his original question rather than answer mine.

"You would be wise to spend time with the other contestants." He turns, waving a hand of dismissal.

"Because you don't want the Tourney to end too soon? I think you already know my choice."

He doesn't react to my declaration, but his jaw clenches, the simmering anger flaring again just beneath the surface. "We neither want the Tourney dragged on too long, nor end it while interest and curiosity still holds the realm."

I know he tells the truth. It's something he drilled into me long before they sent the invitations out. Like everything else my father does, the purpose of the competition for the crown is two-fold. Find a mate. Distract the masses.

But this, the king's reaction, signals that other machinations are at work. Apparently, not all the fae invited are suitable mates. Why invite them? I risk prodding further. Whatever the king is up to, it's toying with my future.

"My King," I call him by the title he prefers from Mother and me, "I know I need a powerful mate, and you want a fae with enough clout to strengthen alliances."

"A king's responsibility is to his kingdom, first and foremost."

"Didi Beechriver's family is well respected." I watch him for any facial twitch. "An alliance with the Spring Court is always acceptable."

My father stills, an almost imperceptible downward turn at the edge of his lips. "Her family could be good allies in the future."

Nothing more, apparently.

"Does that mean Didi is just a pawn, too?" I ask. "No star fae allowed on the throne?"

"Now, son, you know I would never say that." He avoids

making eye contact with me, but he continues. "But it is too soon to be making rash choices. You still have several influential, adoring fae in the competition."

"Too soon? I'm talking about Amberle. *Amberle,* who I've known my entire life!"

"Bridle your heart, Orion. Ask yourself *why* she's here. Remember, Amberle disappeared for decades."

"And she came back."

"True, but it doesn't mean she's not capable of disappearing again."

Sixteen

The once pink clouds of dusk have darkened to a deep shade of plum as I fly back to the palace. The cool air kisses the skin of my arms and cheeks, raising goosebumps and sending shivers of pleasure through me as my wings stretch and catch the wind.

Prince Orion is clearly in love with you. Wyn's words cut through my reverie, and I drop several feet. My heart leaps, but I quickly right myself.

Nonsense. It's not true, I chide my thoughts.

It's not really something you can argue, he'd said when I denied it.

"He's just seeing things," I speak into the night air. "Misinterpreting something that isn't there."

The prince has changed in a lot of ways. But his kindness is nothing more than proof he's matured. He could become a great ruler if something ever happens to his father.

Didi's voice rings in my head, *... obviously the prince is in love with you!*

My serene flight is no longer peaceful as I war with myself. I would fly all night to escape the echo of their suspicions and the way my throat tightens in response. But Gnacia's deadline and the upcoming dinner must cut my flight short.

Focus, Amberle.

As Wyn reminded me, I have a dangerous job, and it's imperative that I have my wits intact. I shove the image of Rion's face from my mind, but feel an uncomfortable fluttering as I trip on the memory of the look he displayed when we last parted. It was a painful smile right before he marched off to talk to his father about what happened on the ship.

I chew on my lip, silently praying to *Vejo* that the prince can successfully convince the king to let me stay. But I can't control what happens in that conversation, so it's urgent that I also find something to prove my worthiness to remain in the Consort Tourney—or rather... to remain in the king's employ.

If I fly back to my sitting room's window, the winter magic will probably be waiting as soon as I leave out my door, so I opt to enter on the small balcony that overlooks the lavender fields. The one Wyn and I spoke on when he first disclosed that he's also working as a spy for the king.

Landing lightly on the rail near where it meets the wall, I conceal myself against the face of the palace, listening for any fae and feeling for winter magic.

The air is quiet, without the buzzing, tingling sensation.

Good. No magic.

I still have time before I'll be expected in my rooms to prepare for dinner—an hour, perhaps—but that doesn't mean the other contestants aren't already having their faces glittered and their hair arranged. In fact, I'm gambling that the powerful Princess Shay will be primping rather than spying. I make my way through the halls to the contestant quarters, sticking to the shadows and making sure I'm not being followed or watched.

I intend to go to the winter fae wing. Frost is clearly dangerous, even if she wasn't a part of Juniper's death. Perhaps I'll finally get lucky and get a clue to help me uncover her accomplice. As long as I don't make a mistake.

The curse is constantly on the back of my mind, although it seems to only cause me to spill my every thought, so I shouldn't worry about its return while I silently spy. And oddly, it hasn't struck in a while, but I can't depend on my good fortunate to continue.

As I pass by the autumn wing, my ears prick at the mention of my name. I can't say I'm surprised. They've only attacked me with glaring looks lately, but I knew that wouldn't be the end of it. It's probably Tierney and Cerule. My intention is to ignore them, but when I hear the prince's name and my heart does a little stutter; I can't let this opportunity to eavesdrop pass by.

Maybe I'll still learn something to bring to Gnacia.

Creeping down the hallway, I see the two autumn contestants. I'd know Tierney's delicate, white butterfly wings anywhere, and the petite, thin form with burnt orange hair that hangs to her knees is clearly Cerule. The two of them slip into a room and shut the door. I check to ensure I'm not followed as I near the door, but when I press my ear against it, I can only hear muffled voices.

I quickly survey my surroundings, considering my options. My eyes gloss over the concealed entrance to the passageway where I found Juniper. I can't even look at it for fear of overwhelming feelings.

Juniper. Thinking of her reminds me of yesterday when Gnacia took me into Juniper's vacant room. I scurry to her door and quickly pick the lock with a hairpin. It's ridiculous how easy it is, but apparently the king assumes creatures are passing through the guard stations. Once inside her dark rooms, I pray that her massive window actually opens. I fist the crystalized sunbeam around my neck, ready to cut the glass if needed.

I grin, noticing an adjacent breakfast room with a wide balcony. From the positioning, I calculate the balcony is shared with the next suite—the one the two gossiping autumn fae just entered. Perfect.

I crack the door, listening for Tierney and Cerule. Hearing

nothing, I peek out, relieved to see the wrap-around balcony is connected, like I'd hoped. A warm glow spills out from the window of the next suite, along with mumbled voices from inside.

I fly up to the small ledge over the next room's doorway, finding a comfortable perch. I smile; from here, their voices ring out with clarity.

"I've asked my servants for a bluebell-colored dinner gown for tonight," Cerule says. "I need to stand out if I'm ever going to get time alone with Prince Orion, and they said it was his favorite color."

"Then I hope they deliver."

"What about you? What will you wear?"

Muk-muk. A rattling sound draws my eyes to the balcony rail where I see a squirrel. With beady eyes, it looks up at me, then shouts something in squirrel-speak.

I press a finger to my lips and widen my eyes at the small creature. *Shush!*

It's probably futile to think it would listen, but maybe it will just go away. But then my heart lurches. One of the gifted familiars at the last Invitational was a squirrel.

Tierney received a squirrel.

The rodent hops down from the rail, then rushes into the room, still now chittering—and likely warning Tierney that there are eavesdropping ears.

"I don't think it matters. I don't even know why I'm still here," Tierney says, sounding bored even as the squirrel keeps chirping.

"Why do you say that?"

The squirrel lets out a loud squeak. "Well this, for one. A squirrel? The prince obviously doesn't know me. And as much as I'd enjoy being the crown princess at the end of all this, I don't think I could stand being tied to Orion." Tierney's familiar screeches again, but less enthusiastically. "The only way I'd take the crown is if I could get rid of Orion."

I stiffen, straining to hear the next words.

"You wouldn't." Cerule's voice shakes.

"Juniper said he's not fit to rule Faerie."

The squirrel squeaks again, and Tierney curses at the creature. "Useless gibberish."

I breathe a sigh of relief; grateful Tierney is ignoring its warning.

"But we don't know why." Cerule sounds desperate. "I don't really care if he has something dark from his past, or if his magic isn't as strong as mine, or even if his childhood friends are star-fae. I think Orion is kind and handsome and—"

"What? Do you think *you* have a chance with him? Haven't you been paying attention, Cerule? Didn't you see the disgusting display on the ship today?"

"B-but you just said it was Amberle's fault!" There's fear in Cerule's voice, and her words sound a lot like a flavor of denial. She sounds hurt, too. "You said she was the reason they went overboard. You said she was trying to kill him or something."

"I said *I hope* that's what the king thinks. Honestly, I don't think the talentless star fae could kill a sprite, let alone the prince. But as intimate as their conversation was before their little swim, I wonder what they talked about *in the water*. Away from the listening magic. There's definitely something suspicious about Amberle."

I concentrate on breathing calmly as my pulse spikes. *They don't know I'm here. There's no need to panic.*

Tierney's tone softens when she continues. "Maybe you will have a chance if we can dig up some dirt on her and get her eliminated. I mean, she left quietly. Disgraced, perhaps? And where has she been all these years? Clearly, she has secrets."

Not good. It will be problematic if *anyone* is paying particular attention to me or looking for ways to get me kicked out. I inwardly groan; I'll have to take special care and cover any tracks I leave. Thoroughly.

"They have a shared past." Cerule's voice drops, and I lean

closer to the window. "Do you think he's been in love with her since they were younglings and none of us even have a chance?"

"I doubt it. Until the Consort Tourney was announced, Prince Orion was destined for Princess Arielle."

"That doesn't mean he didn't love Amberle anyway." *Ugh.* Cerule is still stuck on her suspicions about me. "Sometimes we want what we can't have." Her voice is wistful.

I wish she would stop.

The breeze picks up and lifts strands of my hair.

Does Cerule love the prince? Is that why she's focused on me?

"Maybe she put some sort of magic enhancement on him," Tierney suggests. "An infatuation spell?"

"But she's star fae, there's no way she could have—"

"That doesn't mean someone else did it on her behalf. Don't count yourself out, Cerule. You still have a chance."

"But there are ten of us left. And Amberle—"

"Nine. I don't *want* the prince. It's time to stop pretending that I do. From now on, until Prince Orion sends me home or I feel like it's time to send myself home, I'm focusing on helping you win."

I can't see Cerule's face, but I imagine the smile and encouragement she feels from her friend's words. It should make me glad that Tierney is 'pulling herself', even unofficially, from the competition. But is Tierney really walking away? She's as competitive as anyone, despite her dislike of Rion.

"Besides, one of us should win," Tierney adds.

I stifle a laugh. Tierney *is* competitive—and with Cerule as queen, her loyal, helpful friend would reap more than a few benefits, like access to summer magic, sensitive information, and every social function in the kingdom.

My mood sours, realizing she'll become more observant while in the service of Cerule.

By the time I see the air spirit, it's too late. Her form is nearly transparent as she flies with the breeze along the face of the palace, hidden from view until she rounded the vacant balcony. Quiet as the wind, there was no way to avoid her.

"Baaaaad." Her words are a cross between a whisper and a hiss. I recognize her immediately by her orange sunset glow that is nearly invisible in the dark of night. An arm's length away, we face each other. It feels like she's boring into my soul with her eyes—eyes that have no iris, no pupils. *"Noooo, noooo."*

She's Cerule's gifted sylph from Rion.

Without another word, the sylph melts into the room, carried by the wind. Ready to warn the autumn fae about me.

I don't hesitate and jump straight up, flying wherever the wind will take me the fastest. I need to find an alibi—nowhere near here. I pivot and aim for the spring contestants' wing. Floating in through a vacant balcony that leads to the spring corridor, I drop into a crouch just as I hear a commotion carried on the wind. I slip around the corner, knowing Cerule or Tierney are on the autumn balcony, and they have summoned guards.

And they probably tasked the sylph with hunting me.

I take a breath and smooth down my skirt, as if I'd just come in from a leisurely flight, as I listen and feel for magic. I sense a touch of winter magic, but it's not immediately near me. That *might* benefit me.

I run my fingers through my hair and force myself to look serene as I stride for Didi's room. She wanted to hear about my date and she might give away loads of information about the other contestants.

Lifting my chin as if I'm expected, I march forward, nearing my friend's room. When a familiar form strolls in my direction, I blink, slowing, making sure he's not a mirage.

Prince Rion sees me and tilts his head, before breaking into a curious grin.

My heart lightens at the sight of the prince, and I immediately wish to learn how the conversation with his father went. Then the realization of where we're standing hits me like a wall of water far colder than the deepest waters of the Sea of Neptulus.

We are in the spring corridor.

Rion walks toward me. I feel the winter magic, but distantly.

"What brings you to this floor of the palace?" he asks, calmly.

"I could ask you the same," I say, wishing seeing him didn't make me feel like I was suddenly flying, making my wings instinctively flutter.

He points over my shoulder. "Is it—? Did Wyn take you to the healers?"

I beat my wings, once a bit more slowly, noting how his attention slides from them back to my face. I'm not sure which fuels my smile more: his regard or my recent, exhilarating flight. "Yes, it's healed."

His eyes drop to my lips and linger for a moment before glancing at my wings again. "I'm glad to see it. Have you tested it? Have you flown?"

"A bit, yes." *And bumped into a sylph.* I roll my lips together, hiding a nervous smirk.

His earlier ease melts as his hands carefully clasp in front of him. "I was having a little chat with Didi Beechriver."

My throat tightens as a heaviness presses against my chest. *What was he discussing with Didi?* As my spirits plummet, I hide my disappointment by finding a wall ornament to stare at—a swirling tangerine-colored glass blown in the shape of the sun. "Oh? I was headed to talk to her myself."

Rion leans closer, bringing the fresh scent of citrus and sunshine with him, and sniffs, snapping my eyes back to him. "You still have seawater on you." He scrunches his nose, then lifts a hand. I think he's about to touch the tips of my still-damp, salt-crusted hair hanging over my shoulder, but he seems to think better of it and drops his arm. "You might want to bathe," he teases, pinching his nose. "Perhaps you could speak with Didi later? At dinner?"

"I'm fully aware of my appearance, Prince Orion," I flippantly quip, trying too hard to ignore my disappointment. "My memory of today is still fresh in my head."

The prince's mocking smile falls along with his chin as he bows his head slightly in a nod. "As is mine."

I want to ask him what happened with his father. Am I staying or has the king had enough of my presence in the competition and at the palace? Rion's posture and mood and distance suggest their conversation didn't go well. Or perhaps the king simply insisted I leave, and Rion is uncomfortable seeing me unexpectedly.

We stand for several pregnant moments. His lips part as if he wishes to say something. I want to pry about his conversation with the king, and with Didi, but the bubbling churning in my gut is making my thoughts tumble with chaos.

"Amberle, I..." Rion finally starts, his eyes on the floor and a stone plummets through my core. With just two words, Rion has all but admitted in his tone that I might not be long for the Consort Tourney.

I look away, focusing on the sun ornament again. I hate the cheeriness of it and the way it shines brightly, reflecting the light of the sconces.

"Was your conversation with Didi pleasant?" I force felicity in my tone.

His eyes snap to mine, studying my expression.

"You are fond of her?" I ask, managing a smile.

He tilts his head. "She is a cordial fae..."

"And would make an amiable queen consort?" I hate the way it comes out as a question and suck in a breath.

"I suppose..." His eyes narrow. "Is that what you want? For me to pick Didi?"

"I..." But I can't answer.

"Because she isn't my first choice." The prince drops his chin again, but the warmth of his voice sets my heart aflutter, and a ribbon of light twirls inside. He won't meet my eyes, but I can't keep my eyes off him. I watch the way his walnut hair falls just over his brow, the way his mouth creases at the edges and hint at the buried smile.

When his simmering, golden eyes finally lift and lock, my breath catches. I'm anxious and nervous and a ball full of anticipation as I wait to hear what he says next because if he means what I think he means... and it's clear now that I'm—

No.

My chest tugs. It's painful and pleasurable all at once and is followed by a shiver that runs from the crown of my head spreading down and outward through my limbs—my arms, my legs, my wings.

No. It can't be. It's impossible.

And I still don't know where I stand after Rion's talk with his father. I can't even think...

"What did your father say?" I attempt to divert my thoughts, to prompt him to answer the question I'm dying to know, but my voice comes out in an airy whisper. Like Cerule's sylph.

My eyes are drawn to his lips, which press tightly together in some form of displeasure.

"Is he... sending me away?" My throat tightens. "Because I don't want— I mean... if I have to—"

"No." Rion rushes forward, gripping my shoulders. His forehead pressing down. "He assured me you won't be punished for my actions today."

I exhale in relief, but he doesn't let go of my arms. My nostrils fill with the citrus scent that wafts from the skin at his throat. Now I'm breathless for a different reason. His fingers tighten with an intensity in his gaze I wasn't expecting. But then his face twists. He's at war with himself over something.

"Go on. What were you going to say? If you have to... what?" His voice is rough, an almost desperate edge.

"I... Prince—"

"Rion. To you, it's just Rion." His eyes seem to spark with golden fire and his words cause a swelling in my chest.

"Rion I—I'm..." *I'm falling for you.*

One eyebrow arches high.

"I uh..." I drop my gaze to his lips and wonder what they would feel like, pressed against mine, but I catch the settling of his features and doubt creeps in.

His expression is serious. Sober. But his voice is warm when he says, "Amberle..."

My eyes lift.

"Amberle, I'm in love with you."

His tone is so soft, so reverent. I almost wonder if I heard or only imagined his declaration, but I can't help the upturn of my lips when I register the look of unadulterated adoration. It's overwhelming. Heady.

The swelling feeling punctures straight through my ribcage and I suck in a breath as his face drops near my ear. I melt, wondering what his lips would feel like on my skin. I lean closer when my voice whispers in my head.

I'm a liar.

Jerking back, I yank my hands away as if I've been scorched.

The pained look on his face reflects my confusion, as if I've just taken a hammer to my once-cold heart, shattering it into a million pieces.

I'm a spy. My duplicity is as twisted and vile as the darkest fae.

I shudder, my conscience condemning me.

"But there are still ten left," I whisper an excuse as my mind reels.

"Yes, and my father instructed me to spend time with the others." He steps back and presses a palm against the wall, leaning on it for support. "But..." He searches my face, a shadow of fear crossing it before he blinks it away. "I don't want to spend time with them."

He steps toward me again, slowly. He watches my expression as he draws closer, but when I unconsciously move forward, he encircles his arms around my waist. The warmth of his hands pressed against my lower back induces such a feeling that I can't help but let the action slide me even closer.

"I know who I want," he breathes, leaning his face—his lips down toward me. Gripping the sleeves of his shirt, I'm too terrified to pull him toward me or push him away. "I know my choice and I'll send them all home tonight if that is your wish."

My heart quickens, pounding with a mix of desire and dread. "No!"

Rion will hate everything about you when he learns the truth.

Panic floods through me, making my fingers and toes ache with the sudden rush. His promises are sweet, but I remind myself that his affection is a threat to my father's life and possibly mine, too.

I gently push away from him before his lips can meet mine, cursing myself all the while for letting it get this far. "You cannot let them go now!"

I've been a deceiver, and an observer of life, for long enough to know I want an honest relationship built on truth... if I were ever to marry. Rion's affection is shallow, without loving the full, nuanced fae I've become; when he learns about my bargain, he'll lash out, like he'd done as a child. He's changing, but I know him, and he'll never forgive me.

Still, seeing the hurt on his face, I can't help but soften my voice. "At least not yet. We don't know who killed Juniper or who else is conspiring with Frost."

He releases me and steps back, blinking.

"Besides, perhaps your father is right?" I manage a weak smile even as the hidden, tender part of my soul begs me to wrap my arms around him and pretend I could live this fairytale life. "I've changed since we were younglings. You might be confusing the fae before you with the one you used to know. So, it might be good for you to get to know the others."

Rion's face hardens to stone. "Perhaps you're both right," he says, moving past me. "You should go wash up for dinner."

My throat aches and the raw edges of my heart burn cold as winter ice with each step as I make my way to the summer corridor. But I shove it down deep and refuse to question what I've just done.

~~Allowing him to grow too close.~~
~~Pushing him away.~~

Instead, I think about the rosemary-infused bath awaiting me and fool myself into thinking it will wash away all the events of today before I must plaster a smile back on my face for dinner.

But when I arrive at my door, something feels off and my senses heighten.

The winter magic is absent, but something is wrong.

I turn the knob—noting it's not locked like I left it—and push my door open. My room is lit only by the moonlight streaming in through the still broken window... revealing a figure standing as a silhouette against it.

I know exactly who she is before she says, "Funny that

Cerule's sylph caught a spy outside her window, and the pane of *your* window just happens to be cut, Amberle."

Because who else would have access to a locked room other than someone who grew up in the palace?

"What are you doing here, Mora?" I ask.

"That's *Princess* Mora to you," the summer royal says, with a wicked, self-satisfied smile. "And I just want to talk."

Eighteen

Princess Mora lifts her hand, and the chandelier illuminates as she controls the tiny light-wisps overhead. She's making a spectacle—she's demonstrating her strength with magic. Abilities I'll never have. The languishing speed of which she releases the wisps, allowing them to respond properly to my entrance, seems to match the drifting night air in from my cut window, which gently lifts the dark curls around Mora's face.

Unlike me, she's ready for dinner. Her hair is pinned up with tendrils that skim her bare shoulders. Her deep burgundy dress is a backdrop to the orange and yellow thread, woven in shapes of clawing flames. I don't know if it's her appearance—her sophisticated hair arrangement, the sharpness of her features, the cut of her dress—or the bold act of sneaking into my room, but Mora has suddenly become very grown up. She's become a formidable threat.

The once irritating young princess, just a pesky thorn in my side, is a terrifying contender for the prince and the crown. She's also a bona fide danger to my remaining in the palace.

"Why has your window been cut, Amberle?" she asks, folding her arms and lifting a self-satisfied dark eyebrow.

"They did not design it to open, and I wanted to fly."

Her lips twitch. "I thought you had an injured wing."

"Then you'll know I didn't get very far," I say sarcastically. But she'll figure out soon enough that I'm healed, and I don't miss the opportunity to throw her off this little game she's playing. "If you must know, Wyn took me to the royal healers earlier today at *Prince Orion's* request." I lean on the prince's name, knowing it will get under her skin.

Mora's eyebrow straightens and her arms tense. It worked. If I can keep Mora off balance, she'll leave frustrated. So, I push more.

"If you thought I couldn't fly, why would you assume my cut window was for my escape? Maybe someone wanted to spy on me, too?"

"I might have, but you just admitted it." She shoots the flippant reply.

I lift my shoulders, acting as if I couldn't care less.

She marches toward me, dropping her arms and narrowing her eyes. "Why didn't you just go out the door if all you wanted to do was fly?"

I shrug again. "You should know the answer to that, Mora," I pause, letting the slight to her intelligence wriggle through her gut. "I'm guessing you only visited my room when the winter magic assumed you'd be preparing in your chambers. I, too, occasionally need a break from the winter magic constantly following in my wake."

Mora's jaw clenches. I bite the insides of my cheeks to stop myself from grinning at her ire. As a youngling, this would be the part where the summer princess would scream, clench her fists, and stomp her feet before marching away to tattle. She'd find anyone who would listen to her complaints about the *mean, pathetic star fae* who was harassing her again.

Instead, she stands taller, lifting her chin and looks down her nose at me. "Stop dodging my questions, Amberle. Were you the one eavesdropping on Cerule and Tierney?" she asks. "The one Cerule's sylph caught?"

Sylph's limited communication makes it impossible for them to make any meaningful identification. The sylph's simple mind probably flitted to another topic moments after I'd flown away. Even so, someone or something has rarely caught me as a spy in the past. But I've never gone into such a dynamic situation before, either. With the king keeping me in the dark on too many secrets, this was by far my riskiest venture. But I'll do anything for my father.

For more than one reason, it's imperative that I get Mora's attention off the spy. Off *me.*

I let out an exaggerated sigh, as if the princess is a mere annoyance, and not the threat I fear she's becoming. "I just came from speaking with someone I'd rather keep private, if you understand my meaning."

My heart lightens at the fear I see in her eyes, but she doesn't flinch. Instead, she blinks away her concern and her nostrils flare.

"I wouldn't put it past you to have a tryst with a servant you met in the palace," Mora says, her words dripping with malice. "Let me guess, a page? One of the leprechaun gardeners? Or the hobgoblin in the tower?"

Kenna, my human servant, enters from a servant door. I don't know if Mora notices her because she steps to my vanity, frowning at my bottles of colored pigments, combs, perfumes, and my few possessions as she continues. "Perhaps a dirty *kelpie* keeper?"

I suck in a breath, appalled. Mora grins. Father started in the palace working as a *kelpie* keeper. He worked up to his place of status as one of the king's advisors but spent years mucking out cabyll ushtey and kelpie stalls in the beginning of his service. Did Mora know?

Of course she did. The devious, wicked grin forming on her lips tells me she's been holding that minor, but potentially damaging fact in her satchel until the moment it would throw *me* off balance.

My face hardens. "You should leave. I must prepare for dinner."

Kenna scurries to my side, her face pale, just as Mora thrusts her hip into my vanity, knocking everything askew.

"I have a human servant, too," the princess says. "Distasteful, but at least I only have one. And he's not a slob. Though I do make him crawl." She turns the full weight of her glare to Kenna.

The human girl drops her gaze and moves to pick up the items from the table. My heart hurts for her and I bend down to help.

"You will avoid Prince Orion tonight at dinner." Mora's words are a command, not a question.

I snap back to standing. "That's ridiculous—"

"You will stay away from him," she snaps, then slides a glance to my window, then back to me. "Or I'll tell him and everyone else about your cut window. The fae can assume the rest on their own."

I bite down on my tongue. *Let her talk,* I remind myself, leaning on my experience as a thief. *Let her spill the next part of her plan.*

"You won't speak to him, you won't approach him," she demands. "There will be no lingering glances, no smiles, no conversation between you." Mora smiles. She seems to wait for me to ask what the consequence will be. But I won't give her the satisfaction. She continues. "If you do, I'll tell the other contestants and all of Faerie that you have newly healed wings and a penchant for spying."

"Even if someone knows otherwise?" I fold my arms, remembering my small interlude with Rion in the hallway. He became the perfect alibi after the incident with the sylph. And if I'm pressed by inquisitors, I can bring up my meeting with Wyn in the gardens before that. It'll be easy to pretend I haven't left out an important hour of my evening—the one that included the very deed she's accusing me of.

"I'm assuming a servant is going to keep your secret," she smirks. "Even if he has to blackmail you to keep it quiet."

"There's no need for Wy—"

Kenna bumps into me, then straightens. "I'm so sorry, Amberle. Please forgive my clumsiness."

I blink, surprised I'd let that information slip. I had no intention of telling Mora about meeting Wyn. Kenna saved me from spilling it. "F-forgiven." I stutter. "Of course."

Mora's face turns two shades of red, her hands fisted. For a moment, I wonder if steam will come out of her ears.

"If you don't heed my words, Amberle, I'll make sure you regret it." Her gaze drops to Kenna, an obvious indicator at who she'll hurt first.

My stomach drops, but I say nothing as Mora turns on her heel and storms to the door. I sit down, pretending I don't fear the princess will turn around and literally stab me in the back. I inhale slowly with closed eyes, waiting to hear the door close.

"For the sake of everyone, you should bathe," Kenna says, forcing a tight smile.

"You didn't deserve that treatment, Kenna."

"I know," she says as she and I finish righting the vanity. "But I appreciate you saying it."

"I appreciate you bumping into me when you did."

A real grin breaks out on her face, and she winks. "You think that was an accident? I thought I rather blundered it."

"Why?" I ask, surprised.

"I could tell she was getting to you," she says as she prepares my bath. "I'd rather roll around with the pigs than serve Princess Mora. She can't become the next queen. Please don't let that happen."

"I'll do what I can. I promise." And I'm sincere. Mora is already a tyrant, and I can't bring myself to imagine what she'd do with a crown.

Nineteen

I can't enjoy my short-lived bath for all the turmoil of thoughts whirling in my head. I quickly ponder what I learned from Cerule and Tierney before Cerule's sylph saw me. The king wants information and now I have some.

I know Cerule cares for Rion. I don't get the sense that she has any intention of hurting him. Tierney is vicious and I won't put it past her to use Cerule, but of all the fae in the kingdom, Cerule might be the one friendship Tierney actually cares about. Could she secretly be working with Frost? My gut tells me no.

My mind flits back to Rion in the spring corridor and I wonder what he was doing there. The most obvious answer is he was there to quietly court Didi. Even though Didi is the contestant I'm rooting for, my stomach knots. I push thoughts of him away, jump out of the basin, and call for my attendants.

My simple dress is the color of pale candlelight. The sleeves extend from my shoulders down to my wrists and flows into a draped neckline. Gold embroidery decorates the bottoms of my tight sleeves and near the hem of the skirts. Full coverage will hide the few minor scrapes I picked up during my flight while flitting like a shadow near the castle walls.

Kenna weaves my still-damp hair in a simple braid down my back with gold ribbon threaded through. Posey adorns my wrists in raw gold bangles with enough impurities to prevent them from burning my skin, then dabs color on my lips.

I'm the last one to walk into the dining room, drawing all eyes toward me. I catch brief glances of scrutiny and jealousy among some, and guarded smiles from others. As usual, it's only Didi who looks openly pleased to see me, but I can't meet her look because Rion stands near her. Knowing they're about to be seated together chills something deep inside me, and I can't seem to shake it out. I don't look at the prince directly, but the heat of his gaze is enough to flush my cheeks.

I'm in love with you, Amberle.

My pulse quickens and I'm forced to look away quickly and act as if I didn't see him at all. I remember all too well his pained expression when I told him to spend time with the other contestants. Of course, he did that before I'd suggested it—with the very fae he is standing with now.

"Amberle! I so enjoyed our chat earlier." Mora sings from across the room with convincing warmth in her tone. "Come! I've saved you a seat next to me." When I glance at her, I see the fire in her eyes—the threat—to match her dress. Of course, she's trying to keep me from the prince. I'll play her game, but only because she's seated with two fae I rarely have the opportunity to analyze.

I don a smile for Mora and walk toward her table. Lady Pepper and Princess Shay look surprised as I approach their group. I take the seat between Mora and Lady Pepper and ensure that I look genuinely pleased.

The summer princess pats my hand when I've seated and explains to the others, "You know Amberle lived in Isi Aura as a youngling. She and I have a lot of history."

Neither of our table mates comment.

I avoid their gazes by unfolding the napkin and placing it on my lap.

"It was kind of you to give others a chance with him," Lady Pepper says in a low tone with an edge of bitterness.

"It was Princess Mora who ensured it, Pepper," Princess Shay says. I glance across at her and catch one arched eyebrow and a pursed mouth. She watches me with obvious scrutiny. "Although I didn't know Mora had the power to do it."

"I told you, Amberle and I have history," Princess Mora says, turning and smiling sweetly at me. It's a little too sweet and sours my stomach.

Shay ignores her and keeps her gaze on me. "What did you talk about in the water with him? How did you get him to jump in after you?"

"She's bewitched him somehow," Pepper says. "Look, she sits with us and he can't keep his eyes off her." She gestures at the table where he and Didi and few others sit.

At the mention I can't help but glance up at him, instantly locking eyes. I've known him for too long to assume he's looking at me with warm adoration. He's annoyed. I squirm, knowing why.

I snap my gaze away. "He won't select me. I've been rude to him too many times."

I press my lips together, realizing it's the second time I've spoken without thinking tonight. I swallow back the fear crawling up my throat; the curse is active, again. For how long, I can only guess.

"So you say," Lady Pepper laments. "But by the way he's storming over here, it seems there's little point in the rest of us even trying." She stands and vacates her seat, leaving the one next to me open.

Rion slides into it. "I wanted to greet all the contestants tonight," he says as my heart thrums. I can smell the citrus wafting from him. I can feel his warmth. "With the king and queen absent this evening, I thought we could have a more casual dining experience. It would please me to have time with all of you." His knee moves close to mine as he talks and it's all I can do not to nudge my leg to press against it. Mora doesn't need to know. I bite the edge of my lower lip and pray I'm not prompted to speak.

Princess Shay drapes her hand across the table, palm up and gestures with her fingers that Rion take her hand.

He does—the winter princess has forced the expectation—but as he leans forward, his knee pushes into mine and sends a shiver up my spine, tingling the back of my skull. He quickly adjusts, putting space between us. My chest twists at his recoil, but I basically pushed him away earlier tonight.

And I'm not here for him, I remind myself.

"You're welcome to eat your meal here with us," Shay says, lowering her eyelashes and smiling seductively. "Lady Pepper can take your seat over there." She nods her head to the other table.

Rion casually takes his hand back from Princess Shay and turns to me when he says, "I would like that, but the others might be upset."

Sharp nails dig into my opposite arm. The one closest to Mora.

"Amberle has had her time with you today, Prince Orion," Mora says, digging her claws deeper. "She can give up her seat for you and offer your condolences to the others. I think she'd rather sit with her friend, the other star fae, anyway."

"I would hate to displace Amberle that way," Rion says, taking the hint and rising from his seat. "After we eat, I'll spend quality time with all of you."

Mora's grip pierces deeper, enough to draw blood. I can feel it.

Do something, she seems to say. More importantly, I have no idea what confession I could make in a room full of vengeful competitors. As much as I want to spy, this is a risk I *really* cannot take.

"No, you stay here, Prince Orion," I say, hoping my voice doesn't sound like a wounded yelp and stand, pulling my arm from Mora's grasp and immediately clutching it with my other hand. "I'll tell them you'll spend time with all of us."

I don't intend to take his seat. I race for the exit to make sure this night doesn't end in disaster. I'll come up with an excuse later. But I'm stopped before I can leave and dread spreads like winter frost.

"Where do you think you're going?" Gnacia asks.

Twenty

Clutching my arm where Princess Mora dug her nails into my flesh, warm blood seeps between my fingers.

"After a day away, I thought you'd be eager to spend time with the other contestants at dinner," Gnacia says, tilting her horns to the side and offering a false smile for the winter magic. She blocks my way to the exit.

"I think it would be best for all of us if I retire for the night." A trail of blood runs down my forearm, so I adjust it to prevent it from dripping down the front of my pale-yellow dress. I should have worn a darker color.

"You cannot tell me you are too fatigued."

I squeeze my arm tighter. *Not really, but neither of us wants me spilling that I'm a spy.* "I just need a moment to collect myself. Would you excuse me?"

Gnacia's jaw tightens. "I will escort you so you can find your way back."

She doesn't trust me. The faun nearly pulls my hand away from my bleeding arm when she leads me out the door and down the hallway to a small washroom. The winter magic doesn't follow.

"Your deadline is nearly up, Amberle." Now that we're not

being watched, Gnacia's tone is void of any civility. "You should talk with the other fae and getting as much information about them as you can. King Estelar is set on sending you home."

"Mora suspects I was spying on Tierney and Cerule," I say, pouring a pitcher of water into a basin. "She's blackmailing me to stay away from the prince tonight, or else she'll tell everyone."

"And how did she find out?" Gnacia hands me a linen. She doesn't ask where the claw marks came from. Maybe I'm not the first in the competition to be on the receiving end of Mora's silent attack.

"I had to cut a hole in my window to get out without being followed by the watching magic," I say, dipping the cloth and wringing it out. "She broke into my room. If you want me to be successful, I need guards in front of my doors. You left me vulnerable."

She lifts a hand to her forehead. "Fine. But prove to me you're not a terrible spy."

The last thing I want Gnacia to know is that I'm plagued again by the curse that makes me blurt information I need to keep secret. So I focus on what I can tell: the conversation between the two autumn fae.

She actually looks almost impressed when I conclude their conversation with my impressions, but she doesn't let me off the hook for the evening.

"You don't have to speak to the prince in order to speak with everyone else," she presses. "You may have cleared Cerule to be a viable potential mate for the prince. Tierney and Frost are not, but is Tierney a physical threat, like Frost? There are still eight contestants you need to vet, including Tierney. I would advise that you get as much information as you can before you're cast out."

I nod, but don't look at her as I dab at my arm.

"Make sure to cover *that* up." Gnacia points at my arm.

"Make sure you get my window fixed. I want one that opens."

Gnacia pauses and I suspect she's keeping some choice, threatening words to herself. Instead, she raises a brow and slips out. Everything about her signals that she doesn't fear me—she speaks with the king's authority. I must do all I can to impress her, not irritate her, while still pressuring her to aid me.

To get the maximum use from my evening, I'll stay close to Didi. She's the only fae with an ounce of kindness, and she's nonthreatening and bubbly, so the other fae open up to her.

On my way back to the dining room, I find a tie-back from one of the draperies to wrap around my still bleeding arm. The wrap is a deep crimson, so it doesn't exactly match my candle-light-colored dress, but at least any blood soaking through won't be noticed.

The seat next to Didi is open, so I try to keep my head down as I head toward it, but I don't miss the questioning look Rion throws at me.

What's wrong? His obvious concern jump-starts my heart, but when he rises, I shake my head.

Please don't. I want to say. *Don't approach me.*

He frowns, but looks away and sits next to Mora and Shay again.

"What's going on?" Didi asks when I've seated.

"The Prince and I switched seats." I say with forced brightness.

Luna blows out a breath and River's shoulders drop. They're disappointed—and rightly so—but Didi only looks worried.

"What's this?" she whispers, shifting the ribbon on my arm and revealing some trailing blood. Her eyes widen.

Hastily, I cover it again. Before the spring star fae can ask more questions, several servants enter with trays of meats and cakes and fruits piled high. They place the trays in the center of each table in the room, and the fae all reach forward to fill their plates.

"So, River, have you had much time with Nixie?" Didi asks kindly, scooping food to the wooden tray in front of her.

"I swam with her early this morning," River says with a smile.

Nixie must be the name of the seal the prince gifted her at the last invitational.

I busy myself choosing meats and cheeses and putting them in front of me, hoping the selkie will relax and spill hints of her true character.

"But I wish I could bring her inside," River continues. She looks longingly at the spider on Luna's bare shoulder. I didn't notice it until pointed out, as Luna's dark familiar is brilliantly camouflaged on her perch. The purr of Didi's cait sith beneath our table is nearly a rumble on the floor at our feet. Didi drops her attention to her food, her ears flushing.

Wanting to take the pressure off Didi, I carefully think through my words before I speak, "I have not seen my cabyll ushtey since last night."

"But you had *time* with the prince," River points out.

"And you took him away from us just now," Luna huffs, turning to look at the table he now sits at.

My eyes follow hers, and I accidentally catch Rion's eye. *Again.* His expression opens as if he wants to have a silent conversation across the room.

But I snap my eyes to my tray and put a piece of sweetmeat into my mouth. It seems everything about this competition is one massive obstacle after another to getting the information I need for the king. I was away most of the day with the prince and unable to speak to any of the contestants and now, between my curse and their jealousy making them wary, I'm stuck.

I pause my chewing, thinking through the date with Rion. I was honest with him, but not because of the curse. My tongue didn't start running away until I returned to my room after my flight. After Mora appeared. I refuse to look at her, even though I want to. I put away that information to scrutinize another day and turn my attention to assuaging the other fae's dislike of me.

"There are still nine in the competition," I say after I've swallowed, using the same logic I used with Rion. "There is plenty of time for him to spend quality time with everyone."

"You mean ten," River says, confused.

"Excuse me?" I ask.

"There are ten of us still in the competition," River corrects, glancing at the others for confirmation and getting nods before turning back to me. "You're already counting someone out. Who?" She glances widely round the room.

I didn't include *myself*. Didi stares at her plate, her ears turning more red. I laugh off River's comment, hoping Didi doesn't think I assume *she's* not a tenable candidate.

"Wouldn't you like to know?" I wink at River, as if I'm not hiding the fact that *I'm* the pretender I've already discounted.

At my comment, Luna grins, as if she's hoping to reveal my secret. The scary thing is, I might actually spill the truth if I'm not vigilant.

"Anyway, I imagine I won't get any time with him for a very long time," I reassure them all. And if the king sends me away tonight, I might not get time with him ever again. "Definitely not tonight."

"You can't believe that," Didi assures me. "Do you see how many times he's looked over at you, Amberle?"

Yes, he looks at me in frustration, at best.

"You're the favorite," Didi says, a hint of sorrow in her words. "Every one of us knows that."

You're not helping, Didi.

"Amberle will not win," Luna says, causing my heart to crash against my ribcage.

"Whyever not?" Didi asks.

As my pulse thunders violently, I wonder what Luna knows. She could've discovered any number of things that would shamefully end my time here.

The question is, which one?

Twenty-One

I don't dare speak. Not after Luna's announcement to Didi and River that she is certain I will not win the Tourney. I keep my head down, looking at what remains of my dinner, but I can't eat either.

Didi and River await Luna's explanation too. The winter fae speaks the truth—I cannot win because I'm not an actual contestant. But is it because she knows the truth? That I'm the king's spy planted as a mole? Or does she have another reason for doubting my position here?

But following Luna's line of sight to Princess Shay at the other table, I see her meaning. "Politically, one of the princesses makes the most sense." She glances back at us. "It's just a question of whether Prince Orion will lean more toward the more powerful alliance in Princess Shay, or if he'll insist on one of his own."

"You mean Princess Mora?" Didi asks.

She nods.

I sense the winter magic strengthening, and I wonder what Luna's angle is. We've said several things that will be fodder for gossip for days. Years. I've said a few things that will raise some eyebrows, for certain. But I really don't care as long as I keep my cover in place and free my father. There's a chance Luna might be so used to the magic that she's forgotten the king and all of Faerie will hear her words. Perhaps she's hoping attention will raise her popularity in Faerie, putting pressure on the prince to go on a date with her—it's the same reason he took me on a date. Public interest.

"Why do you think the rest of us are here if he was always going to choose one of the princesses?" Didi asks, giving me a side-long glance.

Luna lifts her shoulders. "That's a good question. But, I could be wrong."

"So, you believe the competition is legitimate?" Didi says.

Luna picks up a berry, but mumbles something and whirls her finger around before popping the fruit into her mouth. I feel a sudden warmness, not as if from heat, but as if the cold was sucked away.

"I do, but we're not all on equal footing." Luna swallows her food, then continues quickly, barely moving her lips. "Frost knows it too, because she's trying her hardest to put herself above Shay."

With surprise, I realize the watching magic is gone, but clearly, we have little time.

"Frost?" I prompt, taking advantage.

"Well, no one knows it, but Frost's servants weren't the ones assigned by the palace," Luna says. "Somehow, someway, Frost managed to get her own personal servants the permission to attend her. Even Princess Shay couldn't do that—although I don't know if it occurred to her to try."

"How is that a problem?" River asks. I don't think she's realized that Luna has manipulated the magic because her tone is still conversational, but I'm grateful because it's a question I want answered too.

"Because she's getting messages out to her influential family. I think she's searching for extortion-worthy information. She may have already found it. All I know is her family isn't above *pressuring* the high court into forcing Prince Orion to choose Frost."

"To what end?" I ask, feeling creeping tendrils of fear entrap my heart. *To marry and then assassinate the prince?*

"To form a marriage alliance with the prince, obviously. To get the crown. To bear an heir for the high court."

I shove away the uncomfortable feeling that came with her last words and focus on the meaning. *So... not a threat to the prince.*

"Would she go to extremes to get the crown?" I ask. *Like kill someone who might be a threat? Like murder Juniper?*

Luna levels a dark gaze at me. "Going to extremes is how the Niege line became such an influential family in the Winter Court."

The air cools again as the winter magic flows back into the temporary bubble Luna made for us. The conversation remains superficial for the rest of the meal, vacillating between guessing who will get the next date, and theories about which contestants have been watched most by the realm. I smile and nod through it all. No one seems to mind my silence.

When the plates and trays are cleared, I am about to excuse myself when Rion stands. Hearing his voice, all the fae quiet, their attention on him. He's looking at me when I turn, but I can't read his expression and he looks away just as quickly.

"I would love a chance to have some time with each of you before we retire for the night. It is not a requirement," he says, landing his eyes on me and not blinking or turning away as he continues, "But I would love for you to join me where we can more comfortably talk."

I rip my gaze away as heavy dread sinks to my toes and the room erupts into bubbling, chittering excitement from the others. The prince said it was not required, but there was a clear expectation—especially for me—to take him up on his invitation.

But I don't have to see Mora's careful glance at me as a reminder that *I cannot talk to him.* Not without her fulfilling her promise to make my servant's lives miserable. Or let slip her suspicions about me spying on the autumn fae. Not to mention the curse. If I talk to Rion in private, it can't be tonight.

So as I follow behind the fae, trailing as the last one to leave the dining room, I contemplate what excuse I can use to get away before it's *my* turn. When we near the prince's chosen destination, I scramble to form a solid excuse that none of Faerie will question. When I round the door, the last fae to enter, the prince stands just inside the doorway, greeting each contestant. His eyes search my face, then drop to the make-shift bandage on my arm.

"Amberle, I had hoped that I could speak with you first," he says, reaching out for my hand, wrapping his warm fingers around mine.

"Actually, Prince Orion," Wyn says, approaching. "There's something quite urgent awaiting Amberle."

I turn to Wyn and want to throw my arms around him for saving me from Mora's attention and my cursed tongue.

"And it cannot wait?" Rion asks, his tone softening. I feel his eyes land on me, then back at our friend.

"It cannot." Wyn's tone has an edge of anxiety. He won't look me in the eye.

"What is it?" *Is it my father?*

"Follow me, this way." Wyn pulls me away from the prince. "You should get back to the others, Prince Orion." He calls back.

Rion nods and swallows hard, but turns to face the others in the room.

Wyn finally speaks after we're out of earshot and the winter magic fades away. "Someone wants to speak with you." Wyn picks up his speed, hurrying down the corridor. "It's Princess Arielle."

My heart leaps at the thought of seeing Princess Arielle again. I didn't realize how much I've missed my friend.

There's so much I want to tell her, so much I want to talk about. Most importantly, if she's been watching the Tourney from outside the palace, since she'll have a different perspective. Perhaps she'll tell me what she knows about the other contestants. Any observations could be helpful in determining which fae might be most suitable for the prince. And who might be dangerous.

After all, with only one set of ears and eyes, I can only be in one place at a time.

"I realize pulling you away and giving you even less time to obtain information seems unwise," Wyn says. "But the princess insisted. She demanded that it be tonight. Now."

I offer him a reassuring smile, though her urgency is unsettling. "It is for the best. The curse has struck me again. I might spill secrets. My actions—I might misstep..."

Wyn stops and briefly touches my shoulder, halting me too.

"I heard about the sylph," he says, quietly. "But it cannot point to you as the eavesdropper."

"Still, it was too close."

"Amberle, you got away."

"Yes, well, Mora suspects something."

Wyn smiles and tilts his head with folded arms. "I think you can handle Mora. You always could."

"She's grown up." I frown. "She's smart and devious. I cannot underestimate her."

Wyn's smile falls, but it's replaced with resolve, not fear or frustration. "Stories of the *Silver Shadow* have reached every corner of the realm. Her name commands awe and respect throughout all of Faerie."

My throat constricts, but I remain silent. He speaks to my fears. I feel as if I've somehow failed *her*—the previous version of me who was good at thieving and spying. The one who, along with my young friend Clay, ruled the streets of Rosewind.

"But the *Silver Shadow* works under the protection of anonymity and darkness. She works in the corners of society; in places no one thinks to look." Wyn pauses, waiting for me to look at him again. I do. "Here, you're on display with none of the protections the *Silver Shadow* is used to."

"And yet?" I wait for the coming reprimand. In the garden earlier, Wyn had emphasized caution in my dangerous position. Yet, I've only made things worse in the space of a few hours.

"And yet?" Wyn's smile returns with a pinch of confusion between his brows. "And yet, the masses love you as a prospective match for the prince. I assure you; they suspect nothing."

"How can you be so sure they don't suspect me?" I ask, sliding past the part where Wyn thinks the masses might accept me at Rion's side—because it won't ever happen. "And even if Faerie hasn't figured out the truth, what about the other contestants?"

"They fear you. They're jealous because they fear the prince is in love with you."

There it is again. Why must he continually bring *that* up? I ignore his last comment and turn the topic back without letting my response to his words show. "And Mora?"

"Don't worry about Mora. We'll figure something out. Come. Princess Arielle awaits."

We travel up two flights of stairs to the royal guest quarters of the palace. Perhaps they have housed away the princess from the others to prevent questions about her being in Isi Aura again. Yet when Wyn opens the door, it's vacant of any fae.

"Where is she?" I scan past the closed, thick curtains and simple, tucked bed with a single pillow.

Wyn crosses room and opens the doors of a heavy armoire, revealing only a familiar disc.

"Is that..."

"A winter communication disc, yes." He places it on a table next to a high-backed chair.

She's not here.

"Where did you get it?" I ask as my heart sinks. "Who knows you have it?"

"I won't be thrown into the stocks for having it, if that's what you're asking." I surmise we're in Wyn's rooms, not the princesses. "They provided it to me since I am working for the king."

Yes, and so am I, but they didn't provide me with a spying disc or special flint to flit around the palace undetected, I think bitterly. I am supposed to work in secret, and Wyn is not, yet more eyes watch my every move while Wyn can move about essentially invisible. Perhaps that's why the king trusts Wyn to keep his magical tools a secret from Faerie.

"Let us communicate with Princess Arielle Lieawarin," Wyn says to the disc, and within moments, a shorter, spectral version of the summer princess appears on the table.

"I'll make it quick, so you can get back to the prince," she says, pushing a section of her long, golden hair back from her shoulder and her sunset-colored wings flutter slightly. She looks regal—as always—in a gown of deep navy. She turns to Wyn. "Thank you for fetching Amberle."

"Of course." He bows low. When I glance at him, there's a hint of emotion in his face, but it disappears before I can read it.

"It seems the curse has fallen upon you again," Princess Arielle says. "I've been watching."

"You noticed?" I groan, putting a hand on my forehead and closing my eyes.

"Did you ever figure out the object the hex was put upon?" she asks, jarring my memory of our conversation in the library—what seems like so long ago—after the labyrinth trial when I had stolen away to find out anything I could to rid myself of the curse.

"No. I admit the curse has been absent for so long, I mostly shoved it from my mind."

"Until tonight, when do you last remember suffering from it?" The princess gets right to the point, and I'm thankful for her focus and determination.

But at her question, another, not-so-fond memory slips into my thoughts. "My foolishness in the garden that night with the prince." I cringe and let out a miserable laugh. "When I fell all over him and admitted to him and anyone who listened that I was cursed."

Arielle's small projection eyes widen. "I remember that night, but I don't remember you mentioning the curse."

"The ki—they cut it off, so no one saw." No need to bring the king into the conversation. Arielle needn't know everything I'm tied up with—like Wyn does. For her own safety.

"That's good. And it gives us a place of reference to figure out what it is." The princess paces on the table. "Do you know when the curse returned?"

"Tonight!" I say.

Heavy footsteps sound in the corridor outside the room. My heart jumps and Wyn abruptly inhales.

"I'll handle it." Wyn hurries out the door, ensuring we aren't interrupted. Or discovered.

After he leaves, Princess Arielle stops her pacing and grips her chin. Her sunset wings stretch slowly. "It wasn't before you were on the ship with the prince?"

"No..."

She tilts her head and looks at me strangely, but then waves it off and paces again. "Alright, when did you notice it was back? What was your first mistake?"

"Wait." I step closer and fold my arms. "Why did you think the curse was back sooner? During my outing with Rion?"

She stops walking again, but won't look at me.

"Princess Arielle..." I can't command her to tell me what's in her thoughts, but hope our friendship is close enough that she will anyway.

"Obviously I was not there..." she says, gesturing with her arms then pauses for another moment before clasping her hands in front of her and looking up at me with intensity. "But as a spectator, it looked very much like I was watching two fae fall in love."

Now I look away, but feel her studying me. Suddenly, I'm glad she's *not* here in person.

"It's apparent to all of Faerie that you are his choice, Amberle," she continues. "But the way you just spoke when you called him *Rion...*"

My eyes jerk back to her as my pulse surges, but I blow out an exasperated breath to cover it. "Yes, it's what I called him when we were younglings. Surely you remember?"

She frowns and tilts her head forward.

"You and I are friends," she says. "And Wyn is ensuring no one can hear us."

"Right..." I frown and glance at the door.

"Meaning you don't have to be afraid to tell me the truth."

I don't know if it's her assurance or the curse, but I sigh and suddenly the words spill out. "You're right. I think I'm falling for him."

Her grin is contagious, and I can't help but mimic it. But with it comes a painful, horrible realization that whatever happens next, it won't end well.

I'm falling for him.

Falling in love with the prince was *not* part of the plan.

Foolish, foolish, Amberle.

I cover my face with my hands and groan.

The door swings open and Wyn returns. "It was patrolling guards, but they suspected nothing."

But the way Arielle's smile falls when he enters, and the tension in Wyn's shoulders as he straightens, makes me think he isn't telling me everything. And maybe Arielle knows something too.

"What's wrong?" I ask, looking from Wyn to Arielle. "What's going on?"

Arielle shakes her head in innocence. "I've been *here* talking to you. Why are you asking me?"

I turn back to Wyn.

"I assure you; it is just as I said. Although, they did mention that if I saw you, I should bring you back to the group soon. It's very late, but the prince wants all the contestants in the same room when they announce the next trial."

My stomach hollows out. Another trial.

Twenty-Three

Another trial.

Not a date or an outing or even a group of fae decorating for some upcoming festivities. Wyn said the prince is announcing another *trial*. Tonight.

I shouldn't be shocked. When I agreed to work for the king, he said there would be trials and competitions I would have to take part in. He also said I should do well in them to ensure that my ineptness isn't a reason to be eliminated.

But if this is anything like the labyrinth trial, I must be prepared for other fae to sabotage me the way Clove did in the maze.

Clove might be gone, but I've gotten to know the other Tourney contestants since then. And although I won't be the fae chosen by Rion in the end, I've set myself up as someone to beat.

"Have you said what needs to be said?" Wyn asks, pulling me from the roiling thoughts that now plague me and back into the room.

My eyes snap to him as I think on mine and Princess Arielle's conversation—who stands on the table as a winter magic projection—when he stepped into the hallway.

I admitted to Arielle that I have budding feelings for the

prince. My cheeks burn with the memory, but Wyn wasn't privy to that part of our conversation. He refers to the curse.

I shake my head and close my eyes, pushing away the revelation Arielle pulled out of me and focus on the task. It's now even more important that I rid myself of the curse.

Focus.

As much as I want to blame my actions on the ship today with Rion on the curse—as Arielle alluded—I'm confident it wasn't active then. And though I'm frustrated that a sylph alerted the autumn fae to my presence, I wasn't caught. The *Silver Shadow* wouldn't have taken the risk in the first place, and I'd escaped. "The curse came back tonight."

"The curse would reactivate almost immediately after touching the offending object," Arielle says. "So, what happened tonight?"

"The first sign of the curse returning... was at dinner," I tell them.

"And before dinner?"

"I was in my room, getting ready."

"Did anything unusual happen?"

"Yes, Mora broke into my room." I glance at Wyn again, then back at the projection of the summer princess. "Do you think she has something to do with the curse?"

"Could she have contaminated something in your chambers?" Wyn asks.

"The curse caused you trouble even before you came to Isi Aura," Princess Arielle reminds me. "I don't remember Mora leaving the palace in the weeks leading up to the Tourney."

She could have had someone else do it for her. But I realize Mora didn't know where I was. No one did. And even if the younger summer princess knew, she wouldn't know that I was going to be a contestant of the Consort Tourney. Or have the foresight to do something so well played out. "You're right. It couldn't have been Princess Mora."

Arielle paces again. "Is there something you touched that maybe you hadn't touched in a while?"

"She bumped some things off my vanity." I think about the glass perfumed tinctures and make up. "My attendant helped me pick it up."

"It would be something you likely brought with you," Arielle presses.

My hand flies to my throat, gripping the crystalized sunbeam that has hung around my neck since it replaced the object that hung there before it.

The key Clay gifted me.

The key I touched while thieving for the fae who wanted deeds to human lands in a trunk owned by the fae with a frown and a lion's tail. Nightfell.

"There was a key I brought with me—I picked it up as I was putting everything back."

"That must be it!" Arielle says, with a clap of her hands.

Next to me, Wyn is beaming at her projection.

My thumb and finger run over the smooth pendant. "I replaced the key with this when Rion gave it to me. But I wasn't wearing the key during my outburst in the garden, and I only touched it tonight. It hasn't been on my person."

"From what I've read," Arielle begins, "it's proportional to the length of time worn. So, if you'd worn the object for a week, the curse would linger approximately a week after removal."

"But I only touched it for a brief moment tonight."

She nods. "Typically curses last *at least* until the next sunset. Be careful."

"I touched the key after dark. Are you saying it might linger until tomorrow night?"

"It's possible."

I groan inwardly. I cannot bury myself in my room for an entire day. Not with another trial coming up.

"At least we have an answer," Wyn says. "I'm afraid I must get you back to the prince and the others. I'll personally remove the key from your room immediately."

"Can you handle the curse for one more day?" Arielle asks, sympathetically.

What choice do I have? I straighten. "I must."

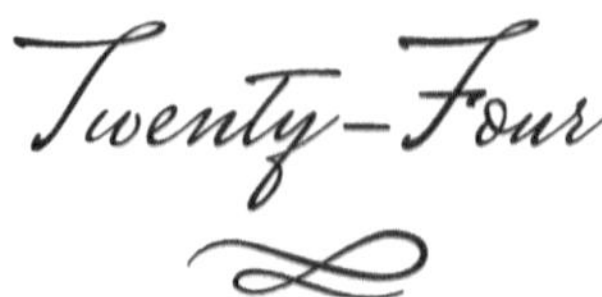

Twenty-Four

Only the sounds of mine and Wyn's steps echo through the corridors as we make our way back. I'm lost in my thoughts. How can I endure this curse for one more day, what will the next trial be, and most importantly, how I feel about a certain walnut-haired, cat-eyed fae I met in the Rosewind market what feels like centuries and moments ago all at once.

Until I uttered the words, I didn't recognize my growing feelings.

When we descend the stairs, Wyn breaks the silence, "I shouldn't be surprised it happened, especially since I thought your position in the Consort Tourney was legitimate in the beginning, but you must proceed with caution."

"So, you think someone knew I was on the invitation list and wanted to sabotage me? Is there any way to postpone the trial?" I ask, feeling a tightening in my chest. "You're right. Dealing with the curse for one more day will be very tricky."

"That's not what I meant," Wyn says with a meaningful look. "I mean the very obvious fact that you're catching feelings for Prince Orion."

"I uh..." I scramble to come up with something, anything, to contradict him, but merely ask, "Did you hear my conversation with Princess Arielle when you were in the hallway?"

"No. Amberle, I've been *observing* you." He drops his volume. "I've seen the way you look at him. Falling in love sets you up for unnecessary risk. It might be too late to remain unemotional, but you must be careful."

I keep my expression still even as an upheaval of emotions surges in my chest. "You're right. Only someone who can be with the prince, with the king's blessing, should allow themselves to fall in love with him. Anyone who did otherwise would be a fool. A fool who'd put themselves in incredible danger."

A line of concern etches into his forehead, but he nods. "I'm glad we're in agreement."

I want to assure him I know what I'm doing, but I can't quite form the words. We walk the rest of the way in silence.

***

My gaze instantly falls on Rion's when I enter the sitting room where he and the other contestants are gathered. The prince's brows pinch together and before I can tear my glance away, he mouths, *is everything alright?*

I manage a smile and nod; grateful my face can lie even if my lips can't.

He sits on a chaise with Cerule. Her back is toward me, but she's gesturing with one hand as she speaks to him. She chatters on, seemingly oblivious to the prince's body language shifting away with her every syllable.

A warmth begins at my core as I remember my admission to Princess Arielle only moments ago.

I'm falling for him. But... I can't.

His lips move, saying something to Cerule. My brain doesn't catch up with the situation until he rises, his focus on me. I feel Princess Mora's eyes boring into the back of my skull, scrutinizing my next move. I fist my hands, mentally grasping for some solution to this very public meeting.

He approaches and I wipe my clammy palms on the sides of my skirts as if I could rid the ache of wanting to talk to him into the soft fabric, pushing my dangerous feelings away in one action. Rion's eyes reflect the smile on his face and my heart trips.

But before the prince can close the distance between us, Nieven Morphyra enters in a cerulean-colored suit that matches the exact tone of his skin. I can't help the audible sigh that escapes at the announcer's timing.

"Come! Gather 'round," Nieven says, gesturing widely with his arms. The prince pivots and strolls toward him. Didi and Lady Pepper rise from their seats to obey.

"It's been an eventful day—" Nieven gestures at me, still just inside the doorway. "And night—" He gestures to the others. "For our prince. It's very late, and the sun has nearly risen again, but before we allow Prince Orion and his ladies to rest, we wanted to announce the next trial."

At his words, another figure enters the room. The royal visitor sends every set of shoulders straight and every fae who wasn't already standing to their feet.

A collective whisper of her name—*Queen Siora*—flutters through the room. The high queen steps next to the announcer, imbued with her elegance and her beauty. Her *regalness* radiates from her glittering jeweled crown down to her delicate silk shoes.

The sight of her hits me like an ice block, forcing me to blink several times and press my lips tightly together.

"If you are Prince Orion's choice," the queens says, addressing us as a group and lifting one hand toward her son with a shining glimmer in her eyes. She looks at him, her countenance lightening with joy in a way my mother once gazed upon me. "If you become his mate and his bride, then you might become the high queen consort someday."

The queen looks at Nieven, who bows slightly. When Queen Siora looks back at us, I feel the power in her gaze. As a child, I admired her and was never nervous in her presence. But now I know better. As kind as she was to me, with a flick of her finger, I could disappear—and there would be no questions.

"As the high queen, in addition to being a support for your king, you will also have some political duties. Some of those duties will be to meet with other court royals, and while they will often come to you, in some cases, you will have to go to them."

Cerule turns to Tierney and whispers something, and I see Lady Pepper shoot Princess Shay a look. The latter merely nods. She knows what the queen speaks of.

"For your next trial, we will assign you a court capital that you must travel to the quickest and safest."

Interesting. A race.

"And since it is often imperative that your travels are unknown so that assassins and robbers and even doting subjects cannot interfere, you must be secretive and travel in ways that you will not be caught."

So we must travel like shadows. Like ghosts. The winter court and their glamours will have the advantage. Even so, finally, this is a task where my skills of being invisible will excel.

"May the swiftest, most clever fae win." The queen smiles, then twists on her heel and walks back the way she came. Before she exits through the door, she looks back once, her eyes sweeping over all of us. I might imagine it, but her gaze lingers on me for a moment longer than the rest.

I wonder what she thought of me all those years ago. Was her kindness a part of her nature as a queen toward a young subject? I wonder what she thinks of me now. If she knows about her son's feelings toward me. If she guesses my feelings for him. But her expression is unreadable.

When the queen is gone, the announcer claps his hands—still wearing his performer air—and says, "But... do not fret, because you won't be traveling alone."

A few fae release held breaths and the room collectively sighs with relief. This is good news for them, but my excitement plummets.

"You will be in groups."

Inwardly, I groan. Even if I'm paired with someone who doesn't hate me, such as Didi, I won't be able to fully use my skills. Not with other contestants watching.

"Get some rest. We will gather you in secret and inform you of your target locations when the trial begins."

When the announcer leaves, the room erupts into chaos. Fae talk over each other as everyone speculates which courts they will be assigned to travel to. *The Winter Court is the farthest*, some argue, *and would be unfair to send one group there while another only needs to travel to Herdan in the Spring Court.*

I'm not watching them, I'm watching Rion, who goes to the door the queen and announcer left through and talks to someone on the other side. After a moment, he walks back into the room and I feel the crackling energy of the watching winter magic rush past me and toward the same door.

He patiently waits.

It doesn't take long. Within seconds, the winter magic dissipates and completely flees the sitting room. The hair at the back of my neck and the edges of my wings tingle with nervous anticipation.

"If I could have a private word," Prince Orion says. His voice is neither loud, nor demanding, but the seriousness in his tone silences the room completely, and every set of eyes turn to him. "I asked that Faerie not see this part because they already have a head start to thwart you during this trial."

"What do you mean, *thwart us*?" Princess Shay asks, stepping forward.

He glances at her with unbridled concern that he sweeps over the rest of us.

"That announcement was public." The prince points to the doorway where both the queen and Nieven exited. "When my mother must travel to another court in secrecy, the rest of Faerie doesn't know about her movements. Yes, there are dangers that are always lurking, but her loyal subjects are unaware."

Didi glances at me as if for reassurance. I manage a small smile.

"I have heard rumors that some of you..." Rion's eyes drop to the floor. "Are well-liked among the fae." He pauses and closes his eyes. "And some of you are not."

Whispers amongst the contestants ignite.

"Are you saying that we could be in danger because some of the fae *don't like us?*" Tierney asks.

"Or they could slow us down because they do?" Princess Mora asks, glancing at Lady Pepper.

"I fear that both are a possibility," the prince says, standing straighter. "I had hoped that the announcement of that trial would be more vague because now the fae might watch for you."

"But you did not announce where each of us is going," Shay says, stepping toward Rion and placing a comforting hand on his arm. "We appreciate your concern for us." The winter princess lifts an upturned hand at all of us. "But that should provide some comfort. Faerie is large and the fae cannot block all roads. It is just imperative that we all do well."

The girls converge on the prince, offering their reassurance that they will succeed in preserving each other's safety. I remain where I stand, afraid of what I might do or say if I approach him.

Their words satisfy Rion, because his smile returns and his posture relaxes. "It's been a long day and night. Let us retire so you can prove your words."

I'm dead on my feet and the first one to turn toward the doorway. The others are reluctant, but don't linger much longer and turn to follow.

"Amberle, wait," Rion says when I've almost passed the threshold.

I turn.

Mora catches my eye, but I pretend not to see the look that screams, *talk to him and I'll tell everyone that you have newly healed wings and a penchant for spying.*

"Could I have a word?" he asks.

I nod. Not knowing how I can outright say no with a direct request, but vow to keep my lips closed.

The prince watches the others file out, many of them giving him curious looks before turning toward the hallway, but none protest.

"Are you alright?" he asks when we're out of earshot, his tone has changed. It's warmer and fills me with bubbling sunshine that I force back down.

I can't.

I look away from the golden depths of his eyes that search mine with such intensity and nod again.

I cannot say yes because I'm not okay. Mora has threatened me if I speak to him. I've also just learned that I'm cursed for at least another day, and this next trial could end in disaster. If I'm too good at traveling invisibly, the astute fae observers might connect me to my true identity. And if I'm not, vicious fae who hate seeing a star fae on the arm of their beloved prince could mob me.

But most of all, there's the giant, grotesque, monstrous *div* of a problem that I'm falling in love with someone I can never be with.

I cannot say no because then he'll want to speak longer and I'm afraid I might spill all of it.

The gentle press of his hand lifts my chin upward, and I'm compelled to look at him again. My silence doesn't matter. He can see the lie. I know it by the way his face contorts into a frown that chips away at my heart.

"What is it?" he whispers, his voice breaking. "What's wrong?"

I can't tell you. I want to say but fear the curse will twist even that. So, I bite the inside of my cheek hard enough to taste blood, close my eyes—which squeezes out a single hot tear—and shake my head.

The prince releases his grip on my chin. "Get some rest then."

Twenty-Five

Moments after my head hits the pillow, I'm startled awake. But when the servants yank aside the curtains, full light streams through the window. I'm surprised at how deeply I slept.

"Come!" Posey says as she approaches with a pale blue dress. "They've summoned you for the trial."

Those words push the last bit of grogginess and fatigue from my limbs as a jolt of anticipation fills them.

"Any rumors about who is on each team?" I ask Posey as I push back my covers.

"Of course, but it's impossible to say if any are true." She lays the dress on the bed and hands me a glass of sparkling water.

"I just hope I have partners who can be... discrete," I say and take a sip.

Posey snorts a laugh. "That rules out most of them."

"I wish I was doing this challenge alone."

"How am I not surprised?" She flashes a wry grin. "But remember, these contests are more than they appear at first glance."

"Maybe the king wants to see who can play well with others?" Kenna suggests.

"The fae? Not likely," I say.

"Kenna could be right," Posey says. "Alliances are important,"

"Or the king wants to know who the best saboteur is," I say, thinking of Clove's antics in the labyrinth. "That is how Gnacia earned her position."

Although it might've served the king's assistant, it didn't serve Clove in the end, since she's no longer a part of the competition.

"Then you must be on your game today," Kenna says.

She's right. But the one positive note in all this teammate-nightmare is the opportunity to watch the contestants I'm paired with closely. I already know that Frost is trouble, but what about Princess Shay? And I barely know the underwater fae, River. Perhaps I'll be paired with one of them and can figure out who deserves to be with Ri—the prince.

The thought of his name sends a shiver radiating from chest and tingling outward to my crown, the edges of my wings, and my toes. I cannot allow my feelings for him to trip me up, and I force myself to focus on the upcoming task. Kenna helps me out of my nightclothes, and I step into the dress that feels like the same fabric I wore for the maze trial. Comfortable and easy to move in.

"Don't I get to bathe first?" I ask as clasps are hooked, and sashes are tied.

"There isn't time," Posey says, ushering me to the vanity. Kenna brushes through my tangled tresses. "They're expecting you now."

I remind myself that it doesn't bother me. When I thieved, I was lucky to have clean water to wash my face and hands each day. If I wanted a full body cleaning, I had to sneak where I shouldn't go—the lukewarm leftovers of a manor house that hadn't yet been emptied, or a freshly filled bitter-cold trough in a kelpie stable—or a trek to Oris Lake.

I can't let myself get accustomed to palace life.

While Kenna braids my hair, I recall what I can of the capitals. The Spring Court would be the easiest assignment. I know the roads, and I spent time everywhere from the breathtaking cherry blossom trees to the derelict spring fae hovels. The capital, Herdan, is larger than Rosewind, but not much different. It's also the closest to Isi Aura, but I can't hold my breath that I'll be that lucky.

Avala, the Winter Court capital, is the furthest away. But taking advantage of the shadows and darkness that became second nature in my former life might allow me to avoid being ambushed by doting—or hating—fae.

I imagine the Autumn Court capital, Graycrest, might be the most challenging. First, because I've never been and I'm not familiar with the landscape or the best routes. We might have to cross the sea or skirt the Harsh Lands to get there. But it's not as far as Avala.

With my luck, I'll be sent to Autumn.

Kenna finishes the braid, then twists it into a tight bun at the nape of my neck, her deft fingers working quickly and ensuring not a single piece of my silver hair escapes the cage she constructs.

In less than the time it takes an autumn fae to tear down what a spring fae can create, I'm ready and ushered out the door. Without a word, I'm briskly led through the palace to the exit near the beach that leads to the Sea of Neptulus, where Luna Diables waits.

She eyes me, and I note she wears the same pale blue dress. Although the color of the fabric looks nearly pure white against her dark elf complexion and matches the smattering of white freckles across her nose and cheeks. We must be teammates.

Luna scowls and folds her arms. "I suppose it was too optimistic to hope they would pair me with another full fae so I might actually win this trial. I figured my odds were favorable since there are only two of you."

I don't bother responding. She wouldn't be complaining if she knew my alternate identity. And I hate to admit that I am pleased to be paired with a winter fae. Her ability to manipulate shadows will come in handy wherever we're sent.

The familiar clopping of Gnacia's hooves approach us from behind, so we turn to greet her.

"I applaud your ability to get here quickly," the faun says to us. "Not everyone is quick to rise and endure a rushed dressing."

I bite back a snarky retort. This morning was leisurely compared to being thrown out of bed because my hideout was discovered or ransacked. My small apartment over the bakery was definitely not my first as a thief.

"Yes, well, we are ready. Are you here to tell us where we're going?" Luna asks.

"Not until your team is assembled."

Luna and I glance at each other.

"How many others?" I ask, trying to keep the tension from my voice. More contestants will only provide more opportunities to fail.

"Just one."

A moment later, the thin, petite form of Cerule Rostina emerges from the palace and joins us. If I must work with an autumn fae, I'm glad it's her and not her friend, Tierney.

"Great, now we can get started," Gnacia says, clapping her hands.

I feel for the winter magic that has uneasily become so familiar lately, certain it must be present or soon-to-be present to watch as the king's assistant announces to all of Faerie where the three of us will travel to. But it's happily absent.

"First, some business," Gnacia says. "The prince was concerned about this trial being broadcast while it was happening. He worried zealous fae might overtake you and thwart your progress."

I glance at Luna, relieved, but only get a huff and a scowl. Being a winter fae herself, the watching winter magic must not bother her. So I look at Cerule, but she doesn't meet my gaze.

"But the king promised Faerie that they would see the Consort Tourney, so the events of this trial *will* be shown... later."

"Yes, so tell us. Where are we going?" Cerule asks.

"In order to make this trial as equal as possible, each team is given the approximate appropriate time so that all will reach their destination all at once so that a winner can be determined." Gnacia offers a rare smile. "If they are successful."

"What do you mean?" Luna asks.

"Well, I mean, the team assigned to travel to the Winter Court will leave before the team assigned to the Spring Court."

It surprises me they are attempting to be *fair*. It isn't a common trait of the fae.

"Another factor in the attempt at equality, each team will go to a court that *isn't* the heritage of any of the teammates."

I can't help the smile that spreads. Since I'm a summer fae—half, but still summer, Cerule is autumn, and Luna is winter, we must be going to the Spring Court.

"Which means they have assigned your team to travel to Neptulus."

"Wait!" Luna blurts.

"You can't possibly mean..." Cerule says.

And I finish, "the *Underwater Court.*"

Twenty-Six

Fear and dread pours over my skin and the waves of the sea are suddenly a roar in my ears. As if taunting me.

"The *Underwater Court?*" Luna asks, as if I didn't just say it.

"But that's imposs—" Cerule starts, but cuts herself off.

For once, I feel truly in sync with two of my fellow contestants. I point at each of us. "None of us have gills."

"We cannot *breathe* underwater!" Luna says. *Again,* as if I didn't just imply it.

"Has the queen *ever* gone to Neptulus?" Cerule complains.

"Doesn't the fish court always come to her?" Luna says.

Luna isn't chided for her slang insult of the underwater fae. Calling star fae *halfling mutts,* or the *impure,* is overused and rarely corrected. But calling the underwater fae *fish* is usually cause for punishment; the underwater fae are *full fae,* after all.

"No, they do not always come to her," Gnacia says calmly. "In fact, they have an entire annex—albeit a small one—within their palace reserved specifically for fae who cannot breathe underwater."

"Then how do they get there?" Cerule ask.

Gnacia smiles, but looks at me when she answers, "None of

the parties are receiving instructions on which route to take. But when you begin at the right place and at the right time, your path will appear."

"That hardly seems *fair*," Luna whines, then folds her arms and pouts.

"Yes, well, I imagine you won't be intercepted as easily as the other groups, since your available courses are much more varied," Gnacia points out.

The winter night elf puffs out her chest, defiant. "Except we might not even *get* there—"

I yank at Luna's arm, pulling her with me and cutting her off. "She isn't going to help," I hiss. "We'll have to figure this out ourselves."

Cerule falls into step with us as I pull Luna down the beach. We're only a handful of steps before Luna yanks her arm from my grip.

"There's no point arguing with her," I say.

"But it isn't fair!" Luna says, moving to stomp back up the beach to confront Gnacia.

"Amberle is right, Luna," Cerule shouts, stopping her. When the winter fae turns, Cerule continues. "Arguing with Gnacia will only waste time."

Luna folds her arms and cuts her a glare. "Fine then. Do you have some sort of *grand* plan, Cerule?"

Cerule glances at me once, then gestures that we follow her to the shore. Luna huffs with each step, but we don't speak while walking to water's edge and stop. Standing side by side, we sandwich Cerule and watch the waves break on the sand. But she doesn't speak right away. I don't think she has a plan.

"Well?" Luna asks, shifting her body toward the autumn fae and letting her frigid impatience seep into the air with heavy iciness.

"We could ride cabyll ushteys?" I suggest. I still haven't had a chance to ride mine, let alone name her.

Crunching steps approach us from behind. Perhaps Gnacia is coming to help us after all?

"And then lose the competition because we became its meal?" Luna says. "That's a horrible suggestion, and it doesn't solve the problem of getting to Neptulus before we drown."

"Luna could create an ice flow for us to float on," Cerule offers. "And I could use my wind magic—"

"*Again*, we have no way of getting *underneath*," Luna cuts her off. Neither of them seems to hear the footsteps approaching us. "Even if we could locate Neptulus, have either of you ever been to the Underwater Court? Do you know where it's located?"

"There are several tunnels to access it," Rion says, and I involuntarily gasp. I didn't expect it to be him. He stands directly behind me and the surprise of it being *him* and not the faun makes me stumble backward—toward the surf—as I turn to face him.

"Prince Orion!" Cerule says, with a sickly sweet tone. "To what do we owe the pleasure of your presence now?"

He doesn't look at her and catches my eye, but I look away quickly. It doesn't deter him and he glides toward me, but I keep my focus on my teammates, studiously looking away from him. He and I will never be together. We cannot be together. It won't work. The king won't allow it, so I cannot allow my conflicted feelings for him to have any chance to grow by getting lost in his golden eyes.

I must dissuade him, too. Somehow.

His eyes still rest on me when he says, "I shouldn't be giving any of the team's hints, but the tunnels are not well known."

"Tunnels?" Luna asks.

"Yes, air-filled tunnels for fae traveling to the Underwater Court who can't breathe underwater."

Cerule's expression is unreadable. "And how do we find these... tunnels?"

The prince turns to her. "The entrance of one is near the eastern tip of Terpsichore."

Gnacia mentioned the winter magic won't show the events of this trial to the masses until *after* they have happened, but I can't help but worry that the very nature of tunnels to access Neptulus could give the underwater fae plenty of opportunities to thwart our journey—with little chance for us to evade or escape.

"We would need a way to get to the island," Luna says, contemplating.

Cerule lifts a finger to speak.

"I know!" Luna interjects. "I could create a boat out of ice for us, and Cerule could propel us with wind."

"What an excellent idea," the prince says. He's impressed, and it shoots a pang of... something through me. Jealousy? Maybe.

I shrug it off, but when he angles toward me and I feel the full force of his gaze again, my face heats, and my stomach flutters as if caging dragonflies.

Stop, Amberle. You cannot feel this way about him. It won't work. You're here to pair him with someone else. You work for the king. You're doing this for your father.

With significant effort, I pretend his attention isn't affecting me.

"Cerule came up with that plan first," I say, ignoring Luna's glare. I can't be with Rion, but that doesn't mean I can't point out which fae are the bigger slaugh bulbeggers.

"You could come with us, Prince Orion," Cerule says, sidling up to him.

"As much as I'd love to join you," he says, "I've already broken a rule of this trial."

"Then it won't hurt to break another." Cerule has his arm in her grasp and a sultry tone in her voice.

He pulls away in one motion. "I'd hate to disqualify your team because of my actions."

My resolve fails and my eyes find his, causing a jolt behind my ribs and a flush up my cheeks.

But there's something behind his eyes I recognize now. It's a hint of discomfort—pain. The imagined, trapped dragonflies turn to shame as I recall the way I spoke to him last night. But by the time I open my mouth to say something, *anything,* he's broken the spell, excused himself, and is walking away.

I push the uncomfortable feeling from my mind as Luna expertly creates an ice craft with what looks like little effort. She molds and forms the ice into a wide, canoe-like boat with a bench in the center and a taller one in the back for Cerule to sit and use her wind magic to propel us across the sea. The three of us board the make-shift iceboat and with a flick of Cerule's wrist and a *whooshing* of wind, we're heading toward the islands of Euterpe and Terpsichore.

We travel for several hours causing strands of my hair to escape from the tight bun Kenna crafted. And although we're still in the summer heat, the combination of the ice I sit on, the added winter magic from Luna to keep the ice from melting, and Cerule's fierce winds, I'm freezing. Rubbing my hands along my bare arms to warm them, my teeth chatter and my body is wracked with the occasional shiver that rushes up and down my limbs and spine.

"*Ugh*, you're so useless," Luna says when my teeth clack against each other hard and swiftly enough to draw her notice. "It's a good thing they didn't send you to Winter, right?" She rolls her eyes.

I don't respond.

"Cerule and I are doing all the work while you sit there sniveling because you're *cold,*" she continues. "I've been in the Summer Court for ages during this Consort Tourney and I haven't complained once.*"*

"Yes, well, you have ice magic to keep yourself cool, Luna," Cerule says. "Since Amberle is half-fae, she can't create her own summer fire to warm herself. Not like Princess Mora or Lady

Pepper can." Her words sound kind, but her tone is condescending.

"True, but she's still useless. It's hard to forget her outing with the prince and the disaster of him falling overboard. Lemons?" Luna turns back to me and scoffs. "Did you really think lemons would save him?" She shakes her head and laughs once.

If she was watching, she would know that isn't how it happened, but I imagine many of the contestants saw what they wanted to see. Painting me as a villain who tried to murder the prince furthers their position in the Tourney.

"And you're such a fool for him," she continues.

I feel the color drain from my face.

"We all see it. It's pathetic."

Can they? Do they *all* see how much I've fallen for him?

"But you won't be the one in the end. Halflings don't belong on the throne—any throne."

She's not wrong.

Desperately, I try to hide the next wave of shivers, but Luna has made the air even colder with her frigid attitude and it causes my entire body to shudder.

Luna laughs, but doesn't berate me again.

* * *

We ride in silence the rest of the way to Terpsichore. I'm the first one to jump from the boat and walk up the sunbaked beach. I plop down, sitting with my legs outstretched to warm as much surface area as possible, but think better of it and raise my knees to sink my toes into the sand and rid their numbness. The warmth is so welcoming, I nearly groan in pleasure. I lift my face toward the sun and love the way the heat feels on my cheeks and arms. I absorb the warmth into my wings and feel it spread throughout the rest of my body, ridding all shivers and teeth chatters.

Cerule also jumps from the boat, but she remains standing. Luna extends the ice of her boat to grip the sand so it doesn't float away, but doesn't move onto the shore. Likely preferring the ice to the summer island.

Minutes later, I've warmed enough, and I rise and walk along the beach, looking for any sign of these *tunnels* Rion spoke of. But the beach looks the same as any. Sand and shells and water.

"Where is this *tunnel?*" Luna asks. I turn and note that she hasn't moved from her spot and has an impatient hand on her hip. Cerule walks in the other direction, looking out and down into the water.

I stop and peer into the depths, but only see more sand and rocks and a bit of coral as it gets deeper, then it drops off and I see nothing more than deep blue.

I turn back to Cerule and Luna.

Neither of them can fly, so I push off the sand and rise into the air with my dragonfly wings flapping rapidly to gain altitude. Maybe I can spot the tunnel from the air. I relish flying without the pain I'd lived with for too long during the Tourney. If we weren't in the middle of a race, I would love to leisurely fly around the island, catching updrafts and glide around in the summer sunlight.

Every second we take to locate this *tunnel* and make our way to Neptulus is another second the other teams have to get closer to *their* destinations. So I focus back on the water and the island, looking for anything resembling a tunnel.

But again, all I see are the varying colors of blue and green in the water and nothing on the land.

As much as I'd like to stay in the air, I glide down, landing on the sand next to Cerule, who seems to have given up her search by foot. She stands with arms crossed and a furrow between her brows.

"See anything?" she asks.

"Just water," I say.

"Perhaps... it's further inland?" Cerule suggests.

"If a tunnel started further inland, wouldn't we *see* it trailing down into the water?" Luna says.

"I looked," I say. "I saw nothing." I turn back toward the sea, racking my brain for any ideas. Could the prince have been wrong? He wouldn't deliberately lead us astray. But then something occurs to me, and I realize that Gnacia *did* give us a hint. She said something about the right path *and* the right *time.* Rion directed us to this tunnel, but maybe it isn't the right path because it's the *wrong* time. "High tide."

"What?" Cerule asks.

"It's high tide. I imagine the tunnel won't reveal itself until the water recedes at low tide."

"Meaning?" Luna asks with a tilt of her head.

"Meaning, right now it's under the water." I point.

"Yes, but didn't you *look?*" Luna asks. "You said you saw nothing but water."

Cerule looks at me expectantly.

"Perhaps it's deeper."

"So we have to wait until low tide?" Cerule asks, deflating. "When will that be?"

"I'm not exactly sure," I say, my mood also deteriorating. "Several hours at least."

Luna grips the sides of her head in frustration. "It took us *several* hours to get here! The group assigned to the Spring Court might already be there!"

"Gnacia said they gave each group an appropriate amount of time..." Cerule reminds us, but Luna is right, and I don't want to sit around waiting until low tide, either.

"Well, someone should swim down there to see if we're at least in the right spot," Luna says, eyeing me.

Cerule looks at me, too.

They want me to do it.

"I mean... we *know* you can swim," Luna adds with a smirk. "We all saw it."

Hardly. No winged creature is a strong swimmer, and our "extra limbs" are easily injured when wet, but Luna is right. I was useless in getting us to the island and I might've flown for a few moments in search of the tunnel, but it wasn't enough to pull my weight. Not after both Cerule and Luna used their magic for *hours* to get us here. I still cannot fathom the reason we were divided into teams for this trial, but I walk toward the water with my chin held high and pray to Vejo that I don't meet my end while attempting to be a team player.

I step into the water, wading until the cool water is up to my waist. I pull my wings down tight against my back as the waves splash my torso and face. Without a glance back, I press forward, take a deep breath, and dive into the sea.

Twenty-Seven

Water *whooshes* into my ears, cutting off all sounds from above. I'm glad to have a moment of peace from the icy cruelness of Luna and the ignorant condescension from Cerule.

The saltwater stings my eyes, but I push through the discomfort to search for the tunnel Rion spoke of. It's just like my search from the beach and the air. Sand, a bit of coral, and midnight blue that only gets darker the deeper it goes, but no tunnels.

Needing air, I push to the surface, take a deep breath, then dive again.

I pull my useless wings as tight to my body as I can, but the gossamer acts like a mini sail, slowing my swim. The pressure pulls at my back, and I worry about re-injury. But I push away my doubts, reminding myself that my wings are strong. I've swum before and I was in the water just *yesterday* surrounded by lemons and keeping the prince from drowning.

I'm almost out of air again when I spot *them* and terror grips me.

A pod of sirens—perhaps twelve or thirteen—swim further down with their orange and red and violet hair streaming behind them, appearing as silk.

I halt my descent and stop moving completely. If I draw the attention of even one, they could sing me to my death.

They're slow-moving, leisurely. Panic rises as my lungs feel near-to-bursting. They haven't looked my way, and my body screams for oxygen. I take the risk, slowly propelling myself to the surface while keeping my eyes glued to them.

My anxiety eases as I rise. They didn't spot me, and the surface is moments away. But a siren with deep burgundy—nearly brown—hair pulls away from the group and ascends, too.

My mind wars, arguing to hold perfectly still. But my body wins out, and I kick to the surface. I break through the surface and hungrily gulp the air.

The siren pushes through too, so I freeze where I am, treading water. Her back is to me, thank Vejo, but I have little doubt she would attack me if she discovered my presence. I draw lower, keeping my nostrils above the waves, hoping to avoid her notice.

The siren lifts her head skyward. Is she gazing into the heavens? Or perhaps just feeling the warmth of the sun on her face the way I did when we first landed at Terpsichore?

"Amberle!" Luna calls from the shore.

I snap my head around.

The winter fae cups her hands around her mouth and shouts again, her entire body practically pointing right at me. "Did. You. Find. It?"

Does she not see the underwater fae? Does she not realize that drawing this siren's attention could become extremely dangerous for me?

Anger and fear spike in alarm inside me, as I realize Luna has found the perfect way to have me cut from the competition. Death by siren song. An *accident.*

Something yanks on my legs, and I immediately suck in a mouthful of water as I'm back under and suddenly face-to-face with the large, yellow eyes of the siren.

I kick away and propel back to the surface, then hack up the water, horrified that the last thing I'll hear is her song. I'm vulnerable, desperate. I spot Cerule, her back to me, while Luna watches my undoing with fascination. I shoot her a glare, not wanting her to relish a star fae's weakness in the face of death. But instead of a graceful end, my body violently rids more water from my chest.

I sense the siren behind me. I can barely breathe, let alone fight. Pressure supports underneath my arms, keeping my head above water.

I wretch again, and finally I catch my breath. My mind somewhat clearer, I realize the siren song has never sounded. The siren is keeping my head above the surface. *Is she... helping me?*

I move from her grip and turn toward her.

"You're Amberle Kindra," she says.

"I am."

She recognized me. Maybe that explains her assistance?

"What are you doing here?" She glances up at my teammates on the shore before looking back at me. Somehow, her already large eyes grow larger. "They sent you to the Underwater Court? That is your assignment for the trial?"

"Yes."

"Then why isn't River Lyn on your team?"

I attempt to shrug as I continue to tread water. "Gnacia—the king's assistant—said none of the contestants were sent to their own court."

She nods as if she understands and gestures at our surrounding. "But why are you *here?* You cannot breathe underwater. There are no access points here for the air fae. At least not right now."

"So, there is an access point here? Ri—*er...* we were told about a tunnel at the eastern tip of Terpsichore. That's why we're here."

She glances at the shore—at my teammates again—then back at me. "Yes, but not until it's low tide."

I deflate. I was right. Why did the prince send us here if we can't even access it? "Are there other tunnels we could reach *now?*"

"Several. In fact, there's one straight across on the mainland that's often accessible." She points south, straight across the sea. "It's the one the royals usually take."

Why didn't the prince send us there? I wonder. Did he not realize this one would be underwater now?

"Several mer folk are at those usual locations," she continues. "River Lyn's supporters are stalking the accesses near the palace, waiting to cheer her on. If some of the mer and selkie had seen you three instead, well, that would've been entertaining." She flashes a grin, her green pointed teeth on full display.

"The prince said some fae don't like certain contestants," I say, hoping to get a little more information from a fae outside the contest.

She pauses a moment before responding. "Yes. That's true."

I remember too clearly that all names were called with excitement, except mine.

"Many of them are not keen on a..."

"You can say it," I prod.

"On a star fae winning the crown."

Noted. I wasn't welcome. My team might have been delayed, or worse, if we had traveled that usual, easier royal path. Because of me. Perhaps *that's* why Rion sent us here. Although I imagine he didn't expect us to run into deadly sirens.

"Well, you aren't the only ones who feel that way," I say. "But I assure you, the odds of a star fae landing on the throne are very low."

"Oh. I didn't say *I* didn't want it," she says it as if I should have guessed it.

"*You* wouldn't mind having a *halfling mutt* as your possible future consort queen?"

She moves closer to me until our noses are near touching. "No, because I'm—as you say—a *halfling mutt* too."

I pull back. "You're star fae?"

She flashes a self-satisfied smile. "It's why I came to the surface. I needed some air. Of course, I'm half-siren so I *can* survive underwater unlike a summer star fae, but it makes me uncomfortable to be too long without a lungful of fresh air."

"How long?"

"I can last for weeks if I must. But whenever my pod travels near the shore or the surface, like we are today, I take advantage."

"Amberle!" Luna calls again, and Cerule shouts my name right after.

"It's lovely talking with you," I say. "I'm glad to know there's at least one star fae with underwater heritage."

"Oh, we're not as rare as you think. Sirens fall in love with human men almost as often as they kill them. Unlike the mer and the selkies, sirens are probably the most accepting of the star fae. And we're not sad about the possibility of a star fae being our queen someday." She adds with a wink.

The sentiment unexpectedly warms me, but I don't want to dash her hopes by telling her the prince won't choose me in the end. So, I get back on task. "Do you know where the access point is? The tunnel?"

"Take a breath. I'll show you."

I obey and she dives, then grips my wrist and pulls me with her. I tuck my wings again, but being dragged by a siren—even half-siren—is much quicker than swimming myself and soon she's pointing at a perfectly round opening surrounded by coral. It's far down. Too far. She pulls me back to the surface.

"The tunnel keeps the water out with underwater magic," she explains while I refill my lungs. "So if you can get to it, you'll be able to breathe once you cross the threshold."

I'm afraid we won't be able to reach it, but I don't mention that to her. "How long until low tide?"

She glances down, then up at the sky. "Ten hours at least. And I'm afraid that tunnel is never fully on the surface. Air fae must always swim a little to reach it. I think it's why they prefer the one on the mainland."

"They don't enjoy getting wet?" I guess.

She smiles, and her jagged siren teeth don't seem quite as menacing this time. "Precisely. Good luck."

She dives, and I swim to the shore to update my teammates on our predicament. My hair hangs in a heavy, soggy clump at the back of my head. I remove what's left of the pins, releasing my tresses to fall freely down my back as I trudge through the surf toward the beach.

Cerule sits on the sand and leans back on her hands while Luna paces. She holds a long stick that she likely found further up the beach near the edge of the jungle.

"Why didn't that siren drown you?" Luna asks, pointing the stick at me like a sword. She sounds disappointed.

"She recognized me," I say, not wanting to divulge everything the siren said. Specifically, that she's also half-fae.

"I bet the king ordered that no one harm us during this trial," Cerule says. She doesn't move from her spot on the sand.

"Lucky for us," Luna says with false relief, swinging her stick, then planting in the sand and resting on it like a cane. "Well? Did you find it?"

"The siren showed me where it is."

"That was kind of her," Cerule says. "I'm sure you would have struggled to find it on your own."

I bite my tongue. Mostly because she is right. "But it's too deep for us to swim to until the tide gets lower."

Luna lifts the stick, turns and swings it around a few times. I think she plans to toss it high in her anger, but she keeps it and turns back with her free hand on her hip.

"There's another across the sea we could access now," I continue.

"Then why didn't Prince Orion send us to that one?" Luna asks, pointing her *sword* at me again.

"Should we re-board the boat?" Cerule asks, standing and dusting the sand off her hands and skirts.

"But the siren said that one is likely swarmed with other

underwater fae," I say, holding a hand up. "I think the prince sent us here to avoid that."

"And *lose?*" Luna turns again and throws her stick like a spear. It doesn't go far and flops into the sand, lifting a puff of dust with it. "I don't know about you, but waiting for *hours* seems like the best way to lose this trial."

I stare at the discarded stick. I feel like it might be the answer to something, so I turn back to the water.

"But what have we really lost?" Cerule asks. "We weren't told if there was a reward for the team who arrives at their assigned court first."

The siren said the water magic pushes the water out of the tunnel.

"Cerule, it's obvious," Luna says. "Why are we in this tournament?"

If we can just make it to the tunnel...

"For the prince?" Cerule asks.

I look at the stick Luna threw like a *spear.*

"Exactly," Luna says. "I imagine the winning team gets quality time with him. Like the maze trial."

"Luna, what can you do with your ice?" I ask.

"What do you mean, *what can I do with my—*"

"Can it only remain in the first shape you make it?" I ask. "Or can you manipulate it once it's formed to change?"

She walks toward me with both arms folded and her chin lifted. I feel the air chill as she nears and pushes her face close to mine. She's trying to intimidate me. "I can do *whatever* I want with ice."

"The siren said there is air in the tunnel. Water magic keeps the seawater out so if we can just get to the tunnel—"

"You said it was too far to swim," Luna interrupts, then turns to Cerule with an incredulous look.

"It is," I say. "But if you shot a long *spear* of ice that spanned from here to the tunnel to cut through the water, stopping just inside the tunnel, then widened it and hollowed it to create—"

"To create an ice tunnel," Luna interrupts. "We could walk, or slide, right down!"

"Yes."

"Show me where the entrance is." She stomps toward the water, but stops just before a wave can wash over her feet.

"You might have to get wet," I say.

Luna stares at the water, as if she could part the water with the sheer force of her glare. "I'll do anything to win."

Twenty-Eight

I bite the inside of my cheek, hoping Luna can work quickly. The dark elf moves her hands to form an icicle as Cerule stands next to me, clutching her hands together.

The ice grows and lengthens into a long spear. Luna tips it forward and one end pierces the water. It appears as if she stops, but her brow is furrowed in concentration. I look again, and notice the ice-spear is lengthening, traveling down to the tunnel opening that leads to Neptulus, deep in the waters of the sea.

"Do you think he's watching us?" Cerule asks dreamily.

I look at Cerule who is twisting one of her long, burnt orange locks around one finger. She stares at the sand as she continues, "I mean, Nieven Morphyra said the broadcast would be delayed, so perhaps he's not watching us right *now*, but do you think the prince will see us working so hard to win?"

I frown. I hadn't thought about that possibility, but I don't feel the winter magic. "I imagine the magic is trained on him. Since Faerie can't watch *us* right now, I bet it's following him to keep them entertained."

"I hope we win," she says absently, still twisting her hair and clearly not listening to my answer. "I think it's the best way to have a chance with the prince. Earning time with him. He would've chosen Juni at the end if she hadn't died."

The mention of Juniper smarts. I wonder if Wyn has found any more clues about her death. I should have asked when he pulled me to talk to Arielle.

"You think so?" I say, though I disagree. Juniper was convinced her loved her, but I never saw evidence of it.

"Of course! She earned time by winning the labyrinth trial and he was falling in love with her during their date." Cerule's tone is sickly sweet. "She said so herself."

"Juniper was powerful and clever," I say, watching Luna.

The winter fae now stands knee-deep in the water, with the ice beam cradled in both arms. I would move closer but the icy wave I feel, even where I stand, is as much as I can bear at the moment. Especially since I will soon be surrounded by ice if Luna's tunnel works.

"Maybe I should do what you did," Cerule says, drawing my attention back to her.

"What did I do?"

"In the garden? Tierney said it was pathetic—and maybe it was, but you can't help that." She reaches out as if to pat my arm but drops it when I flash an unintentional scowl. It doesn't faze her. "Still, it worked, and you got time with him."

"That isn't why—"

"It was a smart move," she interrupts, flashing a forced smile. "But King Estelar is smart too. You cannot win, of course, but I'm sure the king would have made it appear like you had an equal chance. There was no need to throw yourself at the prince in the garden. You would have had a moment with the prince before they cut you from the competition."

There's no point arguing with her because she's probably partly right. But I'd almost prefer Luna and Mora's outright cruelty rather than her condescending pretend kindness.

"I'd rather earn the prince by winning this trial," she continues, "but if I don't, maybe I need to think of something drastic to get his attention."

I wish I could excuse myself from this painful conversation. From where we stand, Luna is leaning back, straining under the weight of the growing ice, but she remains stalwart. The diameter continues to widen, so I move to help her, but she sends me a murderous look.

"Getting time with Prince Orion won't necessarily endear yourself to him," I say. It's a knee-jerk response, but I'm frustrated I can't escape Cerule.

"Right. Nearly drowning the prince was terribly foolish, but I'd use my time more wisely." She sighs. "I'm certain he would fall in love with me the way he was falling for Juni." After a pause, she asks, "Would you accept me as the consort princess?"

It catches me off guard. None of the contestants have asked that question, but it forces me to consider it. Despite her haughtiness, Cerule wouldn't be the worst candidate. I just hope she would impart some *kindness* to the star fae and be the influence on Ri—

I can't. I can't think of it until I must. "There are still ten of us left."

Cerule turns to watch Luna. "I know I'm not the obvious option. Not like Princess Shay or Lady Pepper. But I think I'd be a wonderful queen."

She might not be the worst option. My stomach churns as I consider she might be the *best* option. I almost ask her about policies she might change that impact star fae, but I clamp my mouth shut. Her actions have already shown that she thinks we're inept and have the intelligence of a sylph. All I can do is prove to her that star fae are capable allies. I *might* be able to make her doubt her preconceived notions. Maybe.

Luna is hollowing out the beam now and rests it on the sand as it grows. It's almost time. I'm impressed with the sheer majesty of Luna's creation. I've seen plenty of winter magic, and this is something truly spectacular.

"Well done, Luna," I call out a compliment.

She hisses at me, flashing her teeth, like I'm some wild animal she wants to shoo away.

"Now I just need to think of something big to catch his attention," Cerule ponders, and by the tone in her voice, she's wanting ideas. "I think I'll do it even if we win."

I want the conversation to end, so I step toward Luna as I say, "I thought Tierney was going to help you since she doesn't care for the prince. She's bold and corrosive. I'm sure she'll have some ideas for you."

Oh no. I slipped. I only know that information because I was the one spying on their conversation. I continue walking toward the winter fae, cringing, but wipe it from my face immediately. It was bound to happen. Arielle said the curse could affect me today since I touched the key last night. I just hope Cerule wasn't paying attention, again.

A shiver rushes through me as I near the finished tunnel.

"It might be a little cold, Amberle," Luna says, flashing a self-satisfied smile, gripping the edge of the ice. "I hope you can handle it." She's obviously pleased with her work. "Cerule, let's go!" Luna ducks into the tunnel.

I will myself to move forward, toward the entrance. The air chills with each step. If I'm to enter the Underwater Court tunnel, I must first endure this one made of ice.

Cerule slips past me and follows Luna.

I'm right behind her and when I look inside, I see the retreating dark forms of Luna and Cerule. The tunnel is dry, but I'm still wet from my time in the water, so it feels like my bones are turning to ice the moment I step inside.

Part of me would prefer to swim instead.

I stopped trying to silence my chattering teeth ages ago, but my jaw is so tight it aches. My arms wrap tightly around me, but it hasn't helped the painful numbness that has spread through my fingers. I can't feel my toes or the edges of my wings.

I'm forced to move slowly through the never-ending tunnel. Darkness surrounds me and I can barely see my hand in front of my face. I can't risk slipping or colliding into the ice walls for fear that my still-wet wings will freeze to the tunnel wall. So, I keep my wings tightly tucked and shuffle my feet, feeling my way through the descending tunnel.

I lost sight of Luna and Cerule when the darkness deepened. But as the former's affinity is anything frigid, her pace was probably more of a skipping frolic to Neptulus. She's likely already there sipping cocktails with the Underwater Court monarch, Queen Morvenna.

Drops of water occasionally splash on my forehead and my bare arms. I worry that Luna's creation is melting. This is the summer's sea, after all. But I can't force myself to move quicker. The ice above my head groans and whines, and I pause. A cracking sound is followed by several tiny streams of water ahead. And behind. I continue forward. I must. I pass under a thin waterfall of frigid water, following it as it slides into the depths beyond.

The roar from below comes before an icy air blast tears at my dress and frozen wings, stinging the skin of my cheeks and the tip of my nose. For a moment, I can't breathe. The burst of ice-wind seems to have frozen my every muscle. The very blood in my veins. It's unbearable. Then a second gust follows. I want to curl up and cry. But the freezing air passes, and I take a stuttering breath.

This is for my father. I'm doing this for my father. I close my eyes and picture us together again. Then I grit my teeth and continue forward, forcing my limbs to respond. I realize the fracturing ice is silenced and the stream of water at my feet is now frozen.

It must be Luna down below, keeping the tunnel intact. My image of her and the queen vanishes.

After a few moments, as I continue forward, a dark form

comes into view and when the tunnel levels, I see Cerule standing. Waiting.

"Luna sent me back to see if her re-freeze slowed you more—"

As the words leave Cerule's lips, another, louder roar rushes up the ice tunnel with such a force and much colder than the last that it knocks the autumn fae off her feet and she collides into me, sending me sprawling backward. I wave my hands to catch myself, trying to keep my balance, but I can't stop my momentum on the slick ice. I tilt and slam into the tunnel wall.

"Oof!" Cerule says at my feet. I can't see her well, but she quickly gets up and throws a glance over her shoulder, down the tunnel. "Was that necessary?" she shouts into the darkness, but she doesn't sound particularly angry. "Let's go before she tosses another one at us."

I try to right myself again and am met by a sharp, stinging, *stuck* feeling. The part of my wing that still has feeling in it stabs with pain.

"I can't move."

"C'mon, I'll lead you. I know you're cold. I could hear your chattering all the way down the tunnel, but the Underwater Court tunnel is warmer."

"No, Cerule, I can't. I'm stuck." I'm glad the panic doesn't bleed into my voice. "Luna's ice blast pushed my wet wing into the ice. It's frozen to the wall."

Not again. Why have my wings been such an encumbrance in this Tourney? Until returning to Isi Aura, my wings had not been injured in at least four *decades.* This is the third time something has happened.

"Then let's get you unstuck."

"No! You cannot just pull it free," I cry. "It'll tear, it'll—"

"Stop! I'll just decay—"

That's even worse! Rotting my wing until it's free? "Please don't—"

"Will you let me finish? I won't kill your wing. I'll decay the *ice* around it."

I'm heaving big, gulping breaths. "You can do that?"

"Well, most autumn can't. But I inherited a pinch of winter magic from a distant relative. Enough to melt the ice a bit. Obviously, my real talents lay in autumn destruction and wind."

She feels in the darkness to where my wing is attached to the ice, then moves it higher, palming the space just above my frozen wing.

"I know you were the spy," she says quietly, moving a section of her long hair behind her shoulder and out of the way. The closeness of her mouth to my ear as she works on the ice sounds like an angry hiss.

The hairs on the back of my neck stand to attention as a shiver not related to the cold travels down my back.

But I turn my face to hers, challenging her statement.

"How else would you know Tierney has no feelings for Prince Orion and that she means to help me with him?" she asks and tilts her head in my direction.

She *was* paying attention when I slipped.

"You're a halfling," Cerule says as if it's reason enough. "You'll do anything you can, even cheat to win the crown."

She's wrong, but I don't dare say so.

"You could leave me here," I say instead.

"I could, but Tierney calculated that anyone who crosses you is eliminated."

"You didn't get me stuck to the wall."

"Yes, but I know you're friends with the prince and if I help you..." The autumn fae wills me to look at her, but I can barely make out her features in the dark. "You might tell him I helped. Perhaps you could persuade him to consider me, since you know you can't be with him."

Of course. She would never help a fae out of the kindness of her heart. Cerule—just like all the fae—wants something in return. A bargain.

"If you help me without injuring my wing, I'll be sure the prince knows of your kind act."

I feel the ice moving, pulling apart from itself until in one motion, my wing falls forward. My wing looks fine, thankfully, but a chunk of ice is still attached to it.

"We'll get Luna to melt it when we reach her," Cerule says. There's no rush of water, so she removed my wing and the chunk of ice while keeping the tunnel intact. "You can thank me with your recommendation to the prince," she says before spinning and marching down the tunnel.

I follow and feel a rush of joy when I see lights ahead and realize I'm close to the entrance of the tunnel that will lead to Neptulus. The one the siren pointed out. The tunnel that is most definitely warmer than this one.

But Cerule has slowed to a stop.

"Keep going!" I say, frustrated that she's not moving. We're so close!

"Luna is gone!" she says. "That selfish brat left us. She'll be the first one to arrive."

I pass Cerule and grab her wrist, determined not to arrive much further behind. The last thing the realm needs is to witness a star fae shivering, half-dead, and coming in last.

Twenty-Nine

RION

The chill of the winter magic keeps pace with me as the clomp of my boots sound through the darkened path. Nieven Morphyra appears to be a part of my retinue, walking at my side, but it's all part of the illusion since he's not actually with us. In reality, the announcer is standing in an open-air upper room of the summer palace with the Neptulus Sea behind him as the sun dips below the horizon. It's his projection that hovers alongside. But to Faerie, it looks like we're together.

Nieven's projection will *greet* each team as they reach their assigned court. But I want to join one group in person. I could not sit and wait as the contestants moved further from Isi Aura as I sat on my cushioned chaise eating tartlets. Keeping busy, no, *moving* will distract me until this dangerous trial ends and brings everyone back again.

And bring *her* back again.

"Prince Orion, could you give us a hint?" The announcer asks. "We are on the edge of our seats, wondering which court—which *team*—are you surprising?" He flashes a toothy grin and a wink at the audience as if their unheard cheers and shouts will convince me to divulge.

"As you said, it's a surprise," I say, forcing cheer to keep the irritation out of my tone. "And Faerie doesn't know the teams yet. I wouldn't want to ruin the fun for the fae across the realm, now would I?"

At my side, Wyn ducks his head, hiding his smile. He's a full arm's length away and slightly behind me, strategically staying out of the sight of the winter magic, but I know he finds this whole thing comical. It's the fourth time the announcer has tried to get me to spill my destination or any clues about the trial.

"Our prince is right," Nieven says. "My fellow fae, it's almost time to reveal what has transpired thus far: the gathering of teams and announcements of their assignments. But I have a secret to tell..." He pauses for dramatic effect, then his projection leans further away from me with a hand cupped around his mouth when he says, "In real time, some contestants have already arrived!"

That's news to me. I lengthen my stride and quicken my steps. Has *she* arrived?

The luminescence creatures that huddle in the globes above seem to brighten as we get closer, illuminating our pathway.

When Nieven's image disappears, off to greet the teams, the winter magic evaporates. I know it's only a brief reprieve until we arrive at our destination, the court capital.

Wyn senses it too and steps closer. "Might I speak freely, My Prince?"

I resist the urge to flash a side-eye. Wyn has never asked permission to speak. It must be for appearances. For my guards' sakes. "Do you want to speak freely? Or privately?"

"Both, actually," he admits.

I nod, glance at my guards, then stop walking. My forward guards take the hint and walk several more paces, and the ones behind fall back.

"You must be careful with Amberle," he says after a pause. "I sense a... a spark, a fondness between you. There's no denying it."

I grin like a foolish youngling. I know my feelings for

Amberle, but it pleases me to hear our friend sees something on her side too. "I haven't exactly tried to hide it, have I?"

"Yes. But Rion, I don't think she's in a place to commit to an actual relationship." His eyebrows pinch together with worry. "You deserve to be with someone who can. Someone who can fully be there for you, despite your feelings."

"What makes you think she could not be exactly who I need?" I fold my arms and step back.

"Amberle deserves to be with her perfect mate, too. Someone who understands her life and can give her more privacy than what a prince can afford. Fae marriages, even for us halflings, can last centuries."

I see. My fears about him having feelings for her might be true. Does he speak out of jealously? "Do you have someone in mind for her?"

Namely, you?

He frowns. "No I—"

"You know Amberle as well as I do. You grew up with her, too. The two of you were some of the few star fae at court. You must've grown... close." How can I blame Wyn if his feelings for our mutual friend have grown deeper? What if he has fallen for her, too?

"Listen, Rion." Wyn directs a piercing stare at me. "You're right. Amberle and I have always been close. We understand each other on a level that a royal never could."

At least he's jabbing me from the front and not stabbing me in the back. I lift my shoulders, bracing myself for the declaration that he loves her. Piecing together our recent conversations and his actions fall into place. It was too painful for Wyn to be around when the Tourney began, so he didn't accompany me to Isi Aura. He couldn't even watch from where he was hiding as I courted her until he felt forced to in order to investigate the death of Juniper Faeven. And his outburst in my rooms that I *'just marry the girl'* was out of heartbreak and frustration.

But Wyn cocks his head to the side and pinches his eyebrows

in curiosity. "But it was never more than that." He grins. "You thought I *loved* Amberle?"

My lips twitch as the tension cracks.

He laughs. "Amberle is great. She is. And yes, I love her, but no." He pauses and makes a face. "Just... *no*. Not like that. I love her like a dear friend. Like a sister, even. But there is nothing romantic between us."

I roll my eyes, but feel the relief slough off my shoulders like autumn leaves.

"But I still mean what I said," Wyn says, sobering again. "Because I do care about her. Amberle is a half fae without noble or royal blood. You're not doing her any favors by giving her so much attention. You're making things hard for her."

The knife twists in my chest. I fear he is right. That, or my father has gotten in his ear.

"It's hard to hear, but you know it's true," Wyn says.

"You're right." I'll have to ease the king, the other contestants, and the realm to accept who will be my ultimate choice. Especially with nine other fae remaining in the competition. It might be time to cut more soon so it doesn't bring up so many questions when I spend too much of my time with Amberle. But I'll have to play my part more convincingly in the meantime. Play act like I'm trying to care for the others. "But I'm already ahead of you." Only because my father insisted. "It's the reason I chose *this* team to surprise."

"For no other reason?" Wyn gives me an accusing look of disbelief.

"I'm trying to get to know other viable contestants. If I'm ever destined to *feel* something for any of these fae, I must spend time with them. Attempt to form a connection."

He doesn't look convinced, but nods anyway.

After a pause, I ask, "Have you discovered anything about Juniper's murder?"

"Nothing that points to who might have done it," he says.

I nod. "Did Amberle show you where..."

"Yes. I'll keep you informed."

I nod again.

"My concern for Amberle isn't the only reason I wished to speak to you in private." Wyn inhales deeply. "I've done some digging into Ilthuryn Kindra's whereabouts."

"Oh?" It hasn't been long since I asked Wyn to look into Amberle's father. Only two days. But it's been nigh a century since the Kindra's left the Summer Court under the cover of darkness—never a good sign. Whatever happened, my father never spoke of it. Amberle said she's in the competition for her father. Perhaps she's hoping she'll do well enough to earn trust with the summer advisors, perhaps enough to find him another position in the palace? Or perhaps another court would hire him? When I speak with her father, I'll be able to find out.

Wyn's face darkens and my insides churn.

Is he dead? Was there an incident? And if so, does Amberle know? I'd hate to be the one to tell her, but I'd have no one else tell her if something terrible has happened to her beloved father.

"Yes," my friend says. "It took furtive bribery and strict secrecy, but I've learned where he is."

My mood lifts. Wyn knows his location. Where he *is*. As in presently. He hasn't died.

"But... you won't like it."

I suck in a breath. Bracing myself. "Tell me, Wyn."

"Ilthuryn Kindra is in... the Gray."

The Gray Vault? By nature, the fae are dangerous and cruel, but the Gray is a dungeon reserved for only the most heinous crimes and the most blood-thirsty, vicious fae.

So why is Ilthuryn Kindra locked up in the Gray?

Thirty

I'm nearly thawed by the time Cerule and I spot the spires of the Underwater Palace in the distance. The chunk of tunnel ice stuck to my wing clunked to the ground ages ago. My footpads are silent in the Underwater Court tunnel that continues to descend at a steep decline into the darkening waters. Their world is blurred through the water barrier around us. I prefer baking beneath the summer sun, of course, but this tunnel is a welcome change to Luna's icy version. Part of me is relieved the winter fae left us behind, but I sense Cerule bristling.

At first, being surrounded by the depths of the Sea of Neptulus was disconcerting, especially when I spotted enormous sharp-toothed creatures I'd only ever seen in picture books as a youngling. But now I only see the beauty of it.

The ocean floor nears, and I realize they expertly carved the rock below into ornate buildings. A school of mer younglings flit out of one of the larger pink corals. Their attention is on us.

The tunnel flattens out and Cerule quickens her pace, muttering encouragement to herself, "I won't be last. I won't be last."

Below our feet, the sprawling underwater capital city of Neptulus goes as far as I can see—which, granted, isn't much.

Between the darkness of the murky water and the movement of the ocean against the barrier, it's hazy. The castle grows unbelievably large, the spires easily twice the height of the Isi Aura palace. If not more. The walls are made of an opalescent material of shifting pinks and blues and greens. Mermaids, selkies, and fish swim past the many spindle-thin archways, disappearing into the depths of the palace. I am awe-struck. On the ground floor, a long, wide corridor leads to a massive glass dome. At the entrance of the corridor, a stone plaque attached to a rusted anchor reads: The Annex of Neptulus, the Reception Hall for all Air Fae.

Air fae. Meaning, air-breathing fae.

Cerule squeals and disappears down the corridor in a flurry of bubbles. Instinctively, I leap after her and I'm sucked into a whirlpool. Before I can truly panic, I'm slammed down in front of soaring salmon and peach hued coral arches—the entrance to the annexed glass dome beyond.

Cerule stands with wide eyes, gazing at the translucent wall. For the first time, we are on equal footing, unsure, and out of our element. With the flick of a wrist, this very tunnel could collapse, or the annex could be flooded, and we'd drown. I've never felt so small and vulnerable before. Perhaps that's the point.

I shrug off my discomfort like I've done a thousand times before, and step under the coral archway. Cerule follows. Inside, everything is bathed with a turquoise glow created by the luminescent creatures that cling in clusters outside of the transparent walls all around. I'm surprised to see spring cherry blossom trees and yellow-leaved aspens of autumn in a small garden in the center, while fish and marine life and mer of all colors flit around the walls beyond.

How they keep living plants that need both air and the sun alive is impressive.

The pathway winds along the barrier wall. A juvenile mermaid with a jade-colored tail that matches the shade of her hair presses her face against the glass until her nose smushes against it. She cups her hands around her eyes to peer inside. Her face alights when she spots Cerule and me. She pounds her palm on the glass, then waves. I'm not sure if she's pleased to see me in particular, but lifts a hand waist high in a greeting. The autumn fae grins and waves wildly in response.

Luna stomps toward us with fury in her expression. With her is another intense wave of frigid air that penetrates every pore of my skin and sends a violent shiver from my crown to my toes. It spurs another murderous glance from the winter fae. She's not amused by my misery anymore.

"Where have you been?" she demands, not stopping until her toes are nearly on top of mine.

Trying not to freeze to death, I want to spout, along with a string of curses about how it was *her* fault I was quite literally stuck to her ice tunnel.

But Cerule places an arm between us and gently pushes me backward—as if I was the one who invaded Luna's space.

"There was a complication, Luna," Cerule explains in a soft tone. "You must remember, Amberle is only half-fae and has many difficulties that you and I don't."

I grit my teeth at the insult, but force a neutral expression.

"Well, because of your *complication*, our team might lose!" she says. "Even though I was technically the first, apparently, we must arrive *together* to complete the challenge." She punctures me with a glare. "I suppose I'm glad the siren didn't drown you after all." Then she spins on her heel and storms forward. "Come! Now!"

Cerule and I follow, and around the bend of the glass, we find an entrance door made of wood that has seen better days. Perhaps from a shipwreck? Inside, I immediately feel the heady, buzzing winter magic trained directly at me. I probably look like I've been half-drown in a slushy-ice lake, but I can't do much to remedy that now.

Strange creatures flit into 'walls' of coral as we pass through the winding corridor, but a few stop their chores and stare as we pass. The inside of this place is a maze, but Luna leads us into what looks like a massive ballroom with underwater fae clustered around the edges of the room; their attention is on the massive projection of Nieven on the opposite side of the room.

Shells and skeletons of different sea creatures are embedded in the tiles of the floor, and a round, arched dome overhead is buttressed with what looks like the rib bones of a whale. Chandeliers seem to dance, but it's small will-o'-the-wisps adding to the blue light.

This must be the ballroom where the underwater fae host—as they call us—*air fae.*

"Ah, finally! The rest of Luna Diable's team has arrived in Neptulus!" the projection of Nieven Morphyra says, again dressed in opulence, wearing a suit of crimson adorned with matching gems. "Cerule Rostina and Amberle Kindra!" He's surrounded by projections of other contestants.

Meaning... our team was not the first. Meaning, we've lost. Hopefully, we're not *last.*

"Making you the *third* team to complete the trial!" Nieven continues.

But third doesn't earn more time with the prince...

Cerule must be so disappointed.

On the projection, I spot Princess Shay and Didi. And Mora. I groan inwardly at the sight of her and pray she isn't on the winning team.

Underwater fae stand around the edges of the room. I turn my attention to the reception hall and recognize the recently eliminated Lily and Aqualis speaking to the projection of River—who is still in the competition and obviously on a team that arrived before mine. I also notice the elusive underwater princess, Nerine, standing near her aunt, Queen Morvenna, ruler of the Underwater Court.

We quickly learn that of the four teams, Princess Shay and Didi were the first duo to arrive at Graycrest, the Autumn Court Capital; followed by Princess Mora and River at Avala in Winter. I'm impressed by the latter. Avala is quite a distance to trek through unforgiving terrain. Or so I've heard.

One team has yet to arrive. Tierney, Lady Pepper, and Frost were due to arrive in Herdan any minute, so the rest of us were instructed to wait patiently.

Clearly the duo teams had more success in this competition, but I can't help but wonder if the king helped along the contestants he wanted to earn the victory.

Namely, Princess Shay and Didi.

I speculate if Princess Shay is King Estelar's favorite to win in the end. If I were the king, I'd rather have her allegiance than her ire. Plus, she seems to get along well with the queen.

The heaviness of the watching winter magic makes my already itchy, salt-encrusted skin more irritated, so I move to the outskirts of the room where Lily and Aqualis stand. The magic lessens until it becomes only a slight vibration.

"I'm pleased to see the two of you here," I say, acting as if my desire to speak with the former contestants is the reason I moved away from the group.

"Yes, well, we thought River might come to our court, and we wished to show our support," Aqualis says, then walks away without another word, leaving Lily alone with me.

"Don't mind Aqualis," Lily says, looking at me with her large eyes. "She's still bitter that she was cut from the Tourney."

"It was only days ago," I say. "You must feel the same."

"Yes, I had hoped I would stay longer, but Aqualis and I knew we were not truly in the competition. The prince barely glanced at either of us. There are so many others with a better chance of being on the throne." Lily points her head toward River, who has moved to stand next to Princess Mora. "I imagine River won't be long for the Tourney either." Her candor is unexpected.

"You never know, maybe she and the prince will form a strong, romantic bond," I say and hate that even the hypothetical statement causes the edges of my vision to blur and my afflicted heart to twinge with unwarranted jealousy.

I cannot allow my feelings for him to affect me so much, I remind myself even as the mere *thought* of Rion fills me with warmth and dragonflies fluttering pleasurably in my stomach.

Lily forces an amiable smile and aims a pointed look. If we knew one another better, I might read her silent inference. "I don't know if you're right, but it doesn't seem likely."

The projection images of the last team enter the room. First Tierney, followed by Frost, and then Lady Pepper. None of them look as bedraggled as I feel, but I imagine traveling to the Spring Court wasn't too harrowing. It is curious how the closest destination from Isi Aura took the longest to arrive.

Again, I can't help but wonder if they did not design the timing and the obstacles along the way with a specific winning team in mind. Or a specific contestant.

"And that, my fellow fae, is the end of this trial!" Nieven Morphyra says, with arms spread wide. He turns in a circle, addressing the entire realm.

"What do we win?" Didi's projection shouts, and I grin. Even if this was a rigged competition with Princess Shay as the fae to win, at least my friend was on the winning team too.

"Excellent question, Didi," Nieven says, flashing her an amused smile. "But I imagine the answer is obvious?"

"More time with Prince Orion?" Didi asks, hopping and clapping with glee.

"Precisely!" The announcer clasps his hands together out in front of him. "At dawn, Princess Shay and Didi Beechriver will embark on a romantic two-on-one outing with our beloved prince." He turns his head and looks at the air. "And since viewing this trial was delayed for you fae watching, the date begins... *now!*" Nieven lifts his arms above his head with dramatics, then lowers them quickly, and the thickness of the magic recedes.

With his theatrics dropped, the king's entertainer looks around the room at the contestants, explaining. "Faerie has just now begun watching the action of the trial, so from this moment until the prince's date tomorrow with Princess Shay and Didi, you will not be on display."

Without another word, the announcer and all the projected fae disappear.

Luna doesn't waste a second before storming in my direction with an accusing finger aimed at me.

"You!" she shouts across the grand hall, not seeming to care that everyone can hear the way her voice bounces and echoes all over the domed ceiling. "You! You pathetic, useless *impure* halfling! *You* are the reason we lost!"

Stunned, I try to slow her embarrassing rant. "Luna, I—"

"You're such a miserable little *slaugh*," she interrupts, "you couldn't handle even a tiny bit of ice! What an inept, sniveling, waste of fae blood—what little you might have running through your veins at all! You don't deserve to have a drop of fae blood. You're an embarrassment. A black mark on this prestigious opportunity to become the high queen. I hope Prince Orion sees how incompetent you are and cuts you from the competition immediately."

Queen Morvenna clears her throat, silencing Luna's rambling verbal attacks. But it doesn't stop the daggered look the dark elf pins on me.

"My niece, Princess Nerine, and I would like to invite you three to a special meal we have arranged."

"How lovely!" Cerule says, quickly skipping away from me. She follows the queen through an arched door on the other side of the room.

I don't move right away, not wanting to turn my back on Luna. The large eyes of the underwater guests stare, their attention flitting between Luna and me. Most, if not all of them, are full fae—I'm an outcast among outcasts, alone and without a single friend.

From the corner of my eye, I realize Princess Nerine is waiting for us, so I feel obligated to move forward. I shift so Luna isn't completely out of my sight.

"Walk with me, Amberle," Princess Nerine says, closing the gap between us and threading my arm through hers.

It's a bold statement, a single sentence and movement that says volumes. I warm to her kindness immediately. The winter fae huffs behind us, her shoulder slamming into me as she passes, quickening her step to catch up with Cerule and the queen.

"Are you sure you want to be seen with a... what did she call me? *A sniveling, pathetic halfling—*"

"*Who doesn't deserve the fae blood that runs through her veins?*" Princess Nerine finishes and laughs, stopping to turn and look at me. "She's certainly creative with her words. And yes, you are just the fae I want to be seen with."

"Can I ask why, Your Highness?"

She's a pretty underwater fae with the typical large eyes and gills across her throat. But the elegant blue and green scales that run up her arms and behind her ears are a trait only the royal family possesses. It makes me wonder why she wasn't selected as a contestant for the prince.

"Many will deny what we all see. Perhaps I have the benefit with my naturally large underwater fae eyes, but it's clear, my little half-fae friend, that you are a serious contender to be our ruler someday."

Summer heat rises up my cheeks and I'm forced to look away at the sides of the hallway to hide my discomfort. I focus on the decorated clear walls adorned with glittering shells and draperies of dried red and violet seaweed.

But a devastating realization soon overshadows the feeling. While many of the fae abhor the thought of me becoming the prince's mate, a handful of fae have expressed their desire for me to win or, at the very least, their assumption that I will.

And the list of them continues to grow.

If several have expressed it to me, there might be more than I imagine around the realm who also wish for it. If the king catches wind that enough fae want *me*—a half-fae thief—at Rion's side...

Dread fills my limbs, and my throat tightens. I can't even think about what King Estelar might do if he thinks I'm a real potential candidate. A threat. I keep my head turned, looking out into the sea, feigning interest in the harmless fishes that surround us and try to ignore the pit of fear eating through the walls of my gut.

No. The king won't find out. I quickly form a plan. First, I must obliterate any sign that I'm falling in love with Rion. Second, I must dissuade Rion and Faerie from believing that our union is possible. Hopefully, he'll have some romantic spark with Didi tomorrow. Or Shay.

My wings and arms grow heavy.

Most importantly, today, I will study Luna and Cerule. I must prove I'm a brilliant spy. And the next time I see the prince—

"Prince Orion!" Princess Nerine's jovial tone echoes along the walls.

I look for a projected image of the prince down the hall. But there is no fuzzy outline of him, or the view of objects behind him through his transparent image.

Rion is here. In Neptulus. In person.

Thirty-One

The prince can't be here now. I'm not ready to see him. A mixture of horror, excitement, and guilt war inside me as I absently stroke a hand down the length of my hair, feeling the way the stickiness of the saltwater clings to my tresses. I've had no time to mentally prepare myself to push him away. Perhaps my current physical appearance will help?

But my horror turns to irritation; I can't believe I've allowed myself to fall for Prince Orion Illuminae—the *crown prince of Faerie.* But I did. And I shouldn't have.

And I must end it.

Logically, it's clear as light wisp's wings what I must do. Still, the ridiculous part of me wants to revel in the intoxicating feeling a little longer and imagine that we *could* end up together. A dangerous fantasy knowing that with one conversation, Rion will know I've been lying to him this *entire* time. A conversation more likely to happen if the king learns that some fae want me to win. Surely, I'm a glutton for the punishment.

This delusional fantasy isn't wise. Not if I want to see my father again. Not if I don't want to rot in the dungeon next to him.

The prince is here, in the Underwater Court, so I shouldn't delay the inevitable. This is my chance. It must be now.

But I'm not ready for it.

"We did not expect you here tonight, Prince Orion," Princess Nerine, says, looking at me expectantly.

Apparently, I've forgotten how to speak at the sight of him.

"I cannot remember the last time you visited us here in Neptulus," she says.

"Yes, I should have notified the queen I was coming," says the prince. He speaks to Nerine, but his eyes fall on me and all his proper, arrogant-like, princely edges soften with such unabashed adoration that I'm forced to look away. Knowing what I'm about to do feels like a thousand slashes across my heart.

"But the team that came here didn't win the competition," the princess says.

"Yes, but my obligation to the winners doesn't begin until dawn." He smiles. "I didn't want to spend the evening in Isi Aura alone, so I chose a group to surprise."

"Well, I'm afraid it's not much of a shock that you chose this one." Princess Nerine eyes me, then winks. "Come. Join us for dinner."

"Your hospitality never disappoints, Princess."

Instead of a dining table to sit around, a buffet of foods is arranged in the center of the Underwater Court's version of a dining hall. Chairs line the edges of the room, which doesn't encourage the guests to talk with one another, being so spread apart. Still, clusters of fae stand with their plates of finger-foods in casual conversation while others sit in various tight groups, some talking intently and others eating in silence.

As the princess and I walk toward the buffet, the room quiets and all heads look behind us. We turn and see that the Underwater

Court Queen has entered, with Prince Rion beside her. With the initial shock waning, I note that his hair could use a trim. It sticks up in places and brushes over his right eyebrow, but the strange lighting in this room gives it a richness not seen in the summer sunlight.

Rion's eyes twine with mine, but I quickly look away and back at the underwater royal.

Queen Morvenna gestures for the princess to stand beside her, then says, "We are pleased to have three of the Consort Tourney contestants dining with us tonight." The room of important underwater fae erupts into polite applause. "They might not have won the trial of being the first ones to arrive at our court, but it speaks well of them that they got here at all."

Good-natured laughs sound from several nobles at her compliment. Across the room, Luna stands taller, staring intently at the prince. Cerule is just behind her, staring open-mouthed at him for a moment before she catches herself and shuts it.

Princess Nerine says, "Our chef has prepared only the best underwater *dishes*—as you call them above-water—and we are happy that many of you are already enjoying yourselves."

The queen touches the princess on the elbow with affection, then gestures to the prince. "And to our delighted surprise, the crown prince has also joined us tonight. He cannot stay long since he must soon meet with the winners of the trial, but we are honored by his presence tonight."

The princess walks back to me when the queen has finished speaking and I direct my focus on the food, so I'm not tempted to look at the prince again.

I fill my plate with different types of slimy, raw seafood that Princess Nerine recommends, then the two of us pick chairs near the corner opposite the door.

"I know it must not feel this way for you," the princess says, breaking the hard shell of a sea creature with lots of legs, revealing the soft edible meat. "But it's been quite entertaining to watch the Consort Tourney unfold." She takes a bite and gestures at the prince, who is flanked on both sides by Luna and Cerule. He leads them to sit near us along the wall, perpendicular to where we sit. The winter fae on one side and the autumn fae leaning in on the other.

"Yes, watching females throw themselves at the crown prince lends for plenty of entertainment," I say, and pop a piece of red-something into my mouth. I'm not sure what it is, but it I like it despite the strong taste of salt. "This is delicious."

"I'll tell the chef." The princess smiles. "She will be so pleased that *the* Amberle is a fan of her work."

I can't help but grin. I could actually imagine myself being friends with the princess. And maybe we will be if I can escape the Tourney unscathed. The princess angles her back toward the prince and my teammates to face me more directly.

"I must admit," she says. "Watching the two of you together has been my favorite part of the competition. I meant what I said about my assumptions. I think you might be the one in the end."

I shift uncomfortably in my seat. She can't be thinking of that. *No one* should be thinking of that.

"Your outing on the ship yesterday—"

Cerule laughs, drawing my eyes to the three. Cerule's hand grips the prince's forearm and her head is thrown back.

I look back at Princess Nerine.

"Don't worry about them. Everyone saw the way he looked at you and spoke to you yesterday." She leans closer and lowers her voice. "I bet he's looking at you right now."

Like a spider is drawn to a vampire, I can't help that my gaze automatically flits to him, and sure enough, I catch his eye again.

My stomach flips and I jerk my attention away. The entire exchange is too temptingly pleasant. My treacherous heart begs to lean into the warm sensation. He's with *them* but looking at *me*. Part of me screams that he cares for me, and we can make it work.

But I can't. I can't allow myself to enjoy even a bit of this emotion, as delicious as it is. I won't be *the one*, so fanning the flame is cruel. It's beyond all missteps, mistakes, and blunders I've made in this competition so far. It's *perrifool* and... and dangerous.

The princess is grinning broadly when I look back at her. She pats my knee. "I actually wanted to ask you a question about something."

I have questions for her too, but I'm not sure how to ask. "Oh? What did you want to ask?"

Princess Nerine's smile falls. "It's about something you wore early in the—"

"Amberle!" Rion calls, interrupting her. We both turn toward him. "Come closer." He beckons. "Bring the princess. Cerule asked a question, and I want you to hear the answer, too."

"We were actually in the middle—" I start, but Princess Nerine ignores my excuse to decline him and pulls me to my feet. At her signal, a servant hurries over and moves the chairs closer to the prince and the other contestants.

I'm happy for the excuse to be near him, but hate that it makes me happy. I can't be happy about it. I shouldn't.

"That's better," he says, looking at me when we've moved. I'm sitting across from him. If I pushed my toe forward, it wouldn't take much for him to do the same and make our shoes kiss. This close, the warm gold of his eyes fills a sunshine warmth in my core that at once eases my discomfort, as it also warns me of how much hurt is in my near future.

"What did you want us to hear?" I ask, wishing to get this over.

Cerule grips the prince's arm again. "I asked Prince Orion why he sent us so far away to the tunnel across the sea when there was another, *closer* tunnel."

"Yes, *apparently,* there's a tunnel just east of Isi Aura," Luna says. "It was above the water during the race, so we wouldn't have needed an ice tunnel to reach it."

I already know this thanks to the siren I met. She also told me the other tunnel was likely swarming with fae who don't like half fae. Or the idea that one might win the crown in this Tourney.

Real or not. I think I already know the reason Rion sent us to the lesser used one.

"I told you about the tunnel at Terpsichore because the easier, closer one was bombarded with waiting fae," the prince says. "I wanted you to go the route you'd be less likely to be interrupted."

Cerule nods. Satisfied. But Luna still bristles.

"We appreciate your concern for us, Prince Orion," Luna says. "But since Amberle was on our team, going the longer way cost us the win."

He turns toward her. "Are you criticizing my advice to take the safer route?"

"Oh no!" Luna grips his arm, mirroring Cerule, and smiles sweetly up at him. "I'm not blaming you at all! The halfling just held us up, is all."

Rion takes a breath and the corner of his left eye crinkles. I'm almost taken aback that I remember his look of pre-meditated sparring.

"Another part of this trial was to see how well each of you could form alliances and work together," he says. His tone is bright, and I'm impressed. He's come a long way from his shouting as a child. Even so, there's still a challenge in the statement.

"We worked together brilliantly!" Cerule says. "Luna built an ice boat, and I used wind to propel us to the island."

"Yes, but while Cerule and I did all the work, Amberle wasn't exactly a team player," Luna says. "Remember Cerule? She complained of being cold the entire time."

"Sure, she was uncomfortable, but she flew around to search once we arrived at the island, then dove in the water to locate the tunnel for us," Cerule points out.

"Yes, but it was a siren who actually showed her where the tunnel was," Luna adds. "And then *I* created an ice tunnel to meet with the underwater one. *I* made it possible for us to arrive at all."

"You cannot blame Amberle for the magic she doesn't have, Luna," Cerule says, leaning forward to pat my knee like a pet.

Princess Nerine adjusts in her seat.

"She's only a half fae and did what she could," Cerule says, earning a smile from the prince.

A sharp pang pricks my chest. I know his appreciative smile is in thanks for her kindness. But even if it was more than that, I must remember that the prince could choose worse than Cerule.

"Yes, well, *I* kept the tunnel frozen long enough for us to get to safety," Luna says, looking at me, then turns back to the prince. She can see that Cerule has captured his attention and wants it back. "Amberle took so long, I had to freeze it a few extra times. If I hadn't, it would have melted and filled with water."

"Did Amberle tell you that one of your ice blasts froze her wing to the ice?" Cerule asks Luna.

It's subtle, but Cerule's chin lifts in self-satisfaction, and I remember what she said in the tunnel when she helped me. *Tierney calculated that anyone who crosses you is eliminated.*

Is she trying to point out that Luna potentially sabotaged me?

Luna laughs once, then says, "Serves her right for taking so long."

Cerule pulls on the prince's arm. "But *I* helped her get free." She looks at me. "Didn't I, Amberle?"

"Yes." I nod. "Cerule was very kind to stay with me. She freed my wing."

Rion's eyebrows twitch. He doesn't respond to me or Cerule, but turns toward Luna. "You would willingly hinder your own teammate?"

"The test was about efficiency in travel. I wanted to be the fastest." Luna shrugs and smiles.

"You didn't answer my question. Was it intentional?" he asks.

"She made it, didn't she?" Luna gestures with a hand directed at me. "Amberle is here. In one piece."

"But did you *know* what your ice blast would do to her?" He's keeping his voice steady, but I can hear the subtle rise in emotion. My chest twinges in a different way.

"The tunnel was leaking, Prince Orion," Cerule says, patting his arm. "So the first two blasts were warranted. Luna is right, the tunnel might've filled with water or even collapsed." She leans forward to look around the prince at Luna directly. "But the last blast wasn't necessary. It was stronger and colder, and the tunnel was already safe from any flooding."

"What are you saying, Cerule?" the prince asks.

"That I think Luna sent the last one because she was frustrated with Amberle's slow pace," she says. "Amberle struggled with the cold on the ice boat, and I think Luna punished her for her vulnerability and for not keeping up."

I adjust in my seat. I don't like appearing weak, but that's exactly what Cerule is saying.

"Well, I think this Consort Tourney is ingenious, My Prince," Princess Nerine says. Her tone is bright. She's trying to direct the conversation elsewhere. "These trials you've designed to test your would-be-mates surely bring out the strengths and weaknesses of each contestant, don't they?"

"That is one of their purposes, yes," Rion says. He seems glad for the change in tone and the princess's inclusion in the conversation, but he appears distracted by something or someone behind us.

Luna sits taller in her seat as Wyn walks into my line of sight and leans toward the prince. I expected he'd be nearby.

"Prince Orion? A word?" he asks.

Rion stands and walks with Wyn away from the group.

"The trials of this Tourney also show each fae's true nature, doesn't it?" Princess Nerine says when the prince is out of earshot. She looks at Luna.

"If that's true, what do you think it means that you *aren't* in the competition, Princess?" Luna asks. "Why don't you tell us why non-royals such as River and Lily were invited to the Tourney, and you weren't?"

I fight the urge to slap her across the face in defense of my new friend.

"How do you know she wasn't chosen, Luna?" the prince says, returning. "Maybe Princess Nerine declined the invitation."

"Better for us," Luna says, putting back on her gracious attitude reserved for the prince. "Princess Nerine would have been fierce competition."

The prince doesn't comment. Instead, he says, "Sadly, I must go soon, but I wanted to speak privately to two of you before I do. Luna? Could I speak to you for a moment?"

"Of course." She rises with a self-satisfied smile and takes the hand he offers.

"Amberle." Perhaps it's my imagination, but his voice softens slightly when he says my name. "I'll only be a moment, but I'd like a word with you, too."

I nod as my throat tightens. A moment alone. I'm out of time. I must quickly formulate a plan to keep him close enough to not get sent home, but distant enough that I don't lose my head.

Thirty-Two

Cerule watches the prince and Luna walk away with longing. "Why doesn't Prince Orion wish to speak with *me-e?*"

"You could follow them and ask," Princess Nerine suggests, glancing at me with a side-long look.

"I'm sure Prince Orion will speak with you soon," I offer, then drink from my water glass. "He is trying to get to know all the contestants."

Cerule gives the underwater princess a contemplative look—ignoring my comment—then rises and rushes after them.

"The sheer agony of not getting enough attention from the prince is utter torture," I say with exaggerated anguish.

Princess Nerine laughs.

"Declining your invitation to the Tourney saved you from a similar fate," I say.

The princess nods but rubs the scales along her arms absently, the sudden tension palpable. "I didn't decline. Prince Orion was cleverly deceptive with his words."

"But he said—" I stop and try to remember.

"He said, *how do you know she wasn't chosen? For all you know, Nerine declined.*"

"You're a princess," I say. "Why weren't you chosen?" But I recall that Mora wasn't chosen at first and she, too, is a princess. I took her place. It was more important for the king to have his little spy—*me*—in the competition over Princess Mora. Not that it matters now. Mora still snagged a spot.

Is another fae in the competition over Princess Nerine? And if so, why?

"I don't know." Nerine sighs. "Queen Morvenna thinks King Estelar didn't want his son marrying into the Underwater Court."

It seems plausible. I know more than anyone that the king is directing the prince's choice of mate.

Or... could one of the underwater court contestants be the other spy and the reason they didn't choose Princess Nerine? If it's true, who is it? Gnacia said I was only guaranteed to make it past the first elimination. Aqualis and Lily stayed through the first Invitational, but the prince eliminated both at the second. Was the other spy one of them? Or is she still in the competition? Could it be River?

"But the king had to pick three from your court, so why not you?" I prod. I want to learn about her fellow water fae while I have the princess's ear. "What's so special about the others?" I lift my glass to drink again but realize it's empty. The exertion of getting to the Underwater Court has left me parched.

Princess Nerine takes the glass from me, then shifts her body, blocking the sightline of the cup from the rest of the room. Her brow furrows and her jaw clenches, but my glass is magically refilled.

"Aqualis has traces of the royal bloodline, so they didn't snub the queen's family entirely," Nerine says, handing back my glass. "And since River is a highborn selkie with ties to humans, she was also an obvious choice."

"And Lily?" I drink from my glass.

Nerine sighs. "Lily is showing signs of possessing seer power."

"Seer—" I choke on the water as the word registers.

"She can see things that will happen in the future."

My mouth drops open.

"It's the most powerful water magic, but only a few possess it." The princess forces a smile. "But the strength of magic isn't determined by blood. It doesn't care if you're royal or common. With the discovery of her extraordinary magic, Lily Strom will never live commonly again. The queen is happy to have her back at court."

Perhaps Lily's seer power was the reason she wasn't upset about being cut from the Tourney. At least not like Aqualis was. Maybe Lily *knew* she wouldn't win because she saw it. She said River wasn't long for the competition either. Was she just saying that because she believes none of the underwater fae has a connection with the prince? Or because she knows the truth and knows River will be eliminated soon?

I'm afraid to ask.

"Perhaps I wasn't chosen because my magic is weak," the princess laments, but doesn't seem overly distraught about it. "Using water droplets in the air to fill up your glass is the extent of my power."

"It's still amazing."

"Most underwater fae could fill this massive space in moments." Nerine waves a hand, gesturing at the room. "Many can move a river, change its very course. Several can shift entire ocean tides." She pauses. "Lily can see the future, but I... the only thing I can do is fill a glass."

"Well, I don't have strong magic," I say as if it might ease her pain. I don't add that I'm also star fae and by that reason alone, I wasn't destined to have powerful magic.

"Yes, but you have been a wave of clean water, Amberle. Without magic." Her lips curl into a sad smile. "While I don't like being snubbed, I have enjoyed watching you. The king had to seem fair, I suppose, by placing you and the other star fae in the competition. For appearance's sake, perhaps? I'm sure you and the spring fae are in the Tourney for a reason."

I don't think the king cares about appearances or fairness, but bite my tongue because Princess Nerine is perilously close to questioning the real reason I was chosen.

"But it's in the past." She waves a hand. "I quickly came to terms with my future without Prince Orion."

Wait. Did she want a future with him? I shift in my seat, feeling a pressure in my chest. How many fae have feelings for Rion?

The princess places a hand over mine and she gives me a bright smile this time. "Don't fret. I've never thought of him romantically. And although I have a deep respect and friendship with many air fae, I would have been miserable living above water."

"I didn't—"

"But even if I did, it's clear that he has eyes only for you."

The pressure lessens and intensifies all at once. She thinks I'm in love with Prince Rion. But she's also struck a nerve. Princess Nerine came to terms that she and the prince don't have a future together. I *know* Rion and I don't have a future together. My head knows it. When will my heart realize it too?

I must change the subject. "Now that we're alone again, what were you trying to say earlier? Before we were interrupted?"

"Oh! Yes." The princess leans closer to me with her head bent and lowers her voice. "I only caught a small glimpse of it because you kept it mostly hidden beneath your dress, but before the prince gifted you the crystalized sunbeam..." She points at the sunbeam beneath my throat. "You wore a key around your neck."

My mouth goes dry, but her look of intensity keeps me from drinking more water, so I merely nod.

"I just wondered why you wore the key because I recognized it, and it isn't something that should be worn. *Ever.*" Her expression seems exasperated. "But our conversation will have to wait... *again.* The prince's companion is coming to interrupt."

I turn and see Wyn approaching us.

"Find me afterward," Princess Nerine says, signaling a servant to whisk away our plates. "We should speak before the winter magic watches you again." She flashes a smile at Wyn. "I assume you're coming to take her away?"

He bows. "Prince Orion wishes to speak with Amberle."

"Since you are taking away my new friend, *Wyn Firetail*, then you must keep me company until she returns."

"I would assume nothing less," he says, jovially responding to her obvious flirtation as he offers his hand to me. "Allow me to escort Amberle to the prince, then I'll return."

"I'll be waiting," she says, and winks.

Thirty-Three

Wyn and I make our way out of the dining room and he leads me to a set of stone stairs. I grip the smooth, mother-of-pearl coated rail as we ascend.

"Why can't more fae be like Princess Nerine?" I ask. I tell myself I'm just making conversation, but really, I'm trying to distract my thoughts away from the conversation that's coming. What does the prince wish to say to me? Do I have the strength to resist more declarations of adoration? Do I have the strength to push him away? Do I have the strength to ignore the desires of my heart and make him believe I don't feel the same?

"The princess is actually tolerable," Wyn agrees. "Like she wasn't born with a golden rod up her—"

"Wyn!" I cut him off.

"What? It's true," he says, his shoes clopping heavily against the stairs as we climb.

I resist the urge to smile. Without knowing I needed it, like a good friend, he knew exactly what to say to get my mind off my warring heart. "Princess Nerine reminds me of Arielle, but with less..."

Wyn's arm tightens as we near the landing. "Less... *what?*"

"Not less. The underwater princess just seems more... carefree. About most things." She seemed troubled by her lack of magic, but was otherwise very cheerful.

"Princess Nerine has had her own troubles, like every fae, but she carries her burdens differently." He stops on the landing and turns to me. "I know you promised to rejoin the princess afterward, but Prince Orion and I both agree that you should depart the Underwater Court with us—"

"But the underwater princess and I just became acquaintances. It would be rude to leave without a goodbye," I say, making an excuse to stay.

"Amberle, it's for your protection, and the others, really."

I check over my shoulder and lower my voice. "She has information for me. I cannot leave until we speak."

Wyn shakes his head. "Amberle, Faerie already knows the Underwater Court was your assignment and we expect some fae might try to intercept you on your way back."

"If it's that dangerous, why is he still keeping me around?" I lament even though I know the answer.

Wyn stops walking, halting me as well. "Do you *want* to be eliminated? As soon as you have the information the king needs, he'll gladly let you go."

I pull my arm from Wyn and walk forward toward one of the round openings that looks out into the sea and watch tiny yellow and blue fishes pick at the coral around the edges.

"But you should know... he loves you."

"I know," I tell the fish.

"Then for his sake, if you ever had positive feelings toward him, *ever,* please, *please* be kind."

I turn back to Wyn, but my throat is so tight I cannot speak. His face is pale and drawn with open concern. His lowered shoulders scream the truth he knows: I'm a spy. Rion is the crown prince. We cannot be together.

The realization of why Wyn's not letting me lie to myself about the prince's feelings crashes down on me harder than any wave. Rion and I are headed for an emotional tsunami and, as our friend, Wyn is trying to steer the ship away from the shoals.

"Orion will still be on display to all of Faerie as he navigates a broken heart while picking his *second* choice."

"I don't want to leave yet," I say, my voice breaking.

He nods. I don't know if he sees the torment that roils within me, that the prince won't be the only one nursing a broken heart once I'm sent away, but I hope my careful composure hides it.

"Then you should travel with the prince's retinue back to Isi Aura, Amberle."

I bite the edge of my lower lip and shake my head, unable to speak as I swallow my emotions.

"Do you know what it's about?" he asks, frowning. "What information does Princess Nerine have?"

I pause, but realize it's better if he knows. "She said she recognized that key I used to wear."

Wyn's eyes widen. "The one that—"

"Yes."

He grips his chin. "Do you think she'd tell me?"

"I'm not sure. How well do you know her?"

"Maybe I can get her to talk," Wyn says, pointing down the hallway. "The prince isn't far. There's a door there on the right adorned with black pearls. Do you think you can find it?"

"Yes."

"Keep your conversation with the prince quick. Gnacia will have my head if I don't get him back by dawn."

"What does he want to talk about?"

Wyn's eyebrows twitch inward briefly. "I have an idea, but he should be the one to tell you."

My heart drops, but I press forward, walking down the hall as Wyn's footfalls disappear down the stairs behind me.

Cerule exits a door on the right—likely the one the prince is behind—with an exuberant grin that quickly falls when she sees me.

"You'll find out soon enough, but Luna was just cut," she says with faux sadness as she walks toward me. She clutches her hands in front of her to hide her obvious excitement, but there's a clear buoyancy in her step.

"Oh?"

"Prince Orion said he was looking for someone who could be a leader and work well with others. Luna proved she could do neither."

"He told you this?"

"Yes. He said he didn't need to speak with me because I'm still in the competition. Oh!" Cerule's eyes widen, and she covers her mouth with both hands in dramatics. Then she talks around her hands. "I wonder if that's why he wants to speak with you? Do you think...?"

A wave of terror rushes through my body. *Is he planning to send me home too?* The ever-present sliver of fear that he has learned the reason I'm in the Tourney rips into a chasm. Or perhaps he, too, has realized that we can't be together and so wants to cut me before his feelings get too deep. However, the rational part of my mind argues that Rion has something different, if not equally difficult, to discuss.

Cerule grips my hand. "It will be easier for me with you gone, but I'm glad you were on my team for this trial." She strokes the back of my clutched hand with her other one as if I'm destined for the executioner's block. "Working with a star fae will surely show my capabilities despite the handicap I dealt with." She keeps stroking, but is mostly talking to herself and staring at nothing. "And since the prince clearly has a fondness for the star fae, my kindness to you will only make me look better in his eyes."

"I should get it over with, then," I say, attempting to pull my hand away, but she holds it fast.

"Remember what we discussed in the tunnel when I freed you?" The autumn fae looks at me again—intently—with a warning smile.

"You want me to tell the prince that you would make an excellent choice as his mate."

Her tiny fingers are strong as she crushes mine.

"You want me to say that since he and I obviously won't be together, he should choose you?"

Cerule presses her lips together and pats my hand once more, then releases it. "I won't forget you, Amberle Kindra."

Then she walks away, brushing her long orange hair over her shoulder.

I take a deep breath, then walk toward the door decorated in black pearls. They resemble the shine of raven eyes and seem to stare at me with judgment. I have so many sins, I don't know what they are judging me for.

I ignore them and knock. "Ri—Prince Orion? It's me. It's Amberle."

"Come in."

Thirty-Four

I turn the conch shell doorknob, the ridges of it digging into my palm, and swing the door inward.

Inside is a small sitting room with salmon-colored cushioned chairs and a long white chaise along one side. But that's where the familiarity ends because the ceiling is bubble-like and curves until it reaches the floor. It's not made of a tangible material like stone or glass, but is simply a barrier of underwater fae magic, merely keeping the sea at bay. After my conversation with the princess, I briefly wonder how many fae possess the magic to make these air pockets. I imagine several rooms like this one exist in the annex for visiting *air fae* like Rion and me.

Prince Rion stands in the center of the room, clasping his hands in front of him. His posture is tense. He seems nervous.

It makes me nervous.

I feel for any sign that the watching winter magic is present, but feel nothing. Still, one cannot be too careful, so I form my words carefully. "Cerule said you eliminated Luna."

"I did." The very sound of his voice sends a thrill through me. "She was not right for me."

I shake it off. "Did Faerie get to see?" *Are they watching us now?* "Or will you announce it later?"

"Faerie is watching the events of the trial. Luna's elimination will be replayed for them after the trial concludes."

Which means this conversation could also be recorded somehow and broadcast later. Especially if he means to cut me, too. I suck in a breath.

"Why did you cut her?" I ask, keeping my voice steady. Cerule told me the reason, but I want to hear it from him.

"I did it because she hurt *you*—" His voice breaks, and he steps forward.

I hold a hand up, stopping him even as a ribbon of light twirls inside me and my heart melts. Then I whisper, "Are we..." I close my eyes. It hurts to look at him when his golden eyes burn so brightly. When he looks at me as if I'm worthy. As if I'm a royal, or... or a *goddess,* in his eyes. When he looks at me as if I'm *his.* I keep my hand raised as if supporting the space between us when I ask, "Are *we* being watched?"

"No."

My eyes open, and my hand drops.

Rion glides toward me and takes my hands in his. The warmth and the pressure of his fingers gripping mine send a jolt across my skin that causes my voice to leap into my throat.

"We are alone," he whispers.

I don't mean to, but I sigh with relief knowing we aren't on display. Part of me believed what Cerule said, that he *might* eliminate me next. The magic would be here if that's why he summoned me.

He cocks his head to the side. "What's wrong—" He stops, then pulls his arms toward himself so I'm forced to step closer. "You didn't think..."

I shake my head and pull a hand away to wave it off like it was silly of me to even entertain it. "Cerule just said—"

"No! I just wanted to tell you something the others shouldn't hear. Amberle." He runs his free hand through his walnut hair— it's even longer than I thought, and is a strange hue beneath the filtered sunlight through the hovering sea. "I'm *not* eliminating you. *Ever.*"

My head feels fuzzy as the intensity of warring emotions intensifies and makes me dizzy. All at once, I am filled with fear and elation and confusion, and headiness.

"I just have to figure out a way to get my father to agree," Rion says, unfocusing his eyes and looking over my shoulder. I hope he is so distracted that he doesn't see the look of sheer horror mixed with unadulterated joy that crosses my face at his declaration that he's keeping me indefinitely. I'm struggling to wrap my head around it. Rion thinks I'm the one? That of the ten—no, *nine*—fae who remain, he intends to end it... with *me*?

I imagine my hair sticking to my face, my saltwater-encrusted dress, and my perfumed scent of fish. How can he endure being near me at all?

I lift my eyebrows, erasing my other visible emotions when he looks back.

With his free hand, Rion runs a finger—light as wingtips—across my brow and down along the side of my face, pushing away one of my stringy clumps of hair. His touch sends a fiery heat along my skin that runs down my neck and spine, causing me to shiver. And smile.

He smiles too.

My pulse speeds, and my cheeks burn, but I try to keep control. "What did you want to tell me?"

I don't push him away, so he moves his hand to wrap around my waist, pressing his palm and splayed fingers against the small of my back, just beneath the edge of my wings. They twitch, suddenly feeling hyper-aware of the closeness of his touch. Then, he releases my hand and wraps his other around me, too. The movement pulls my face closer to him as he lowers his.

"I've told you how I feel," Rion says, ignoring my question and pressing his forehead against mine. He closes his eyes. "You *know* how I feel."

"You did." My heart hammers in my chest. "I do."

"Tell me you still hate me like you always have," he whispers. There's a hint of agony around the edges. "Tell me you'll never forgive me. Tell me... you don't love me."

I want to melt in his arms, to give away to temptation. But I can't be that selfish.

"Rion I—" But my voice catches in my throat. I can't say it. I can't say I hate him, that I'll never forgive him, or that I don't *love* him because it's a lie.

His eyes open, and he looks at me with an expression full of question and disbelief and surprise and hope and... and...

It only takes a tiny motion to bridge the distance between our lips until his gently press against mine. Electric heat rushes through my entire body, feeling the warmth of his summer-kissed mouth. I'm so surprised by the kiss that my arms instinctively wrap around his neck, pulling him closer to me and kissing him with a hunger I didn't know I had.

And I realize I'm *beyond* falling in love with the fae I met in Rosewind. With the *crown prince*. The realization moves my hands into his hair, running my fingers through his too-long locks. His arms tighten at my sudden enthusiasm, but then he breaks off the kiss.

"Kisses can be lies," he murmurs, keeping a tight grip on me but squeezing his eyes tightly shut. "Are you lying to me? Tell me you hate me."

I bite down on my lower lip. "I can't."

His expression doesn't change, and his eyes don't open. "Tell me you'll never forgive me."

I bite harder, tasting blood. "I... can't."

"Tell me..." The prince inhales deeply, then exhales shakily. "You don't love me." His eyes fly open, assaulting me with the molten gold of his irises and his dilated, nearly round pupils.

I close my eyes and release my own shaky breath. "I-I... *can't.*"

I'm scooped back into his arms with a kiss so fierce it's like basking in the summer sun. He tastes of citrus and light and smells of plumeria in bloom. I'm rendered lightheaded and nearly powerless to stop him. But I do. I must. He releases me.

"Rion, we... we *can't*." An urchin's spine pierces my heart at the irony of using that word again. "The king would never—"

"The king sent you an invitation," he whispers, pressing his forehead against mine again. "He allowed you to be in the competition, and surely there's a part of him that can be persuaded to allow me to make my own decision. My choice. Even if you came to be a part of this for another reason."

I push him away more forcefully, and he immediately releases me, allowing me to step back and put distance between us. It clears my head.

"Amberle—"

I raise my hand again, stopping him. I can't look at him, so I close my eyes again. "Rion—*Prince* Orion—it will never work. For whatever reason your father allowed me to be in the competition... he'll never let you pick me."

He doesn't speak, so I open my eyes to see if he heard me.

He shakes his head and turns away, rubbing his arm absently.

"You know I'm right," I say.

"N—" he chokes out, and angrily grips a handful of his hair.

"See?" I whisper, my voice breaking as a painful crack fissures inside my chest. "You can't deny it. You know it's true."

The muscles of the prince's neck tighten. His jaw clenches. His fists do too.

My eyes burn, but I force myself to remain in place and not turn away because I must fulfill a bargain I made.

"P-perhaps..." I begin a statement that feels like acid on my tongue. "Cerule Rostina would make a good choice?"

Thirty-Five

RION

I study her, trying to ascertain whether she's serious.

How can she bring up the autumn fae at a time like this? How can she suggest someone else when I just confessed I never plan to cut her from the competition? When I just kissed her!

"Now isn't the time to be discussing other contestants." I want to talk about us, her and me.

"But Cerule might be an excellent choice for you, Rion," Amberle says with a tightness, and what I imagine is thinly concealed desperation. "During the trial she was—"

"It's too late to convince me to look at someone else." I don't want to hear about Cerule. "You've already won over my heart, there's no one—"

"It doesn't matter!" She lifts her hands, throwing her hair behind her shoulders, then knots her arms across her chest. "You know your father will never allow us to be together. You can't deny it. So, you must consider which one of the others would be best for you and the realm. You must stop thinking of me."

She won't look at me, but I stare at her with tight knuckles burning at my sides and teeth clenched. The mention of my father reminds me about his comment not long ago. *She hasn't told you yet? Good.* What hasn't she told me? And does it have anything to do with her pulling back now? Does it have to do with her insisting my father won't let me choose her?

Fury fueled by blazing summer fire threatens to consume me from the inside out, because she's right. The king won't allow me to be with the fae I love.

It's a tragic irony that I inherited the summer heat *from* my father.

But I refuse to give up.

"Never," I say in response to her plea.

Her wings twitch and it gives me hope. If my nearness to her has even a fraction of the effect hers does to me, she cannot resist forever.

But she's not wrong about the obstacles in our path.

My father might have controlled picking the Tourney Contestants—Princess Nerine's odd lack of invitation showed that he was involved in the Choosing much more than I realized—but selecting my mate and bride is supposed to be my choice.

I'm not so naïve to believe the illusion of full choice, but even illusions can be manipulated.

"Perhaps it would be best if I—"

I bridge the gap between us and stop her words by gripping her arms. She cannot give up hope. It will take careful strategy and scheming, but we can figure out a way. But, if Amberle gives up and pulls herself out of the competition, it will be a thousand times more difficult to achieve a happy ending. "Don't say it. There must be a way, just... just give me some time."

Wyn knocks once before letting himself in.

I lower my head, but don't remove my hands from her arms. I don't know when I'll be able to touch her again.

"Prince Orion, Amberle, my apologies," Wyn says. "But we really must depart soon."

Amberle steps back, forcing my arms to drop.

"It's fine, Wyn. We were finished." She walks toward the exit and says something to him in a low tone.

"Wait," I say, stepping forward. "Just another moment."

Another moment before I'm thrust back into the public and forced to pretend I'm considering all contestants. Another moment with Amberle without scrutiny. Another moment to hold her in my arms again, to breathe the scent of her hair again, to... feel the softness of her lips again.

Amberle's face crumples briefly, but she quickly puts her features back in place. "Really, Rion—"

I look at Wyn as if he could help me convince her to stay, even though he was the one who reminded me of my damned schedule. Wyn's expression is tight, but there's a pity in his eyes as he looks at Amberle. Then I remember there's something else I need to tell her. The thought tears at my throat and floods my heart with dread.

"Actually, there is one more thing," I tell Amberle as I look at Wyn, hoping he gets my meaning. "Something I cannot say while we're being watched. It was the thing I wanted to talk to you about."

Wyn nods, then excuses himself. "Please be brief, My Prince."

When the door shuts, I look at her. She watches me with a little impatient expectancy, but doesn't protest.

As much as I don't want to be the bearer of bad news, I wouldn't dream of sending her this message by letter, and it's not something I would put on Wyn's shoulders. I cannot delay in telling her, and I can't let the deep sapphire-blue of her eyes distract me or stop me from getting it out. So, I breathe in and close my eyes when I say, "It's about your father."

I expect some version of *what about my father?* But she says nothing. I open my eyes and see she's gone pale, which only looks worse with the hovering sea-filtered light dancing across her skin. Bridging the space between us with only a few strides, I reach for her hands and squeeze them gently. Her fingers are cold, stiff, but she doesn't pull away.

"I asked Wyn to locate him. I wanted to speak with him and see if I could learn the reason—" Cowardly, I duck my head. "I just thought it would be best coming from me, but you should know that your father—"

Amberle yanks her hands away and steps back. Her wings flick briefly while she twists her mouth to hide whatever emotion crosses it and looks away. I fear she's about to excuse herself, to run from the room, to run from the competition, but she seems to force herself to stay and finally whispers, "What about my father?"

"Amberle..." *My darling,* I want to add, but can't bring my lips to say it. "Your father is in the Gray."

Her eyes snap to me and her entire body stills as she stares. Her features are unreadable, but it must be shock or confusion or devastation. Perhaps a mixture of the three?

"The Gray?" Her lips move, but the words are hardly a whisper.

I brace myself, ready to comfort her, let her vent her anger, or whatever she needs. I prepare to assure her I don't know the reason for his imprisonment, and that I just learned of it myself. I mentally run through all the things she might ask, or for an emotional outburst.

But she balls the fabric of her skirt into her fists and rushes out the door.

Thirty-Six

Wyn says my name as I pass him, but I'm so blinded by the traitorous tears and deafened by the twisting agony that rips through my chest and slashes at my heart that I can't decipher what he says after it. I'm so shaken by the news of my father my thoughts are a jumbled mess and I stumble. But my wings—though stiff—catch me before I nose-dive into the floor. Miraculously, I make it to the stairwell in a semblance of one piece.

If I were an autumn fae with the ability to decay my skin with acid tears streaming down my face, it wouldn't be half as painful as what I feel right now.

"Amberle!" Wyn's grip on my arm surprises me. I didn't know he'd followed. "We really must go—"

I yank my arm away. I cannot be bothered with silly things, such as keeping the prince's precious schedule when I've just learned the fate of one of the most important fae in my entire existence.

But Wyn doesn't protest and doesn't reach for my arm again. "He told you." Pause. "I thought you might have an inkling—"

"That my father was in the *Gray?*" My voice cracks roughly on each word. My intense *devastation* ripping through my vocal cords. "I knew he was in prison, but I didn't know..." My voice gives out completely as more tears stream down my face. My promise mark burns.

Wyn frowns, looks at the ground, and clasps both hands behind his back. "Does this change things, Amberle?" His tone is low. Tentative. "Are you... pulling yourself out?"

I look down the dark stairs when I say, "Why should I stay?" *What's the point?*

But the pain of those words wrench themselves with such force through my veins it feels as if they've stripped them from the inside. Leaving would—*correction*—leaving *will* hurt too.

"For the reason you agreed in the beginning," Wyn says.

I expected him to say, *For Rion.* But I imagine he knows better than anyone the exact flavor of *complicated* and *doomed* and *impossible* this mess I've agreed to has become. When I look at him, it's not because I'm shocked.

I should have known.

"If you do what the king bargained, it could free your father." Wyn doesn't lie, but his words aren't convincing either.

"No one comes out of the Gray alive, Wyn." I frown as more burning tears well. My lip trembles. "You know that."

My friend places a gentle touch on my shoulder and leans down to look me in the eye. "Just because no one ever has doesn't mean no one ever will. You mustn't give up hope."

"What if he's already—" I wrap a hand around my throat.

Wyn pushes my hand down. "He's not."

"How—"

"The king is desperate for this Tourney to end the way he intends." He lowers his head and his voice. "Why else would he employ two undercover spies, then bring me in? He'll do anything to get the results he wants. Including fulfilling a bargain to free a fae from the Gray."

"You just proved how futile it is, Wyn! Why would he care to free my father when he has others to rely on?"

He grips my arm again. "No. You're not giving up. This isn't over, Amberle. Sure, King Estelar had the power to remove you from his employ early on, but you and I both know the prince isn't letting you go anytime soon. You have the upper hand in this. You have more power over your and your father's fate now than you did in the beginning. Lean into that."

I stare at him, soaking in his words. Wyn is right. Rion said himself that he never plans to let me go. His declarations and the fervent kisses we just shared are proof. I can't obsess over the way that knowledge makes me feel, but his affection affords me opportunity. Regardless of my reasons for being a part of it.

Guilt wraps around my gut like the crushing jaw of a cu sith. My initial goal of balancing the line between amiable-enough-to-remain in the competition and keeping myself emotionally distanced failed.

He's fallen. I've fallen.

"But I didn't mean—" I stop, searching for my words. "It's not the way I..." I can't finish. It's not the way I *wanted? Expected? Hoped?*

"Of course it wasn't." Wyn releases his grip on my arm and steps back. Studying me. "Will you stay?" he asks.

I nod once, rubbing the side of my eye to ease the burn of my promise mark. It diminishes a little. Then I repeat his words. "This isn't over yet."

"Good."

The position my father is in seems even more impossible than it did an hour ago, but it's likely he's been in the Gray this entire time. I just didn't know it. Instead of worrying that he might have been exiled years ago, already buried in another realm, my mind settles on one indisputable fact: the king made a bargain with me. If I fulfill my end of it, he'll have no choice but to fulfill his.

"What did you learn from Princess Nerine?" I ask, wiping the tears from my face and standing straighter.

Wyn's expression falls. "She'll only speak to you. Find her, then meet us at the main entrance."

I nod.

"And make it quick."

The pain and devastation of my father's predicament doesn't ease, but I regain control of my human side. After talking with Wyn—or rather, after being scolded and brought back to my senses—I compartmentalize my emotions as I make my way back to the gathering to locate the princess. I can't free my father if I cannot keep my head in the competition. One step at a time: speak with Princess Nerine; leave with Prince Rion and his retinue; return to Isi Aura; then plot out my next steps.

I've barely walked into the gathering before the princess approaches me.

"You're back," Princess Nerine says. "Come, we must speak quickly and privately." She links her arm with mine. I don't argue and walk with her. "Wyn Firetail explained—and I agree—that you shouldn't be traveling back without their protection." She leads me back to the stairs I just flew down, but instead of climbing the steps, the princess leads me down a corridor in the other direction. It's a long, round tunnel with nothing but the push of water magic keeping the sea at bay. It's similar to the enormous dome and the room where Rion and I spoke and... kissed.

When we've distanced ourselves from the main part of the building, it feels like we're just strolling along the seafloor the same way the spring fae walked the streets of Rosewind. I can't help but reach out to touch the *walls* as we walk. My fingertips graze the barrier, passing through it and into the water and skitter along the surface as if I sat above in a boat and dragged my hand while sailing across it.

When we've walked in silence for a while, Princess Nerine pulls me to the right and through a trickling waterfall—drenching me again—that leads into a small sea cave.

"I asked that this be cleared of water before your arrival by someone I trust," she says, releasing my arm. "We won't be over-heard in here."

As my eyes adjust to the lower light, I notice the sparkle of precious stones imbedded in the rock and coral. Reds and blues and greens blink even in the lower light. I didn't know such stones formed at the bottom of the Sea of Neptulus, but I haven't had the opportunity until now to look around down here, either. The thief in me calculates the most efficient ways to free the stones and conceal them for potential clients or pawn them for coin.

But I focus on the underwater princess—ignoring the streaming water flowing down my hair and down my legs—and ask her the question I came here to learn the answer to. "What do you know of the key? You said it should never be touched."

"Let alone worn for an extended period of time." Nerine uses her hands as she talks, more animated now that we're alone. "I was shocked when I noticed you wearing it because I thought it was retired."

"Retired? What do you mean?"

"Well, it was magick'd to negatively affect the actions and strengths of those who are unlucky to touch it. It causes the victim to reveal things and say things they wouldn't otherwise speak."

That sounds a little too familiar.

"How do you know all of this?" I ask.

"Centuries ago, notices were circulated in the courts to prevent other unfortunate victims from becoming hexed by its powers."

I clutch the top of my dress and nod, grateful for the great pains and secrecy she has taken to tell me what she knows. I wish I could tell her she might be helping me save my father's life, but of course I can't. Maybe someday, if everything goes well, she'll put the pieces together and be happy for me.

"The effects of it were so subtle, most victims never learned what cursed them," the princess continues. "They did not know it was a hexed object, and many thought they merely had a bout of bad luck, or an ailment."

Again, very familiar.

"So the key was shrouded in mystery and inflicted incredible damage before it finally came to light that it was used as a political weapon." Nerine walks toward me with a heaviness in her step. "An extremely dangerous weapon that was used to blackmail, steal power, and start wars."

"Until it was retired," I say.

"Exactly. That's when pictures with information about the key were spread around the realm in all noble circles so it could no longer be used without extreme subtlety and concealment."

Wyn's reminder to make this quick buzzes in my head. "I want to ask more questions, but I should go."

"Of course."

The princess leads the way, and I follow her back through the waterfall. The stream of water pouring from my hair and my dress had slowed to a steady drip, but is now streaming again in earnest.

"What did the prince talk to you about when you left?" She pauses outside the waterfall and tiny beads of water lift from her dress and hair and move to join the ocean 'wall.'

I suppose it's the perks of having water magic, even if her clothing is still damp and sweat lines her brow. She takes a deep breath and turns to me with an expectant, raised eyebrow that flushes my cheeks and forces me to look forward again.

"It was good then?" she asks. "It's unfair that I won't be able to watch it later since I assume no magic recorded it?"

My smile is large when I look at her and notice her lower lip juts out into a pout. I shake my head.

She pulls at my arm, stopping me in the middle of the tunnel. "Repay me for the information? Tell me what happened! What did he say?"

My thoughts immediately turn to my father and the devastating information I learned. I can't tell her any of that, nor do I want to burst into tears.

"Please?" It's a powerful word. A near binding one.

But there is one thing I can say. One thing that fills my breast with sunshine and citrus and... hope. One thing that ignites my being from the top of my head to the tips of my wings and toes. "Prince Orion..."

"Yes?" Her already large eyes widen as she takes my hands in hers, practically dancing a jig in the hallway.

"He kissed me."

Thirty-Seven

My confession to Princess Nerine permeates my thoughts and demands my attention as I make my way toward the main entrance. An underwater servant guides me through a tunnel to meet up with the Summer entourage. And Rion.

He kissed me.

So much happened while I was in the Underwater Court. All within *hours*. Between discovering my father's fate and learning about the extensive history of the cursed key I unluckily came into possession of—I haven't had time to process that kiss.

Rion. *Prince* Orion. The fae I grew up with, the fae I've hated and avoided and never even thought about once in all my years away from the palace, kissed me. *Rion* kissed me.

And I kissed him back.

An electricity skitters down my neck and along my wings all the way to the tips at the memory. At the way his hand felt pressed firmly against my back; at the way he said, *"I've told you how I feel. You* know *how I feel"*; at the way he tasted of citrus and smelled of summer flowers.

I cannot think of it, though. I shouldn't.

Even now, the news of my father's situation overshadows the

memory with a heavy darkness. Though that kiss will likely haunt my dreams for the rest of my life, I don't regret it. It was a moment of escape, yes, but it was also a reminder of the reason I'm here. With well-deserved guilt. But like Wyn said, I cannot give up now. I must do all I can to free my father.

But that kiss...

I enter an enormous dome where several coral arches glow with brilliant light. I imagine each one leads to a tunnel that exits to various locations in Faerie. A group of guards and other summer fae wait near the center one, speaking quietly. The prince's retinue. I spot Wyn and walk to greet him.

When Rion enters, the room turns to him as if he's sunshine in a cold cavern. He strolls toward those waiting from a different direction, but for a moment, I catch his eye. The dark cloud shrouding me, hiding my brokenness, is permeated by a light that seeps through the cracks and finds a way inside. Rion's smile is small, but it rivals the dawn. I can't help but look away or else be blinded by the brightness that threatens to blossom with hope that he can actually do everything he promised. Hope that my father won't meet his end in the Gray—or that he hasn't already been exiled and sent to an early grave. I also look away because Cerule Rostina is hanging on the prince's arm and chittering in his ear.

When we've joined the group, one guard speaks to the prince, then directs several guards to walk through the tunnel, with Prince Rion and Cerule behind them. Wyn gestures for me to follow next to him. We're flanked by guards on the side and behind as we exit. Just past the coral is another flurry of bubbles; we're sucked in, then spit out on the other side.

The tunnel looks like the one Cerule and I entered through with groups of bioluminescent creatures providing light from above as we leave the underwater city and traverse into the depths of the sea. The glow creates an eerie atmosphere that increases the unease I already feel about the day's revelations.

The group is quiet except for Cerule and the prince, though

the autumn fae does most of the talking in an animated and lively voice. I can't make out their conversation, but I'm not sure I want to hear what they're saying either.

But I am desperate to know about my father. First, I feel for the winter magic. Feeling none, I choose my words carefully, leading Wyn toward my true intentions.

"Wyn," I say, stepping closer to my friend. "I feel fortunate to get reacquainted with my old friends, like yourself, as a contestant." The guards are close, and I cannot give away even a hint of what I'm talking about.

"Yes, it has been nice to see you and Princess Arielle." Wyn speaks overly casual, obviously suspicious of my comment.

"How is your family?" I ask, hoping the inflection in my voice and the emphasis on my words will tell him what I'm asking. *Is my family okay?*

My knowledge of the Gray tightens around my throat like a hungry serpent. I've never seen it, never visited—I had no reason to—but rumors of it gave me nightmares as a youngling.

Before Wyn responds, a tingling sensation makes its way across my scalp as a long-buried memory surfaces.

I bound in through the door of my family apartment and see my father studying a stack of missives while sitting in his favorite chair.

"Papa!" I say, rushing forward and moving his hands away so I can crawl onto his lap and grip his shoulders "I want to go—"

"Amberle, I'm—"

"You said I can't interrupt your work when you're in your office, but I'm allowed when we're in our rooms." I drop my hands, then lift my chin, widen my eyes, and attempt the haughty look Prince Rion perfected as an infant.

Father's smile raises his thick, silver eyebrows. He sighs, then sets the papers on the small table beside him. "You're right, Lark."

I can't help but flash a triumphant smile, then place my hands on his shoulders again. "I want to go..." I pause. "To the Gray."

Father's smile falls, and he moves my hands from his shoulders. "Where did you hear about that place?"

"Wyn said his father went there to escort that autumn fae who tried to assassinate King Carpus. I thought an autumn fae couldn't be held in a prison because they could rot anything that holds them, but Rion said—"

"Prince Orion," Father corrects me.

"Prince Rion said the cells in the Gray are made specifically for each fae they hold. For autumn, maybe it's rusted metal and blackened vines and decayed plant matter. The guards put a silver ring around his neck to prevent him from decaying anything." I twist my face at the macabre description, but it doesn't quelch my curiosity.

"His Highness is very knowledgeable."

"He said the summer cells are extremely hot and the prisoners are held in a metal cage over a pool of lava." I gesture with my hands. "He said the water cells are lined with seaweed and shells with a pool of water in the center with the prisoner held in an enchanted bubble suspended in it. Surrounded by water, but they can't use it.

"It's like the criminals are surrounded by things they can normally use with their magic, but they're blocked!" I scrunch my nose. "Wyn thinks they go mad."

"Lark." Papa says my nickname with a loving tone. "Your descriptions of the Gray sound very, um, romantic, but the reality is terrible."

"Don't worry, Papa. I'm not afraid."

"I know you're brave, little Lark, but the Gray isn't a place for someone with human blood to visit."

"Human blood, why?"

He places a hand on either side of my head and brings my face closer to his. "I will not fill the precious mind of my daughter with images and experiences that will traumatize and haunt you forever. But it's nothing you need to worry about. They send only the most heinous criminals to the Gray. What that autumn fae did was rare and heinous. I doubt another fae will be sent to the Gray in our lifetimes."

"My family is well enough," Wyn says. "My mother wishes my father would stop gambling so much on div fights on Erato Island. But he's enjoying his retirement."

Obviously that's not what I want to know. I shudder, imagining my loving father trapped in his own metal cage and suspended over a pool of lava.

"So, your father is doing well, considering?" I can't help the little crack in my voice.

I hate that I hope my father is still in the Gray. The alternative is worse. I'd discovered what my father had sensitively kept to himself all those years ago. At the end of the criminal's sentencing, they're sent to the human realm.

Between the weakened fae state and the human's superstitions, fae never lasted long. If my father isn't in the Gray, he died in the dungeon or is in the human realm withering away with old age. Star fae age at the same rate as humans in their realm, which is why we rarely visit.

Wyn watches the guards ahead as he chatters about his mother's cooking. My irritation rises. Wyn isn't an idiot. He knows I'm prodding for information about my father. Not knowing is torture, so why isn't he spilling a single secret?

I cut him off mid-sentence, "How long ago did you see your parents?"

How long ago did you verify my father's location? Even if he'd been sent to the human realm a week ago, my father could've traveled to some unknown town. But beyond that, how much time has passed? A month? A season? Time between realms is tricky.

"Did you see them in person? Or did you send—"

"Amberle Kindra," he says. "I know you're trying to distract yourself right now. You see the prince and Cerule, and it's bothering you. But I'm sure you can find more productive things to focus on." His voice is abrupt and clipped. His words feel like a cold slap in the face, with no hint of familiarity or friendship between us.

Yes, I know. I need to find out about the contestants. It's easy to say and hard to do.

I fall back, briefly feeling more alone that I did the day my father was taken. But I remember my place as a 'contestant' of the Consort Tourney and force myself to lift my chin and walk two steps ahead of Wyn, as if I'm someone special.

But how do I move on without even a hint about my father's situation? How do I keep focused on my task when my fears hijack all hope?

My throat aches as if I've been screaming when I wake up sweaty and shaking. Immediately I'm wrapped in the comforting arms of Papa, who soothes me by stroking my hair and pushing the plastered locks away from my face.

"Shhh..." he croons. "It was just a nightmare, Lark. It wasn't real."

I open my eyes and see the comforting sandstone walls of our small apartment. I'm still not used to the dry air of Sandtide, but it's become home. With Papa, I'm home.

"B-but I dreamed they locked you in the Gray! Papa, you aged like a struck match, turning to flame and then to blackened charcoal in a blink. It was horrible!"

He pushes me outward to look at me. His face is stern, but full of love. "I have never, *nor will I ever do something that will cause me to be thrown in the Gray. Trust me, Lark."*

"But we ran from the palace. We left in darkness, and I've seen the way you glance over your shoulder wherever we go." We left years ago, but it didn't take long for me to realize what that meant.

Papa sighs. "I want you to listen to me carefully, Amberle Kindra."

My eyes are glued to his at the use of my full name.

"I didn't want to worry you, but there are some fae who are looking for me."

"But why? Are you in trouble? Did you do something wrong?" My voice squeaks.

He doesn't answer my question. "If I am caught," he pauses. "I may spend some time in the summer dungeon, but that is all."

"But you're good! If they want to arrest you, they're wrong! I'll come after you, I'll—"

"No!" It's the sharpest he's ever spoken to me and it shuts down all arguments. I finally feel the graveness of the situation. "No." His tone is softer. "You must promise me, Amberle, that you will not come after me. If I am taken, you must disappear."

"But—"

"Promise me, Amberle." Papa closes his eyes and sets his jaw.

"I... promise," I say.

Father's features soften and he smiles when he opens his eyes. "And I promise, little Lark, that I'll never set foot in the Gray."

My father broke his promise.

I sink into the lavender-infused water of the copper tub in my washroom, feeling warm for the first time since setting off in that frigid ice boat that carried Luna, Cerule, and me to Terpsichore at the beginning of the trial.

My maids chitter like house wrens in the other room about the *unfairness* that befell me and my team, while the winners, Princess Shay and Didi, had it comparatively easy, riding on horseback to the Autumn Court.

"I'll admit," Kenna, my human maid says, "it was clever the way the princess acquired the horses. And she and Didi were obviously sore and tired once they reached Graycrest—"

"Especially after traversing both the Harsh Land and the Autumn Woodland," the spring maid, Posey, interjects.

"Yes, but Amberle's team had to navigate getting *underwater!*" Kenna continues. "Shouldn't they receive extra merits for that? It doesn't seem fair."

Fairness isn't the point. I sink lower in the bath so the hot water is just below my earlobes. *The fae aren't known for being 'fair.'*

"I, too, am disappointed Amberle wasn't on the winning

team," Posey says. "But the task was to be the first ones to arrive at their destinations, and her team wasn't."

"One word. *Underwater.*"

"They also chose a trickier route," Posey says, resigned. "If they'd just gone down the coast toward the Carbonne Channel, they would have found an easy passage."

I sink lower again until my head is fully immersed to drown them out.

When my bones stop hurting with cold and I've washed away the salt and sea, my maids help me dress. Kenna weaves my hair in an intricate, twisty braid that hangs down my back.

"Why take such pains to make my hair look so lovely, Kenna, when I won't see the prince or the winter magic today?" I ask, admiring the human's work in the vanity mirror.

"I know you aren't scheduled to see him, but Prince Orion has a way of fitting in time to see you when it's unexpected," she argues.

Posey is no help when I look at her. She only offers a smug purse of her lips and a shoulder lift.

"I cannot believe you still don't see it!" Kenna jests. "The prince traveled to the Underwater Court to see *you!* He knew that was your assignment and didn't care that your team wasn't the first." She shoots a side-eye at Posey, who frowns and shakes her head.

I glance between them. There's something more Kenna wants to say, but Posey is trying to keep her quiet. It would have been less likely to pique my curiosity if Posey hadn't responded at all.

"What is it?" I ask.

Kenna lifts an eyebrow at Posey, who relents with a head tilt as if to say, *go ahead and tell her.*

"We just wondered—" She stops when Posey shoots her a glare and a headshake. "*I* just wondered if the prince took advantage and snuck some private time with you after the trial. While you were in the Underwater Court."

I can't help the flush that rises into my cheeks, but these two cannot know about my conversation with Rion. Or the kiss. Maids talk, and one slip from me would spread like wild summer fire from mouths to ears—all the way to the king.

If King Estelar ever suspected the possibility of actual feelings forming between Rion and me, he'd have my father immediately sent to the human realm. Or worse. Either way, I'd never see him again.

"You'll soon find out what the prince did after the trial ended," I say, attempting to deflect. "But I assume you noticed my 'team' for the trial didn't return intact?" Understanding colors their faces, and I excuse myself and slip out of the room before they can ask more questions.

The recorded images of the trial are winding down and I imagine Luna's elimination will be shown soon, but as much as I'd like to watch her humiliation, I know Princess Shay and Didi are about to embark on their date with the prince. Meaning, Shay will be occupied and won't be a threat to discover me using the projection disc in the upper room of the library. I plan to take advantage and do some long-overdue spying.

I take longer than I wanted to travel there because I'm forced to act like a contestant of the Consort Tourney by meandering through the corridors as the winter magic watches. Entering the library through the main doors, I pretend to read the spines of books in the library. I pluck a few from the shelves as if I'm killing time while the prince embarks on his date with the winners, but I'm really checking for witnesses in the room and feeling for any unwelcome winter magic. As expected, I'm alone—all eyes are on the date.

I race up the stairs, checking over my shoulder one last time before entering the small room at the back of the library, then barricade myself inside by shoving a book cart against the door. I waste no time in asking the disc to show me Frost Niege.

The air above the disc materializes until I see the corridor that mirrors the one my room is in. The Winter Court corridor. But no Frost. I curse. She must be in her room where the magic is barred.

Before I can voice the name of my next target, the magic moves. It glides along the floor, drawing closer to a closed door until it halts. Blocked. But it doesn't give up. I hold my breath as it slides along the invisible barrier along the wall until it finds an 'opening'. A weak spot. Everything goes dark as it passes through the wall and within seconds, it opens to the outside of the palace, hovering in the clear night air. Spinning slowly, it turns toward a balcony and moves forward.

I exhale and move closer, as if it will assist the magic. But again, it stops. Blocked again.

But I see her now. Sprawled on her enormous four poster bed surrounded by thin blue gossamer curtains, Frost lays with her white hair fanned all around her and her massive cu sith lying next to her.

They're both asleep. Frost snores quietly.

The sight makes my eyes heavy, and I realize I haven't slept since before the trial began. I wonder how Rion is faring on his date. Surely Didi and Princess Shay had time to rest since they were back in Isi Aura long before we were, but we walked a long distance back through the tunnel. I shake off my exhaustion and thoughts of Rion and focus on my father.

It looks as if Frost fell asleep on top of her bed and pulled one pillow out of its perfect placement. Next to her bed is a framed photo of her family, a jewelry dish with her sunbeam pendant gift half buried inside, and an open letter. She looks almost innocent, curled up next to her familiar. But as soon as the thought crosses my mind, I remember the ice in her voice as she told her unknown partner she didn't kill Juniper because *killing her would be prema-*

ture. Meaning, she's not against murder once she learns *which contestants are in the way.* I shudder, my every instinct warning that she's dangerous. But Frost won't reveal anything about her nefarious plan while asleep, so there's no point watching her longer.

Next, I ask to see River. The scene evaporates and is replaced by the sunlit beach just down from the palace. The waves roll and spill over onto the sand with frothy surf, but other than a scurrying crab, I see no sign of the underwater fae. I see no one.

Perhaps it's like it was with Frost and the magic needs to move around or through something for me to see River, so I wait. Willing the magic to find her. But it doesn't move. Still, I wait.

After several moments, I ask the disc again, but my words choke when I see a disturbance—a small splash—in the distance. I squint and lean forward to see the smooth, dark hide of a large seal, followed by a smaller harbor seal. I recognize the smaller one as the seal the prince gave to River at the last invitational. As a selkie, River can shift into the form of a seal, so the other seal must be her.

I know better than most that the magic can't travel over water. I curse at my luck but watch for several moments, hoping the selkie will soon return to shore. But I doubt it's likely. The night Rion gave her the seal, River soaked her dress in her excitement, caring more about her new pet than her clothes or appearance. There's no telling how long she'll stay out there today. With the prince on a date with others, she has nowhere to be.

Taking a deep breath of frustration, I ask the magic to show me Tierney and pray she isn't out of reach or sleeping. The sea dissolves into a path in the garden lit by varied shades of blue *will-o'-the-wisps.* Immediately, I spot Tierney—with her squirrel perched on her shoulder—and Cerule. The latter's sylph hovers just behind her and I'm grateful I'm not actually there for the air spirit to discover me again.

I settle in and watch as the two meander through the hedges

—holding my breath when they pause at the location where I threw myself at Rion.

Kisses can be lies...

...Then lie to me.

I shake off the memory. That night feels like ages ago, but still makes my insides squirm.

The two remember it too and take the opportunity to laugh at my expense. Calling me *pathetic* is an understatement. But they don't dwell on it long and continue moving as they discuss the contents of a letter Tierney received from home. From what I can tell, it's mostly gossip from the inner circles of the Autumn Court. *So-and-so is rising in rank, but that's only because she impressed King Carpus, who promised her a betrothal to what's-his-name.*

I wait for them to discuss the date, for Cerule to lament that she hasn't had time with the prince, for Tierney to insult Didi as one of the winners of the trial— *anything* pertaining to the competition—but Tierney leads the conversation and clearly doesn't care to discuss anything outside the Autumn Court as they make their way back inside the palace.

I practically sigh in relief when they enter the autumn corridor and shut themselves inside one of their rooms.

It's discouraging that I've learned nothing new, but I'm not ready to give up.

I clear my throat and ask the magic to show me Lady Pepper. I know very little about the summer fae. She's quiet and doesn't stand out in any way—good or bad—but it's prudent that I make sure she doesn't have any banshees in her wardrobe.

The projection dissolves once again and is replaced by the image of Lady Pepper sitting in a small palace sitting room. *Good, she's not sleeping or hiding from the magic.* She is preening, fiddling with the feathers of her left wing to clean or straighten them. I stretch my left wing out and glance at it. My dragonfly wings might be thin and more easily injured, but I don't wish they were bird's wings and full of feathers like Lady Pepper's. Too much upkeep.

She isn't alone. Also in the room is a winter fae with gray horns, and hair the color of dirty snow—I've seen her around the palace—and... Princess Mora. Lady Pepper's pink wisp hovers next to her, but the princess's raven is nowhere to be seen.

The winter fae seems to look straight at me and I sit back as if she can. But her face merely scrunches, then she shakes her head and walks from the room.

Princess Mora shudders. "Are all winter fae so cold and eerie? Why are they even here?"

"They're assisting with the winter magic," Lady Pepper says without looking up. "The king wants the Tourney well-viewed. Did you think the winter fae projected their magic all the way from their kingdom? They have representatives here, invited by the king. Who knows, perhaps we're being watched right now?"

My stomach leaps, but I know she isn't talking about me. She is assuming the organizers of the Tourney might want to make her conversation with a princess available for the masses.

"Have you seen the way Mori and Stjarna have taken to each other?" Mora changes the subject. Stjarna is Rion's raven. *Mori* must be the raven the prince gifted her.

Mori. A play on the princesses' own name. Not very clever, but at least she's named her familiar. I haven't even seen my cabyll ushtey since the prince gave her to me, let alone named her. *I'll remedy that as soon as I'm done here*, I decide.

"They're together *all* the time," Mora continues. Lady Pepper nods but doesn't look up from her wing. "Whenever she's not with me, she's either with him or collecting sticks and things. *I* think she's building a nest... and you know what that means..." Mora wags her eyebrows when Lady Pepper finally looks at her.

"Really?"

"They're in love, I just know it!"

"Lucky her, she doesn't have to compete with other females," Lady Pepper says, going back to her wing.

"I know…" Mora sighs and stares at nothing across the room. "If I didn't have to compete, I'd be with Prince Orion right now, watching the Elementals performance in the amphitheater." Her tone changes and she spits as if she's just eaten a bitter dandelion. "Instead, the *Ice Queen* and that sniveling halfling, *Didi*, are with him."

"I, too, wish I was on the winning team," Lady Pepper agrees and sighs.

Mora turns wistful again. "What do you think they're doing right now?"

"Watching the Elementals perform?" Lady Pepper sounds hesitant, as if it was a trick question.

"I saw them perform once. They didn't impress me." Mora's shoulders bob slightly. "I could do grander things with *my* fire and light magic."

"Oh, I absolutely believe you could, Princess, but wouldn't it be thrilling to watch the growth and decay of the spring and autumn performers?" Lady Pepper's tone is dreamy. "I've never seen them, but I hear the weaving of fire and water and ice is quite the sight."

"I suppose…" the princess muses. "But when would I have time to use my magic in order to entertain others, anyway?"

"Exactly," Lady Pepper agrees, but then exhales. "It must be romantic, though. Sitting next to him… maybe he holds your hand or puts an arm around your shoulder…"

I adjust in my chair. Listening to Mora discuss the romance of ravens and Lady Pepper's assumptions about the prince's date are not topics I'm keen on hearing more about.

"I'm sure he's not doing any of that," Mora says with confidence, though I can hear of hint of doubt in her tone. "Princess Shay cares more about appealing to the high queen and Didi has probably snuck off to write another letter to her sister or request a winter projection call with her father." She rolls her eyes.

"Perhaps she's homesick?" Lady Pepper frowns.

"Then she's not fit to be the mate of the prince. If she can't cut the apron strings, how could she possibly be a potential queen?"

I have seen no sign of Didi being homesick, or missing her family, but I have spent little time with her lately. I'll have to check on my friend.

A raven flies in through the window and lands on the floor near Princess Mora.

"Have you been off with your *loo-oove*, my pet?" she croons.

Kraa!

"See?" she says with a wide grin. "They were made for each other." She looks back at her familiar. "Just like Prince Orion and I were. You should have seen the way he—"

I've heard enough of this, but there's only one name that comes to mind when I ask the winter magic to show me someone else.

The scene dissolves and is replaced by swirling fire and ice in a majestic, elaborate, weaving dance. Three silhouetted figures sit just a few seats below in the grand palace amphitheater.

Thirty-Nine

I hug my arms tightly against my chest, but I can't look away. I should change the projection again. I should see if Frost is awake; I should see if Raine has gone back to shore; I should watch *anything* but this. But I can't bring myself to change it.

Didi leans close enough to Rion's shoulder that her fiery curls spill down his arm and part of his back. Princess Shay sits on his other side, her back and shoulders locked, but she's also sitting close to him.

My gut twists, and I shift in my chair until it screeches against the floor. The sound forces my gaze to look away briefly, but it doesn't last. Nothing can capture my attention in this small study room in the Isi Aura library the way the prince's interactions with a powerful winter princess and a charming, bubbly star fae does.

I could shut it off and walk away. I want to run and burn the image in front of me from my memory. But I won't squander this opportunity to spy.

I look back at the projection. The performance in the amphitheater is mesmerizing. Ribbons of light swirl around a sprouting tree, maturing before my eyes. Vibrant shades of vermillion burst from the branches. The air turns to sparks, snow-like lights drift as the leaves flutter downward. The cycle shifts from life to sleeping death. I swallow, suddenly discomforted despite the beauty of the show. My attention turns back to the prince and his dates.

Mostly because the watching winter magic has moved closer to the three of its own volition, as if it knows Princess Shay is about to tilt her head close to the prince and say, "Could we take a walk, Prince Orion?"

The magic has pivoted until I'm looking at the pair straight on. Seeing the way the light plays along his features and turns his hair to gold makes my breath catch and my heart leap.

The prince lifts a hand toward the stage. "But we'll miss the performance."

Her gaze flits down to his mouth before returning to his eyes. She smiles. "We've both seen the Elementals perform, Prince Orion, yet we've had very little time for just the two of us since this Tourney began."

He won't go for it. He'll make an excuse to stay. I'm sure of it. Intrusive thoughts push through. Hopeful thoughts. *He doesn't really want to spend time alone with anyone but—*

Stop.

Princess Shay moves to look around the prince and speak quietly to Didi. "You don't mind, do you?"

My friend's smile is forced, but there's a challenge in her eyes. "I do. But just know that if you steal him away now, I'll demand time with him later."

"I'd expect nothing less," Princess Shay says, impressed, then looks at Rion. Her dark eyes shine in the reflection of the light show they all ignore. "We should both have our time with him."

He'll protest, saying that they both *won the competition and therefore the three of them should stay together. He won't—*

Rion stands, but I can't be surprised. I shouldn't be. Not really. It might not be how I hoped he'd respond, but no matter what he's said, this Tourney won't end with me. Prince Rion must explore his other options.

Princess Shay threads her arm through his and the magic trails as they walk up the steps to exit the amphitheater.

My thoughts war. My heart aches that he might entertain a future with someone else, even as my head knows he's playing the game—as he should. But I cannot even think that way. I cannot feel jealousy because it will never work. It can't. Not without great sacrifice and disregard for my father's life. And I won't sacrifice my father.

But it's more than that.

For a moment, I believed Rion was right about having the persuasion to change his father's mind. Or I wanted to. But even if King Estelar agreed, allowing Rion to pick me at the end of all of this *and* release my father... I'd have to tell Rion the truth.

I'd have to tell him why I came here. I'd have to tell him it wasn't for him, but only for my father.

I've told so many lies. He'll be humiliated. Heartbroken. He'll hate me for it.

My eyes burn, so I focus back on the scene in front of me.

The prince and princess walk out of the amphitheater and make their way to the gardens. I'm struck by a *rightness* I feel in seeing them together. Two equals, though from different courts, walking side by side through the summer night. I feel like I'm watching the beginning of a powerful union—summer and winter—who could unite and peacefully reign over Faerie for a millennia or longer. I can't make out their words, but I'm struck by their familiarity. Princess Shay hasn't spent much time with the prince in the competition, but they clearly have a relationship that must've grown in the decades I was away from Isi Aura.

I catch the tear before it trails down my cheek. There's potential between them. I can see it. A friendship. A kinship. A romance.

I may have fallen for Prince Rion, but I've been smart to keep a wall around my heart. Yes, for a moment I was tempted to believe this thing between us could have a happy ending. But it won't. I can't. Between the king and the lies I've agreed to let Rion believe... I will never be with him.

I must focus on what I came here for.

"That's enough," I say, then shut off the disc and leave the room.

I'm dead on my feet as I make my way out of the library and through the corridors, desperate for sleep, but my mind is also running as if on the wheel of a mill. Never stopping, always moving with the pouring thoughts that keep it spinning around and around.

It's a never-ending flash of memories and thoughts and feelings. Princess Mora bragging about her raven. The trial. Didi's hair flowing over Rion's shoulder. Princess Nerine's kindness and information about the curse. Luna's ice boat. The pearls on the door that led me to Rion. The way Princess Shay looked walking with *him*. Frost's cu sith. The kiss.

I make it to my room and push it open, grateful my maids are elsewhere and rush to lie face down without changing my clothes. The instant my body crashes into the bedcovers, sinking into the mattress, my thoughts ease and I feel the pull of unconsciousness dragging me down.

It feels as if it's been only moments since I laid down, but the light has changed when I feel the sharp, jabbing edge of a missive beneath my cheek and my body and mind instantly awake.

Is it from Rion? I wonder as I rise with a start and lift the note to read whatever sweet words he might have for me—even as my mind wars that I shouldn't want for such things.

But it's not from Rion. It's a letter from Gnacia.

When you've had adequate rest, come see me. - Gnacia

My disappointment is immediate. I attempt to dismiss my feelings and lay back down, but the interruption was enough to scare any hope of sleep away. I'm pulled into another thought spiral—imagining the date still continues. And if so, what Rion and his dates are saying to each other. If—as Lady Pepper imagined—he drapes an arm around Princess Shay or laces his fingers with Didi's. If he looks at either of them with the warmth of his golden eyes, or if they move a lock of his too-long hair away from his face.

Eventually, Rion will realize that appealing to his father to choose me is impossible. He'll come to terms that he should look at someone else for a mate and a bride. And if he is to be happy with the fae he ends up with, he should try for a real, genuine relationship.

It might not be this date tonight, but it will happen eventually with one of them.

That thought alone is enough to force me off the bed and escape out the window. Gnacia can wait.

I wanted to see my cabyll ushtey, anyway.

***

The last time I was near the stables that house the court cabyll ushteys was mere hours before my father and I fled Isi Aura. The creatures always fascinated me, and I spent nearly as much time peering over stalls and peeking through the cracks in the doors as I did hiding in the lavender fields and stealing pastries from the kitchen with Princess Arielle.

Descending toward the greenish-brown roof, I land silently just in front of the main double doors, take a breath, then walk inside. The smell in the air reminds me of the Underwater Court. Salt and fish. Before my eyes can adjust to the darkness of the stable, several pairs of crimson-red eyes turn and focus on me. I step back.

Despite my fascination, those eyes are a reminder that water horses are lethal. I remember the oft-spoken warnings I heard as a youngling that always ended with some variation of being drowned for their meal.

As my eyes adjust, the equine faces come into focus, each claiming a pair of red eyes. Each is also secured behind an iron stall door.

"Have you come to see her?" asks a tinny voice.

I whip my head to see a small, bright-eyed brownie wearing the palace uniform, complete with the king's gold insignia. He wipes his hands on a dirty rag.

"It's been ages since he picked her for you," he continues. "I thought you'd come sooner."

"I've been otherwise engaged," I say.

"I know." His smile lights his face. "I've been watching the Consort Tourney too. I know the prince has kept you very busy." He winks, igniting a flush in my cheeks as the kiss in the under-water court immediately comes to mind.

But the stable brownie either doesn't see or doesn't comment on my unease.

"Come. She's just down here." He leads me down the row of stalls. Not all are occupied, but I can't help but stare at each of them as I pass. A deep red stallion with white spots digs its hoof in the dirt, but the motion doesn't distract my eyes away from the thick sinewed muscles of its legs and shoulders and neck. Seaweed hangs from the mouths of two identical blue-green mares a few stalls farther down. They chew slowly, almost lazily, until I catch their eyes watching me with their predatory stares. I shudder and look away.

We continue walking past large and small water horses, and when the brownie pauses, I do too.

"Here she is," he says.

I'm immediately drawn to her as she approaches me. Without thought, my hand reaches out to rub her smooth, pale snout the way I did the night Rion gifted her to me. Her red eyes close and she lets out a low *huh-huh-huh* of pleasure. Just like that night.

My thoughts clear, and it's just her and me. All the complications and trials and obstacles seem to melt away. It feels as if I've been wrapped in a quiet, safe cocoon. Her name comes to me.

"Aquene," I whisper. *Peace.*

There is no competition. I am not a thief or a spy. My father doesn't need saving. The threat of the king doesn't exist.

I can be with Rion.

"Aquene. Is that her name?" The stable fae interrupts my thoughts.

"Yes." I answer without taking my eyes off her.

Aquene bobs her head as if in agreement.

"Have you ever... ridden a cabyll ushtey?" the brownie asks.

"No," I say, and everything comes crashing back. Clenching my teeth at the pressure in my chest, I don't look at him when I say, "I was hoping I could ride her now."

The fae is quiet. In my peripheral, I see him glance out the window before turning back to me.

"It's still light out. I'm sure it won't be a problem."

Forty

The brownie walks silently behind me as I lead Aquene down the beach. I didn't ask that he come with me, but I don't send him away either. He knows I've never ridden a cabyll ushtey. Maybe he's following to give me some tips. My hammering heart silently thanks him.

"The cabyll ushtey's magic will bond you to its back," the brownie says as we near the water.

"Yes." *So I've heard.*

"It will keep you from falling off, but will also prevent you from escaping if she decides to—"

"Yes, I'm well aware." I stop and turn toward him, trying not to show irritation—only a front for the terror and anxiety that lies just below the surface.

Aquene catches my eye, but the crimson color doesn't look nefarious or sinister on her. It looks more like a precious gem—a ruby—that hints at nobility and loyalty. There's power behind it, but I don't feel her dangerous nature directed at me.

Those could be my famous last thoughts, but the warmth and ease I feel disagrees.

I spot movement down the beach and see River walking in the shallows toward shore. She's alone—an opportunity I cannot miss. My heart pounds, knowing I need to intercept her. And not while in the water riding Aquene. My familiar is new to me; it's too risky to be with a potentially dangerous contestant *and* a wild creature.

"You know, I don't think I will ride this morning," I say to the groom. "I no longer need your assistance."

The stable fae's eyebrows pinch. He thinks I'm a coward. "Taking it slow with her is wise," he says. "Would you like me to take Aquene back to the stables?"

"No. I want to spend some time with her." I need an excuse to hang out near the water, talking to River.

She snaps her jaw. A reminder that the instant Aquene touches the water, her hook nose will form and sharp teeth will emerge. The brownie's advice is actually practical. We'll take things slow.

"Even that—"

"Do you have any other tips?" I ask, filling my tone with superiority. I hate speaking that way, but in my peripheral, River has almost reached the sand. I can't be stuck talking with this groom and miss the opportunity to catch her.

"Just... they like seaweed. It's a treat for them."

"Seaweed." I look back at Aquene. "I'll find some for her. You may go."

The groom nods, then turns and walks back the way we've come.

Without thinking, I whistle and gesture with my head that Aquene should follow me down the beach toward River. No one told me to do it. It just seems like the right thing to do to direct her. As if by instinct, my cabyll ushtey obediently follows.

The pale blue of Aquene's land form hide seems to shimmer like a rainbow in the summer sun. I'm curious to see her other form—her water form—one day soon. When Rion gave her to me, he said her hide shifts to a darker blue that matches the color of my eyes.

The underwater fae glances at me as we approach, but says

nothing and turns to face the sea. River's seal, *Nixie*—I remember her name from a conversation before the trial—lies on the sand with her eyes fixed unblinkingly at Aquene. I stop briefly, wondering if seals are on a cabyll ushtey's diet. But Rion gave the two water creatures to River and me within moments of each other, and there was no mention of danger or keeping them apart then.

Aquene leans forward, like she longs to be out in the water and cares more about the sea than the harbor seal. Satisfied there won't be a problem between our familiars, I continue walking toward River.

Keeping her face toward the Sea of Neptulus, River lifts her arms outward and causes what looks like an explosion of water that expels from her and looks like a firework. When the blast settles, I realize she is now completely dry.

She glances at me again, but turns to her seal when she says, "You should never walk with your water horse behind you like that."

I look at Aquene, almost expecting to see a maw of sharp teeth ready to rip my head from my shoulders, but she just glances at me the way she always has in the short time we've been together. With connection and trust. I feel it in my gut that my cabyll ushtey would never hurt me.

When I don't respond, River continues, "That's how they get you. Lure you with complacency and make you feel like they're not a threat. Then they'll grip you with their teeth, sling you on their backs and dive into the depths—"

"To drown me. Yes, I know." I've heard the warnings my entire life. It's one thing about the cabyll ushteys that is so intriguing. Riding the back of a creature that could as easily make you its meal as it can give you a thrilling experience.

Logically, I know it's true, but my heart assures me not to worry.

"Have you been out all day?" I ask, changing the subject.

Gnacia asked to see me soon so I need something, *anything* I can take to her. I remember River lamenting the night we all spent time with the prince—when Mora blackmailed me and ordered that I not speak to him. River complained she hadn't had time with the prince. Was her disappointment because of a competitive spirit, or does River have genuine feelings for him?

"I enjoy spending time with Nixie," she says without looking at me.

Aquene shifts to have one ruby eye facing land and the other facing the sea, then stills as if observing something.

"Of course. I've tried to find things to keep my mind off the date too," I prod, with the assumption that she went swimming to avoid watching or thinking about the prince with Princess Shay and Didi. "I get it now. It's difficult when he's spending time with the others." I hate the way my voice catches on the word *difficult*. I can't lie, and although telling the truth now serves my position undercover, it's not something I wished for when I started down this path.

Her head snaps to me.

"That's not—" Her voice catches too. She can't say it because it's a lie. But that still doesn't tell me why or what she *does* wish for.

Aquene shifts again, capturing my attention. I look out at the water and see that something is disturbing the water. Whatever it is, it's just below the surface, so I can't make out what it is.

"They're wild cabyll ushteys," River says, folding her arms and gesturing her head toward them.

My pulse spikes.

"I knew they were out there when I was with Nixie, but they didn't bother us. They stayed in the depths." She doesn't take her eyes off the area. I wonder if she can still see them. I strain to see them, seeing nothing but a growing churning in the water.

"Do you think they followed you to shore?"

River looks at Aquene, then at me. "No."

"Then—"

Aquene steps toward the surf with slow, marching steps.

When the saltwater hits her hooves, her hide darkens, beginning at her legs, then spreading upward. She stops when she's a few paces into the water. Her mane lengthens and turns the color and texture of deep blue seaweed.

"Aquene," I say, but she doesn't move. Forward or back.

When the color moves up my water horse's neck and into her face, the shape of her snout lengthens and shifts. It curls and hooks downward. I don't need to see to know her teeth also morph into sharp points. Lethal points.

A loud chirping sound crosses the water expanse. I don't need an explanation from River to know it's coming from the wild cabyll ushteys.

What are they doing? I wonder.

"Now is not a good time to ride her," River says, glancing at Aquene. "Especially since you're..."

"Inexperienced?" I finish.

"Do what you want, but I'd rather not explain to Prince Orion why you're no longer in the competition." She looks at me. "I don't want to win that way." But without another word, she lifts her hands forward, cupping them as if holding invisible balls and a wave forms. But it doesn't come inward. It begins at the sand then rolls out, collecting water and power and increasing as it moves until it rises nearly half the height of the outer Isi Aura tower before crashing over the wild cabyll ushteys' location.

When the wave settles, and a smaller one ripples its way back to shore, I hear another sharp chirping sound, then frantic splashing as the water horses retreat to the depths. I still can't see them, but it's what I assume.

Aquene seems satisfied, because she returns to my side. I try not to think too hard about the fact that she hasn't returned to her land-form yet and the only thing between her sharp teeth and my flesh is her hook nose and a small bit of space.

"You scared them away. How?" I ask River. I can't hide the awe in my voice at the powerful water magic I just witnessed. "They're water creatures. Your wave shouldn't have hurt them."

River turns to me. "It didn't." She waves another hand, and the water flies off Aquene, forcing her to shift back. River doesn't seem affected by the amount of magic she's used. She doesn't even break a sweat. Not like Princess Nerine did when she filled my water glass. "But they know what I can do."

"I don't—"

"Meaning, they also know I can take it away from them just as quickly."

But cabyll ushteys can survive on land, I want to argue. *I don't—*

"And I could drain the very blood from their veins if I wanted-ed." She answers my silent question.

I take a steadying breath while River looks at the rising sun. Finally, she gestures to Nixie, signaling she should return to the water. "I'm going back to the palace," she says to her familiar, then turns to me. "I imagine the date is over by now."

River has officially freaked me out, but I force myself to ask one last question.

"And you're hoping to get some time with the prince?" I prod.

"He's proved to be tolerable for an air fae, even though I will miss Neptulus terribly if he chooses me in the end." She shrugs. "But... it will do wonders for the relations between our courts."

Calling the prince an *air fae* is just one more reminder that the underwater fae see themselves as separate from the other courts. Being in this competition is a personal sacrifice for the greater good of her court. A match with the Summer Court would pull the Underwater Court to the inner circle.

"So yes, I plan to seek him out, but he might be sleeping. They've had him on a rigid schedule with the trial, so I might as well sleep, too." She looks at Aquene. "Do you need help returning your cabyll ushtey to the stables?"

"I'll be fine," I say, wondering why she even offered, and why she forced my water horse to change back to her less fearsome state. She was helping me. Why? Then I remember the reason

Cerule helped me in the ice tunnel. I wonder if Tierney's suspicion about being on my good side and not letting me get hurt to keep favor with the prince has spread among the other contestants.

Without another word, River leaves me.

Slowly, I walk along the beach with Aquene. I worry that she'll yearn to get in the water and abandon me. But although she looks at it longingly from time to time, she doesn't complain and remains at my side. I make sure her head is always in my line of sight, though, and not behind me, as River suggested. Better to be safe than sorry, especially as I really don't know Aquene.

The waves pushed some seaweed up to the edge of the sand further down the beach, so I pull handfuls of it up onto the drier sand for Aquene to snack on. Before I can even wipe my hands, she digs in. I'm glad for the tip from the stable fae and I'm content to watch as she happily eats.

"They told me I might find you here."

My heart jerks against its tethers as flames rise up my neck.

It's Rion.

Forty-One

I press my hand tightly against my galloping heart and turn around to face the prince. "You startled me."

His smile is forced, and I notice the dark circles beneath his golden eyes—the pupils are thin slits—and the way his too-long hair hangs limply over his forehead. He looks about ready to collapse.

"Did the date just end?" I ask. Did it go all day?

The prince frowns, then places his hands on his hips and looks at the sand. "No. It ended hours ago."

"What are you doing here? Have you slept since we've been back?" I itch to step forward, to touch his face, to will his eyes to meet mine and smooth the worry creases streaked across his brow. But I refrain and bunch my hands at my sides.

Rion shakes his head, then looks up. "I tried, but..." He runs a hand through his limp hair. "Well, I rarely sleep well." He inhales deeply. "I've never told you, but for as long as I can remember, even as a youngling, I often wander the palace hallways in the dead of night because I can't sleep." He pauses and studies me. "Especially when there's something pressing on my mind."

Something pressing... "Was it... did it have something to do

243

with your date with P-Princess Shay?" I ask and hate the way my words trip. "Or with Didi?"

I know he's supposed to find connections with the actual contestants, but I don't want to hear about the progress of his relationships.

"No. It was about what you said in Neptulus." Rion steps toward me, causing my stomach to flip.

So... not about Shay or Didi...

Neptulus was where we—

He stops a few paces away. Close enough to reach out and pull me into his arms, but he clasps his hands behind his back instead. Keeping a firm distance between us.

"You were right," he says. "I delusioned myself into thinking you could be my choice because the king chose you to be in the competition. But that's not the real reason you were chosen. It shouldn't have taken me this long to figure that out."

Sweat forms at my brow and at the back of my neck. Does he know the truth? Has the king told him why I'm really here? I look at Aquene to hide my discomfort, feigning interest in watching her quietly eat the seaweed I'd gathered.

"I suspect it was to appease the star fae," he says, drawing my eyes back to him. "Sure, Didi Beechriver is also a star fae, but placing two of you in the competition is less obvious than one."

"Right." I'm relieved at his assumption, but it makes my guilt spike. There's not even a small part of him that suspects the truth. It doesn't even occur to him.

He reaches forward and takes my hands—which sends a spark through my fingers—then he pulls me closer. A comfortable warmth radiates from my chest at his touch. "But I know my father well enough to know he won't let me choose you." Rion's eyes flash with brief pain, then he twists his mouth. "At least not now."

His eyes search mine and I fear and hope he's about to kiss me despite his words. He shouldn't kiss me. I shouldn't let him kiss me. But I want him to.

"Damn, I want to kiss you right now," he whispers, as if reading my thoughts. "But I can't. It's not fair to either of us."

The prince drops my hands—creating tiny fractures in my heart—then steps backward, placing his hands securely out of reach behind his back again.

"I'm a prisoner to my station as much as you are. If not more." He flashes a bitter smile. "As the crown prince, you'd think I could choose the girl I want. But you were right." His eyes close and his voice breaks. "I hate that you're right."

The cracks in my heart widen. The edges burn with such intensity that I close my eyes against the wave of agony that erases the fleeting warmth and comfort I felt when he touched me a moment ago.

It's for the best, I tell myself. It's what we talked about in the Underwater Court. But knowing it logically doesn't erase my devastation. A part of me hoped he'd say to hell with what we should do and insist that we enjoy stolen moments and kisses in the shadows. We could live on borrowed happiness until we figure out the next step.

But we shouldn't. Like he said, it isn't fair to either of us.

Isn't fair to him. I've built our new relationship on a bed of lies instead of honest truths. A happy ending was impossible from our first palace conversation.

My throat seizes, preventing me from speaking.

"Amberle, there are things about me even you don't know."

More than his insomnia?

"I would share them with you, but it would hurt my family. My father and my mother. Just trust me that I know my father loves me... in his own way."

I nod and think of my first meeting with King Estelar when he found me in my apartment above the bakery. Although he wanted control over his son's choice, he also wanted someone whom the prince could love. It seemed foreign to me back then, knowing Rion's character as a youngling, but he is clearly a romantic.

But it also leaves me questioning just what he's keeping from me. What other obstacle I'm not aware of that might make our situation even more impossible?

Rion shifts his feet, adjusting his stance while looking down, then rolls his shoulders before his eyes come back to me.

The tension is palpable. It makes my blood feel slow and thick. My limbs are weighted and heavy.

"I meant what I said," he says. "I will talk with my father and do everything in my power to convince him to let me choose you."

He pauses and my heart stops.

"I love you, Amberle," he says, "I want to be with you..."

Even his words hurt. Another twinge cuts deep in my breast. But I also clearly read his tone. He loves me... but?

I feel as if I'm teetering on a cliff. Ready to tip and plummet.

He exhales through pursed lips. "This is for the best," he says, almost as if to himself. "I have no plans to eliminate you from the Tourney, but I've decided... to let you choose when you leave." He closes his eyes and whispers, "If you choose to leave."

What?

"If at any point this gets to be too much for you..." he explains, shifting his stance again. "Let me know, and I'll release you. I'll let you go."

My eyes burn. I didn't realize how much it meant when he said he was never cutting me from the competition until he took it away.

Just like that.

"You can signal to me that you wish to leave by removing your —" He clears his throat. "Your necklace." He points at the soft glowing crystalized sunbeam that has taken permanent residence hanging just above my heart.

I grip the pendant in my palm and blink a few times.

"But know I love you," Rion says, stepping toward me and reaches to take my hands, but stops himself and fists them at his sides.

I fist mine too. The crystal cuts into my fingers.

"I love you, Amberle. That will never change."

I straighten my spine. "Is that what kept you awake?"

"There's something else. I'm working on a way to get you into the Gray to see your father."

An explosion much like the water expelling from River bursts inside me, filling my arms and wings and legs with a tingling sensation that is at once full of terror and joy and... and intense, all-encompassing love for this fae. I throw myself at him, wrapping my arms around him in a gleeful hug.

Realizing what I'm doing, I push myself away from him, jerking backward. I shouldn't. I... can't.

"Sorry," I mutter.

"I'm not."

"Rion, that's..." I tilt my head forward. "Dangerous. Even you shouldn't be asking for such things."

Rion ducks his head, looking at me through his hanging hair with concern and unaltered adoration. "Trust me. I've been doing this prince thing for a while." His smirk is enough to fill every dark corner of my thieving, deceiving soul with light. "Don't act so shocked, Amberle. I'd do anything for you. But only if you want it."

"To see my father?" A sort of horror crashes like River's wave at the thought. Never in my life have I ever wanted to see the inside of the Gray. Let alone see what it has done to my father.

"I understand if you don't want to see your father in there. And yes, it will be risky."

But I have to say yes. I must verify that he's alive and okay. The words won't leave my lips, but I manage a nod.

"Are you sure?" he asks.

"Yes. Please."

Rion reaches forward with one hand and takes mine. "I cannot guarantee that I'll be able to get you in. But I promise I'll try."

A promise. A bargain.

It takes more strength than I have to release my fingers from his. So he does me a kindness, releasing me. And then I watch as he walks up the sand.

Forty-Two

In Aquene's stall, I stroke the velvet smooth space between her eyes. She lets out a low *huh-huh-huh*. My water horse closes her eyes with each stroke, as if in a trance, docile and calm. Some distant part of me remembers the fierceness of her water form, but the frightful sight of her is nothing compared to the crushing conversation I had afterward.

Every word Rion said was necessary. Utterly, devastatingly logical. Every non-touch, every non-kiss, space-between-us was for the best. I touch my crystalized sunbeam with my free hand, running my fingers over the smooth planes to remind myself it's still there, as if I'm worried it will disappear of its own volition and accidentally cue the prince to send me away. Perhaps I should find some sturdier cord to string it through to ensure I, alone, have the power to signal when I wish to leave.

Not wish. When I *must* leave.

If I could, I'd never take it off. *Ever.*

But some dreams are impossible. Reality is inevitable. Just thinking about that future day feels like a gut punch, so I refuse to think about it.

I say goodbye to my familiar—marveling at our growing

connection—and walk slowly to the palace. My throat tightens and I chew on my lower lip with a new realization. When I leave the palace, I'll need to find a safe place for Aquene. A few ideas come to mind, but none of them are as nice as the palace's facilities. Of course, I'll give her the option to go into the wild, but I have a feeling that won't be her first choice.

Gnacia's note said I should see her after I rest. Likely she meant *immediately* after I awoke. I imagine she'll have plenty of words for me after taking a detour to the beach, but I can't bring myself to hurry. I've learned things about the contestants, but each bit of information I gather and report only brings me closer to the end.

I know the path between the stables and the palace almost as well as I know the maze-like hallways of the Isi Aura palace, but it seems somehow changed. Perhaps the trees have grown taller, or the shadows have grown darker, but I feel a frigid coldness in the air that shouldn't be present this far north of the Winter Court.

Goosebumps skitter up the back of my neck, and I stop in place, rigid and alert.

I reach out, feeling for any sign of the watching winter magic. It's absent, but the feeling of impending *something* doesn't dissipate, so I duck to the side of the road in a thick grouping of trees and crouch down to conceal myself. Then I wait and listen.

My half-fae ears prick at the sound of hushed voices further up the path. Remaining to the shadows and keeping my body low to the ground, I move toward the voices, using the quiet fluttering of my wings to silence my feet.

A brief rush of anxiety fills me with concern that I'll be caught because of the curse, but my swift calculation reassures that it's finally worn off. I was in complete control of my words while talking to River on the shore. I gleaned information about her motives for being in the competition without making a fool of myself—or getting the blood of my veins drained.

Then with Rion... Yes, I threw myself into his arms when he

declared he wanted to get me in to see my father, but I know it resulted from my feelings for him, not a controlling curse.

The morning light filters through the trees with brilliant rays. I move to ensure none of them point directly at my position, but my sunbeam suddenly glows with the charge of sunlight. I shove it beneath my dress to conceal it right as a familiar voice pricks my ears. "I fear she has an excellent chance at winning."

Frost Niege.

My pulse quickens at my luck. She's awake. She's talking to someone. And she doesn't know she's being overheard.

"Princess Shay? But she's one of our own, she's—"

"She's a threat to my position," Frost snaps.

I don't recognize the second voice, but he's clearly a male. My first thought is that he's a servant, but his tone and his words are anything but submissive.

"Is there something else you wanted to say?" Frost's voice is filled with venom and authority.

"It's just..." the fae says, then steps into my line of vision.

I duck lower and flatten my wings so there's less chance he'll spot me. I note that he wears all black and has the black feathered wings of a winter night fae. I don't recognize him. I haven't seen him around the palace or the competition.

"It doesn't seem like Princess Shay is the one you should worry about," he says.

I freeze and feel an icy chill rush from my crown to the tips of my wings and the bottom of my toes.

I don't dare move for fear of being heard, but my colorful wings could give me away if they paid close enough attention.

"It's pretty obvious to everyone, and it seems the prince doesn't care to hide the fact that he prefers the summer halfling."

"Amberle?" Frost scoffs loudly.

"Pardon my bluntness, but it's very clear that he loves her."

That painful twinge I felt down at the beach twists in my chest.

"Love has nothing to do with it," Frost says.

"But—"

"Do you really think High King Estelar Illuminae would allow his son, the *crown prince,* to be wedded to a *halfling?*" Frost's cold tone isn't surprising, but it doesn't make the slanderous term smart any less. "A mutt? A nothing? Let alone bed her and create little royal nothings?"

"But the princess..."

"The Niege family employs you, Bane. *Not* the princess. If I marry Prince Orion, it will raise your station." There's a forced cheerfulness that sounds so strange coming out of Frost's mouth. "And remember, if I marry Prince Orion, I will immediately become your *high crown princess.* And someday... your high queen. You would do well to obey me."

"Yes, my lady." He bows low, then his demeanor shifts. "The Onyx have arrived."

"Are they in hiding?"

"No." He sounds pleased. "Jessamine requested more winter fae. She carefully crafted her words, saying that more winter magic will benefit the outcome of the competition. She just didn't say *whom* it would benefit."

"Clever girl." Frost laughs once. "And they fell for it?"

"Yes. They agreed."

"Stupid fools."

"They're distracted by something. They aren't paying attention."

"So, if they aren't hiding, where are they?"

"In plain sight. They're proper guests, stationed around the palace, ready for your signal."

"Good. They won't need to wait long. My signal will come tonight."

"My lady, something this delicate should be carefully planned, I do not think—"

"The longer we wait, the more time we have for mistakes. And the more time *they* have to put into place anything that can thwart it. We cannot afford that. It must be now."

"Yes, my lady."

"After tonight, Princess Shay Malov will no longer be a contender in the Consort Tourney."

Forty-Three

My muscles cramp and the foliage scratches at my skin, but I hold my crouch. I don't dare move for several moments after Frost and the black-winged fae leave the area for fear of being caught. But moreover, because I'm stunned at the nefarious plot I overheard.

Frost Niege intends to remove the winter princess, Shay Malov, from the competition? Her *own* princess. The fae are cruel and conniving and self-serving, but some loyalty to one's own court is typically honored. *Typically.* And I doubt Frost's coordination with the mysterious Onyx—which sounds like a mercenary group—means a peaceful removal of Princess Shay.

I fear this *signal* they spoke of will ignite something violent and bloody.

Why didn't they eliminate Frost sooner? Why was nothing done when I first warned the prince and Gnacia about her?

It's unwise to question the actions taken, or not taken, when I brought the high court the information on Frost, but she is clearly a fae they should have paid more attention to.

When I finally move from my cramped position, I rush through the forest, staying off the path until I'm closer to the palace. I shake the sand and leaves from my skirts and walk with a gliding pace toward the royal wing.

If anyone asks, I've just come from the beach and cannot be delayed; Gnacia demanded that I report to her directly, after all.

But it's all I can do to not fly through the hallways and hide the anxiety and tension just below the surface. I don't know who is watching or who is working with Frost. I keep my face forward with a guarded expression, but my insides swirl with an aching feeling of haste and terror for whatever awaits us today.

I rap on Gnacia's office door and am immediately beckoned inside. Shutting the door behind me—and keeping the watching winter magic out—I turn toward the irritated faun, ready to spill everything.

"Did you oversleep?" Gnacia asks with one hand hitched on her hip.

"I—"

"Don't fumble for a clever turn of words." She lifts a hand, silencing me. "I know you went to the beach. I hope it was worth it."

I adjust my shoulders and stretch my wings. I won't cower at her sour mood. *Well* worth it. If I had not gone to the beach this morning, I wouldn't have the urgent information I learned on the way back."

Gnacia drops her hand and gestures that I sit. "Pray tell?"

I'm filled with so much nervous energy that I merely glance at the chair and remain standing. I stitch my thoughts into something coherent, not wanting to spew everything in one breath.

With pursed lips, she seats herself behind her cherry wood desk and steeples her hands together. "Whether or not your information is good, your father won't be freed if you don't divulge what you know, little bird."

My father. I know better than to admit knowing he's in The Gray, the worst place in all of Faerie. Possibly the worst place in any realm. As his daughter, it's my responsibility to earn his freedom. The weight presses down more than ever now that I know his true circumstances. A shudder raises the tiny hairs at the back of my neck.

But for once, I realize, I might have everything I need to free him.

Intelligence of Tierney and Cerule, Princess Mora and Lady Pepper, all that is resourceful information. But I also know of River's immense power. And greatest of all... I know of Frost's impending treachery.

"Yes, and I believe I have enough now to free him," I say boldly. Time is limited, but I cannot waste this moment.

Gnacia hitches an eyebrow and tilts her head, gesturing again that I sit.

I obey, but keep my chin high and my spine straight.

"Tell me what it is, and I'll determine if it's enough." Her words are clipped. She's still annoyed with me.

"No. I want a vow," I say, keeping my tone firm. "I know what I have is enough to free my father and I want you to vow that you'll persuade the king to free him and—" My voice catches, and my eyes burn. To calm the sudden aching in my chest, I reach up and grip the crystalized sunbeam in my fist. I don't need her influence to tell the prince to send me home. I can signal the request myself.

"Amberle," she says with a chiding, condescending tone. "You know I cannot vow on the actions of the king, nor that I can presume to persuade him of anything. Tell me what you know, then we'll discuss—"

"The king gives power to those he trusts." I poke at her pride, but my words are also true; insights I learned as a child. "And surely he trusts you more than most. Surely there is *some* type of evidence or intelligence that's worth my father's immediate release?"

Gnacia narrows her eyes, indicating thoughts churn behind them.

Part of me wants to reach across the space between us and

shake her roughly to hurry her acquiescence because time *is* limited. But I refrain. Thank *Vejo* my curse is gone.

"But if, as you say, this information is so vital, why should we let you leave?" Gnacia's tone shifts. "We might need your assistance further." She smirks, but sounds doubtful that my information is as useful as I imply.

She's right. Especially now that my curse is gone, I could be an especially excellent asset for them to keep the tolerable contestants safe. To keep Rion safe. To ensure the prince ends up with a fae who won't kill him on their wedding night. They might need me. She doesn't know that I have the power to stay or leave when I wish, but I don't intend on telling her. "You still have another spy," I say. "Besides, you don't want me here for the interviews. That could be ruinous for both of us."

Gnacia taps her quill on parchment, waiting. "Fine. What *incredible knowledge* do you deem worthy to end your bargain?"

"To end my father's imprisonment."

"Yes, of course," she says, waving a hand. "That was the bargain. To free your father."

I take a breath, then briefly tell her what I know of the others—that Cerule obviously has feelings for the prince, but Tierney can't even tolerate him. That River has strong water magic and Lady Pepper is vapid but wouldn't be the worst choice. I tell her Princess Mora is a tyrant, but I must admit, is no physical threat to the summer royals. I tell her I still believe Didi is a wise choice and though I still know little of Princess Shay, she appears honorable and regal and might be a promising candidate. Most of them could prove to be fine picks, I realize. My heart sinks.

"While I applaud your espionage skills, none of that is enough—"

"I'm not done," I say. "I saved this part for last because..." I take a breath. "You'll want to notify the guard immediately."

Gnacia shoots up to her hooves and clips around the desk. I definitely got her attention. "Then why did you not say it first?"

"It's Frost," I say. "She has organized winter fae loyalists right *here* at the palace. I overheard her speaking with one of them about something that will happen tonight."

Gnacia's face pales. "What do they intend?"

"I don't know the specifics, but she wants Princess Shay out of the competition. She thinks the winter princess is her greatest threat. Her exact words were, *'After tonight, Princess Shay Malov will no longer be a contender in the Consort Tourney.'*"

Without another word, Gnacia walks toward the door, but in another bold move, I grip her arm. Stopping her.

"I've done my part." I ask, a little winded. "Will you do yours?"

Her violet eyes pierce through me with urgency and obvious distraction. "If we do not need your further assistance, it is enough."

It is enough. The words shift the weight on my soul. And I won't be bullied into staying beyond my contract.

"You have another spy. Use them."

She presses her lips together. She doesn't want to relent, but says, "I promise to speak with the king and the prince. The other spy should be enough."

I release her arm and she flees the room.

My limbs are frozen. I should leave too, but my legs won't move. My wings won't move. I'm finished. This terrible bargain I never should have entangled myself with... is finally over. At this point, there are only formalities left. Gnacia seemed confident that she only needs a conversation with King Estelar and Ri—I squeeze my eyes closed and shove down the painful twinge in my heart at even the thought of his name—Gnacia only needs a conversation with the prince and I'll be freed. *My father* will be freed.

We can escape the tight, pressing grip of the high court and finally... be free.

As if hearing the word, my extremities ease from their stone-like-state and I can finally move my legs again. The last thing I want to do is fake a pleasant conversation with any other contestants, so when I leave Gnacia's office, I hurry to my rooms to pack.

In the halls, I sense the winter magic stronger than I ever have. I tell myself it's because I know Frost is planning something terrible, but I can't shake the oppressive weight in the air. Yes, I informed Gnacia all I know about Frost's villainy, but my gut instinct is that the summer royals will be protected first, leaving Princess Shay vulnerable.

I remind myself that Shay has her own guards; they might protect her better than the high court. Yet, will they receive a timely warning? Will they be given a vague message or be told the attack will come from within their own court? In good conscience, I can't leave it up to chance. I rush down the halls, using the haste and speed of my wings, straight toward the div's den: the personal quarters of the powerful Winter Court.

Forty-Four

As I round the staircase, leading from the fourth level to the fifth, I brace myself for whatever I'll encounter. I've already seen increased winter fae prowling the palace as the competition has worn on, but I expect to see more.

The fifth level is where the summer quarters, *my quarters,* are, but the other end of the corridor belongs to the Winter Court. Until now, any fae I passed might assume I was heading to my own rooms, but as soon as I reach the landing and turn the opposite way, I'm in potential enemy territory. Any servant or fae I see might work for Frost. Although she dismissed me as a threat to her position, the others working with her—such as the black-winged fae—suspect the growing feelings between the prince and I. They might not hesitate in removing me from the competition of their own volition.

I am just a lowly star fae, after all. Less than nothing.

"Amberle!"

My heart slams against my ribcage, but then swells with recognition of her voice. It's Didi. I've missed my friend. All thoughts of Princess Shay momentarily vanish, and I turn to see her following me up the stairs. She wears a simple green dress. Her red braids fly behind her.

"I've searched for you," she says, slightly winded when she catches up. "It's been too long since we've seen one another."

"It has," I say. My smile is genuine, though I still feel the urgency to talk to Princess Shay.

"I was about to get a late lunch," she says. "Would you join me?"

"I actually..." I want to say yes, but cannot delay speaking to the winter princess. It's unwise to be cryptic about my reasons for declining Didi's invitation or else it'll create more suspicion, so I glance up the stairs and tell her part of the truth. "I must relay a message to Princess Shay."

"Oh." Her expression falls.

It's crucial that I warn Princess Shay, but I realize whatever is coming tonight could be dangerous for everyone. I must protect Didi and keep her out of harm's way if I can. "But you and I need to spend some time together," I say, filling my voice with excitement. "Let's do that tonight! You can come to my room, or I'll come to yours. We'll order rainbow tartlets and that tasty mulberry wine I've heard about." I grin and build on the energy, hoping to persuade her without giving away that I'm desperate. I don't want to hear about her date with the prince, but I should. I *need* to hear about it and pray the prince is growing a healthy relationship with her. He may not love her, but if there's potential after I... I can't even finish the thought, but add, "Then... you can tell me about your date with Ri—*Prince* Orion."

Didi pulls her braid forward and fumbles with it. "Well, I had hoped to see him tonight," she says, staring intently at the ends of her hair. "We had such a lovely time..." After a momentary hesitation, she seems resolved and flips her braid behind her again, then looks up at me. "You're right. We need to spend time together. One of us could be cut from the competition at any moment."

"Tonight then?" I ask.

Didi nods. "Tonight. Ever since Juniper told us about that mulberry wine at the beginning of the competition, I've wanted to try it."

I feel a twinge of regret at the mention of fallen autumn's name. Wyn said I should stop investigating Juniper's murder, but I can't help but feel guilty for failing her. I wonder if he's learned anything since discovering the note. I've been so focused on everything happening to me—The trial, the news about my father, my tumbling feelings for the prince—I've given no thought to solving her murder.

"Then we will get some," I say.

"I look forward to it."

"So do I."

Didi turns and returns down the stairs. I wait until she's rounded the landing and is out of sight before climbing the rest of the way to the fifth floor. When I turn toward the Winter Court wing, I take a breath and my pulse thunders through my veins. Winter fae guards line the hallway, filling the space with a frigid chill, but none gives me more than a cursory glance until I reach the room belonging to Princess Shay.

A guard with blue-tipped black hair and pointed elven ears moves in front of the royal's door before I can knock.

"The princess isn't receiving visitors," he says, stern and tight-lipped.

"I think she'll see me," I say and fold my arms, then lean on one leg with feigned confidence.

The guard lifts a brow.

"She'll be stunned that I, Amberle Kindra, the lowly *halfling* contestant, wishes to speak to her. Her curiosity will *insist* that you let me in."

He studies me for several moments before answering. "The princess isn't here."

My stomach plummets. "Oh? Where is she?" I had hoped to speak to her in her rooms so she could immediately warn her guards. I had hoped for privacy because, well... she's bound to be dismissive if surrounded by her cohorts. "It's important that I speak to her."

"For the safety of the princess, I cannot tell you her whereabouts."

I ground my teeth and clench my fists. "For the safety—" I stop my words before I can insist that speaking with Princess Shay is *for her safety.* Because although this guard stands in front of the princesses' door, that doesn't mean his loyalty lies with her and I must remember that. This could be one of the Onyx members working for Frost. He could be a danger to Princess Shay's safety while posing as one her guards. It makes me wonder if his answer is cover for not actually knowing her location. "Very well," I amend, but don't let go of the frustration on my face. "I'll see if I can locate her *myself.*"

I turn and walk back the way I'd come. Who would've thought that I'd be going out of my way, on a mission, to warn the winter princess of anything? But if it came to the prince choosing between Princess Shay and Frost Niege as my future queen consort, I'd choose the former.

Frost might be kicked out of the competition after my revelatory conversation with Gnacia, but my warnings weren't heeded the first time. Until Frost is gone, she's a threat. And if she's willing to go to treasonous lengths to cut down her *own* court for the crown, she'd surely be a tyrannical high queen. Once the crown is on her head and she's wedded to the prince, would she hesitate to *rid herself* of her husband if his ideas don't align with hers? I can't risk finding out.

I don't know Princess Shay's favorite areas of the Isi Aura palace and since the palace is massive, I need help to locate her. Time is limited. So I head to the library to use the princess's own magic to find her. If she's there, all the better because although I'll be caught knowing about her secret winter magic disc, I can warn her and hopefully prevent her from being hurt... or worse.

When I enter the secret room on the upper level, it's empty. Without breaking stride, I ask the disc to show me where she is.

An image appears and shows the green-skinned princess with

piled curly dark hair sitting with several of the contestants eating an afternoon snack downstairs.

Including Frost.

But at least she's safe and I know where she is.

"You know we have to hate you a little since you won quality time with Prince Orion," Frost says with a sneer disguised as a half-smile.

A feeling of icy, cold dread pours over my head and spreads down my arms and shoulders. She told the black-winged fae, Bane, to await her signal. Might she give it sooner than she said?

I'm frozen as I watch Didi join the group and sit next to the princess. I should have accepted her invitation! Then I wouldn't be running all over the palace looking for Princess Shay. But I didn't know the others also decided now was a good time to eat. I should rush down there immediately, but it will get the attention of the entire room if I insist on pulling Princess Shay aside when she's never given me even a fleeting look of respect, let alone friendship. I must strategize.

"Yes, but there were two of us," says Princess Shay, sliding a quick glance of approval toward Didi. "Neither of us had the amount of quality time we wished for."

"But hate us anyway," Didi says, looking at Frost and laughing. Then she shares a knowing smile with the princess. "I think the prince enjoyed his time with both of us, so you may count us as a threat." She holds her head high with a self-assured grin.

No. No, no, no. You cannot say that, Didi! I want to shout at her. She cannot let Frost think she's a serious threat! My friend must know she's throwing herself at the div! She's cutting off chunks of herself to feed to the biloko! Shutting off the disc, I rush from the room. It takes all the will I have to keep my pace hurried, but not frantic. I cannot draw suspicion from the fae I pass on my way to the dining room, but I must get there before Didi digs her own grave.

When I reach the doors to the dining room, I close my eyes and take a deep breath before walking inside. I plaster an easy expression that I hope will reveal nothing to the other contestants. Then, I walk inside and eye Didi on my way to the buffet table. I hope she hasn't said anything else to anger Frost since I left the winter spying disc in the library.

Didi spots me and rushes to my side. "The prince ordered cryspes for us this afternoon!" She squeals and takes a plate, then piles the sugar-coated pastries onto it and holds it up to me.

Did he remember I love them so? I wonder as I take the plate from her hands and feel a warmth that the prince took the time to request one of my favorite treats.

"My father always makes them on special occasions and for celebrations," Didi says and my glee wanes.

Perhaps Rion requested the cryspes on Didi's behalf.

I force brightness in my voice when I say, "How thoughtful of Prince Orion to have the kitchen make them just for you."

"That's the funny thing. I don't remember telling him about that small tradition, but I must have. We did talk about my family."

"How do you know it was the prince who requested them?"

"Because of this note!" Didi lifts a small parchment that leaned against the platter and hands it to me.

When was the last time you had cryspes? - Prince Orion

A thrill rushes from my core down all my limbs. *He remembered.* Rion asked me that exact question with those exact words as we danced at the revel what feels like so long ago. I thought he intended to kiss me that night.

That was also the night I first learned that Frost had malicious intentions to ensure she wins the Tourney. Which brings me back to my task.

I glance at the table crowded with the contestants.

"Oh, and Princess Shay was just here," Didi says, sounding chagrined as she licks sugar from her fingertips. "But she left."

My stomach drops. *She's gone?* I study all the faces and see that all the fae who were present while I spied with the winter magic disc sit in their seats, except the winter princess.

With horror, I realize Frost is gone too.

Forty-Five

When I overheard Frost's instructions to the black-winged fae, she said the attack would be tonight. But I have a sinking feeling the timeline is flexible.

"I know you wanted to talk to her, but you've just missed her," Didi says.

Lifting a single sugar-sprinkled cryspes from the plate, I give it back to her and try not to snap when I ask, "Where did she go?"

"To the gardens, perhaps?" Didi lifts a hand to her chin. "She said she is taking tea with the queen soon." She gestures with her hands. "But she wanted some fresh air—"

Taking the lone pastry with me, I hurry toward the exit. Didi shouts something about coming too, but I can't have her tagging along for this, so I pretend I didn't hear. I pray she changes her mind and stays with the others.

Flying out the palace doors, I no longer worry about appearing in a hurry. I'm past that. I *must* find the winter princess before it's too late. Floating toward the gardens, I hope Didi was right and Princess Shay is wandering the pathways for some fresh air. When I spot the top of her head walking through the rose hedges with guards trailing in front and behind her, I ease a bit and touch down far behind them. Now that I've confirmed her location, I must force myself to be calm or else she'll dismiss my warnings as overly emotional and delusional—too human to be taken seriously.

The scent of the plumeria blossoms and stargazer lilies sting my nostrils as I rush through the garden pathways. The heat of the sun and the ominous feeling that swirls in my core heightens my senses. I'm not sure when it dropped from my hand, but the cryspes pastry is gone and only traces of sticky sugar remain. I'm so focused on moving forward and catching up to the princess that when I round a corner, I nearly crash into the back of a tall night elf wearing the royal colors of the Winter Court. Black and pale blue. Shadows and ice.

She turns and chills the air. A warning. It takes extreme self-control to keep my stance and not cower underneath her black-eyed stare.

"I need to speak with the princess," I say.

"No one is allowed to speak with her," says the elf as she moves to tower over me.

"Why? I'm a Tourney contestant, not some—"

"Lowly halfling?" It's Princess Shay.

Finally. I nearly throw myself at her and hug her in relief, but control the impulse.

"What do you want, Amberle?" she says dismissively, folding her arms.

I glance at the night elf, trying to signal to the princess that we should speak alone. She either doesn't catch the hint or chooses not to act.

"Could I speak with you privately, Princess Shay?" I ask, trying not to sound subservient, though her station and the air she carries certainly compels it.

"Look, I have an appointment with Queen Siora and I wanted to spend some time alone in preparation. So if you'll just—"

"It's important," I interrupt and move toward her. The night elf's reaction to step between us in an act to protect the winter princess is slightly delayed. Almost imperceptibly. But I notice. And so does Princess Shay.

"Who did you say you came to replace?" the princess asks the elf, but then waves a hand before she can answer. "Never mind. Leave us."

"But Your Highness—"

She flicks her wrist again, silencing her. The night elf bows, then walks down the path behind us. I don't know if the princesses' other guards ahead are trustworthy, but note that we might be surrounded by minions of Frost Niege.

"Frost wants you out of the competition," I whisper too low for anyone else to hear. "I don't know what she's planning, but I fear your life may be in danger."

"Frost?" Princess Shay scoffs. "The Nieges have been friends of the royal family for generations."

"That may be true, but Frost wants to be high queen, and she thinks you are the fae in her way."

Princess Shay narrows her eyes, determining, perhaps, whether what I say deserves more of her time. But our fae ears hear simultaneous sounds at once. I act quicker by hurling myself at the winter princess, shoving her down and crashing into the rosebush a mere moment before an enormous blaze of fire ignites in the space where we stood.

But it's the scream I heard at the same time—Didi's scream—that halts my heart.

Forty-Six

RION

The scream jerks me awake from my accidental slumber.

Amberle. She's my first thought, but I was so deep in sleep, I can't identify who I heard. Or if it was just a dream.

Popping to my feet before I've completely recovered my consciousness, I spill the remains of the peppermint tea I was holding onto the rug as I race toward the balcony. I trip on the way and slam hard into the corner of the armoire before throwing open the curtains. My clumsiness isn't surprising considering I fell asleep in the high-backed chair of my sitting room and not my bed, so the circulation of my legs is tingly and partially numb.

When I lean over the rail, what I see fills me with horror, ripping away any vestiges of slumber. The scream wasn't a dream. Billowing, black smoke undulates into the cloudless afternoon sky. What looks like the aftermath of a fireball burns in the center of the gardens. But I see nothing else from this vantage point. The hedges and the trees obscure too much from this distance.

It doesn't look like fire magic gone wrong by a novice. I would know. No, this looks skilled. Deliberate. My thoughts fill with speculations about who could have done this and why. *Is it connected to Juniper's murder? Or an enemy of the court?* Fire magic could only come from a summer fae, and although rebellion within one's own court isn't unheard of, it seems unlikely. *Could it be an attack on a contestant?* The initial terror spreads to my extremities. *Or are the contestants fighting amongst themselves?*

Whatever it was, *whoever* it was, I must ensure the fae in the Tourney aren't in danger.

I must ensure she *isn't in danger.*

I rush back into my room and toward the door when I hear a commotion of guards thundering through the hallway outside my chambers. It doesn't take long before a heavy fist pounds against the door.

"Your Highness, open your door!" A guard shouts.

"Let us in, Prince Orion," another says. "We must get you to safety whilst we investigate the potential threat!"

I stare at the door, knowing my guards will be furious if I don't answer. But if I do and allow the guards to *get me to safety,* they'll shut me up in fortress-like security, leaving me powerless to do anything. No matter my feelings or insisting that they also save and protect the contestants, they might not be a priority.

I must see to their safety myself.

Reacting, I lock the door and trigger the dormant spring magic. With a *whoosh,* heavy vines fling themselves across the door, crisscrossing and attaching to the frame in several places along each side, the top and the bottom. Then each vine thickens before my eyes. The spring magic won't hold long—the guards will simply employ an adept autumn fae to decay it, or a summer fae who could control the burn—but the security measure was only meant to work in a pinch and slow an enemy down.

Still, it will give me a head start.

Sprinting back to the balcony, I hop over the rail and lower myself down by gripping the ledge. As I hang, pinpricks at my fingertips fight with a faint numbness.

This was a bad idea, I lament, realizing how desperately tired I must've been. Pushing through before my fingers fail and slip, I swing my body and propel myself forward to drop onto the floor below.

It's the balcony to the queen's personal social room.

Only female fae are allowed inside and only those she personally invites. Even the king isn't allowed inside. *I'm* not allowed inside. But this is an emergency.

I crouch on my feet, listening for signs that my mother or any other fae are in the room. I hear nothing, but when I try the door, it's locked. The guards are smart to keep flying fae from intruding on the queen's personal space, but it's created a problem for me. What do I do now? Should I go back up? Or down?

I trip back to the rail, gripping it tightly in frustration as I watch the flames in the garden grow and hear shouts I can't discern. Peering over the edge, I wonder just how much it would hurt to jump—

"Orion!" a panicked voice says from behind me.

My mother.

"What are you doing out here?" Concern bleeds from her voice.

I turn. The queen's golden hair is piled neatly on top of her head.

She beckons with one hand. "Something has happened. Come inside!"

I follow her through the door. "Mother, I must find out if the Tourney contestants are safe."

Her eyes snap to mine. "No, no, no. Orion, you mustn't put yourself in harm's way. I cannot lose you—"

"If one of them is to be queen someday, their safety is as important as mine," I say as I rush to the other side of the room toward the exit.

"You mean *her* safety?"

I stop and turn. One eyebrow lifts along with one corner of her mouth.

"You love her." It's not a question. "I've been watching. And as your mo—" Her voice chokes on emotion, but she clears her throat and regains her composure. "I can read you better than any fae."

I wonder if the king can read me so transparently, but I can't wonder about that now. "It isn't the time, Mother. I must—"

But a familiar pounding on the door interrupts. "Queen Siora! Let us in. There has been an attack."

Regret is written in her eyes. I shake my head, but she turns her face toward the door and says, "Yes, come in."

Vedette, The Epoch Guard, leads four other female guards into the room and my stomach plummets. Vedette's name is legendary throughout Faerie, though I've known her all my life. Always sent on the most dangerous, the most delicate missions, Vedette is one of the courts most valued guards. Last I'd heard, she'd recently returned from tracking down a particularly vicious night elf with a penchant for torture who had recently escaped from The Gray. Her report was that the night elf was *taken care of* and was no longer a threat.

I don't fear her, but I know it will be impossible to evade her to find Amberle and the others.

"Your Majesty," Vedette says, then sees me and her eyes widen. "Prince Orion! We have been looking for you." She looks at the queen. "We must get you both into the Vault."

"No—" I start, though I know it's futile, but I'm stopped by my mother's gentle hand placed on my chest.

"You may take me to the Vault," the queen says, calmly but with authority. "But Orion must see that his guests aren't in danger."

Vedette steps forward. "But Your Majesty—"

"Go with him."

I shoot my mother a glaring look that she ignores.

"Ensure that my Orion is safe, but allow him to learn whether his nine remaining potential brides are also safe."

"Yes, my queen," Vedette says and bows low.

Mother turns to me and cups my face with her hand. "Be safe, my little *Meissa.*"

My little star. Meissa is the name of the star at the head of the constellation Orion and is a nickname the queen gave me when I was a youngling. She rarely calls me by that name anymore, so the use of it is both endearing and manipulating. I know she says it because she loves me. There's no question about that. But she also uses it hoping I will change my mind and put her worries about my safety ahead of my worries about the contestant's safety.

I'm grateful she used her power to give me the choice and didn't insist that I also slink to the Vault. Still, I want her confidence that I'm capable. "I'm grown now, Mother," I say. "And I've been trained to defend myself in dangerous situations like this."

"I will risk my life to defend his," Vedette adds.

"I will be careful," I say, though I know Vedette's vow weighs more than my words, then rush from the room with The Epoch Guard at my heels.

We take back corridors and secret passageways to make our way out of the palace undetected. We emerge right as Tierney and Princess Mora lead a group of contestants from the dining hall. I do a quick headcount.

"Are you satisfied, my prince?" Vedette asks, but I shake my head.

"Only five," I say. "Four aren't here."

She's missing. Amberle isn't among them. I don't have a chance to figure out who else is missing before the contestants notice my presence.

"What's happened, Prince Orion?" Princess Mora says, rushing to my side and clutching my arm tightly. She eyes Vedette, but then quickly looks away.

"I don't know." I ease away from Mora's grip. "Where are the others?"

Tierney and Cerule exchange a glance. Behind them, Frost

stares at me, her brow furrowed. River limps toward me, her hands fisted.

"Mora, you slimy slug," she spits. "You shoved me aside to get yourself out of the dining room first. And then Tierney stepped over me like common trash while guards swarmed to secure the room. Spineless slu—"

"Princess Shay went to the gardens," Cerule says, interrupting.

"You don't think..." Frost's eyes widen, and she clasps a hand to her mouth.

"I'm sorry you were injured, River," I say as I signal for a guard to assist her to the healer.

I step toward Cerule and grab for her elbow. "Was it only Princess Shay who went to the gardens?"

Cerule's face flushes and her mouth opens, but nothing comes out.

I resist the urge to shake her violently when Frost steps forward and says, "Amberle said she was looking for Shay. She left too."

"And Didi followed Amberle," Cerule sputters.

Releasing Cerule's arm, I rush toward the gardens and hear several cries of my name behind me, but I ignore all of them.

Of course, Vedette follows, so I pray to *Vejo* she doesn't stop me and is only coming to help. I must get to Amberle.

Weaving through the hedges, I listen for sounds of a struggle, or magic. *Anything* that will help me find her.

When I round a bend, I see the shine of Amberle's silver hair. She's shivering and looks drenched. Huddled next to her are Princess Shay and Didi. The princess's dark curls are plastered to the sides of her face, but Didi's braids appear dry. Before I can get to them, or even wonder what happened, a whoosh of cold air blasts my face and I'm stopped by a wall of ice that forms instantaneously in front of me. A second later, a boulder that must've been aimed at me crashes into the ice.

Fortunately, the wall holds, leaving us unharmed.

Wait... Vedette isn't a winter fae.

I whip around.

"Don't worry, Prince Orion," Frost says, flinging her white hair behind her while keeping one hand raised to control her ice wall. "That guard is no longer with us, but I'll protect you."

Forty-Seven

My heart thrums in my ears and the intense heat of the blaze burns my nostrils as I untangle myself from the thorns of the rosebush and scramble to my feet. I ignore Princess Shay's protests when I grab her hand coated with ice and pull her with me as I fumble forward.

I tell myself that her ice is a protection against the heat and not an attack on me as my hands burn from what feels like intense frostbite.

But I won't let go, despite the pain.

"C'mon! We must get away!" I say as I pull her to run toward Didi's screams. I must get the princess to safety *and* find my friend.

When a barrage of water pours down like a heavy monsoon, I pull my wings tightly against my body to protect them. They've been wet and injured too many times. I won't risk them again.

We both take gasping breaths as the water pours down our faces, but we must keep moving through the hedges until we find a brief respite under the canopy of a dogwood tree.

The water still finds its way through the branches and leaves to drench us, but at least we can breathe easily again.

"What do we do now?" Princess Shay splutters.

I turn around in place, looking for the source of the water while keeping myself beneath the protective covering of the tree and realize the water isn't pummeling the entire gardens. It's specifically aimed at us. Branches of trees in its path snap like twigs flying in all directions. With the power and force like a high waterfall but in an arc twice as big around as the trunk of the tree, it bridges over the nearest hedge, obscuring the source.

"Whoever it is, they're only attacking us," I say between coughs. Despite holding my wings close, they're still getting soaked.

"But it's not Frost," the princess says, clearly winded. "First fire, and now water? Frost is a winter fae with neither summer nor underwater magic in her veins."

"That doesn't mean she didn't use someone else," I argue, thinking of her mention of the Onyx. I had assumed this *Onyx* comprised only winter fae, but maybe I was wrong. "How strong is your shadow magic? Can you obscure us so they can't detect where we are?"

I expect a heavy sigh, but the hair-dripping princess lifts her hands and tendrils of shadows from all around coalesce and draw toward her in a swirling motion. But as they spin around us, they seem to disappear.

"Let's go," she says.

I still feel exposed. Nothing looks different than it did a moment ago. Was her shadow pulling just a trick?

"Amberle!" she snaps when I hesitate, then grasps my arm and pulls me with her.

It works. The water still pours onto the poor dogwood tree behind us and doesn't follow us. We must be invisible.

Still, it's only a guess and my heart hammers again when we come upon some fae who look like guards—but might be the Onyx undercover. They look through us as if they can't see us. I'm impressed by the princess's magic.

Princess Shay turns to her side and motions with her hands that I do the same, so we pass by without detection. When we're right next to the passing guards, I instinctually suck in my gut and pull my soaked wings close as I fear brushing past them will reveal our position.

We pass by undetected.

When we round a corner, I hear quiet whimpering on the other side of a large bush and motion to the princess.

My anxieties and worries melt when I see that it's Didi. Huddled and crying with dirt streaked across her face.

Princess Shay releases the shadows, and we fall in next to Didi in her hiding spot.

She jerks at first, startled by our sudden appearance, but after seeing we aren't the threats, her shoulders relax, and she throws her arms around my neck.

"Are you hurt?" I ask, gripping her tightly. "I heard you scream."

"No," she says. "I saw a fireball strike over there." She points at the direction the princess and I came from. "A smaller one landed there—" she points at the blackened remains of a flower bed with embers that still smolder. "That's when I screamed, but I dodged out of the way."

Relief rings through my bones, grateful she isn't hurt.

"What's happening?" she asks. "I saw the water too." She points at our still-dripping hair. "Is someone attacking us?"

A gust of wind cuts across my cheeks, then turns counter-clockwise and blasts into my ear with a force that knocks me off balance. I fall from my crouched position hard onto my shoulder. The wind continues to swirl around us, gaining power and collecting debris.

It peels petals from flowers, then rips ferns and shrubs from their roots, flinging them into the air and pulling them in a cyclone-like fury.

I push myself to my feet, trying to keep steady as the bush that was Didi's hiding place is stripped of its leaves as the wind intensifies. When it rips the tiny branches and sticks from the bush, tossing them all around, it lashes slices into my skin. I throw my arms up to shield my face as my drenched hair slaps around me.

Then I see our attacker. Wicked smile and putrid green hair hang from his head in clumps. I know he must be the autumn fae responsible for the violent tornado.

Darkness swirls around us, creating another invisibility bubble, and for a moment, I think Shay kept us hidden. But then the fae uses his decaying power to cause the rest of the healthy foliage to decompose and fall apart so the whirlwind can more easily rip the shrubs and trees from their roots and hurl them at us.

"He knows we're here!" Shay snarls, but the fatigue in her voice makes it sound like a whimper. The shadows still swirl toward us, but they've thinned. Weakened. And I imagine the magic around us has too. The princess lifts both arms over her head and crouches down to better protect herself.

Didi has turned herself into a small ball with her arms covering her neck and head.

I kneel next to the princess.

"He'll just keep the wind going and hope he strikes me hard enough to drop the magic," she says. "We won't make it far."

I watch the swirling wind spinning around us, determining the speed of it and calculating how I would propel myself if my wings were dry. How I would jump into the cyclone in order to land...

"Can you make a ball of ice?" I ask.

The princess shoots me an incredulous glance, but it only lasts a moment before she removes one protective arm from her head and conjures a tiny transparent ball of ice. When it's the size of a cherry, the swirling wind threatens to rip it from her hands, so I move around the winter princess to protect it and use both my hands to shield it.

Sticks and pebbles and a few stones strike me. Each thump is certain to leave me with gashes and bruises, but I ignore the pain and keep the princess's ice ball protected.

The autumn fae's wind rips a nearby tree from its roots right as Princess Shay's ice ball is the size of a melon. It's lopsided, but it must work. I take it from the princess and eye the tree that curves around, careening toward us.

"Distract him," I whisper, keeping the ice ball concealed.

The winter princess nods, then sends ice shards into the tornado, aimed in a trajectory to hit the autumn fae. He dodges them easily, as I expected, but it's enough misdirection that when I pitch the orb into the cyclone, it catches and arcs away from us. Then away from the autumn fae.

"You missed!" he shouts over the cacophony then grins with blackened teeth.

But he's not the only one who understands wind. Just as I planned, the ice ball curves back at the last second and smacks the fae in the side of the head. His body goes limp, and he falls to the ground, unconscious.

I have a split-second to act and dive onto Didi and Princess Shay as the tree whizzes over our heads. It shatters against the ground, throwing wood shrapnel in every direction. Still heavy with water, I flick my wings outward, shielding the other two from most of the onslaught as stinging slivers pierce every inch of my back. Every inch of my wings. I grit my teeth against the stinging pain and fist my hand against my mouth to stop from crying out.

"Amberle, stop!" Didi cries, pulling at my hand and urging me to spare myself, but I don't budge. Better that only one of us endure it.

When it ends, I feel like I've sprouted painful quills all along my backside. I don't dare lower my heavy wings for fear of imbedding the splinters even more.

What do I do now? I wonder, as my muscles ache with the effort. Squeezing my eyes tight against the threatening tears, I feel stuck. Frozen. Unable to move. But I fear the next blow of elemental magic will come at any second.

"Turn around," Princess Shay says quietly.

I can't help the whimper that escapes my mouth and bite hard on my lower lip as a wave of agony washes over me.

Keeping my eyes tightly closed, I say, "I can't."

Through the pain, I hear her moving as icy air slides around me, around the edges of my wings, as she makes her way behind me.

The muscles that hold my wings tremble with the effort and I brace myself for when they fail and cause more injury when they drop. That thought alone helps me hold on a little longer. Enduring the growing ache under the stinging pain.

Then, I feel a quick suction as the water instantly pulls away from my wings and along my back. But the heaviness leaves for only a moment, then increases and an immediate chill replaces it. I realize a sheet of ice lines everything from my neck to my wings to my heels.

Thick dread pulses from my heart to my extremities as I wonder what the princess intends to do next. She's nearly immobilized me, putting me in a vulnerable position and I don't know what's happening in the garden beyond, except that it's gone quiet. My mind spins, and I'm about to fight the brace she's created, when the ice jerks away in one motion, sending another piercing onslaught everywhere the wood shards imbedded themselves as they're removed at once... but it's followed by immediate relief.

I heave a sigh as Didi converges and huddles next to me. My hair is still dripping wet and re-soaks the back of my dress. That, combined with the recent ice, sends my teeth chattering and I have an awful déjà vu of the trial to the Underwater Court. Sitting on a frozen iceboat as it sped across the Sea of Neptulus, then traversing through the ice tunnel.

The reminder sends another violent shiver through me from my head to my toes and I swear the air seems to ice over again. When I look at the princess, she's huddled next to me too. But it's only partly by choice. Princess Shay looks about ready to collapse.

A loud crash rattles the ground and the three of us leap away.

My heart thrums, seeing a massive ice wall has appeared out of nowhere, followed by a large boulder that shoots by us and smashes into it. The ice wall cracks and the boulder bounces back and onto the ground, sending a dust cloud into the air. The boulder could've smashed us, especially with Shay so depleted, but it wasn't aimed at us. And the wall wasn't conjured to protect us, either.

What?

When the cloud of dust dissipates, I recognize the white hair of Frost on the other side of the ice wall and fear seizes my gut.

Because standing next to her is the prince.

<h1 style="text-align:center;font-family:cursive">Forty-Eight</h1>

My wings twitch. The onslaught of attacks pauses, a breath held, but for how long? No more hurled boulders, whirlwinds full of projectiles, or horizontal waterfalls. My nostrils still burn from the smoke of the fire and the water in my hair still streams down my back, but the garden has gone still. Silent.

Crouched next to me, Didi is quiet, but Princess Shay's breathing is labored. The winter princess has spent her energy conjuring shadows and ice, and I worry she won't even be able to stand, let alone defend herself—or us—any longer.

Bracing for the next wave of attacks as I scan the broken trees and shredded shrubs littering the ground, I quickly draw my attention to the ice wall. The prince and Frost's features are barely visible behind the barrier. I can't see the gold of his eyes, but I imagine they're filled with concern. For Princess Shay, for Didi, maybe even for Frost, but also for me.

"I'll protect the prince!" Frost shouts from behind the ice wall. Her voice is muffled, but still coherent. "You should leave the gardens! Go! Hide in the lavender fields!"

So, we should run as far from the lavender fields as possible. I dig my fingers into the mud, pushing back my fear and embracing the fury storming through my blood. Frost's specific directions to the fields feels intentional.

What awaits us in the lavender fields? Clove easily trapped me in the same maze of lavender during the labyrinth trial. I won't let anyone take me or Shay out with a simple spring magic trap and an *accidental* fire... or something worse.

Princess Shay's hair is plastered to her forehead and her exhaustion has carved dark circles beneath her eyes. But she's conscious, and she manages a sardonic, doubtful expression.

"Do you still believe Frost is behind this?" Princess Shay hisses, pushing herself to her feet. I move to help her, but she slaps my hand away. "We should do what she said."

"Wait, you think Frost is behind this, Amberle?" Didi snaps her head to me. "But she's protecting Prince Orion!"

"Yes, of course she wants the prince to think she's innocent. Then, whenever her fae allies get rid of *whichever* contestants she's targeted—" I shoot Shay a meaningful glare, "—he'll think she was a hero. She hopes to rise in favor with him. It's all a part of her plan." Frost is even more dangerous if everyone believes she's harmless, but I don't have time to argue my point. "Let's get away before something else attacks."

I lead them away—back the way we came—although my instinct tells me to run toward the ice wall, toward *him*. It takes everything I have to resist, even though I know Rion isn't Frost's target. Her goal is to win a crown, and Frost can't become a princess if she kills the prince.

But he calls my name and I spin around to see him racing toward me. Then he adds, "Princess Shay! Didi!"

They've already turned too, and when I glance at them, I catch them both looking smitten, hearing his concern for them. My heart twists, but I remind myself that, of course, he should be concerned for all of us. Whatever else I'm feeling, I cannot process it. Not now.

"No, Prince Orion! We must get to safety!" Frost yells, following on his heels.

Before he reaches us, a cool, white mist rises from the ground, enveloping everything it touches, obscuring and hiding everything.

Rion's eyes widen, and he pivots, searching for the culprit right as Frost grabs his arm, stopping him just as the fog reaches shoulder height. Within an instant I see nothing but dull white. My cheeks tingle at the chilling touch of the mist, and I can't even see my fingers until they are a mere handsbreadth away from my face.

More water magic.

"Rion!" I cry but I'm shouting into a void.

Reaching out my hands, I feel for where Didi and Princess Shay stood, praying to Vejo that I'm close enough that I can reach them. If her energy isn't too spent, perhaps Princess Shay could turn this water vapor into ice and clear the air. I have no reason to believe that Didi is one of Frost's intended targets, but she's as vulnerable as I am in the crossfire, and I hope I find her first.

I feel neither of them and only grasp the air with each swipe of my hands. I call out to them, only to hear more silence. But I won't give up. I pause and listen for the slightest mumbles or vibrations and hear nothing.

I test my wings. They're drier than my hair, but tender from the shards of wood Princess Shay pulled from my wings and back. The injuries, though many, aren't deep or serious. I think I can fly.

Crouching down, I ready myself to take to the air—

"Amberle."

I stop and strain my ears to listen. *Was it Rion?* I hold my breath, hoping to hear it again.

"Amberle."

It *is* him.

"Rion!" I feel like I'm shouting into nothingness again, but if I can hear him through this thick fog, maybe he can hear me too. "Rion!"

"Amberle!" His tone has changed. He sounds relieved. "Amberle, where are you?"

"Here! Rion, I'm here!"

Finally, through the mist, the faintest shadow of a form approaches. I step forward and we're together in the fog. His hair is disheveled, but the joy on his face is clear and fills me with a thrill.

"What's happening?" I ask as he closes the distance. His feet nearly touch mine and he leans his forehead downward, only a fingertip away from my skin. His eyes are a deeper gold, nearly brown, and shadows line his face in the low light of the heavy fog.

"I had to see you," he says.

A shiver runs across my skin at his words. "Are you alright? Are you hurt?" I ask. "I was in the gardens when there was—"

"There is something we should discuss." He interrupts and looks away.

"Now? But we're in the middle—"

"I know we had a connection as younglings," he says, talking as if I said nothing. As if we're not shrouded inside a heavy mist with dangers lurking just out of sight. "And I know you had feelings for me, but I think it's time your place here in the Consort Tourney ended."

I step back, putting space between us.

When he looks back up, something seems off. His mouth isn't quite right, and his hair falls in all the wrong places. It could be from the obscurity of the fog, but my instinct tells me it's something else. I fumble with my thoughts to determine what's amiss.

"In fact, I believed that you've bewitched me into thinking I was falling in love with you, but now I know it's a lie." His voice changes pitch and I feel a brief twinge of pain. "I don't love you and I never will. It's time you leave and never return." I clutch a hand to my chest, but the full impact of his words hasn't hit me yet. It doesn't feel real.

"You're just a star fae, a halfling, a *nothing,* and I can't fathom why you were ever allowed in the Consort Tourney. Especially when there were so many *pure* fae who should have taken your place."

Now I know it's not real. Rion would never say those things. The brief hurt evaporates because now I know he's just an illusion.

I keep my attention down, wondering if the fae behind the illusion can see me, or if it's a distant projection. Either way, two can play this game. I lift my eyes, feigning hurt, though I intend to rile.

"Prince Orion, I knew we could never be together for so many reasons," I begin, "but for the sake of our friendship, please don't pick Frost. She'll make for a small-minded queen."

As I expected, Pseudo-Rion's expression flashes to irritation. It is quickly hidden behind a sneer, but I shoved a verbal splinter under this fae's nail. Good.

"Frost understands what it takes to build a powerful kingdom," the illusion says. "She comes from a bloodline who knows sacrifice and loyalty."

"Sounds like she's your favored contestant," I say, fighting to keep the bite out of my voice while I prepare to press the splinter deeper. "What has she promised those who help her secure the crown? Does she not have a place in her court? Or is she a lower noble, tired of licking the boots of her betters?"

The illusion's expression shifts, and Rion looks at me in a way I never even imagined him. His frown twists and his eyes burn with hatred, every line deepening. The illusion has thinned, revealing a glimpse of who is behind the mask. The fake prince's features snap back into place, but he spouts shallow insults.

"You are less than dirt on the bottom of my—"

Stepping forward with swiftness, I move to shove him square in the chest and just as expected, my hands move through the apparition of the prince, dispelling his shadow image instantly and I nearly fall on my face.

I knew he wasn't real, but I can't help but feel a bit of relief at the confirmation.

Winter fae are known for their illusion—*shadow*—magic that can make fae see things that aren't really there. If I am seeing illusions, Didi and Princess Shay might see them too. I must get to them.

With no more hesitation, I take to the air rising above the blanket fog until I'm high above it. It's condensed to one area like the water stream was, but stretches to encompass the entire gardens. Beyond, I can clearly see the lavender fields and the Sea of Neptulus, but everything between it is covered, though it doesn't appear to push past the steps of the palace. Distant screams and shouts carry across the mist from the palace. Vines are flying up the walls and brief flashes of flames spark from inside some of the windows. I pray that Vejo keeps the innocent in the castle safe and turn my focus to those I can help below me.

Flying lower over the blanketed gardens, I watch for any sign of movement. Any flash of Didi's red hair, or the green of Princess Shay's skin, but the fog is still too dense. I'm about to give up and search for them back in the ground's obscurity when I hear a low voice. I dive lower to better hear it.

"Most males would happily marry any royal to raise their status..."

I don't recognize his voice.

"But you are just so *loathsome* in every manner, I couldn't bear the thought of being with someone so weak, so... pathetic."

The conversation is so out of place it must be another illusion.

"Even if it meant I could be a prince of the Winter Court," the male voice continues, followed by a cruel laugh.

I hover lower, close enough I could touch the black hair of the vampire hovering over a crouched figure heaped on the ground. Even from above, I can tell the vampire is attractive and charismatic. *Who is he?*

"I'm glad I escaped you and chose Beatrice as my mate instead," he says with a sneer. "Prince Orion won't pick you either and when you return—"

Charismatic or not, I've heard enough and in one swift motion, I land on top of the vampire's head, moving through his body as it dispels, and the illusion vanishes.

I realize it's the winter princess crouched on the ground with her hands covering her ears. Tears stream down her cheeks and agony creases her face, though her gaze is almost vacant. Lost. Seeing her so weak and broken tears at my half-human heart. *Did Princess Shay love this vampire? Does she still?*

"Princess Shay," I say, gently shaking her shoulders. "Princess Shay, he's gone. He wasn't real." Whoever he was.

But she doesn't snap out of her internal torture. *This goes deeper,* I realize. Getting rid of the illusion wasn't enough. The winter fae are also known for their hallucination magic. The ability to pull their victim into a vision-like trance and make them experience whatever horrors they wish. Whoever attacked the winter princess used *both*. I must pull her out of it before she's lost in her own version of hell forever.

"Shay," I say, gripping the sides of her arms tightly. "I know you don't particularly like me—in fact, I'm pretty sure you *hate* me, but I need you to listen to me right now." I dig my nails into her skin. A little physical pain might help. "You can pull yourself out of there, so just for once, pretend like you would rather see me, the halfling, the star fae, Amberle Kindra, than whoever that cruel vampire is."

Her head rolls back, and she lets out a guttural moan, so I shake her with more force. "No! Whoever he is, he's not worth it. You must return to reality, Princess, snap out of it! Feel the mud beneath us and the cold of the fog. Pull yourself out!"

I grind my teeth, thinking about what the illusion-vampire said to her before I stomped on him.

"Shay! You are strong and regal and definitely not *loathsome*."

"Then why did you choose her?" She whimpers. She's still lost inside her head talking to that loser vampire.

"Because he was a fool!" I say. "He was a coward who couldn't handle someone as powerful and self-assured as *Princess Shay Malov*! Forget about him and think about Prince Orion." My throat constricts, but I ignore it. "He would never say those things to you." The memory of watching Rion and the winter princess on their most recent date comes to mind. "The prince respects you and I think you have a very good chance at winning this whole thing." My voice breaks. Thankfully, she won't notice it.

"Prince Orion?"

"Yes!" Relief fills me. Finally, I'm getting through to her. "He doesn't think you're weak. He sees you as a formidable option to someday being the high queen of Faerie."

"High queen—" Her eyes fly open. She blinks several times, then tilts her head. "Amberle?"

I release my grip on the winter princess and fall back. "Yes."

She holds a hand to her head. "What—"

But then seems to remember.

"Winter magic." Is all I say, and she gives a halting nod in understanding.

"*Ah!* Thank *Vejo* I found you!" Frost says as she emerges from the mist.

I push to my feet, my knees shaking, putting myself between Frost and Shay. Frost is a noble, but I can assume the king invited her specifically because she's powerful. Powerful enough to create an ice wall, cast an illusion, *and* a hallucination. Before Frost can say another word, my hands are already curled into fists.

Forty-Nine

Amidst the obscurity of the fog, I can't tell if I'm staring at the real Frost or if I'm seeing another illusion. But I won't let my guard down. I keep myself between her and the still recovering winter princess crouched on the ground behind me.

"I thought you were protecting the prince," I say, keeping my stance wider than I normally would. I could attack and confirm I'm really looking at Frost, but I'd rather stall and give Princess Shay time to regain her senses.

"The prince is safe," she says, moving as if to help the princess to her feet.

I step sideways to block her. "You just left him?" I ask. "While we're being attacked?"

"Look. A very formidable guard showed up to protect him." Frost sounds annoyed. *Good.* But she pushes back a section of her white hair, feigning nonchalance. "She assured me he was in *very* capable hands and ordered me to get to safety."

"This isn't exactly *getting to safety*," I point out, gesturing at the ominous fog around us.

"I wouldn't leave behind the princess!" Frost lifts both arms in the air, exasperated. Every movement and expression are so very

Frost I'm almost certain it's her, but I let her continue. "I knew Princess Shay was out here, so I ran into the mist to find her. And I found her." She gestures at the winter royal with a hand, palm up.

"We've been attacked by illusion and hallucination magic," Princess Shay rasps from the ground, her voice small. "How do we know you're real?"

Frost's butterfly wings flick as she moves to step around me again, but this time I stop her by gripping her arm. It's solid. She's real. Keeping one arm on Frost to keep her at a distance, I reach back and extend my other hand for Princess Shay to take. Frost's skin bites with cold against my palm, but I hold her firmly away while Shay grabs my hand. I lean to help the princess stand, all while not taking my attention from Frost.

"I've dealt with the illusion magic too," Frost insists as I wait for Princess Shay to steady herself. She's shaky and weak. *Not good.* Especially while we're facing the enemy. It feels like an eternity, but I know only moments have passed when I finally release Frost and stretch my fingers, subtly pumping blood to warm my hand.

"Some powerful winters are among us," Frost adds, and for the first time, I notice a bead of sweat slip down her temple. *Powerful winters.* Like herself? "Come. Let's get out of this wretched garden."

"You still don't believe she's a part of it?" I whisper to the princess, gripping her arm to support her as we follow Frost. I hope to conceal Shay's exhaustion and pray she doesn't pull away from my help again.

"Why would she? She's helping us get out." Shay matches my low volume.

"Is something wrong?" Frost asks, turning back.

Princess Shay sidesteps away from me. "Yes. Amberle thinks this is all your doing." She still sounds doubtful. "She thinks you want me out of the competition, so you orchestrated this attack to take me out."

You're showing her our hand! I want to scream. How does she not see it?

"Frost is no fool. She'd know that an attack on me would put all contestants under scrutiny, including her," Princess Shay says to me. "Besides, Frost can't create fog or throw boulders."

"Exactly." Frost flips her hands palm up and smiles with false incredulity. "I also can't wield fireballs or shoot water."

"How did you know about the fire and water?" I ask, narrowing my eyes to hide my triumph. I might have caught her in her own words. "You weren't there when we were attacked by fireballs."

"It wasn't hard to guess, Amberle." Frost chuckles and links her arm with Princess Shay, then says something about the *simple minds of halflings* before looking back at me. "I could see the flames all over the palace grounds. And by the drowned look of the princess, it's not hard to guess that water was involved too."

Princess Shay won't meet my gaze as she limps slowly forward, leaning hard on Frost's arm.

"You had help," I argue, then hurry ahead of them to turn and speak to Princess Shay directly. "Look, I know you don't like me, but I overheard Frost say that she wants you out—"

"Amberle is so bent on accusing me of all this, could *she* be guilty?" Frost releases Princess Shay, causing her to stumble and fall back. Does Frost even notice? Or is she too caught up in her plan to pin the fault on me?

I itch to assist Princess Shay, but I don't think she'd take my help. I've laid out the truth and Shay still refuses to open her eyes and see the treacherous villain who just attempted to stab her in the back.

"Where would I have access to such a diverse group of *full* fae with powerful magic?" I ask Frost, briefly glancing at the winter princess behind her, who has a curious look of determination in her eyes as she rises back to her feet. "I have no family connections like the Niege's. I'm a *nobody,* remember?"

Frost's eyes flash briefly but turn cold again. Her attention focused on me. She doesn't notice when Shay slightly pivots, hiding her hand behind her back. But I can see what the princess is doing just fine.

"You're right." Frost's tone is full of venom. "There's no way you could have orchestrated this. Only a well-connected and clever fae could pull it off." She pauses, then she quirks a malevolent grin, and she says, "Perhaps *you're* the target. You and that other stupid halfling."

Didi. A spike of worry flashes through me.

"Perhaps—" Frost stops in her tracks, her eyebrows shooting upward in surprise, then she looks at her feet. Next to her, Shay still holds her hand behind her back, tiny sparks forming in her half-open palm, her fingers like claws around it.

Frost's expression changes, becoming unreadable, as she twists her hips to glance behind her. In a snap, Princess Shay whips her arm out from behind her, hurling what I now realize is a ball of ice bigger than my fist. It flies and smacks Frost on the side of the head, splintering on impact.

Frost collapses into the mud. Unconscious. But it's an awkward fall, her feet pulling up a chunk of wet earth and grass below them—Shay had frozen Frost's feet to the mud!

The princess falls to her knees. It's amazing Princess Shay is still coherent after creating *another* ice ball, but her breathing is ragged.

I rush to help her to her feet. "I thought—"

"Only Frost knew about Godfrey's rejection," she says with deep rattling breaths, then pushes my arm away and rises with her own power. "That's how I knew what you said was the truth. Frost was—*as she said*—the *unfortunate* fae who had to break the news to me that he'd chosen Beatrice over me. Luckily, no one else in the court knew of our secret, short-lived romance, so the humiliation and heartbreak were mine alone to bear."

She knew. So when Frost found us after the illusion, Princess Shay *pretended* she didn't believe me. I knew the winter princess was admirable, but that was incredible. Epic.

But I'm also heartbroken for her after witnessing that illusion of Godfrey and the effect it had on the princess.

"So, Godfrey." I prod. "Do you still..."

"Love him? No, it's been decades, but seeing his face even if it wasn't *him*..."

"Brought the feelings back?"

"The feelings of rejection, yes." She takes a deep breath. "There are still nine—" She glances at Frost. "Or *eight* contestants left in the Tourney, but I fear..."

Frost groans on the ground. She'll wake soon. I know what she fears, but we don't have time to discuss it.

"Come. We should go before Frost comes to," I say, gently pulling at the winter princess's arm.

She pulls away again and stands over Frost. "I must bind her better. I froze her feet to the ground, but thawed the earth enough that it wouldn't break her ankles as she fell. I should freeze the rest of her—"

"No! You'll render yourself unconscious. You've pushed yourself too hard."

Princess Shay turns to me and grips both of my arms with her hands. "No. We can't let her get away. I won't collapse."

"But Princess—"

The winter princess releases me and lifts her shaking hands above the prostrate Frost. Spider-web like cords of ice snake across Frost's body in a crisscross pattern from her head to her toes. When her body is covered, the cords thicken and freeze together until the traitorous winter noble is encased in a tomb of ice.

Princess Shay's hands drop and she sways. For a moment, I think she might walk under her own power out of this mist. But she crumbles to the ground.

I curse under my breath, quickly making a plan as I jump to Princess Shay's side. As I expected, she's unconscious but still breathing. *Thank Vejo.*

"I'll fly for help," I whisper to the winter princess as I squeeze her hand.

I release her and get into a crouch, preparing to fly above the mist, but the creaking whine of cracking ice stops me. My heart freezes mid-beat, dread crawling up my spine.

No. Frost is exhausted from her expenditure of power. Exhausted. She'll be dazed if not unconscious for at least a quarter hour.

As much as I tell myself it's impossible for Frost to wake up and melt Shay's work, I step toward the ice-cocoon and bend over to see better through the mist.

And one of her steely eyes snaps open.

Fifty

How *long does it take a winter fae to undo winter magic?* I consider as I shoot skyward above the mist. Frost is awake and I know she's spent a lot of energy, physical and magical.

But she's awake and Princess Shay is not.

I just pray the princess's ice trap lasts long enough that I can find help before Frost escapes and accomplishes her deadly goal.

Where is the watching winter magic? I wonder and reach out to sense for it. Maybe someone has seen the exchange and is coming to help? But, no, I feel nothing.

I scan the still thick fog, ignoring the stinging pain in my wings from the thousand small pieces of wood Princess Shay removed. They'd still be imbedded into my skin if it wasn't for her help.

I don't know who I'm hoping to find. Rion, obviously. And Didi. But I really need a palace guard. Frost said she left the prince with someone formidable and although I don't trust her word, I don't think he was the target.

He's safe. I tell myself.

Knowing enemies infiltrated the palace grounds causing the

carnage and chaos, if I call out for help and I'm found by the wrong fae, I won't survive. And neither will the princess.

But I'm out of options, blind and far from the palace. So I take the risk.

"Rion!" I scream, my voice bouncing back at me. Am I flying toward the palace? I think so. I press on, shouting Rion's name, praying he'll hear me.

Then the mist thins. I slow my pace, but my heart thrums. A water fae created the mist. Are they nearby?

The mist evaporates, pulled away and leaving a narrow strip of earth and sky clear. And I spot her. River. She gives me a respectful nod and the tightness in my chest lightens and I exhale. I can almost tangibly feel her powerful magic at the edge of the mist.

Perfect.

Can she reverse the magic further? Or even thin the fog? I fly down and land next to her, silent as she concentrates. Her hands are raised, and the fog is dissolving, slowly, further around us.

"This isn't how I want to win," River says, echoing what she said on the beach.

"Or maybe you don't want to win," I say.

The others, including River, don't know what's happened. They don't know about Frost's treachery. They couldn't have missed the fog, but most fae would have allowed us to perish, lost and pummeled by fireballs.

River shakes her head. "Oh, I want to win. By using my magic to defend an attack, it will only raise my status in the eyes of the crown."

"Okay, then. Can you do it faster?" I ask, then point. "And in that direction?"

She looks at me. "Look, it's not like liquid water—"

"Princess Shay is in danger and Frost needs to be stopped," I interrupt.

"Frost?"

"That direction." I point again and give her the short version.

River's already large eyes widen at the story as she works. I trust River, but the never flustered fae's response of surprise further confirms she wasn't a part of the conspiracy.

River takes a deep breath and begins lifting fog skyward. Moving it. She's changing tactic, speeding up her work. She'll get to Frost and Princess Shay soon.

Can River trap Frost more permanently, especially after her magical expenditure? Would Frost only need to freeze whatever water River throws at her? I need Frost's antithesis—a summer fae.

Flying back up, I'm still limited to a small perimeter, but from this angle I realize River has thinned the mist further out beyond the cleared space. I can almost see the outline of the palace behind us. A flash of a fire burst sparks east of where I left Shay and I fly directly toward it, hoping to see friendly faces.

The shadows of two fae move through the mist, so I take a chance and hover closer and see tossed walnut-brown hair. A thrill crackles across each nerve from my center to the tips of my wings. I stumble mid-flight, but quickly right myself.

It's Rion. And someone is with him.

Cutting through the fog, I land near enough to be seen.

She's on me just before I realize who she is. The planes of her face have always been sharp and jagged, but her skill with a blade —which is now at my throat—and her fealty to the High Court rivals no other fae.

Vedette, the Epoch Guard. I haven't seen or heard her name in more than half a century, but only because I haven't been in Isi Aura—or out of the shadows—for very long.

"Amberle," she says, removing the blade and stepping back. A trail of blood runs down her temple. Immense relief fills me, knowing this trusted guard is protecting the prince.

Rion rushes to me. His hands grip both shoulders and feel hot through the fabric of my sleeves as he inspects me for injury. "Are you hurt?"

I shake my head, but can't voice it because it's not true. But my wounds are nothing compared to what others are suffering and I don't want the focus on me.

"Frost is behind this attack, and she's about to kill Princess Shay," I say as I pull out of his grip and reach for his hand.

"What?" Rion gasps.

As I guide the pair, stumbling through the mist, I tell him and Vedette about Frost's actions. My heart is beating so hard, it pounds in my ears.

I nearly stumble over Frost, who is now sitting up, her attention on the last bit of the cage over her legs. Steps away, Princess Shay is awake, but laying on her side and groaning. The prince is next to her in an instant, checking her pulse.

"Is everything alright, Princess?" Frost asks, donning her facade again for the prince and Vedette. The last bit of her cage cracks and she kicks free.

She scrambles toward the princess, but before she can get too close, the Epoch Guard slams her foot down, blocking Frost's progression.

Frost looks at the prince with confusion, feigning innocence, then darts a glare at me. "Did she say I was to blame?" She turns back to him. "Don't you have some rule about the contestants turning on one another? Because Amberle is determined to sully my reputation—"

A look passes between the prince and the Epoch Guard. His hand is now on Princess Shay's shoulder, but he flashes a signal with his fingers.

An explosion of light momentarily blinds me, and I lift a hand to cover my face. Then I hear it. The buzzing, whirring sounds of light beams.

Living in the summer palace most of my life, I've seen this rare magic more than once. I know exactly what it is, and I'm immediately filled with fascination and trepidation.

When my vision clears, several luminous beams sprout from the ground, forming a symmetrical structure around Frost Niege. The radiant beams—thick as my forearm—converge to create four solid walls of dazzling, golden light, their brilliance and color reminiscent of the elusive light wisps. Each beam acts as a vertical bar, meticulously aligned to form a cage.

Opposite of shadow magic, light magic—summer magic—excels at trapping a winter fae.

Additional beams are arranged in a grid-like pattern and lay across the top, sealing off any escape from above—built to trap a winged fae like Frost.

The prince and the Epoch Guard hold their hands up, working in tandem, controlling the light magic and keeping Frost trapped inside.

Inside her new cage, Frost drops all pretenses. Her nostrils flare and her teeth now boast fangs that press against her lower lip. I pray the king will put her in the lowest reaches of the dungeon and lose the key because she's staring with pure hatred. At me.

Fifty-One

I want to run to him. I want to wrap my arms around him and never let go. To kiss him. I want to tell him that whatever stupid, foolish, *cowardly* reasons I thought we couldn't be together doesn't matter. That him being a royal and me being a nothing doesn't matter. That the Consort Tourney *doesn't matter.* That the king... to hell with the king.

But I don't.

My life was nearly snuffed out due to the evil scheming of a selfish winter fae who wanted the throne and whose objective didn't even bother to include me, except that I was in the way.

But my feet won't move.

Of course, Princess Shay leans heavily on his free arm while the other aids Vedette in keeping the light-cage at full strength. River is close by, moving more of the mist skyward. With everyone working and spent, it isn't the time for me to seek comfort from Rion.

But I want to.

After Frost is contained, Vedette sets off a series of crimson and silver fireworks into the sky to signal our location and request for additional guards. She's not taking any chances, and for that, I'm very grateful. Vedette's flares might also attract the enemy, but ever since Frost confronted me and Shay in the mist, the attacks have stopped.

"Perhaps I should take Princess Shay to the healers?" I offer, feeling restless and needing to do something useful—I need to stop pining and lamenting over the prince I can never have.

"The healers in the palace? You should see something first." River pivots, then swipes both hands outward, pushing aside the curtain of mist above and revealing the spires of the palace not far off. Wisps of smoke pour from several windows, but look like the tail end of a recently extinguished fire. River pauses her magic to turn to me. She looks fatigued, but nothing like Princess Shay. "The guards have pushed back the attack. It was almost over when I started clearing the fog. Whatever they were trying, it obviously failed."

"It makes sense," I say. "Frost and her followers needed a distraction. They needed Faerie to believe you were collateral damage, not the primary target. Otherwise, the investigators would've quickly homed in on the contestants and figured out Frost was nearby."

"Healers can't do much, anyway. I just need rest," Princess Shay says.

I try hard not to focus on the way she leans on him. "Are you sure?"

She smiles at me. Not in an annoyed, *can't be bothered to listen to a halfling*, smile. But in a weary, *I know you mean well, but I'm perfectly content leaning on the handsome prince's arm*, smile.

A smile one might give to a *friend*.

I nod, then look at Rion, who glances at me but doesn't smile, before he focuses back on the light cage. My heart splinters.

"I'll look for Didi," I say, then flick my wings to test their soreness now that the excitement-of-murderous-winter-fae has ebbed. They hurt, but not enough to keep me from flying.

"I'm sure she scurried away to an excellent hiding place," Shay says, clearly attempting to soothe me.

But I'm not assured. "I should still find her and tell her the threat is gone."

Shay doesn't protest more, and neither does Rion, or anyone else, so I crouch down to fly, but when I leap, I see it and nearly fall face first into the mud. At the edge of the newly cleared mist, only a stone's throw away from where we've been all along, I see familiar red braids sprawled in the dirt.

Didi!

Panic tears through my center and I rush to her while jagged fingers of dread dig beneath my ribcage and steal the air right from my lungs. She's laying lifeless, curled over herself.

"Didi!" I cry out, pushing her shoulders gently so she falls on her back.

The surrounding mist is immediately sucked away, and River soon falls to her knees right next to me. She supports Didi's head as it lolls to the side. My hands work without me thinking, wildly inspecting her for injuries.

Was she a victim of illusion magic? Has her mind been broken from the intrusive hallucinations? But then I feel it as I brush over her hand that clutches her middle. The space between her fingers is wet. Sticky. Covered in blood.

Carefully pulling her hand away, her palm is slick with more of it. And her dress...

"Oh, dear *Vejos!*" River shrieks at the sight. "She's dead!"

I can't breathe.

My name is Didi Beechriver. What's yours?

My vision blurs and I pull the spring star fae—my *friend*—upward as if embracing her will bring her back.

· · ·

I'm glad to meet you, Amberle. Aren't you excited to see who is chosen? Isn't this romant—

Didi gasps against my sleeve and everything comes back into focus. I loosen my grip and cradle her against my shoulder.

River sighs in relief. "She's not dead."

"You're not dead," I whisper and cover my hand over hers to help staunch the blood.

But Didi gives me a resigned look of sadness that freezes me to the core, colder than anything Frost could ever throw at me. In this life or the next.

"You're. Not. Dead," I say through gritted teeth.

"She needs a healer," River shouts over her shoulder to the prince. But none of them can fly.

"I'll get her to one." I say and don't let go as I push up from the ground and hold her tightly with every ounce of my remaining strength as we ascend toward the palace.

Fifty-Two

My wings scream as I push myself higher. My trajectory wavers as I strain to keep moving as warmth seeps against my torso. Beyond the fog line, the palace is a stark contrast to the crystal-clear blue sky. The palace is blackened and partially decayed on one side, malevolent smoke rising from the second floor. The grounds are a wreck, bushes stripped of their leaves and strewn across what was the lawn, but now is a muddy, unrecognizable mire. But the palace is silent. No cries of terror, no cacophony of magic clashing. I suspect the fighting is over; the time needed for distraction, over.

"Hold on, Didi," I growl through my teeth. My arms shake, but I won't let her go. I won't. "Just hold on. I'll get you to a healer and everything will be fine. *You're going to be fine.*" I feel like I'm assuring myself more than her.

I fly toward Kali Islandwort—my healer friend—but realize the royal healers are closer. Carrying Didi through the lower levels to reach Kali will take too long.

"Amberle, I should—"

"*Shhh.* Spare your energy." I grunt and suck in a breath, willing my arms to hold on. "We're almost to the royal healers."

"No!" Her anger surprises me. I glance down as her frown quickly turns to a wince. Sweat beads on her brow and she's pale. Too pale. Still, she continues. "Just a..." Didi mutters as her eyes cross. "Games."

"You can tell me all about the *games* after you've rested—"

"Amberle!" She pulls at my dress, jerking me to look at her again. "Spy!" She slips and I nearly drop her.

It takes three times as much effort to re-focus on my determination *not* to tumble from the sky. Thanks to my recent visit to have my wing healed, I know where to aim—the same floor as where the king resides. But unlike the smoke billowing below, the royal infirmary appears safe and intact.

Almost. There.

I slip through the balcony doors of the infirmary and fall to the floor, barely rolling over Didi after she lands hard on her back to avoid crashing on top of her. Then I lay there helpless for several excruciating moments as my muscles—my arms, my wings—twitch and burn and refuse to move.

My breathing roars in my ears, but I'm ready to direct the twin dark-haired elves to help Didi first. However, my expectation of the healers rushing toward us doesn't come.

I hear nothing.

When my muscles recover some, I push into a sitting position, but my eyes tell me immediately what my ears already did. The infirmary is vacant. There's not a healer in sight.

Of course. With an attack on the palace—whether distraction from Frost's actions or a direct attack—the healers will be scattered, busy helping others.

Turning to a half-conscious Didi, I crawl to her side.

"I'll be right back," I say, gripping her shoulder. Forcing her to look at me. "I'll find a healer."

Kali's children are star fae. She'll help Didi. I'll find her.

But Didi grips my arm with strength I didn't think she had and pulls me closer. "Don't go—"

"It'll be okay," I assure her, gently attempting to release her grip on me. "I'll be quick—"

"Amberle, listen!" She rattles.

I stop. Stunned by her ferocity and sudden lucidity, despite her ashen face.

"I'm fading. I feel it," Didi says. Not in terror or sadness, but factual, as if commenting on the weather.

I cannot ignore the crimson pool spreading beneath her. Did the flight make her injuries worse? "No—"

"Zzzt!" She silences me. "I must tell you this before..." She doesn't finish her sentence. "The contestants are pawns in this game, all hoping to be a queen." She eyes me, willing me to understand something unspoken. I feel the watching winter magic and sense her need to be cryptic. Games. Pawns. As a spy, I'm certainly a pawn in the king's game.

"But two are not pawns. Two cannot reach the other side of the board and become a queen. They are rooks." Didi points between her and I.

Wait.

No.

It's impossible.

"Yes," she says, her lungs rattling. "Here's what I've gleaned from my observations—"

"Later, Didi," I shush her. "You *must* allow me to find you some help." I don't care if she's deceived me this entire time. She absolutely *cannot die.*

"No. Just listen!" She pulls me closer. Harder. Then severs her volume. "Juniper wasn't killed out of jealousy or to aid a contestant's chances at winning the Consort Tourney."

Yes, I already know this.

"Juniper knew something, so she was silenced."

Yes, Wyn and I deduced there was some sort of secret. But my assumptions cannot be correct. Didi knows more than I expected of a mere Tourney contestant, but she cannot be the other—

"Of course, you know because..." Didi pauses. "You're the other spy in the competition."

My heart thrashes against my ribcage and my mouth forms an *O* that I cover with one hand.

"I'm not saying I'm a better spy than you." Her smile is weak but satisfied. "But my skills are varied, and I was careful not to make mistakes—" Didi sucks in a breath, bracing against an invisible wave of pain.

"Here's what you don't know. I know who silenced her."

I can hardly think between Didi holding onto my arm with a vice-like grip and my instincts blaring for me to get help.

"The royals," Didi whispers roughly.

I blink, stunned at the accusation.

"Amberle, you must do what you can to ensure—"

"No!" My throat knots and my voice catches. "Now we can work together!" I take her hand in mine and grip it tightly. "We can *both* ensure—"

The stomping beat of boots rushing into the room captures my attention and I snap my head to see Wyn coming. For a brief, imperceptible moment I have hope that a healer is with him, but he's alone.

Still, he can run for help.

"Wyn." I gulp down a steadying breath as relief fills me. "It's Didi. She's hurt. Go get help."

But his eyebrows furrow, and he approaches slowly as if he didn't hear me. When he kneels next to me and takes Didi's hand, he won't even look at me.

"Wyn! She needs help." I move to stand. I won't be as fast— but I must act.

Wyn grasps my arm, stopping me. "Amberle, it's too late."

"It's not, look she's still—"

But when I look at my friend—the spring fae who was the first to befriend me before any of this started, the one who forced me to act less like a spy and more like a contestant without my even realizing it. The one true competitor who helped me many times without revealing her secrets. Didi Beechriver, the star fae who should have been the one to end up with Prince Rion because of who she was and what she could have done for the star fae in all of Faerie—is gone.

The spark of light that glows from the eyes of all living is extinguished.

Fifty-Three

Posey answers another knock on my door, but I don't glance up to even acknowledge Gnacia. Is she early? I can't be bothered to track my appointments anymore.

I keep my chin in my hand as I gaze unblinking and unfocused out the window. Days ago, I hoped each knock would bring Rion to my chambers, but the endless visitors have only been inquisitors interrogating about the attack and Gnacia to prep me, then accompany me to each interview.

I've barely had a moment to grieve my fallen friend. Now I feel numb. Perhaps I have the endless questions to thank for shoving me into numbness.

"Amberle?" Posey asks, though we both know I don't have the choice to refuse Gnacia.

"I thought you said we were done for the day," I say to Gnacia without turning.

"Actually, it's the winter princess and the underwater contestant." Posey sounds chagrined.

I twist and see Princess Shay standing just outside my chambers with River by her side. Shay's tight curls hang loose and she's wearing a peach-colored dress that falls to her ankles and wrists. It doesn't have the usual adornments or baubles—and she isn't wearing any expensive jewelry or combs—that accentuate her station, but the fabric looks like it was picked with comfort in mind. It's not typical attire for the winter princess.

River's iridescent purple and blue dress has no sleeves, but the shiny material fits loose around her curves and resembles a nightgown.

The princess appears physically healed, but the drawn expressions and dark circles under their eyes reflect exhaustion I feel in my bones. I imagine they've been subjected to the questioning too.

I stand and beckon with a hand. "Let them in."

A slight smile forms on the princess's face as she and River cross the threshold into my room.

"I wanted to talk," says Princess Shay, then she turns to my maid. "Perhaps you could send for some refreshment?" But then she looks back at me with respect and deference. Posey is *my* maid. She isn't ordering Posey to do anything, but deferring to me.

"Yes, Posey, could you have the kitchens send something up?"

"What would you like?" she asks. But I'm weary of answering so many questions and cannot answer another, even inconsequential ones.

"Let the cooks decide," Shay suggests.

I nod to Posey, and she closes the door behind her.

Shay walks slowly around my chambers, taking everything in with hands clasped behind her back. River remains where she stands and watches her.

"All was not created equal in the Consort Tourney," Princess Shays says, mostly to herself.

"Well, since you're royal and I'm a star fae, I'm sure it's seen as fair."

"It was just an observation," she says with disapproval, then walks toward the window with purpose and studies it. She lifts her hands and cold winter magic spills through the room.

"What are you doing?" I ask, moving away from the sitting area and closer to River.

"I'm ensuring we won't be overheard."

The way River visibly relaxes matches the relief I feel on the inside. She entered with the winter princess, but clearly doesn't know the reason for this tête-à-tête between the three of us.

When the princess finishes with the window, she walks toward my door and performs the same magic.

"We can't be overheard in here," I say. "Our rooms are supposed to be free of the watching winter magic."

"After what happened, do you trust what we've been told?" Shay then brushes her hands together and walks toward the sitting area. "Still, you're probably right, but I'm taking precautions."

The princess sits in a plush chair, then gestures that River and I should join her. I take the seat across from her—I'm curious what she has come to say—but River merely moves to the wall beside me with her fingers laced in front of her.

"The Consort Tourney will not be the same." The princess begins.

Her statement feels obvious, but I suspect she knows more of the specifics. As a royal, she has insider knowledge that even River has no access to, and I would have to *steal* to obtain.

"My father, the winter king, wished for me to win the Tourney on my own merits and without assistance or *special treatment*. But now he feels he must intervene for my safety."

I glance at River, who doesn't move, then say, "That's understandable."

"Yes," Princess Shay continues. "Beyond our interrogations and interviews these past few days, I've also been in advisement meetings with my father and the winter council."

"Do they fear the ones responsible for the attack will strike again?" River asks with trepidation in her voice.

"No. The Onyx will probably go underground now that they've failed," says Shay.

"Failed?" River scoffs. "They sure made a mess of things, and one of us was killed."

"But their target was not," I say, meeting Shay's eyes, but she looks away.

"Wait…" River looks at us. "Who—" But she stops herself when she reads our silence. "The Onyx was after *Princess Shay?*" Her tone is in disbelief.

"*Frost* was after me." The princess adjusts in her chair to sit taller, failing to cover the way her voice tripped over the admission. Someone who was, at the least, an ally in her court and, at the worst, a friend who had betrayed her. "The Onyx comprises outlier fae. The ones who dislike or have fallen out with their respective courts. They are a jumbled group of fae from all over the realm with the design to create chaos and take down those in power. Typically, the underlings, the ones who do the grunt work, are the ones hurt while the powerful members are protected. But this time they took a tremendous risk and used the Niege family's aspirations as a cover to go after the high king."

"But I don't understand. Is Frost a member of this *Onyx?*" River asks.

"It's unclear whether they've been entangled with them for long or if this was their first mission," Shay says. "But either way, this was a massive blow for the group. They'll be back someday, but they won't be a problem for a long time."

"How can you be so sure?" I ask.

"They're fae," River answers this time, her voice quiet with understanding. She glances at me with almost a pitying look. "While star fae may not have the luxury of time, the full fae can wait hundreds of years. They'll wait and see what happens after the Tourney before they even *begin* to plan their next move."

"So if the Onyx are no longer a threat in the Tourney, then why does the winter king see the need for extra protection?" I ask.

The winter princess inhales deeply, somberly, then looks between us with heaviness. Something I imagine only a royal can feel. "Because we never suspected the Nieges. But now that their plot has been foiled, we are even less sure of who we can trust."

"You keep saying the *Nieges*," I point out. "You mean her family?"

"Yes. They were all involved."

"Fae will go to great lengths to win a crown." River points out.

"Their aim was higher than that," the princess says. "Once Frost eliminated who she thought was her greatest competition—me—she had only to win the rest of the Tourney, then become the consort princess. If the king had also been killed, she would become the consort queen."

"So *saving* Prince Orion would have won his heart," River adds, tapping her chin. "And the Onyx wanted a puppet queen—Frost."

"After that, she only needed to end my father to become queen of the Winter Court *and* the high queen of Faerie."

River straightens, her arms dropping to her side. Princess Shay rises from her chair and walks to the window. She looks out with her back toward us.

"Prince Orion would never agree to that," I argue. "He would never allow her to just kill your father."

"Who says he'd have to know about it?" River asks.

"He'd stop it. He wouldn't let it happen." I know he wouldn't do such a thing himself, but if his queen went behind his back... River has a point.

"There's more," Princess Shay's tone has changed. It sounds like she's hiding emotion. "We believe she might've also ended the prince. With or without Onyx's permission, she'd become High Queen of Faerie and elevate the Winter Court as the high court."

My blood turns to ice, the truth of the horrifying plot hitting me deep in my gut. I warned Gnacia and Rion of Frost's machinations, but this is more than I ever expected. In her thirst for power, she plotted the cold-blooded murder of the High King, Princess Shay's entire family, and Rion. For me, the stakes were always about my father. But this wasn't just about the Consort

Tourney. It was a massive, bloody chess game for the throne. Just like Didi warned.

"My father thinks Juniper was killed because she learned something about Frost's plot."

He's wrong. The truth shouts at me. *But should I tell her?*

I told the truth to Gnacia and the king, Wyn and Rion. But what good did it do? They didn't trust me. They didn't listen to my advice to send her away. What if I trusted my fellow contestants?

I feel a connection to both Princess Shay and River, a bond created out of terror. We already risked our lives to save each other. My mind reminds me of all the betrayal and lies pushing away from trusting anyone. But yet I *do.* I trust these two fae. Or, at least, I'm willing to give them a chance.

"Frost didn't kill her. Neither did anyone connected to her." The winter princess turns around to face me. I feel River's eyes on me, too.

"I overheard Frost talking to one of them once." I don't mention it was at the revel—the long timeline would invite too many other questions. "They didn't know who killed Juniper, and Frost said it wasn't her."

The royals... Didi's words echo around my skull, but I can't think about that now. Or her.

"Then her murderer is still out there," says Shay, nodding.

"And we have no idea who did it," River adds.

Silence falls over the three of us for several moments before River asks, "Why us?"

"What do you mean?" Princess Shay asks.

"Why are you telling us? Amberle and me?"

Princess Shay waves a hand like it should be obvious. "Without the two of you, Frost might have achieved her goal. You were the only ones brave enough to stand up to Frost and the Onyx."

"And Didi," I say quietly.

"Yes! And Didi, of course." She agrees. "But the others—

Princess Mora, Lady Pepper, Tierney, and Cerule—hid away as quickly as they could. And while I don't blame them for sparing themselves, you two saved me." Her tone has a reverent timbre to it. "I've earned a great respect for *you*." She speaks to both of us, but only looks at me. Almost singling me out. "I feel immense gratitude and as a boon in return, I decided to share with you what I know."

The door handle turns, and Posey walks in with a tray of refreshments. River finally sits on the chaise to my right.

Princess Shay takes her seat across from me again and says, "And... I trust you."

I'm amazed at how quickly the winter princess's opinion of me has changed. She's gone from looking at me as if I'm not even worthy of being in the same room, let alone being an 'equal' in the Consort Tourney, to respecting me.

Trusting me.

It's too bad I'm leaving.

Fifty-Four

Posey and Kenna layer expensive make-up on my face, magically erasing the splotchy marks and dark circles. My hair is coiffed, and my nails painted for tonight's *special ceremony*.

Tonight, King Estelar will address Faerie and make some speech about the attack, assuring Faerie that the culprits—namely Frost and her family—are imprisoned and will be punished. I'm sure he'll say something on the verge of kindness about Didi to appease her family and the star fae. And despite the recent chaos, there will be an Invitational for the remaining Tourney contestants.

Because something as violent as an attack on the palace—and on the winter princess—isn't enough to put a hold on the momentum of the competition.

Which is why I must sneak away and speak with Gnacia. *Before* tonight. I can easily remove my necklace and signal to the prince to send me home, but I must confirm that I fulfilled my bargain. I haven't broken my and Rion's heart and risked my life just to bolt for the door. Gnacia agreed to let me go when six contestants remain. With Didi and Frost gone and my insights on the remaining contestants, I can leave.

In fact, staying only increases the danger for me and my father. Besides, as much as I hate it, Rion needs to move forward with a fae he can actually choose.

As Kenna curls loose pieces of my hair with a hot iron, I run through what I know of each contestant and my arguments about which would be the best to win the crown.

Lady Pepper is—

A confident knock at my door interrupts my thoughts. My heart dances.

Rion?

Posey opens it.

Not Rion. It's Wyn.

But my rapid pulse doesn't ease because his expression is grave.

"Wyn?"

"Will you come with me?" he asks. It's not an order, it's almost a pleading. "It's the prince. He needs you."

Wyn's stride is long, and I'm forced to use my wings to speed my steps to keep up with him.

"What's wrong?" I ask when we're away from my maid's listening ears.

His only answer is a clenching and unclenching of his teeth. "Since the attack, Orion..."

"Orion *what?*" Panic leaks into my voice. "Wyn!" I pull his arm, forcing him to slow and look at me.

But his eyes fidget away.

"Tell me what's wrong, Wyn," I plead. *Tell me what I'm walking into.*

He finally turns to me, then does something I didn't expect. He pulls out his piece of flint and strikes it against the wall. The blue fire creates a bubble of protection, expanding and surrounding us like it did once before, and I know it will make us invisible to anything and anyone outside it.

The mere act of using this special fire magic increases the coiled-up tension inside of me. I have to remind myself to breathe.

When we're completely obscured, I look at him again, hoping that Wyn will tell me what's happening with the prince. But the tightness and worry behind his eyes tear at my insides. Wyn's jaw pumps again before he says. "Just trust that he needs you."

He says nothing more and gestures that we continue walking, the blue fire staying around us.

We pass two guards as we enter the royal wing, and they stare straight past us. Just like Princess Shay's shadow magic. That reminder sends a shudder of concern skittering across my skin. What is so important that Wyn is taking me to the prince's chambers while keeping us hidden?

But when we reach the stairwell, he leads me down. Not up to the royal residences. When we reach the ground level, I expect him to veer toward the exit. Perhaps the prince is in the gardens—no, maybe the lavender fields? Or the shore? But Wyn veers the other direction toward the back of the palace and to the pathways that lead to the lower levels.

Not the lower residential levels, like where servants live, such as Kali. But the secure lower levels. The ones that lead... to the dungeons.

The need for the fire magic suddenly makes sense, but air steals from my lungs as I contemplate what possible reason *Prince Orion Illuminae* would be in the dungeons. I open my mouth to say something, but Wyn—perhaps expecting my need to speak—shoots me a look that silences even my thoughts. Deep creases of worry line his brow and his eyes are filled with such cavernous pain, the sight of it causes my insides to ache with wretched human emotion I don't even know the reason for. I fold my arms tightly against my chest and pull my wings firmly against my back to keep myself from breaking apart.

What is so wrong with Rion?

Vedette, The Epoch Guard, meets us at the entrance to the dungeons. I expect us to pass her, but the flame extinguishes. We aren't subjected to a tongue lashing. Instead, Vedette seems to breathe with relief.

"Were you followed?" she asks Wyn.

"No," he says with an incredulous tone.

"Are you certain, Wyn?" She steps toward him, her voice stern. "No one. Not a single fae can know about this. Are. You. Sure?"

I feel for any watching winter magic, but feel no tingle or buzz. It's not here.

"I'm sure, Vedette."

"Good," she says, then looks at me and her expression softens. "I'm glad you agreed to come."

"What has happened?" I ask, clinging to Vedette's stern demeanor over to Wyn's quiet panic. This *hurts*. Whatever it is. "*Please*. Tell me what's wrong."

Vedette presses her lips together and glances at Wyn, but he shakes his head ever so slightly I almost miss it.

"Follow me," she says, then turns and unlocks the main door to the dungeons and leads us both inside, bolting the door behind us.

Silently, we pass mostly empty cells as we venture farther into the dungeons. My stomach knots. I feel sick when we turn a corner and continue to descend even lower. And when I realize the direction we're heading, my hands sweat, and my heart thrashes against the walls of my chest. We're traveling to the deepest parts of the prison.

Toward the oubliettes.

No.

My feet stop, and I cower away from both Wyn and Vedette.

Is it a trick? Are they throwing me into the oubliette again? I can't. The five weeks I spent in the pit as a youngling still haunt my nightmares. I can't go back to one of those again. I... my breathing hitches in sharp, shallow gasps as I recount the exact words Wyn used to draw me here.

It's Orion. Wyn had said. *He needs you.*

He *needs* me. Did I misinterpret? Wyn didn't say he needed to see me, or that he needed to talk to me, just that he *needs me.* Does he *need me* to disappear? Does he *need me* out of the Tourney immediately?

Does he *need me* thrown into an oubliette? A place... to be forgotten?

And would he use his friend—*my* friend—to do it?

I step back, fluttering my wings, ready to fly if necessary.

When Wyn and Vedette realize I'm no longer following, they turn, and I read immediate regret on Wyn's face. Vedette looks to him in confusion and my friend slowly shows his open, empty palms.

"Amberle," he says with a calming tone, as if soothing a frightened animal.

I step back again, pulling my hands away from his reach and shake my head violently as my eyes burn with unshed terror.

"No, no, no," I say. "*Please* tell me what is happening, Wyn. Please don't tell me you're taking me to—" My throat tightens. "Please. I'll leave. I'll disappear. I'll never—"

"*Amberle.*" His smile is both reassuring and tormented at once. "*Orion* is in the oubliette. I was afraid if I told you where he was, you'd refuse to come."

"Rion? But—" My mind refuses to understand, so I look to Vedette for an answer.

"Prince Orion put himself there," she says. "After the culprit was secured, he... disappeared."

"And Vedette found him there," Wyn finishes.

All this time... Every agonizing second of every interrogation, every sleepless night of mourning my lost friend, every stern look and snapped word from Gnacia...

He was here during all of it?

"Why?" I rasp.

"He's punishing himself," Wyn says with a muted tone.

I blink back tears and stand straighter. "And he asked for me?"

Wyn glances at Vedette, then turns back and shakes his head. "If he knew we brought you—"

"Where is he?" I step forward. "Which one?"

Without hesitation, Vedette beckons with her hand, and I follow close behind. We move toward the lowest part of the dungeon, and I note that the sconces of light are spaced farther and farther apart the deeper we go—as all lower levels of the palace are designed. Vedette ignites a small fire-orb in her hands to light our way, but it burns like a lit candle at the end of the wick in danger of going out at any second as the oppressive darkness encompasses us.

I know her magic is strong enough to keep it brightly burning, but I can't help but wonder if the diminishing light is by design. To keep us obscured from the prisoners we pass, perhaps? Or more likely, some rule about the amount of light allowed in the Summer Court dungeon.

When we reach a heavy door of iron bars, Vedette slips on a pair of leather gloves to protect her skin, then pulls out a ring of metal keys from a small satchel. She inserts, then turns the key with a heavy reverberating *clank*, then swings the door inward, the hinges whining from disuse.

The oubliettes.

The lowest corridor in the palace.

The place where prisoners are sent to be forgotten.

A wave of sensations assaults me, starting with the stale, mold-filled darkness. I breathe through my mouth to keep from retching all over the dirt-packed floor. The air is humid, and the darkness is heavy, and it clings to me like the tentacles of a thousand black octopi ready to consume my flesh.

My pulse surges again. My hands and the back of my neck turn slick with sweat—

. . .

"Get in there!" Captain Shinyfleck shoves me through the iron door before it's all the way open. I cry out when my arm grazes the metal and is instantly singed. If I were full fae, the burn would be worse, but the thought doesn't lessen my pain. I trip over my feet since my wings have been tied to my back and I can't catch myself.

A wretched sob escapes my lips as he pulls me to my feet again, but I bite my tongue hard to quelch it. I won't let them see me cry.

Gritting my teeth, I ask with as much gumption as I can muster, "Does my father know you're throwing me in the oubliette? You know you must notify a family member!"

"You'll be out by this time tomorrow," the captain growls with annoyance. Like I'm a pesky tiny pixie looking to steal a crumb at a summer picnic. "You can tell him then."

"But my father is leaving with the king tonight! They're traveling to the human realm and there's no telling how much time will pass here before they return! It could be a fortnight or even a year!" I try but fail to hide my panic.

I know how the oubliette works. A prisoner is rarely let out when their sentence is over. If they're lucky, a family member or friend reminds those in power that they should release a fae from the pit of forgetting. If there is no one to remind them, then they're left to rot. A star fae would eventually die after several centuries. A full fae would likely live until a millennia passed, and the ruins of the dungeon finally crushed them.

I feel no comfort in being a star fae, but the worst part is thinking that any day could be the day of salvation. And the salvation never comes.

"Amberle?" Wyn touches my shoulder softly. "Are you okay?"

I shake off the memory while shaking off his hand. "Being here just brings back bad..."

Even in the dim light, I can see that he understands. "I'm

sorry. He won't listen to me or Vedette and we don't want anyone else…"

Now I'm the one touching his arm in comfort. "Which one?"

Wyn points into the darkness. "The furthest one."

My pit.

Fifty-Five

There are only three oubliettes, but they are spaced with enough distance in the long, narrow hallway that the screams of one cannot be heard by the others for maximum isolation.

"I'll walk with you," Wyn says and cups one hand upward to take the Epoch Guard's fire orb—that she has changed from pale yellow to blue. It hovers just above his palm.

Vedette secures the door and stands in front of it as we walk into the darkness.

"How did you find Rion here?" I ask after we've passed the first pit. It's covered by a heavy metal plate with only a small opening for air that gleams dull in the fire's light.

"It took a few days, but Vedette discretely employed a winter fae to use the watching magic to locate him. When she couldn't convince the prince to climb out of the pit, she sent for me." Wyn pauses and exhales deeply.

I feel again for any lingering winter magic, but I feel nothing.

Wyn continues, "I thought with enough of my charm and wit —and a bit of time—that he'd snap out and see the foolishness of putting *himself* in a pit. When Gnacia began looking for him to prepare for tonight's events, we knew our time was up and we had to find the one person who might snap him out of it."

"And you think *I* can convince him?" I don't look at Wyn. It's too dark to even try, despite the bit of light he's holding to light our way.

Wyn doesn't respond for several long, heavy moments. "The oubliette was your punishment and... he's in love with you. He'll hate me for bringing you into this, but he must get over it."

We fall into silence and pass the second oubliette. I cannot see the metal cover through the darkness, but the dull pounding from the inside tells me it, too, is occupied. I fold my arms tighter against my chest and press my wings harder to hold back the shudder that wants to wrack my whole body.

As we approach the third oubliette—the one Rion is in— Wyn covers the light orb with his free hand, obscuring it until only tiny slivers of light escape through the spaces between his fingers.

Wyn gently nudges me with his elbow, urging me to continue forward. The terror and the anticipation of willingly climbing down into an oubliette and standing in front of Rion—even if he can't see me—causes my heart to throw itself so violently against my ribcage, I fear it will burst through.

So I press a hand against my chest and breathe deeply. *Willing* my heart to control herself.

Then I step forward.

I can barely make out the edges of the pit, but see it just enough that I don't trip and fall into it. This one is wide open. The metal plate discarded and shoved far away until the next unfortunate fae is brought here to be forgotten.

The hole isn't terribly deep. As a youngling, I couldn't reach the top. But the guards had simply lowered me with their arms, so I knew I could drop myself down now. A fully grown fae prisoner could probably touch the top—and be burned—by the secured metal plate.

When my toes are at the edge, I close my eyes and inhale

deeply, pushing back the nausea that threatens to render me useless in speaking to the prince.

Then, I leap.

My wings extend, but it's a short drop and I land hard on my feet.

The darkness is complete, but I remember the small space. Even if Rion presses himself against the far wall, I could reach out a hand and touch him before my arm is fully extended.

I listen for his breathing, but hear nothing. Surely, he knows someone is here. After spending a few days in this pit, the *silent* approach of Wyn and me would've sounded like a stampede of wild cabyll ushteys to his deprived ears.

I jolt when he speaks. My stomach does too.

"Go away, Wyn," he growls.

"Rion—"

"Amberle?" His voice breaks.

Without thinking, I step forward and reach for him. One hand finds his arm, but the other slams into his chest. I move it to grip his other arm. "Rion, why are you in here?"

He tries to pull away, but in this small space, he has nowhere to go but up.

"They said you're punishing yourself?" I hear my pained, disbelieving tone, and I squeeze his arms tighter.

He releases a shuddered breath. "No one else will."

"Because you've done nothing *wrong*. Rion, the attack wasn't your fault—"

"But I could have stopped it." His voice hitches and a strangled sob escapes, tearing at my insides. Leaving them ragged and burning.

Without thinking, my hand shoots up to cup his face. Hot tears run through my fingers and slip past my thumb.

"I could have sent her home sooner," he says, covering his hand over mine to hold it there. "*You* warned me about her."

"You had no way of knowing what Frost was capable of," I whisper, brushing my thumb across his damp cheek. "You cannot blame yourself." I imagine even if he wanted to send her home sooner, they wouldn't have allowed it.

"First Juniper. Now Didi..."

He aches for them. I hate that it hurts me to hear that he aches for them. I try to slip my hand away, but he holds it tighter.

"It could have been you."

I reach my other hand up to cup the other side of his face and pull myself closer. "But it wasn't."

I sense the motion of his face leaning toward me and I fear he's about to kiss me, but instead I feel the soft pressure of his forehead pressed against mine. My eyes close, though it doesn't matter in this absolute darkness.

His warm breath mingles with mine in the small space between us, and I revel in our closeness and privacy. But if I allow this proximity for much longer, he'll kiss me. Or I'll kiss him.

So I pull back, breaking the moment.

The action causes a flood of my instincts begging me to flee this place. Neither of us should be here. It does no good for anyone. And if the prince misses his father's address, he'll pay for it—in one way or another.

"You have a job to do," I say. "*We* have a job to do."

"The Invitational." He pulls away, far enough that my hands drop.

"Yes." I hope he doesn't hear the disappointment in my voice. "Everyone is expecting you."

He doesn't respond. His silence falls so heavy and abruptly, part of me wonders if he was ever in this pit at all, or if I've succumbed to hallucinating.

"The attack isn't the only reason I'm here."

I don't dare guess what he means, but I say, "Everyone makes mistakes, Rion."

"Not everyone makes mistakes that lands someone you care about into a pit of forgetting."

Now I fall into silence.

"Let alone the fae you've been in love with your entire life."

Entire life. The admission takes me by surprise, and I recoil, knowing how much I hated the prince as a youngling. I avoided him. Dreaded our interactions.

Without a word, Rion gently wraps his hands around my waist and lifts me out of the pit. Despite the warmth of his hands, I know there's a barrier between us built of shared history and hurts. Wyn grabs my arms and pulls me up, then my wings do the rest of the work.

After being in total darkness, seeing Wyn with the blue fire orb suddenly illuminates the entire space and I see Wyn's concern. For a moment, I wonder if Rion will refuse to follow. But he grunts as he hoists himself up and out of the oubliette.

When the prince passes us on his way out, Wyn and I scurry after him and Vedette. The prince uses long strides to speed ahead. He's clearly done talking.

"I told him not to send her home," Wyn admits when the prince is far ahead.

"What?" I slow my pace and Wyn does too.

"Frost. He knew Frost was dangerous, and I told him to keep her."

"You can't blame yourself, either. They wouldn't have let him send her home, no matter what you said."

"You might be right."

"I am," I say.

Wyn frowns. "Amberle, no one can know about this," he says. "Not the other contestants, not your maids, not Gnacia, and especially not the king. As the crown prince—as the *high prince*—no one can know where Prince Orion has been."

"I know. I won't say a word."

"Good. Now I must escort you to Gnacia."

"Gnacia?" Why? I've already told her everything she wanted to know! What does she want now? "Did she say why?"

Fifty-Six

Wyn escorts me in silence. I sense the winter magic watching us now, following us through the corridors until we reach Gnacia's office and the door closes, shutting it off again. Ever since the attack, I've felt it infrequently and only in the rebuilt, common areas of the palace. I've grown accustomed to the lack of it, so now it feels heavy each time I sense it. I breathe easier whenever I can escape it.

The king's secretary sits behind her cherry wood desk with perfectly arranged hair that curls around her horns. Her mouth forms a rigid, straight line, but her hands are empty, clasped together and resting on her desk as if she's been sitting here, waiting for me to arrive for ages. I imagine that's exactly what she's been doing.

Gnacia levels an irritated gaze at me.

"Amberle's tardiness is my fault," Wyn says. "She was... assisting."

"And your task?" Gnacia asks him, sounding doubtful and narrowing her eyes.

"The prince is in his chambers now, readying for tonight."

"Then I'm sure he could use your help," she says, dismissing him with a flick of her wrist.

Wyn was so adamant about my discretion that I'm almost certain Gnacia doesn't know the specifics. Only that the prince was unavailable or unwilling to take part in tonight's planned events, but now he'll play along.

Wyn nods once, then leaves us.

Gnacia unlocks, then opens a drawer and pulls out a document. The paper looks heavier and more expensive than the menus and correspondence stacked on the corner of the desk. And decorating the top shines a gold emblem. The royal insignia.

"Is that..."

Gnacia smiles. "It is."

I suck in a breath. That piece of paper is the key to my father's release. His pardon. With that, he'll be free and we can leave. Tonight.

"But it's not valid until signed by the king, so don't even think about stealing it," Gnacia adds. "I'm afraid it will be some time before I can make that happen, though." She slips it back into the drawer and locks it again.

"What?" I step forward. "I gave you can give you information about each contestant. I've done my job!"

"There's not—"

"I'll even tell you again! Lady Pepper will say yes to whatever you ask, which you should love. She'll never be more than a pretty face, but she's no danger to the prince. Tierney is the opposite. She dislikes the prince and would only set her sights on her own position and power."

"Amberle—"

"Cerule wouldn't be the worst." I run over her words. "She's clearly in love with the prince. And Princess Mora cares for him, but I *beg* you not to let him choose her."

Gnacia stands and lifts a hand. "You must understand—"

I step back. "River is promising. She cares enough about Prince Orion and is compassionate and brave. She helped when the Onyx attacked."

Gnacia frowns, but doesn't interrupt again.

"But Princess Shay cares about the royal family. She understands the duties. She is the best option. There." I take a breath. "I've gathered information about the contestants, I've fulfilled my side of the bargain, now if you will please—"

"We cannot let you go." Gnacia speaks softly, but she might as well have sentenced my execution. "You must know that Didi Beechriver..." She pauses, perhaps feigning to care about my feelings and my grief over my fallen friend. "Well... Didi was the other—"

"The other spy," I finish, wishing I had a glass of water or something to cover the sudden bitter taste in my mouth. "Yes, I know. She told me right before she died in my arms."

"And because we've lost our other spy, you understand setting you free is not feasible right now."

"Not feasible? With Frost arrested and Didi dead, there are only seven contestants, including myself," I say, frustration building in my chest. "We agreed I could leave before the contestants are down to six. It's dangerously close to the interviews of the final five!"

When Gnacia doesn't speak, I walk closer to her.

"Neither of us want me in the *extensive* interviews!" I say, thinking back to the interview with Nieven Morphyra on the ship and how intrusive that felt. I can only imagine his digging into the lives and past of the final five will be tenfold more difficult. And I doubt there will be a sea full of lemons to jump into to escape the questioning.

I try *not* to think about the thrill I feel at being forced to stay in the competition longer, nor the powerful urge I feel to make certain Rion won't do anything else as drastic as throwing himself into an oubliette again. The sooner I leave, the less it will hurt. It's for the best. And Wyn can watch out for Rion.

The faun seems to chew on my words. In case she's unconvinced, I press harder.

"I warned you about Frost and you did nothing," I say. "I told you she was conspiring and yet she was allowed to remain in the competition."

"We lured her cohorts out and unveiled the extent of Frost's family's treachery."

"But most of the Onyx escaped, and... a fae lost her life." Emotion bleeds into my voice, but I don't care to stop it. I'm a star fae with human tendencies and I lost a friend. I don't know if it will sway Gnacia's decisions, but perhaps she'll relent, if only to stop my crying. "Who's saying you'll listen to me again? Even if I stay on and keep being your little spy?" I make sure my eyes are clear when I look at her and add my last—my best—argument, "You promised me I could leave before six were left."

Gnacia stares at me again for several moments. Fae put themselves first. She dug her own grave with our bargain, and she'll jump in if she doesn't fulfill it. She won't risk the consequences if she breaks it.

The faun unlocks the drawer again and pulls out my father's pardon. "I'll speak with the king and advise him to send you home. But I cannot guarantee he will listen. My bargain was to *speak* with the king about letting you go when six remain."

A flutter that is both joyful and heartbroken steals my breath.

"*If* the king agrees, I'll have the advisors recommend to Prince Orion to send you home."

He will. The king wants me gone. I'm a pebble in his silken shoe.

"Okay. Just... is there a way for you to prepare me?" I ask. I need to know if I should remove my necklace or not. My signal to Rion. "I'd rather not be surprised."

Gnacia nods. "I'll give you a sign."

Fifty-Seven

RION

I might be summer fae, but after so many days in the oubliette, I keep my eyes shut against the painfully blinding light of my chambers.

Snip. Snip.

My father ordered the royal healers to attend to me—despite my protests. He didn't care where I'd been, just that I looked haggard and frightful and that it needed to be remedied before tonight. The healers left an hour ago after imbuing me with strength I don't deserve. Of course, I said nothing about where I'd been and even if a healer could do something about light sensitivity, I wouldn't want their help.

Snip. Snip.

A light knock sounds at my door. I ignore it, but a guard marches to check it anyway.

"Let me in, Orion." Wyn's voice is muffled from outside the room.

My eyes open, but I must squint. I glance at the guard at the door, who looks at me expectantly. I signal that it's okay to let him in—Wyn is persistent, so there's no use denying him. He crosses the threshold and reaches me in three strides.

"Why are you here?" I ask, closing my eyes again.

Snip, snip.

"Who ordered the hair trim?" Wyn avoids my question as the irritatingly itchy pieces of my clipped hair fall past my ear.

"Gnacia," I say.

Wyn chuckles and the autumn fae continues cutting.

"Tonight must go smoothly," I sing the phrase I've heard from both my father and Gnacia more than once and open one eye to look at Wyn.

He frowns, then walks to my balcony and pulls the curtains closed. It helps a little and I'm able to open both eyes without too much discomfort. It's a small thing, but I know the real reason he's here. He wants to discuss what happened. Why I hid in the dungeon and why I refused to get out. But I'm not in the mood to talk.

"As you can see, Wyn, I'm getting ready for tonight," I say. "I don't need you here."

"Say the word and I'm gone," he says, but knows I won't.

There's another knock on the door and my advisors enter.

"Leave us," says Alden Fireheart with his ostentatious fire-colored wings. He's followed by Silva Mistdancer, who glides into the room behind him.

"I'm finished anyway," says the autumn servant who trimmed my hair. She waves a hand over the clippings on the floor, decaying them into dust. Then she walks out.

Alden nods toward my guards—who were ordered by my father to monitor me—hinting that I send them away too.

"Wait down the hall," I tell them, then stand and clap a hand on Wyn's shoulder, barely keeping the sarcasm from my voice. "Wyn will protect me."

They leave and close the door behind them.

Alden glances at Wyn, then back at me. "The halfling really should leave—"

"He's staying," I interrupt. "He can hear whatever you have to say."

"Fine." Alden lifts both hands—but keeps an expression of disapproval— then looks to Silva.

He's not usually hesitant to follow my orders. That one small look speaks volumes.

"Can I finally cut Lady Pepper?" I ask. "I cannot abide her a moment longer."

Alden nods. "King Estelar wishes for exactly five contestants to remain after tonight's elimination. With the treachery of Frost Niege and the death of the star fae—"

"Didi Beechriver," I snap. "Her name was Didi."

"Of course. With the two of them out, there are seven contestants left, which means that *two* must be eliminated tonight."

"Two..." I nod and grip my chin. "Lady Pepper and a fae of my choice?"

"Your Highness, Lady Pepper *is* your choice." Alden pauses and I expect him to suggest I whittle the Autumn Court down to one contestant. Cerule, probably. "The other fae you're strongly encouraged to eliminate tonight... is Amberle Kindra."

I narrow my eyes. This time it isn't because of the light.

"The half—the *star* fae has served her purpose," says Silva, stepping forward and eyeing Wyn before looking back at me. "It's time for her to go."

"You're dismissed," I say and lift a hand when Alden tries to explain further.

Without another word, they shuffle out of the room, leaving only Wyn and me in my chambers.

I move toward my wardrobe and pull it open, riffling through my tunics to find a proper one for tonight.

"Amberle?" Wyn says. "Will you really send her home?"

I pause on a pale blue shirt for a moment, but continue flipping through them. "They are merely my advisors for the Tourney. Their suggestions are not absolute."

Only Amberle can determine when she leaves. I promised her that. But I push down the sinking feeling that I'll watch Amberle take off her crystalized sunbeam tonight.

"But they come from the king."

I nod at my wardrobe.

"You would send her home after everything?"

I can't tell if he's angry, but whip around to him. "After everything she's endured, I imagine she *wants* to be free of me!" He doesn't argue, so I continue. "She was in that damned oubliette for *five weeks* when we were younglings, Wyn. *I* did that to her."

"And that's why you threw yourself into it?"

"Yes…. No… The attack was *my* fault—"

"Your *advisors* had information about Frost and none of them, nor I, advised you to send her home!" He walks toward me. "Orion, no one knew what she was capable of. No one knew she was connected with the Onyx."

"Well, Didi *died* because of it. Princess Shay was critically injured. Amberle almost got herself killed because I didn't cut her sooner."

"Despite what you might think, the realm does not rest solely on your shoulders. At least not yet."

"So you blame the king?" I lift an eyebrow.

"No, because that would be treason." He sighs. "But you love her."

"I'm not good for her."

"And she loves you. Don't let her go. You'll regret it if you do." It feels like he's speaking from personal experience, but I don't have time to dwell on it now.

I pluck a dark gray tunic from my wardrobe and shut myself in my washroom without another word.

Nieven Morphyra feigns somberness when the winter magic chills the air and projects his image across Faerie. My father and I stand side by side just behind him as he addresses the audience.

"Good evening, fellow fae," he begins with arms outstretched. "After some respectful silence from the high court and the

Consort Tourney, it's time that we inform you of all that has transpired in the past week." He pauses for dramatic effect. "An attack happened, ladies and gentlefae. An attack on our beloved Consort Tourney contestants and the royal family. And while I assure you we have caught the primary culprits, one of them was someone we've watched for some time, trying to woo our beloved prince."

An audible gasp spread from the handful of summer fae who were vetted, then brought to the palace to sit in as a live audience.

"That's right. Frost Niege, along with her family, plotted to end the lives of a contestant they thought to be Frost's greatest competition. And the Onyx took the opportunity to attack our king."

Another gasp.

Nieven steps aside and gestures toward me and my father. "I assure you that the king was unharmed, as you see him standing behind me, and our beloved prince is also alive and well. But others were not so lucky."

Now, a heavy silence falls over the crowd.

"The king would like to say a few words."

Nieven steps to the side, folding his hands in front of him and bowing his head as King Estelar steps forward.

"First, I'd like to assure you that the beautiful Princess Shay Malov, though seriously harmed in the attack, is now on the mend." King Estelar gestures at the group of contestants to our right and I sense the winter magic rushing over to project them to the realm.

Princess Shay bows her head slightly and curtsies as the king draws attention to her, but my gaze drifts to another fae.

I've kept my eyes away from the group, but I can't help but look now. At her.

She won't look at me and grips her necklace lightly with one hand.

It's still there. She hasn't asked to leave yet. But my hope is waning. Avoiding my gaze, keeping a firm hand at her throat, it will only take a quick jerk to break it away and shatter my heart.

"But you might also notice that another contestant isn't among the group," the king continues. "Didi Beechriver was tragically killed during the events of the attack. I hope the Beechrivers are watching, because I'd like to formally invite them to the palace as we prepare for and honor Didi's short life."

I press my lips together. As the king, he doesn't have to respect my wishes, but I insisted we do something for the Beechrivers—for Amberle—who are certainly grieving much more than any full fae could imagine. I'm grateful he listened to me, even if it's mostly to keep the favor of the star fae. It's the least we can do, especially since we held a memorial for Juniper.

"I'd like to make one more announcement before my son selects the remaining five contestants in his Consort Tourney." The king smiles. "I'm pleased to inform you that date of the Centennial Fae Showcase has been moved up. Originally, we planned for it to begin after the Consort Tourney and my son's happy nuptials, but with recent events, it seemed appropriate to have it sooner.

"King Carpus has graciously offered to host the Centennial Fae Showcase in the capital city of the Autumn Court at the next full moon, in Graycrest."

Cheers ring through the space that surely spurs excitement in gathering spaces all over Faerie. But I'm surprised by the announcement. What else had been decided in my absence?

King Estelar lifts a hand to Nieven, prompting him to take the stage again.

"I am thrilled with this news," Nieven says. "And while the plan was for Prince Orion and his new bride to be the guests of honor at the Centennial Fae Showcase, since the Consort Tourney is still ongoing, the prize has changed. The prince will gift each of the five fae a special invitation—"

Gnacia strides on stage holding a small stack of heavy parchment paper in her hands. She hands all but one to Nieven, keeping one that looks larger than the others. As she walks off to the side again, she holds the document at her side. A royal communication by the look of it, only visible to those of us on display and the king, though everyone's attention is on Nieven.

"—to compete in an event of her choice at the Showcase."

While the contestants keep their composure, it's easy to see the excitement that flutters through the group. And the worry that briefly creases Amberle's forehead.

"Also, as Prince Orion will only have five remaining contestants after tonight, it will soon be time for the extensive interviews held by yours truly as we explore the lives and past of each contestant. One of you will become a high princess and your kingdom wishes to dote on you accordingly." Nieven steps back and holds out the five blank invitations, prompting me to step forward. "Prince Orion? It's time."

I take the stack and position myself on center stage, turning to face the contestants. I look at each of their faces, seeing various expressions of thinly veiled hope and adoration. Some are unreadable, but I read nothing from Amberle. She keeps her eyes fixed just above my head. To the magic it appears as if she looks at me, but her gaze might as well be hundreds of miles away.

Her hand remains clasped around her necklace and I can't help but think about our encounter only hours ago. Our breath mingled in the darkness as she plead for me to escape my prison. My punishment. In those moments, I was absolutely certain she loved me and I wanted to pull her closer. I wanted to kiss her and never let go. She helped me see the light. She pulled me out of that pit. But now she won't even look at me?

Was it all a lie?

Kisses can be lies...

Did I imagine it all?

I try to push it away and lift one invitation, ready to say Princess Shay's name as the first contestant invited to the Showcase and one of the final five.

But my thoughts are still on Amberle.

Do you want to stay? I glance at her again. Her hand still grips the necklace around her throat.

I might have called these ceremonies *Invitationals,* but I cannot bring myself to *invite* any fae who are not... well, *her.*

I put the invitation back on the stack and lift my head to the contestants. "We've gone through a lot this past week, and tonight has been full of emotions with Nieven and the king's speeches, so I'm going to make this simple. I will merely name the two fae who I *cannot* make a match with. Then I ask that the winter magic be immediately cut off."

I look at Nieven, who gestures at the winter fae in charge of the magic. When he nods at me in agreement, I look back at the Consort Tourney contestants.

"Lady Pepper Islandwort." Briefly, I close my eyes as if it pains me to send her away, but I'm bracing myself to look at Amberle one more time before I call the next.

It's now or never, Amberle. Keep the necklace on and I will defy my advisors.

Or... take it off and I'll let you go.

When I look at her, I'm sure she'll do the former, but she's finally looking at me with glistening bluebell-colored eyes and downturned lips.

No.

In one motion, she snaps the crystalized sunbeam from her neck and drops her hand to her side.

My throat constricts and my mouth dries more than the Tumul Desert. But it's the shrapnel of the explosion no one saw and only I felt that makes it hard to speak.

I'm dimly aware of Lady Pepper excusing herself. Amberle wishes to follow, yet I cannot speak the words that will release her.

"I'm pulling myself out of the competition." A voice distantly sounds.

My head jerks to the speaker.

Tierney?

She steps forward, far enough to separate herself from the rest and address my father and Nieven—and Faerie—as well.

"Two fae have been killed in the competition so far. *Two.* And truth be told, we wouldn't make a great match, Prince Orion." She lifts her shoulders. "Plus, King Carpus's advisors will let me enter any competition in the Showcase I'd like." Tierney spins on her foot and calls out. "Pick Cerule!"

I'm speechless and look to the side for help, but only see Gnacia brushing her empty hands as traces of ash fall through her fingers.

"The final five!" Nieven says, rushing to my aid and gesturing at the remaining contestants. "Princess Shay Malov, Princess Mora Rolen, Cerule Rostina, River Lyn, and... Amberle Kindra."

End of Book Two

Keep reading for the exclusive Bonus Scene written specifically for this edition.

Bonus Scene

As promised, the following is a new, never-before-seen scene written specifically for this special edition of Stealing Fae Hearts and Secrets.

It's from Rion's point of view from chapters 32-34. It begins when Rion leaves with Luna in Neptulus to talk to her while Amberle and Princess Nerine converse.

Enjoy!

—Joanna

RION

F iery anger seethes just below the surface as I lead Luna through the Neptulus palace. But I keep my emotions in check and my posture stiff, pretending the feel of her hand draped through my arm doesn't repulse me. Any kind thought I ever had for this fae instantly fled the moment I heard how she treated Amberle during the trial. A previous version of myself would have made a scene in the middle of the banquet hall, but I've tamed that impulse.

Faerie will see and hear me cut Luna with the aid of winter magic, but I intend to keep it cordial and swift. If I wanted to drag it out, I would have waited until the next Invitational to eliminate Luna from the Consort Tourney.

"Prince Orion!" Cerule sings my name behind us, and I turn, grateful for an excuse to drop Luna's arm.

The autumn fae's slippers clack across the floor as she catches up.

"You said you wished to speak to Luna and Amberle in private," she says. "But surely you misspoke because you want a private word with me as well. Don't you, Prince Orion?" She clasps her hands together and looks up at me through lowered lashes.

I force a smile to mask my true feelings. I did not misspeak. My plan is to eliminate Luna quickly and send her away so I can tell Amberle the wretched news I've learned about her father. I dread telling her, but I feel it must come from me. With less winter magic watching, it will give her space and time to process her emotions before she's forced back into the limelight of the Tourney.

And perhaps I can comfort her until Wyn insists we leave Neptulus.

But I cannot tell Cerule any of it, so I improvise. "Come with me now and I will speak to you both."

Neither fae look pleased with the arrangement, but for once I'm grateful that Cerule clings to my arm, forcing Luna to walk behind us up the stone stairs.

Besides, with Cerule in the room, I'll have another witness.

A winter fae waits for us down the hall. His forehead creases slightly in confusion, seeing me with two of the contestants, but my nod erases it, and he gestures to the room he's prepared with winter magic.

Faerie is watching the trial unfold—the recording of it, anyway, delayed to avoid interruption—but they'll see Luna eliminated immediately after it ends. It's all part of the game. Apprising the masses of every decision I make.

Releasing Cerule's arm, I gesture that she and Luna enter ahead of me with my head bowed.

Cerule lifts her shoulder as she turns back to grin at me. Luna's smile when she passes is more subtle, but seductive. Bile rises and I look away.

The room leads right into the sea, but underwater magic shaped like an enormous bubble keeps the water at bay. Inside are two chairs and a chaise.

"Cerule. Please sit a moment while I speak with Luna," I say, pointing at the chaise.

She bounds forward in obedience.

I turn to the winter fae and feel a wave of radiating cold wash over me. My jaw clenches. She's trying to impress me with her icy magic, but it only reminds me why I want her gone immediately.

"Luna," I say, standing straight and gripping my hands tightly behind my back. "It's time that you leave the competition."

Cerule gasps.

"*Leave?*" Luna balks, but the room temperature drops.

"One purpose of the trial was to see who could lead and work with a team," I say. "You have shown that you can do neither."

Luna laughs bitterly. "Just like that?" She clutches a hand to her chest, but drops it immediately and steps forward. "You're cutting me because you *think* I couldn't lead or work well with others? I'm the one who got us here!" She points at her former teammate. "If it weren't for me, Cerule and that *sniveling halfling* wouldn't have finished the trial at all!"

"Enough!" I shout, stamping forward, but stop myself. The winter magic is watching. Lifting my chin, I regain my composure and control. "Luna Diables, I've seen enough. You and I would not make an agreeable match. It's time that you leave the competition."

Luna's eyes darken, but she relents and curtsies low. "It has been a pleasure, my prince."

Stomping away, she throws the door open, slamming it against the bubble-wall. I flinch, but of course the barrier doesn't burst and flood the room with seawater, but merely splashes like a broken branch tossed into a river. The door rebounds as she passes over the threshold, and I notice a thin trail of frost in her wake.

Wyn stands in the hallway, so I catch his eye and silently ask him to fetch Amberle. I won't be long with Cerule. He says something to the winter fae controlling the magic, then leaves to get her.

My heart swells.

"Would you like me to extinguish the magic, your highness?" the winter fae asks.

"Yes. I won't need it while speaking to the other two."

The fae enters the room and snaps his fingers—dispelling the cold magic and the residual frost left by Luna, warming the room even more—then walks out and shuts the door behind him.

Cerule bounces up from her seat and skips to stand in front of me, sliding her hands in mine. My knee-jerk is to release them, but I refrain. Though obviously not my first choice, Cerule is still a contender to be my bride someday.

Besides, I intend to make this conversation quick too.

"Cerule—"

Her cheeks pink. Witnessing my curtness with Luna didn't deter her.

"The reason I didn't ask to speak with you before I must go is because I don't intend to eliminate you now."

Her face brightens and a gust of wind lifts my too-long hair from my neck.

I release her fingers and step back.

"Now, if you would, please leave me so I can speak with Amberle." All the tenderness I feel for Amberle reveals itself when I speak her name, but if Cerule notices, she doesn't let it show.

The autumn fae flips her orange hair over her shoulder and lets herself out.

Leaving me to wait for the fae I wish to see most.

***

The door handle turns and my breath catches. I want to run to her. I want to pull Amberle into my arms and embrace her, but I remain in the center of the room with my hands tightly clasped in front of me.

My stomach sours for a different reason. I must tell her the whereabouts of her father.

Amberle's eyes survey the room before shifting to me—which sets my heart aflutter—and I see her thoughts working through her mind.

"Cerule said you eliminated Luna," she says.

"I did," I blurt. "She was not right for me."

Amberle's mouth twitches slightly, but she quickly masks it. "Did Faerie get to see? Or will you announce it later?"

"Faerie is watching the events of the trial," I say, trying to think of something light to change the subject before spilling the hard truth. "Luna's elimination will be replayed for them after the trial concludes." We only have a little time, and I don't wish to spend it talking about the others.

"Why did you cut her?" she asks, and I see a flash of panic or pain stirring behind her eyes.

What is she—does she not realize the depth of feeling I have for her? "I did it because she hurt *you*—"

My voice catches and I give into my desire to be near her by stepping forward.

Only the gesture of lifting her hand stops me from reaching for her. Her voice drops, "Are we..." Her eyelids tremble downward, but her hand remains as a barrier between us. "Are *we* being watched?"

Air escapes my lips along with the anxiety of whatever I worried was Amberle's reason for keeping me at arm's length.

"No," I assure her.

The word breaks the spell. Her hand drops and her lashes flick upward.

Rushing toward her, I reach for her hands and feel an immediate shock of pleasure run through my fingertips the moment our skin touches.

Holding Cerule's hand the same way only moments ago was nothing compared to this.

"We are alone," I whisper.

Amberle sighs heavily, sounding more relieved than expected.

I tilt my head. "What's wrong—" I pull her toward me, wanting desperately to shield her from all hurt. Her relief sounded more than just worry about winter magic and how she feels she must act when we're being watched.

I run through our conversation thus far.

Luna.

Elimination.

Watching Winter Magic.

Wait. "You didn't think..."

She shakes her head and pulls one hand away to wave it. "Cerule just said—"

Cerule said you eliminated Luna, she'd said. Did she think I wanted to see her for the same reason?

"No!" I blurt almost manically. "I just wanted to tell you something the others shouldn't hear. Amberle." I run my fingers through my hair. I cannot save her from the pain of what I'm about to tell her, but she must know that I'm not giving up on us. "I'm *not* eliminating you. *Ever.*" Even I'm surprised by my declaration because although it's exactly what I feel, I've never said it aloud. Even to myself.

I'm fae. It's the truth.

"I just have to figure out a way to get my father to agree," I say, staring across the room as if I'll find instructions on exactly how to do that.

Of course, I find no such thing and bring my gaze back to hers. Arched eyebrows hover over her wide bluebell-colored eyes. There's no more cryptic or masked expression. No more guessing what she feels for me. I ache to touch her and reach out to run a finger along one of her lifted brows, feeling their softness, then tracing the edge of her cheekbone—and pushing a lock of silver hair away so I can better see her beautiful face.

She smiles, and it lights her features.

I can't help but mirror her grin.

"What did you want to tell me?" she asks, but the question doesn't register because when my eyes flick down to her lips, she doesn't push away.

I move my hand around her back—wanting her closer—and press my palm just beneath the edge of her wings.

They twitch as I do the same with my other hand and lean my face closer to hers.

The fact she knows we're not being watched and still allows my proximity gives my heart flight.

Could she feel for me the way I feel for her?

"I've told you how I feel," I say, pushing my forehead against hers and shutting my eyes. "You *know* how I feel."

"You did." Her words are breathy. "I do."

Squeezing my lids tighter, I ask, "Tell me you still hate me like you always have. Tell me you'll never forgive me. Tell me... you don't love me."

Tell me... because I know it's true, and this is just a wicked lovely dream.

"Rion I—" Amberle's throat stops. And the way she said my name...

Wait... could she...

My eyes fly open, and I search for the rest of her sentence, for the harsh reality that she'll hate me forever.

But that's not what I see.

Could she... love me, too?

Like magnets, our lips meet and an electric heat rushes from my crown to my toes. Her arms circle my neck, pulling me toward her, and I'm lost in this moment of ecstasy. But her fingers comb through my hair, I can't believe any of this is real and an alarm triggers.

I break the kiss, but not my hold on her. My eyes are clamped shut. I cannot look her in the face when I say, "Kisses can be lies. Are you lying to me? Tell me you hate me."

My heart bashes itself against my chest.

"I can't," she says.

This isn't real.

"Tell me you'll never forgive me."

"I... can't," she repeats.

This cannot be. This lovely being cannot love me.

"Tell me..." I chide my traitorous heart for daring to hope and force myself to breathe. "You don't love me."

Rion, look at her. I order myself and finally open my eyes again.

Something happens behind her painfully beautiful eyes right before her lashes gently rest on her cheeks. "I-I... *can't.*"

Warmth bursts from my heart and I kiss her harder, hungrier this time. She kisses me back for only a moment before gently pushing me away.

"Rion, we... we *can't.*" The break in her voice breaks me. "The king would never—"

No! I will not allow this tiny obstacle ruin everything.

"The king sent you an invitation," I whisper, pushing my forehead against hers again. "He allowed you to be in the competition, and surely there's a part of him that can be persuaded to allow me to make my own decision. My choice. Even if you became part of this for another reason."

She pushes against me, harder this time, and I release her. She steps back, putting distance between us.

"Amberle— "

Amberle's hand flicks up to stop me again. Then her eyes shut. "Rion—*Prince* Orion—" Her use of my formal name cuts like a dull razor. "It will never work. For whatever reason your father allowed me to be in the competition... he'll never let you pick me."

Get three FREE short stories when you join Joanna's email list at joannareeder.com

Including
Bargaining with a
Fae Queen
(a Raven Court prequel)

Thank you for reading *Stealing Fae Hearts and Secrets!*

If you enjoyed jumping into the land of Faerie and Amberle's world, please leave an honest review on **Amazon**, **Goodreads**, and/or **Bookbub**. Reviews are essential to indie authors like me!

Review on: Amazon
    Review on: Goodreads
    Review on: Bookbub

—Joanna

Acknowledgments

First of all, thank you for reading this book!

I also need to thank my Kindle Vella and Patreon readers who took a chance on this story in serial form so that it could shine when it was time to wrap it in novel form.

But it never would have come to fruition without the support of my family. From my sweet husband who may not understand my need to tell stories but supports me anyway, and my crazy kids who keep me on my toes, but also understand that mom needs to write.

Also my parents, siblings, and extended family who are **always** supporting me and encouraging me.

A huge thanks to my mastermind group (the Queens of the Quill), my cover designer, Angel Leya, my editor Madeline Mortensen, and my amazing cheerleader PA, Gladys Atwell.

I also couldn't have done it without my dear editor and friend, Kristin J. Dawson, who continues to help me make this story the best it can be!

And thanks to my brand new Ream subscriber: JurassicLover!

About the Author

Joanna Reeder is a USA Today Bestselling author who takes her readers time traveling to the past and through the portals to Faerie (and ALWAYS have a dash of romance!).

She lives with her husband, three littles, a dog, and a cat. When she isn't writing or reading, Joanna enjoys bike rides with her family, vacationing at the beach, and cuddling on the couch with a good movie.

She's a believer in the paranormal (seriously, she has stories!) and her motto is, "A Dr. Pepper a day keeps insanity away!"

If you love time travel and fantasy, sign up for Joanna's weekly newsletter HERE.

You can also chat with her on:
Instagram @authorjoannareeder
Facebook @joannareederauthor